When the Otherside howls

Sorcha found herself wishing very hard that there might be some rules that still remained sacrosanct. A week of strangeness—geists crossing water, geists laying traps and geists summoning sea monsters—was still nothing to this. The inside of the keep's great hall had been laid out to mimic the form of an Abbey, as all Priories were, yet it was burnt to a cinder.

"Whatever happened"—Sorcha swallowed hard to regain a measure of her professionalism—"it happened right in the center of the room . . . and it happened suddenly."

As he brushed past her, Raed raised one eyebrow. "This deal about you protecting me . . . I think I got the raw end of the bargain."

Sorcha resisted the urge to slap him and followed after, moving deeper into the Priory to see what further horrors awaited . . .

Ace Books by Philippa Ballantine

GEIST
SPECTYR

GEIST

Philippa Ballantine

ACE BOOKS, NEW YORK

THE BERKLEY PUBLISHING GROUP
Published by the Penguin Group
Penguin Group (USA) Inc.
375 Hudson Street, New York, New York 10014, USA
Penguin Group (Canada), 90 Eglinton Avenue East, Suite 700, Toronto, Ontario M4P 2Y3, Canada
(a division of Pearson Penguin Canada Inc.)
Penguin Books Ltd., 80 Strand, London WC2R 0RL, England
Penguin Group Ireland, 25 St. Stephen's Green, Dublin 2, Ireland (a division of Penguin Books Ltd.)
Penguin Group (Australia), 250 Camberwell Road, Camberwell, Victoria 3124, Australia
(a division of Pearson Australia Group Pty. Ltd.)
Penguin Books India Pvt. Ltd., 11 Community Centre, Panchsheel Park, New Delhi—110 017, India
Penguin Group (NZ), 67 Apollo Drive, Rosedale, North Shore 0632, New Zealand
(a division of Pearson New Zealand Ltd.)
Penguin Books (South Africa) (Pty.) Ltd., 24 Sturdee Avenue, Rosebank, Johannesburg 2196,
South Africa

Penguin Books Ltd., Registered Offices: 80 Strand, London WC2R 0RL, England

This is a work of fiction. Names, characters, places, and incidents either are the product of the author's imagination or are used fictitiously, and any resemblance to actual persons, living or dead, business establishments, events, or locales is entirely coincidental. The publisher does not have any control over and does not assume any responsibility for author or third-party websites or their content.

GEIST

An Ace Book / published by arrangement with the author

PRINTING HISTORY
Ace mass-market edition / November 2010

Copyright © 2010 by Philippa Ballantine.
Cover art by Jason Chan.
Cover design by Lesley Worrell.
Interior text design by Tiffany Estreicher.

ISBN: 978-0-441-01961-8

ACE
Ace Books are published by The Berkley Publishing Group,
a division of Penguin Group (USA) Inc.,
375 Hudson Street, New York, New York 10014.
ACE and the "A" design are trademarks of Penguin Group (USA) Inc.

PRINTED IN THE UNITED STATES OF AMERICA

10   9   8   7   6   5

To my captain, who helped me through stormy seas

ACKNOWLEDGMENTS

No book arises in the dark, so thanks must go out to the following people: To my agent, Laurie McLean, who is my backbone. To Gabrielle Harbowy, who helped me begin the process of shaping this novel. To my parents and brother, who nurtured the dream and made me whole. To all the friends on all my social media networks, who gave me encouragement and listened to my gripes. To all my podcast listeners, who made me a better writer and have been waiting for this moment.

ONE

The Quiet Before Matins

It was good weather for a riot.

Or perhaps that was only wishful thinking. Deacon Sorcha Faris breathed out the last smoke from her cigar, twisted the remains against the stone parapet and sighed in boredom. A riot was almost as unlikely as an unliving attack. But it was her duty to remain alert for both, so she closed her eyes and let her Center fall away.

Under the gray and altered veil of her geist-Sight, the gathering of humans below her at the Vermillion Palace's gate smelled of nothing more than desperation and dull resignation. However, there was certainly a good crowd of them; perhaps five hundred dispossessed milled about in the snow-covered square.

Straining her preternatural senses as far as she could, Sorcha still found no tang of the unliving among them. Falling sleet was cooling their anger and they huddled against the southern wall because they had nowhere else to go. Their protest at her Emperor's presence was subdued; they knew full well he'd been invited by the princes to rule Arkaym, their continent, but they needed someone to blame for their own misery. The majority of the citizens of the City of Vermillion loved the Emperor, but these people had filtered in from the outlying towns for one reason—they were hungry.

There was, however, nothing supernatural about them. Pamphleteers had been spreading discontent since autumn, and now

their efforts were bearing fruit. Not all of the princes agreed—
they seldom ever did on much, and there were still a couple that
disapproved of her Emperor. This likely would not come to
much. Still, guarding against the signs of uprising was her job;
more than that, her calling.

When she reeled back her Center, the feeling of disorienta-
tion passed quickly. For a novice it would have been a strain, but
Sorcha had been eighteen years a Deacon. This minor use of her
powers was now as simple as breathing. Sorcha might not be a
Sensitive, but she had enough rank to sign this one off.

The recent spate of possessions in Brickmaker's Lane on the
very edge of Vermillion had made everyone nervous, but another
team of Deacons had dealt with those last week. It was as she
suspected: there was nothing to Sergeant Gent's worries. The
palace was built far out in a shallow lagoon. Surrounded on all
sides by water, the royal residence was almost impossible for the
unliving to enter; excellent planning by the previous owners.

This particular gathering was now officially the preserve of the
Imperial Legion—let them decide how best to deal with the ragtag
protestors. Sergeant Gent was once again seeing geists in every corner. Sorcha thought, not for the first time, that he should have at least
tried to join the Deacons—it might have taught him a thing or two.

She briskly pinned back some of the bronze curls that had
escaped her severe bun, and was about to leave her chilly spot on
the wall when she caught a glimpse of a familiar back moving
into the crowd.

After eight years of marriage she could instantly recognize
Kolya, even if she couldn't see his face. What she couldn't understand was what he was doing down there. He hadn't told her
that he was planning to do this—but that was the way of things
between them, and had been for some time now.

"Sergeant," Sorcha barked as she picked up her leather helmet
from the parapet, "get your men ready." Running to the door, she
buckled the helm on tightly.

Kolya might be a Sensitive, but if he took matters into his
hands, he could be surprisingly dogged. Once, it had been an
admirable trait, but his wife now found it overwhelmingly irri-
tating. However, if he thought there was something going on
down there, he was better equipped to find it than she—a mere
Active—was.

Sorcha led the platoon down the stairs. At the bottom, she

silently gestured for them to hang back inside the tower. Muskets and bayonets would be of little use if the unliving walked, and in fact any bloodletting would only benefit a geist.

A quick check of her Center again revealed nothing new, yet through the iron railings Sorcha could make out Kolya's emerald cloak surrounded by the gleam of his own Center in the grayness of the mob. Sensitive and Active, they usually worked as a team, but they'd argued again this morning. For a year they had been living in icy silence, but lately she had begun to crack under the pressure. She was starting to bite back, enraged at his own lack of emotion. So when the report had come in that morning, and she'd been unable to find her husband, she'd decided her Sensitivity was enough for a simple detection.

Kolya obviously thought differently.

"Idiot." Sorcha tugged on her thick Deacon Gauntlets while trying to ram down her surging anger.

"Are we going in, ma'am?" Sergeant Gent, always too eager, was nearly standing on her toes. The usual reserve most people had around Deacons wasn't evident in this particular Imperial Guardsman.

"Only if my husband is right." She paused, choosing her words carefully. "So most likely, yes. At my signal, get those people clear and out beyond the gates."

Gent saluted, but the gleam of excitement in his eye boded ill. Young men, guns and geists were a potent combination. "Sergeant"—Sorcha shot him her best cutting-down-to-size look—"you've got it straight that any—*any*—bloodshed here could bring a rain of disaster down on the Emperor's doorstep?"

He might have been an ambitious young soldier, but even he had to take a Deacon's warning seriously. With a nod Gent turned back to his men to pass on the word, and Sorcha watched the soldiers' faces reflect disdain. Apparently crowd control was not what the Imperial Guard was famous for; it didn't make the ladies swoon or provide for good stories in the barracks afterward.

She saw Kolya's back stiffen as her Center leapt toward him. Sorcha might still be angry, but she was not about to let him endanger his own life. *The other Actives would never let her hear the end of it.*

Kolya's wry observation spilled into her mind. Such leaking was the negative side of working together for so long. It also made marriage that much more difficult.

Ignoring it as best she could, Sorcha lent him her minor Sensitivity while keeping her inner eye open for trouble. The merged vision opened wide like a supernatural searchlight. Their combined strength was unmatched in the Abbey, and now Sorcha could taste what had drawn her husband into the midst of the discontented citizens. The faint tang of the unliving was far too small for her senses alone to detect. So far it was only manifesting as a bitter taste on her tongue.

To the shambling group of ungifted there was nothing different about the air, yet; only the usual stench of the early-morning emptying of chamber pots. But to talented and trained senses, it was like the odor of something rotting in the sun.

The faint whiff of the unliving disturbed her enjoyment of the morning. Deacon Faris hated disruption. She also hated being wrong. Today had started badly and looked to be going downhill; watery surrounds should have meant safety for her Emperor. After all it was the sole reason Vermillion had always been the capital city—building on a lagoon was not the easiest thing. It shouldn't have mattered that the top surface was ice when the protective tides still moved below.

All those suppositions vanished, however, when the geist burst through the surrounding flagstones and erupted into the crowd. Sorcha envisioned some clerk in the Abbey working overtime to do a rewrite of the textbooks—this geist seemed not to care that its presence was breaking all their rules.

"Now, Gent!" Sorcha barked as she vaulted the railing to where her husband was just turning to face the threat. "Get these people back!" Shoving her way through the still-unaware protestors, she flexed her fingers within her leather Gauntlets—letting the crowd become aware of just what they were dealing with.

Each leather finger was carved with one of the ten Runes of Dominion. Sorcha called on Aydien, and blue fire chased itself widdershins around her hands to finish with a surge on each palm where her sigil was carved.

Actives were sometimes accused by Sensitive Deacons of being overly flashy. Sorcha did find it somewhat embarrassing; all the lights and surges of energy that even the ungifted could see. However, it did clear the space around her rather effectively. Those not yet possessed stumbled out of her way, screaming in shock. After three years the locals had developed a healthy respect for the dangers of a Deacon wearing Gauntlets.

Aydien was the rune of repulsion and worked well on both mortals and lower-level unliving. The crowd was scattering in a most satisfactory way, yet the geist was still pouring out of the ground, ready to possess anyone it could. It would obviously require a more powerful rune to affect it.

Letting the first rune flicker out, Sorcha reached for Shayst. The green surge of energy trickled into her palm. With it she touched the essence of the geist, drawing some of it for herself—much safer than taking from the Otherside. Ten faces in the mob turned toward her immediately, pale and slack. The sheen of sweat was already on them; geists could seldom manage the fine mechanics of the human body.

Behind them Kolya's green cloak billowed, standing out brightly against the snow and gray paving stones. He had, as their training had taught them, refrained from the natural impulse; his saber remained sheathed. It was a weapon of last resort and of very little use against a geist. Wind sprang up and whipped his fair hair about him, but his expression remained calm even though this geist was acting as no other the Deacons had ever recorded. With Sorcha now on the scene it was unlikely to threaten him. Actives blazed in the ether when they wore the Gauntlets, while Sensitives barely disturbed it as long as they did not wear their equivalent, the Strop.

The geist-possessed stumbled about, drool falling down their chins, eyes rolling in their heads and wordless groans squeezed from their chests. Already Sorcha could smell the faint odor of shit; another faculty that geists could not control. Overall, being possessed, if one survived it, was an unpleasant and embarrassing experience. Old thin women, pigeon-chested boys and ragtag men were now the geist's weapons in this world.

"Unacceptable," the Deacon muttered to herself.

Watch yourself. Kolya's unneeded warning leaked across their Bond.

His confidence in her abilities, even after all these years, was so reassuring.

Through the enhanced Sight Kolya fed her, Sorcha could make out the swirling vortex of the geist as it embraced the humans. It was growing larger rather than smaller. The power required to control even this many people was immense—in fact, off the scale. Once again, the paper shufflers were going to get a headache over this.

With so many geist-possessed advancing on her, Sorcha de-cided to draw more power away from the vortex and hopefully release a few of them. With her second Gauntlet she called on Shayst once more.

She bucked backward as the power slammed into her spread hands and raced up her arms. Biting down an involuntary groan of pleasure, the Deacon tried to get past the intoxicating sensa-tion. It was like the euphoria of being slightly drunk without the lack of coordination. Her vision sharpened while her limbs filled with strength. Nothing seemed impossible. It was this rush of confidence that could bring down an inexperienced Deacon.

Sorcha held the power lightly, letting it wash over her but never take control. Shayst had drawn a lot of energy, but the vortex was still growing. And the air was getting colder around her, so cold that her face was numb and her teeth ached. It was impressive that she could be aware of such sensations, wrapped as she was in geist-power.

"Unholy Bones," she swore and, unlike Kolya, she drew her saber. The possessed were now only ten feet away. They had nearly the whole Square to themselves. Gent's men had done their job. In the time it had taken them to clear the crowd, how-ever, another dozen had been touched by the geist. Still, it could have been worse. A crowd of five hundred controlled by the unliving didn't bear thinking about.

Her husband's Sensitivity held her to the ground, sharpened her vision and senses enough to make the right choices. Without him she would be blind.

At this thought her husband smiled slightly; certainly there had been precious few kindly words spoken in recent months. He opened his Center wider so that she could now see right into the swirling mass of the geist. The vortex was large, but she could make out its tail, apparently rooted to one spot on the ground.

Sorcha barely had time to register this odd feature among odd features before the geist shifted its attention. The possessed raised their heads, eyes now gleaming pits of blackness. She could have almost thought there were sly smiles on their slack faces. Then the expanded funnel of power rushed out once more—but not toward Sorcha.

Without him she would be blind. She blinked in astonishment, her throat abruptly dry and raw.

Geists were mindless things. They were intent on their own

purposes, which generally involved wreaking havoc on the real world. They reacted only to Actives, never Sensitives, because Actives engaged them. A Sensitive remained almost invisible unless he did something foolish, like trying to use his lesser Active power. Kolya was too well seasoned for that.

Certainly he had seen the geist turn on him, but he must have not quite believed it. Sorcha shot him a warning as well, but there was nothing in the training of a Deacon for this eventuality. In three hundred years of the Order, no Sensitive had ever been attacked. Even in the battle for the Heights of Mathris, when Sorcha had been just newly ordained, there had never been such an event.

She couldn't reach him. Desperation and helplessness welled up inside her. The possessed were pressing in on her; hands grasping, mouths-turned-weapons stretched wide to bite. The geist filled them with as much strength as Sorcha had received, yet she could not afford to spill their blood. Instead she deflected their blows, sliding out of the way of their attacks in the fluid Abbey style of defense. Rolling away as best she could, she felt their fingernails rake her face and hands. Her mind was full of Kolya. She could not see him beyond the ruckus of the possessed, but in horror she realized that he had gone Active. Her heart hammered while her mind shot desperate queries across their bond. A Sensitive relying on their lesser power was like a fine swordsman resorting to clumsily wielding an ax.

Unlike her husband's Sensitivity, her Active power could not be shared with him to boost his own. That was another thing Sensitives accused her kind of: selfishness. At this point, she couldn't help but agree.

Unholy Bones, he wasn't answering. Gent's men would still be busy with the people—besides, she had warned them about bloodshed. Blood and souls would only feed the geist. The soldiers would be standing well back with their hands full of a terrified crowd.

Her own smaller mob had reoriented itself on her. Catching one of the possessed old women in a shoulder lock, Sorcha managed to pitch her backward into the swarm. This brief respite allowed her to catch a glimpse of her husband.

The vortex was around Kolya. He was turning blue with the inhuman cold, and she could feel a great weight on him. The geist was crushing him like a bug against a window.

Her professional veneer cracked; Sorcha screamed in rage. The world abruptly snapped back to color, leaving her reeling. The Bond was broken, and she was suddenly the sole Deacon standing—yet completely blinded.

Unable to feel if Kolya was alive or dead, or indeed what the geist was now doing, she stumbled backward. Her scrambled brain searched through all her training for a solution. What it came up with was unpleasant: she had only one choice. Deacon Sorcha Faris activated Teisyat, the tenth Rune of Dominion.

Far off in the Abbey, heads would raise from their daily work and turn in the direction of the palace. A Conclave of Deacons would be sent rushing to her position. It would be too late.

Teisyat had that effect. Teisyat needed an Episcopal inquiry afterward, followed by months of investigation and "recommended counseling." Teisyat was so dangerous that only the highest-level Actives had it engraved on their Gauntlets, and only after many tests. Even with all Sorcha's years in the Abbey, only two had passed since this last rune had been carved into her Gauntlets.

None of that mattered to Sorcha. Kolya needed her.

A window opened between the Otherside and the real world— it was no tiny pinprick like that brought by Tryrei. Her Gauntlets burned red like lava now, describing the dimensions of a gateway that Gent could have marched his men through side by side. The ground beneath the Square shook. All these things, Sorcha could observe even without her husband because they were happening in her world. Right before the Emperor's walls, the Otherside was making its presence felt.

All other concerns were of secondary importance to Deacon Sorcha Faris. She was deeply occupied in holding that presence back as best she could. The Abbey had good reason to fear the last rune. Teisyat opened the gates to the Otherside, and once they were open, anything could come through.

The gaping void, white and hungry, was sucking at the real world. Only Sorcha was stopping it from letting forth its nightmares.

She stood right at the edge of the gateway and screamed into it. The Otherside was howling back, loud and hungry. It burned her eyes and tore her hair loose. Her skin felt flayed while her voice was ripped away in the rushing winds.

Yet she held on. Her training and talent diverted the power away from the real world toward the geist. While she acted as the shield, the Otherside demanded something for being summoned. Through streaming eyes Sorcha watched as the possessed were ripped away from all around her. A glimpse of slack faces tumbling into nothingness should have caused her a twinge of remorse, but holding out against the pull of the void was all she could manage.

The physical pain stole the breath from her body, but it was the mind that the Otherside attacked the most terribly. Every fear, every terrible moment in her life was brought bubbling to the surface and thrown against her like a missile.

It wanted her to crack and allow it in. Breaking Sorcha was its path into the real world, so it threw all it could against her. Mistakes she had almost managed to forget resurfaced, and dark thoughts she'd suppressed barraged her brain until she could have shattered. *Why did you marry him?* a voice asked, as sharp as a blade against the most unexplored parts of her consciousness.

Sorcha held out her Gauntlets with Teisyat burning like red anger on them. Without Kolya she couldn't tell if the geist had succumbed to the Otherside or not. Yet she couldn't hold out against its pull for much longer. Summoning the last of her energy, she closed her fist around the rune and bent all of her talent to closing the gate.

The Otherside struggled against her, twisting away like a fish on a line, yearning to be free. For an instant Sorcha felt it slipping, evading her strength. Then her deepest training kicked in. The mind puzzles and control exercises, the ones she had thought boring while a novice, the ones that had been repeated until they seemed foolish, were now her final outpost.

Repeating the phrases, following the numeric puzzles, tangled the Otherside's attempts to pull her mind down. It was just enough time for Sorcha to close Teisyat. The Otherside howled, like a great beast finally brought down, and then closed.

Sorcha found herself on her knees. Her hands, wrapped around the flagstones, were aching as though a horse had stood on them. Inside the Gauntlets, blood was beginning to seep. She didn't dare pull them off. Instead she staggered to her feet and toward where Kolya lay crumpled on the ground.

Numbed inside and out, Sorcha rolled him over, her bloodied

Gauntlets staining his emerald cloak. Hers was not the only blood. Plenty of his was pooling among the white snow, shocking in its contrast.

The geist had wrought terrible vengeance on her husband and partner. He was broken, bleeding and lying like a cast-off doll in the spot where he'd been thrown. He was her Sensitive, her responsibility, and this was her fault. She should have protected him. She should have been at his side. Had she made this happen?

"Gent," she bellowed across the suddenly quiet Square. "Gent! Summon the physician. Now!"

Kolya was still breathing; broken and pained though it sounded, he was breathing. Sorcha held him as gently as she could, but knew there was no rune of healing in the Gauntlets. Deacons were not meant for anything but battle. "Hang on," she whispered to him. "Hang on, you foolish man."

TWO

Pleading Kyrie

Raed, the Young Pretender. He heard the courtiers whisper it behind their enameled fans. It was not warm in the castle of Prince Felstaad, so the ladies of his court only used their fans to muffle their gossip; not very effectively, as it turned out. Raed could feel their appraising gazes all over him like warm, wet hands.

Pretender he might be, but he was conscious of his battered clothes in the finery of the castle. It was certainly not the Vermillion Palace, but it was still far more civilized than he was used to. One of the younger ladies giggled, "He's almost handsome," before she was hushed by her elders.

Raed smiled wryly and rubbed his neatly trimmed beard; this had been his one attempt at civilizing himself. Perhaps he should have docked in the town farther down the coast and sent the crew ashore to shop, but part of him bridled at being forced to bow so low before someone like Felstaad. He might not be handsome by fashionable standards—standards that had apparently strayed toward fey, willowy men, if this court was anything to go by— but his blood was still more royal than that of any here.

The seneschal, who had been watching him out of the corner of one disapproving eye, nodded slightly in his direction. Taking his cue, Raed stood up, straightened his frock coat and strode to the towering gilt and oak doors.

Footmen on each side swung them open as he was announced.

"His Highness, Lord Raed Syndar Rossin, Second Vetch of Ostan and Heir of the Unsung."

He was impressed with the seneschal's boldness. The island of Ostan had been reclaimed by the waves in his grandfather's time, so was inoffensive, but to add mention of his exiled father verged on the daring; the man had not set foot in the kingdoms since Raed was a babe. Raed's heart lightened; perhaps his mission here was not so improbable.

Prince Felstaad's court was smaller than those impressive doors suggested, but it was bright with decoration and beautiful ladies. The Prince himself was dressed in charcoal gray, a tall esoteric-looking man among so many fluttering birds. It was undoubtedly an affect that was well studied. This prince had a reputation for calculation, and when he turned his bright eyes in the direction of the Young Pretender, Raed remembered it was well deserved.

A chain of office glittered around Felstaad's neck. The chain, Raed knew, had been presented to Felstaad's father by Raed's own grandfather. It was the Prince's only ornamentation and no doubt had been chosen with care. Raed would have to tread with caution.

Still, he couldn't quite bring himself to give a low bow. After all, he outranked a mere minor prince, even if his current home was a ramshackle ship and his subjects a collection of the continent's castoffs. Raed therefore inclined his head, with no sign of bent knee or flourish.

Felstaad was too much of a master at the art of politics to let any expression darken his face. The correct form would have been to bow, but he made no indication of giving one of those.

All right, then. Raed filed away that pointed insult.

"Lord Raed." Felstaad smiled in an almost kindly way. "Your presence once again brightens our court. What boon do you come to ask of us this time?"

Evil old bugger. It had been four years since he'd last been here, and it had been no boon he'd been asking. Raed had been requested by a neighboring prince to mediate a border dispute. That particular incident, like so many others, had ended in a stalemate, and merely eight months later the Assembly of Princes had agreed to ask Magnhild, King of Delmaire, to send his second son to be their Emperor. They had considered calling back Raed's father, the Unsung, from his island exile, but in the end he was considered too divisive.

Raed knew that factions within the Assembly had worked against his father. In the end it was purely the fact that they knew nothing of then-Prince Kaleva, whereas the Unsung was of a line of kings who had riled and annoyed generations of those warring rulers.

The Prince's attitude grated on him, but he spread his hands and tried to look as inoffensive as possible. "I need a safe harbor, Prince Felstaad. My crew must have fresh supplies. My ship requires urgent careening and repairs."

"Fueled no doubt by a desperate need to remain faster than the Imperial Fleet?" The old man grinned thinly. The joke was in poor taste, but unfortunately very close to the mark. The bounty on his head fluctuated with the times, but it remained somewhat of a problem. Raed smiled smoothly rather than deny it.

"I know that your familial association with my family has cost you dearly in the past, but all I ask is a little time. Your court is far from the Vermillion Palace . . ." It had been years since he'd been in a princely court and yet he could hear himself dipping once more into the language and cadence of its speech. Raed hated that.

Felstaad's eyes narrowed only slightly. "But the new Emperor's reach is long. Brought up in that sweltering court of his father's, he is always looking for the knife lurking behind the curtain. None of us can afford to be complacent."

Raed took a breath, letting his eye wander over the audience chamber. Felstaad was indeed far from the glittering center of the Empire, yet around him he saw signs of opulence; a jeweled clock here and a very fine portrait there.

Such little clues made the Pretender consider the uncomfortable possibility that this prince was doing more than making gestures of obedience to the Emperor; he could be in his employ. To be certain, the bounty on Raed's head was lower this year than last, but perhaps the Prince needed to buy a new toy for his mistress. Anything was possible, yet he had no choice but to take the chance.

Raed gestured to the side, a little away from prying ears. Felstaad paused a second and then joined him in his walk to the window. The Prince was not quite as tall as the Pretender, and off his dais he was forced to look up a little to meet the other's steady hazel eyes. Raed enjoyed that little moment.

"Lord Prince," he whispered under his breath. "The Empire

is still new, the usurper on my father's throne still struggles with the Assembly, and all I am asking is a small harbor in one of your out-of-the-way villages to make repairs." He fixed Felstaad with a calm look. The Unsung might never leave his island of exile, but Raed wanted the Prince to know that was not true of himself; he would not be so easily dismissed.

His host was a political beast and a fence sitter by his very nature. Those sharp eyes measured the ill-dressed man before him; Raed hoped they saw more than his clothes. The Prince smoothed back his small mustache carefully before answering the request. "In the far north there is a fine little town called Ulrich, with a good-sized fishing fleet. The place itself is inhospitable to any but the locals and perchance there you could make good your repairs." He shrugged. "It is also too small a place for me to keep a representative, so I am unlikely to hear of any unusual visits until well into the spring . . . if at all."

It wasn't the answer that Raed had been seeking. He knew of Ulrich only by reputation. Other trading vessels avoided it, as the waters were rough in winter and the harbor was not an important one for fishermen. It was also near the Imperial Dirigible way station, one of the new Emperor's experiments to bridge the vast distances of the continent. Raed had been hoping for a warm-water port in the very south of Felstaad's dominion; his crew deserved it. Yet, by the look on his host's face, this was going to be the only deal on offer.

Repressing a sigh or indeed any sign of his disappointment, Raed nodded. It was nearing late autumn. Snow was already on the ground in most places that got it. If he wanted to make Ulrich before winter truly set in, there was no time to waste.

Felstaad was about to return to his courtiers when he raised one finger to his lips and spun back to Raed. The nasty smile he wore boded ill. "I do hope," he half whispered in a slightly exaggerated fashion, "that this little stay on dry land will not prove inconvenient . . . considering your unfortunate condition?"

Raed's back stiffened, but out of long practice, distaste did not reach his face. The Prince had heard the rumors and wanted confirmation: Raed would give him none. "I can assure you, Felstaad, that my health is not your concern. I shall manage as I always have."

The Prince's jaw clenched a little on such an abrupt dismissal. It was something he was not used to, but what he was referring to went beyond the bounds of good taste and he knew it. The lingering possibility that Raed might one day be a force to be reckoned with held back any further questions. It usually did with these petty princes.

Moving back to his courtiers, Felstaad brushed his coat as if some of Raed's presence had caught on it. "I am sorry that I cannot help," he said somewhat loudly for their audience's benefit.

Such a shoddy dismissal made the Young Pretender want to slap the ignoble Prince right in the face. In the old days, before the foolishness of his grandfather, such an insult would have been met with steel. But those days were well gone, and Raed had to live in these new ones.

He did not bow as he left the perfumed audience chamber. He did, however, wink at the prettiest of the young ladies-in-waiting, the one who had called him "almost handsome." If he ever managed to return in splendor and with the right clothes on his back, he might just change her mind on that particular score.

"Can I get you anything, Deacon Faris?" Arch Abbot Hastler, despite his rank, always asked that question of those who were lucky enough to gain an audience with him.

Lucky was not something Sorcha was feeling right now. She looked up blankly from the embroidered stool on which she sat in the Abbot's inner chamber. "Sweet tea if you have any, Reverend Father."

He nodded and gestured for the waiting novice to fetch some from the kitchens. It didn't take long. Soon warm liquid was poured into tiny white china bowls, emulating a quaint, friendly domestic scene that was at odds with the dire circumstances of the moment. Steam chugged out of the pot and collected on the lavender-colored stained glass window, making intricate and tiny wet patterns. The scent of sugar and roses should have calmed Sorcha, but it instead disturbed her, coming on the heels of yesterday's madness.

After he had poured them each a bowl, the Abbot sat opposite her and they drank in silence. Sorcha felt at any moment she might drop the fine china from her bandaged hands. His chain of office, with each link bearing one of the ten Runes of Dominion and seven Runes of Sight, reflected the weak sunlight into her eyes, occasionally blinding her. His Gauntlets and his Strop

rested on a velvet stand atop the marble mantelpiece. He was the
only member of the Order allowed to practice both disciplines—
even the members of the Circle of Abbots could have only one. It
took quite a man to handle that sort of power.

As such, he was a formidable person to be seated opposite.
Though Sorcha knew Hastler's methods, she still cracked under
them. She broke the quiet first. "So . . . when is the Episcopal
inquiry due to start?"

His bright blue eyes were suddenly aimed right at her and any
pretense of kindliness was swept away. When he had been tested
as a Deacon, it was rumored that Hastler had ranked so high as
an Active and Sensitive that it had been a close call which he
would choose. In the end Sensitive won out, and it was only when
he was raised to Arch Abbot that he had taken up the Gauntlets.
Sorcha felt intimately aware of this fact as she sat pinned under
that gaze. She understood he could literally see right through
her—a talent no doubt very useful in his position.

"Perhaps you should be asking about your husband, instead
of the consequences of activating Teisyat?" His voice remained
quiet, as if they were discussing doctrine rather than the likeli-
hood of her dismissal from the Order.

She tried to keep her tone as level as possible. "I was with
Kolya all night, Reverend Father. I know he will be fine."

"Eventually, perhaps. But he will not be suitable for duty for
several months at least. The geist exacted a terrible toll on him."
The Arch Abbot set down his half-empty bowl and folded his
hands, waiting for her to reveal all.

If he wanted to, he could see everything anyway. Kolya had
mentioned once that sometimes what people didn't reveal was
more telling than what they did. What concerned her, apart from
her husband's injuries and her possible dismissal, was the nature
of the geist responsible for both.

"It wasn't a normal unliving entity," she began.

"Obviously."

"For its size, it should have been immediately apparent, but it
took Kolya and I together to sense it."

"Such things are not unknown."

"But it read our Bond, Reverend Father. It read my thoughts,
and then it turned on Kolya almost as if it could make conscious
decisions. That is supposed to be beyond anything from the
Otherside!"

The Arch Abbot sighed and leaned back in his chair, and this time it was Sorcha who waited for him to speak. Outside, birds could be heard chirping in the orchard, along with the low murmur of novices filing off to their classes and chores. Finally he turned back, his face furrowed with worry. "This, too, is not without precedent."

The fragile bowl in Sorcha's hand rattled as she tried to set it carefully down. She cleared her throat. "I know I am not privy to all the information you receive, Reverend Father, but I would think that such information would be valuable to the Deacons working in the field."

He did not reply immediately, but got to his feet and crossed to his desk. Placing a long dispatch box in Sorcha's hands, he took his seat once more. Looking down, she saw the gold-embossed sigil of the hand grasping many ribbons, the symbol of the Emperor.

"This was delivered before dawn this morning. Don't read it now; the details can wait for you to ponder over, but the essence is that there is a major surge in unliving attacks to the northeast."

"Then the Abbey rides to . . ."

"No."

The bald reply confused Sorcha beyond measure. The Order had spent the first two years of the Emperor's reign darting from hot spot to hot spot. With this continent's own Priories having long fallen into ruin, the land had been overrun with the unliving. The Deacons who had come over with the Emperor had been pushed hard to keep up, but it had been their primary mandate. Yet now, here was the Arch Abbot saying that they would not be venturing out to take care of the matter. For a moment Sorcha was completely lost for words.

When the Arch Abbot spoke again, he didn't add to her understanding. "I am sending you to the focus of the attacks to investigate: a little town called Ulrich. His Imperial Majesty and I both agree that this is the best course of action."

Sorcha blinked. Deacons received their missions from the Presbyter Secondo; to take direction from the Arch Abbot directly was highly unusual. An honor to be sure—but not one that Sorcha felt she should welcome.

She now wished that she had asked for something a little stronger than sweet tea. "But Kolya could take weeks, maybe even months to be fit for duty," was the best she could manage through a suddenly dry throat.

"That's why I am assigning you a new partner before you go."

Sorcha slumped back, nearly embarrassing herself before recovering her balance on the embroidered stool. "A new partner? But no one ever gets a new partner unless their Bond is broken, or . . ." Or if their partner was dead.

"There is precedent for this, too." The Arch Abbot was acting as calm as ever, which was more distressing to her than anything. "And the situation will only be for this assignment. By then Kolya should be recovered."

Arguing with the Head of her Order would be a foolish move, yet Sorcha could feel a tightness inside her stomach and a taste of bile bubbling inside her throat. Her bandaged hands began to ache. Forget that sending an untested team into a hot zone verged on the insane. Never mind that partners trained for months to get perfectly in tune with each other. The Arch Abbot was dropping her into a situation he seemed unwilling to explain.

Hastler was an evenhanded man, one who inspired trust among his Deacons. He was respected by them and by the Emperor. As one of the top-ranked partnerships in the Order, Kolya and Sorcha had always felt in the Arch Abbot's confidence. Yet as she sat across from him, she could see he was physically tight-lipped. What this could mean, she didn't know. She ached for a cigar at this point but decided not to argue. Her husband would have been very surprised.

Still she kept her voice calm as she went on, trying to make the best of a bad situation. "Perhaps if we were allowed to take one of the Imperial Fleet dirigibles, we could accomplish this so much—"

"The Order's ability to demand that one of the Emperor's valuable new contraptions change its route is limited." Hastler's eyes flicked from friendly to flinty in a heartbeat, reminding Sorcha that while he might look like a kindly grandfather, he was far from it. "Only in extreme circumstances would I suggest such a thing."

Sorcha cleared her throat, and glanced longingly down at the empty cup next to her. Her mouth had gone suddenly bone-dry. "I would like to be able to wait until Kolya is conscious at least, if that is allowed, Reverend Father?"

Hastler nodded and tidied the bowls and pot on the tray. At this point, Sorcha didn't have the strength to ponder what exactly could be causing his unusual behavior.

"Go, sit with your husband." The Arch Abbot kept his back turned, staring out the window at the last few stubborn leaves of late autumn as they fell. "Read the report, as well. I'll arrange a meeting with your new partner for first thing tomorrow."

"And the Episcopal inquiry?" she asked.

"There will be none. The matter is being dealt with in a more private manner. Another thing, Deacon Faris." His tone grew distant. "I would prefer it if you and your husband did not speak of the . . . unusual nature of your encounter."

Compared to the strange things she had heard in this room, that was the very least. The calm of the previous day seemed a very long way off. Her only problems then had been an argument with her husband and the overeager Gent.

At the door she paused and turned back for a moment. "Am I permitted to perhaps know the name of my new partner?"

The Abbot's voice contained something she might have interpreted as sadness. "Deacon Merrick Chambers. A bright young man and a highly ranked Sensitive."

She didn't know the name, but if he had been recently elevated from novitiate, then she wouldn't. Sorcha itched for something to smoke or drink, but duty as always took higher priority.

As she left, she passed three other Deacons seated in the ante-chamber ready to see the Arch Abbot—so many audiences so early was enough to pique her interest. Sorcha recognized Durnis Huntro and gave him a quick smile. The somber man looked even less likely to smile back today, and she wondered what his business was with the head of the Order. However, her own issues were more pressing, and she did not stop to ask.

Stepping out into the corridor, she discovered she still had one more audience to pass. Presbyter Rictun, wrapped in his blue cloak, was lurking in the shadows, waiting for her. If Hastler was the kindly center of the Order, then his second in command was the enforcer. It was he who usually gave out the assignments to those Deacons on duty, and his glance down at the dispatch box in her hand was sharp enough for even an Active to interpret. He didn't like it—not one little bit. He was a young man for the role; there were only five Deacons of Presbyter rank in the Order, and yet he was not much older than Sorcha herself. How he had managed to attain such giddy height was a mystery to her.

It could have been his golden hair and good looks; it was most certainly not his charm. "Off on assignment so soon, Faris? You really know how to go through those partners of yours. I would have thought you might be a little kinder to this one, since you married him."

Four partners was indeed above average, but one retirement, one death and one gone mad could not be all put on her doorstep. Sorcha smiled thinly, the lack of sleep and the shock of the Arch Abbot's audience leaving her with very little endurance for the Presbyter's mocking ways. "Kolya will be all right in time."

Rictun raised one eyebrow. "Terrible to get caught in a riot like that."

His fishing was always pretty blatant but this time it was just a little too far for Sorcha. Holding up her orders, she glared at the Presbyter. "Would you like to have a look, is that it?"

His eyes locked with hers, and she remembered all the other times they had argued. Rictun rubbed her the wrong way at the best of times. Perhaps he saw the impatience in her, as his gray eyes flicked away over her shoulder toward Hastler's rooms. "No, you'd better obey the Arch Abbot. But when you get back . . ."

"I'll report straight in," Sorcha snapped, turned on her heel, and indulged in a little tooth grinding as she strode away down the corridor.

This Chambers, whoever he was, had better have a thick skin, because right now she needed someone to take it out on.

THREE

The Giving of Affusion

Sorcha left the Abbot's chambers and strode through the Devotional with a lot more certainty than she actually felt. It was cool in the stone corridors of the building, high-vaulted ceilings perhaps not the best design choice for Vermillion's winter climate, but the building had been inherited much as the Emperor had received his palace.

She passed underneath carvings of the native Abbots who had once ruled here, their symbol of a circle of five stars pinned to their chests. Many of their stone faces had been hacked off. The wars of this continent had not discriminated against those who wanted to protect it.

In the north wing, there were still lay Brothers clambering up scaffolding to install a new slate roof to replace the one destroyed in the fire that had wiped out the remainder of the native Deacons nearly seventy years before. The Mother Abbey's Devotional building had lain in ruin, open to the tender mercies of nature, until Arch Abbot Hastler had brought the new Order to the continent. Now three years of repairs were drawing to a close. Once the roof was in place, only the scars would be visible, not the destruction.

Sorcha paused for a moment to watch the artisans working on the northern rose window—replacing the glass they'd recovered and installing new portions where that was impossible.

"Sorcha!" The familiar voice snapped her out of a melancholy turn of thought.

A tall figure emerged out of the shadows, his hands covered in white dust, his step halting.

"Garil." She smiled in genuine happiness. "What are you doing here?"

Sorcha knew as his gray eyes looked her over that nothing could be hidden from him; the slight slump in her shoulders and the fractional frown on her brow. Yet unlike most Sensitives, she didn't mind him observing her. Garil had been her first partner, but despite that and everything that happened, he still held her in high regard. It always rather shocked her.

"Little Red." He hobbled over to catch her in a rough embrace. "They poked me out of my tiny Priory with some rubbish about needing my skills for this project."

No one since Pareth, the Presbyter of the Young during Sorcha's childhood, had dared give her a nickname, but from Garil it was somehow acceptable. Sorcha threw her arms around him with a laugh until she realized how thin he was beneath the charcoal robes. She could feel every bone. Garil was one of the few Sensitives forced into retirement by severe injury. The perpetrators had not been the unliving, but if she ever found them, they soon would be.

"So how are you, Garil?" She gently squeezed him back, afraid that she might hurt him.

"Ah, you know." He shrugged, an awkward movement. Despite how hard the physicians had tried, his broken pelvis and back had never healed straight. "It still feels strange to wear the gray after so long in the emerald."

He should have stayed in Delmaire but had insisted on joining the Emperor's expedition. He'd been old then, but still one of the great Sensitives of his age. The Bond they had shared as partners had been very strong.

Sorcha cleared her throat, feeling his sadness like it was her own. Being rated unfit for duty and having to wear the charcoal robes of the retired Deacon was something that few ever got to enjoy, yet it was obvious that Garil took no pleasure from it. She could hardly blame him; the heady rush of geist battle was addictive.

"I was in the infirmary when they brought Kolya in." The elderly Deacon shook his head. "Most unfortunate to be caught in a riot like that." His eyes grew distant as he undoubtedly thought of his own dark night in the alley. Why anyone would beat such a kind man within an inch of death was still a mystery.

It was becoming clear that no one was going to mention the geist that obeyed no rules or her opening of Teisyat. It seemed the paper shufflers in the Abbey would be saved any disturbance.

"Yes," she whispered. "Very unfortunate." Glancing up at the beautiful rose window, she attempted to change the subject. "How is the restoration going?"

Garil laughed, a short little sound that contained more than a hint of bitterness. "They really don't know what to do with an old Deacon here." He leaned forward conspiratorially. "I think the Arch Abbot believed I was going a little crazy out there in the wilds, worried I might say too many things."

Sorcha shrugged. "Well, you have a lot of experience, something that we lack this far from Delmaire. You know how to get people to do things."

Garil sighed. "Even our beloved Emperor has spent years restoring the palace—so I should not grumble."

"Then you are following an excellent lead."

Her old partner nodded slowly, but she sensed something else; the elderly Deacon was holding back. At any other time she would have pressed him, but she had enough on her plate not to go looking for trouble. Not today anyway.

In the name of distraction Sorcha tried him on his favorite subject. "Do you think the native Order would appreciate what we are doing to their Abbey?" She said it in jest, trying to get his grim mood to lift, but the old Deacon shrugged.

"They left so few records it is impossible to tell. I do know that when they were cut off here for so long, their ways were rumored to have grown a little strange."

During her training, history had been the bane of Sorcha's life, but now her interest was a little piqued; the looming statues of those who had come before seemed somewhat more than mere rock today. She knew that in the dark ages Saint Cristin had landed in a tiny boat on the new continent and founded the native Order, but that was as far as her knowledge went. Garil had studied everything he could about the founding Deacons, yet even he didn't have all the answers.

The conversation had strayed into uncomfortable territory. "Perhaps if our Order stays here for six hundred years, we too will be considered strange," she offered.

Garil's great bushy eyebrows drew together, and he looked away. "Maybe we already are." His voice was a low rumble, and

Sorcha restrained an inappropriate smile. Her old partner was not
taking retirement at all well.

"You at least have earned some rest, Garil."

"Maybe so," muttered her old partner as he glanced up at his
workers. "But back in Delmaire . . . Well, there are more gray
cloaks. Here . . ." The rest remained unsaid. Here there were very
few old members of the Order.

Garil shifted uncomfortably, and she realized he had more
than his share of aches in badly healed bones. The wintry air
she found pleasantly bracing would not be so kind to him. Her
ire rose toward whichever clerk had thought this a good project
for an old man.

"Surely they don't need you to watch glass getting slotted into
place." She tucked her hand into the crook of his elbow. "Keep
me company to the infirmary?"

He shot a look up at the artisans and then laughed. "These
young people know what they are about, and I could do with
some more tincture for my old skin. It gets so thin, you know."

It would in fact be for the pain, but his pride wouldn't let him
admit that. Sorcha knew full well what Garil was like. Together
they strolled out of the Devotional toward the low stone building that housed the infirmary. A low lavender hedge contained
a physic garden at the front, where lay workers were rushing
to gather the final autumn plants. To the right were the drying
rooms, and the apothecary where potions, tinctures and rubs
were prepared. The scent that wafted out of the open doors was
so soothing Sorcha almost forgot why she was going there.

Garil patted her arm. "I'll let you go and find your husband.
Give him my best."

He was about to wander away, but she held on to him a
moment, a twinge of concern tickling her conscience. "Is everything all right with you, Garil?"

Was it her imagination, or did a tiny muscle near his eye twitch?
"As well as can be expected . . . you know, in this weather." He
rubbed his leg and glanced up as if he was expecting rain. "Well,
must get in." Garil turned and hobbled away from her.

Sorcha stood staring after him for a minute, knowing that
something was bothering the older man. Still, if he had wanted
to talk about it, he would have; they were good enough friends
for that. Once this foolish mission for the Arch Abbot was over,
she'd catch up with Garil and see what was chewing on him.

Inside the infirmary it was thankfully warmer, though it smelled of sage smoke and soap; smells that irritated her senses. The building might be a place of healing, but it always made her uncomfortable—and it was not just the smell. Lay Brothers ruled here, gliding about with silent efficiency in their brown robes. Deacons might know little of healing, but thanks to the library and careful use of sanctioned weirstones, the Abbey's infirmary was the best in the nation.

So good, in fact, that even royalty came here. Sorcha flinched, but the Grand Duchess Zofiya had surely heard her footsteps. The martial sister of the Emperor, used to commanding troops, missed very little that went on around her. A young male soldier of the Imperial Guard was standing stiffly at attention, holding the royal bags and glowing with pride. The Grand Duchess was looking at her gold fob watch, standing by a neatly made bed she had only recently occupied. On her dark brow was a slight but significant frown. It was a face that might have been called sweetly beautiful, if it had not been for a pair of determined, dark eyes. Sorcha knew in public the Duchess had a smile that could melt hearts, but in private she was rather stern. Snapping shut the watch and tucking it into her dress uniform, she turned.

When Zofiya's lips hardened into a firm white line, Sorcha knew that the truth of yesterday's events had reached her—not the tissue of denial the Arch Abbot was selling to the public. The Deacon's stomach clenched.

The royals might have no direct control over the Order, but they still had plenty of influence. Sorcha was sure that she was about to feel some of it.

"Deacon Faris." The Grand Duchess' voice was still deeply marked by the accent of Delmaire. Unlike her brother, she had not taken pains to remove it. Even with her arm in a sling, Zofiya stood ramrod straight as her gaze ran up the length of Sorcha.

The Deacon bristled at being treated like one of the damn Imperial Guard, but she held herself in check. "Your Imperial Highness." She dipped her head to the appropriate level. "I am glad to see you are fully recovered."

Zofiya shrugged, the brass of her military jacket gleaming in the wan sunlight. "Viscount Jurlise was lucky."

Before Sorcha could catch herself, she let out a snort. "Not that lucky—I hear you shot him between the eyes like he was a prize stag!"

Dueling wasn't common in the Empire, but the Grand Duchess was not one to turn away when her brother was insulted. When the two of them were new to their positions, many had disagreed with their appointment. Back then the Grand Duchess Zofiya had spent a great deal of time shooting at the aristocracy. These days there were few who were stupid enough to slight the Emperor within her hearing. The rumor was that her father had been more than happy to send his difficult youngest daughter off with her brother—before his own dukes and earls were decimated.

Zofiya's eyebrow rose, but she made no comment. Perhaps she recognized an attempt at distraction when she heard one. "I understand there was some kind of geist attack outside the very gates of the palace. I hope the Deacons are still capable of doing their job."

The Grand Duchess had seen plenty of evidence that they were. When the Order had sailed with her to this new and troubled land, she and her brother had witnessed plenty of geists being handled. Sorcha bit the inside of her cheek so that observation didn't pop out. "It was an unusual event, Imperial Highness, but we quickly had the situation under control."

"My brother and I count on the Order to take care of these things." She jerked on fine black gloves and shot Sorcha a calculating look. "If there are any issues we should be aware of . . ."

By the Bones, Sorcha thought, *I am not made for this intrigue.* "The Arch Abbot is fully aware, Imperial Highness, and we are taking steps to make sure it will not happen again."

"I should hope so. Citizens being killed by geists at the very gates of the palace is not the image my serene brother wants to convey. People need assurance that we are in control. You can be confident I will be talking to Arch Abbot Hastler further on this matter!"

Sorcha knew there was no retort for that one. The Grand Duchess made her feel like an initiate again, so she merely nodded agreement and stood as still as possible as the other woman strode from the infirmary with her adoring soldier trailing in her wake.

This day was getting worse by the moment. Sorcha sighed, straightened her cloak and tilted her chin up. Facing her husband was going to be easy after a kick in the teeth from both the Arch Abbot and royalty.

Making her way out of the general ward, she paused at the

only locked door in the infirmary. Beyond she could just make
out the wails of the geist-struck Deacons; locked away lest they
wander in their madness. A shudder of deep fear ran through
her—she did not envy their caretakers.

Kolya was in the smaller ward, the place where the more criti-
cally injured were kept. In here it smelled sharply of vinegar,
and there were fewer Brothers. The one at the door was mixing
potions and nodded to her as she came in. Sorcha inclined her
head, but was also taking the time for a deep breath. The atmosphere in here was even more oppressive and silent. The Brothers
moved about on muffled slippers, and the only sounds were the
labored breathing of the patients and the odd moan of pain.

Kolya was at the far end of the room, two of the Brothers hovering around him like bees. She might have faced the unliving of
all types, but seeing her partner and husband lying there gave her
pause. Sorcha found herself on tiptoes as she approached his bed.
The healers made room for her to take a seat at her husband's
side. They continued to bustle around the room, and Sorcha sat
almost motionless and watched Kolya.

The previous day he had looked better. He'd been gray and
pale and bleeding, yet today he was enveloped in bandages and
had sandbags up against his sides to hold him steady. He didn't
look anything like her husband, this still form on the bed.

As she sat there watching him, Sorcha waited to be swallowed
by a tide of emotions. She knew she should feel devastated. She'd
spent enough time in the infirmary to see how wives react at
times like this. But nothing came.

I don't feel broken like I should, she thought to herself. *I don't
feel anything.* The truth was it was more than a year since she had
felt anything real or passionate toward Kolya.

Her had shut her out—quite an impressive feat for a Bonded
Deacon—and yet he had not always been this way. After the terrible ache of losing three partners in quick succession, Kolya had
seemed a safe haven, a smooth harbor in a storm. Only now was
she realizing that she needed something more. And yesterday
morning she had been nearly ready to speak her mind. Now that
chance had been taken away from her. If she believed in Fate,
she'd think him cruel indeed.

"He is quite heavily drugged," Brother Elies, the man charged
with Kolya's care, whispered, making her lurch out of her reverie.
"Yet he is showing signs of brief moments of consciousness."

"Good." Sorcha nodded, daring another look.

"But there are also signs of unliving canker in him."

The Otherside was a dangerous realm, and those who suffered its effects often were left with something similar to mortal poisoning. While Kolya's wounds were life-threatening enough, it was the infection in his blood that would take the longest recovery time.

Carefully she touched the back of his hand; it was swollen and very warm. Kolya stirred. His pale blue eyes roved around the ceiling before finally drifting over to his wife. Yet there was no sign of emotion. His smooth features showed neither distress nor passion, nor anything at all. *Just the same as always,* Sorcha thought bitterly, then, realizing how awful that was, smiled as best she could. "How are you, Kolya?" It was a stupid question; she realized that as soon as it was out of her mouth.

"Oh, you know," came the faint reply. Always so self-contained, even in pain. Her teeth ground together. Absolutely no way to light a cigar in here, nor was there any way that she could continue the argument begun that morning. Like Garil, it was something that would have to wait until she returned, until she could tell him the truth.

"I have a mission. The Abbot has assigned me a temporary partner. I leave tomorrow." She said it quickly.

Kolya's brow furrowed a little. Most husbands and partners would have been outraged, but he only shrugged a bit. "I am sure he knows what's best."

She cleared her throat, feeling her hands growing clammy. "I imagine so, but it means that I must leave you alone."

"That's what we do, Sorcha." As always, it was like pushing against nothing, struggling to get any reaction. Perhaps getting away was a good idea after all.

Pushing her copper hair out of her eyes, she rocked back on the stool. "I should be here with you," she murmured, sounding unconvincing to her ears.

Brother Elies shuffled to the other side of the bed. He had a small bowl of something foul-smelling in one hand. "We need to . . ."

Sorcha hastily stood up. She didn't want to see what they were doing to Kolya, didn't want to hear him in pain. Even their Bond felt faint and half-broken by what had been done to him—like their marriage. "That's all right . . . I . . . I have to pack."

Words that usually came so easily to her lips had somehow dried up. "Be safe," Kolya whispered from the bed.

Leaning over, she dropped a kiss onto his pale forehead, holding back all those feelings that had been bubbling up in her for months. "I will try," she whispered in return.

The Arch Abbot may have done her a favor—but it had only put off the inevitable.

Cleaning up after his new partner before he had even met her was not, Deacon Merrick Chambers decided, a good sign. He stood alone in the bustling Artisan Quarter of Vermillion and opened his Center wide. Presbyter Rictun had demanded that every Sensitive in residence at the Mother Abbey scour the streets for any sign of the geist that had attacked Deacons Faris and Petav.

Around the young Deacon, the bustle of Vermillion went on as if the confrontation at the gates of the palace had never happened—at least to normal eyes and ears. Merrick, however, was not normal.

He saw a huddle of women at the corner of the street by the coopers' yard and could hear their agitated conversation as sharply as if he were among them. Interesting. They were talking of the near riot—with no mention of the geist's involvement. It was not his place to question the Order, but Merrick found the use of magical cantrips and misinformation to hide the truth distasteful. This, along with the fact that Presbyter Rictun had not shared the exact nature of the geist they now sought, left Merrick feeling deeply unsettled. Still, he had not trained for years to throw it all away now; not on the very cusp of acceptance.

Overhead an Imperial blimp passed, its weirstone engines giving off a low hum, the weak winter sun gleaming on its brass fittings. The new airships were still a rarity anywhere outside of the capital city—especially in the countryside where Merrick's family lived. Merrick glanced up at it in fascination. Maybe if he was lucky, one day his missions as a Deacon would take him aboard one.

For now he had to banish all those blue-sky thoughts from his mind. He had a job to do. Pushing his dark hair out of his eyes and turning slowly, Merrick opened his Center wider—searching for the trace of geist among the living.

A humming, soft but insistent, began behind his eyes. People, rats, horses, dogs, cats, even the smallest insect burned in his mind like tiny pinpricks of light. His senses raced over stone roofs, spread out along the streets dedicated to craft and art, and delved below into the sewers. The essence of every living creature, dark or light, was revealed. Nothing escaped Merrick's notice.

Finally he was satisfied. He had done his duty and cleared the section of street he'd been assigned. It was time to get back anyway.

Crossing the Farewell Bridge, Merrick paused for a moment. The Imperial capital was beautiful this early. The sun gleamed on the icy canals and reflected off the faint snow on the rooftops. He loved the myriad bridges that led to the center and could name only half of them. This city was now home, and today he would confirm that. The young Deacon set forth with determination.

His path took him through the Merchant Quarter, packed with wagons, carts and stalls. The scents of exotic spices competed with the stench of horse and man for his attention. Stepping out of the way of haggling merchants and Tinkers, he dropped a shilling into the grubby hand of a tiny girl child who sat in misery near a stack of cartons.

She would be lucky to survive the winter. When she looked up at the young Deacon he tucked her fingers firmly around the silver. "At midday at the Abbey there is food and drink available for free, little one."

When she tried to get to her feet, he realized she wouldn't make it on her own. So tucking the little bird fingers around his neck, he carried her with him. Silently the girl dropped her head on his shoulder and sighed.

Most likely Presbyter Rictun would think a Deacon carrying a filthy orphan into the heart of the Empire unbecoming, but Merrick knew the true meaning of the Order even if his superiors had forgotten.

Together, then, the Deacon and the child passed through the granite gates and into the Civic Center that lay at the very heart of Vermillion.

The houses here were magnificent, belonging to the most aristocratic families; those who could afford to live close to the Emperor. Carriages rattled past full of finely dressed lords and ladies, and his heightened Sensitive smell caught alternating waves of perfume and wig powder. These treelined streets were far quieter and more elegant than the less salubrious sections of the city. However, Merrick, despite having been raised an aristocrat, found them stifling and too pretentious.

He hurried through these parts, until the level ground began to slope upward toward the palace and the Abbey. His pace quickened further as he murmured words of comfort to the little girl.

Once beyond the gates he found Melisande Troupe, Presbyter of the Young, and gave the waif into her gentle care. Only then did he race up the stairs to his cell to prepare.

It was one of many narrow rooms in the dormitory with only a small bed and a pine dresser in it. Though members of the Order had few possessions, the top of his was scattered with tiny cogs and tools. Merrick had always been fascinated by mechanics, and in fact as a child he had dreamed of being a Tinker's apprentice—that was, until his father's death.

Now he pushed this little project of his away. Today was the beginning of his new dream.

After washing his face and neck and combing his hair, Deacon Merrick Chambers wiped his palms down the length of his tunic for what felt like the fifth time in as many minutes. Then he stepped out of his chamber.

Despite the season, he was sweating as if it were high summer. His little errand had put off this moment, but now the stress and terror came rushing back full force. The cause of it was his new partner; She Who Must Be Obeyed. The one time Merrick had met her as an adult, his tongue had stuck to the roof of his mouth; speechless was not the young Deacon's normal state.

As he adjusted his badge of rank and prepared for their second meeting, he remembered those sharp blue eyes. The most famous Active in the Order would have been a good target to fall in love with—beautiful, powerful and unattainable—but for Merrick that wasn't an option. Deacon Sorcha Faris scared the shit out of him.

Unlike many of her fellow Deacons, Merrick had seen her power unleashed to its fullest. He was also one of the few who had lived to remember the experience. Usually he managed to forget that night, but today as he checked his uniform in the mirror at the top of the stairs, it was unavoidable. The scars were still evident in the ancient stone of his family's castle. The place where his father had died was marked at the top of the grand staircase by five long gouges.

"And now she's your new partner." Merrick took a deep

breath. She couldn't know; he'd made sure the Abbey would never find out his real name, and it was unlikely she'd recognize him. He'd been only seven and not allowed to meet the explosive young Deacon come to test his father. Yet he had seen it all, hidden in the chamber above.

Taking the spiral staircase down, Merrick practiced keeping his Center still. As long as he did, Deacon Faris was too weak a Sensitive to catch any stray thoughts. He didn't anticipate their partnership lasting long enough for them to actually build any sort of deep Bond.

The Arch Abbot and Yvril Mournling, Presbyter of Sensitives, were waiting for Merrick in the Chapter House.

Merrick had seen little of the Arch Abbot himself during his training, but he'd spent many hours under the stern gray eyes of Presbyter Mournling. Though the older man was a member of the Presbyterial Council, he still made time to teach the advanced classes to the Sensitives. The corners of his mouth lifted in the faintest of smiles when he saw the young Deacon—the newest member of the Order. Arch Abbot Hastler held a long wooden box in one wizened hand. Actives had their Gauntlets, but the Sensitives were not without their toys either. Hastler opened the container.

"Name them and control them." He spoke the words of the final test.

Merrick swallowed hard, though he had repeated the Litany of Sight hundreds and hundreds of times. He held his hand over the box and its contents.

> *Sielu, I see through another's eyes.*
> *Aiemm, the past is real.*
> *Masa, the future is a puzzle.*
> *Kebenar, I am open to the truth of all things.*
> *Kolar, this soul has wings.*
> *Mennyt, no path is locked, even to the Otherside.*
> *Ticat, the name unspoken, the purpose in shadow.*

Merrick glanced up. That last rune would never be spoken of in the presence of anyone but a Sensitive, and his mouth still stumbled on that final phrase.

But Presbyter Mournling merely nodded and then spoke the words every Sensitive hoped to live by: "See deep, fear nothing." His smile was cheery, but somehow did not reach his gray eyes.

With a deep bow Merrick took the contents of the box. Made of thick brown leather—the Strop might have at first been mistaken for a wide belt; it did indeed have a pierced length on one end and a buckle on the other. However, on closer examination the Strop was tooled with the seven Runes of Sight. The only other decoration was his personal sigil that he'd carved laboriously from obsidian, set on a brass loop and which would sit, once the Strop was in place, between his eyes, and above his nose. This rock-and-metal setting could also be slid up by virtue of the loop to rest higher, against the third eye. Though it held all the Runes of Sight, wearing the Strop was necessary only to invoke the final two. The Strop blinded the Sensitive to the real world but heightened his exposure to the unliving. Thus, it had to be used with more caution than the Active's Gauntlets. Its hidden purpose, the one only Sensitives knew about, made it more powerful than the dazzling gloves.

After receiving the blessing of both of his superiors, Merrick got to his feet. The Arch Abbot's hands shook as he closed the box, but his eyes were still sharp. "Don't let Deacon Faris see your nerves, young Deacon. Remember, we wouldn't be sending you if you were not equal to the task."

This would have been comforting had Merrick not known more about her than Hastler possibly could imagine. He merely smiled at his superiors and nodded.

Deacon Sorcha Faris was waiting for him in the rectory. She had her back to him when he entered, making a good display that she didn't care. Merrick made no effort to conceal his entrance, so her pretense was obvious. She was wearing the dark blue cloak of the Active, and when she turned around in an almost lazy fashion, her Gauntlets were clearly visible tucked into her belt. It wasn't the norm for them to be kept there within the bounds of the Abbey, but then, this, too, was probably for his benefit.

She was of average height, but that was the only thing average about her. The bright auburn curls, which she usually kept tied up, lay on her shoulders and down her back. Perhaps she had heard he was younger than she and was trying to look a similar age. Her face was deceptively soft and beautiful, but when she spoke, the strength of her personality changed that perception. It was another weapon in her arsenal and Merrick was sure she knew how to use it.

Among the novices, Sorcha Faris was something of a regular

conversation starter. She'd been one of the youngest Deacons to gain full rank, yet had been among the last to receive Teisyat. Hours were whiled away trying to decide why that might be. Merrick, more than most, had a good idea.

What he'd heard, and what he believed was actually true, was that she had power in full measure, but that her control was sometimes in question. It was just the ultimate irony that he was being partnered up with the one Deacon who gave him nightmares.

And now she was looking him up and down. He didn't need to be a Sensitive to know what she was thinking. *Unholy Bones, they've teamed me up with a child!*

It was his dark curly hair and maybe the touch of Ancient blood in him that did it. Everyone always assumed he was only a teenager, when in fact he'd seen twenty-three years his last birthday. Sorcha might be in her late thirties, but she still bridled at the assumptions she'd obviously made about him in the first thirty seconds. Age had nothing to do with competence as far as Merrick was concerned.

"Haven't we met?" she said, eyebrows knitting together in an expression that wasn't totally related to memory recall.

For a second he froze, and only Deacon training kept shock off his face. Then he realized what she must mean. "You taught a basic class in structure of the Gauntlet in my second year."

She grinned in a somewhat feral way. "You asked a question about Teisyat, didn't you?"

At the time, Merrick recalled experiencing the same sick feeling that was building up in his stomach now, but he had indeed asked the question. He couldn't be sure that she remembered what it was, but he did. *How much control does the tenth Active Rune require?*

She hadn't answered, just glared. It had been innocently asked, though, for at that moment he'd had no idea she was having problems with that very same issue. Now he decided just to shrug and take refuge in the "I'm just a Sensitive" act.

"Well," Sorcha sighed, "we better get this over and done with."

Merrick's heart leapt, racing like a jackrabbit's, but he held his hands palm up to her. The bustle of Deacons and lay Brothers at the door suddenly seemed like it was calling to him. If he just darted out into the corridor, he could join them and get away from this moment.

He took a quick, nervous glance down at his hands; mercifully, they were still dry.

Placing her palms down against his own, she locked eyes with him. Hers were the darkest blue he'd ever seen, with an almost-black circle right round the iris. For an instant nothing seemed to be happening, and then came the tug.

It was his first partnership; he knew it was her fifth. She was not gentle, but then, he'd not expected her to be. The wrenching pull broke him free of the real world. He was plunged down into Sorcha Faris, spiraling into her eyes and consciousness in a way that actually hurt. He could feel the bright gateway within her, that place through which the Actives drew power from the Otherside. Inside her head, it burned hot and white and large, and it seemed ready to consume all that he was.

With a stifled yelp, Merrick returned to his own body. The Bond was formed, fragile and not at all comfortable, but definitely there. It would take some time for him to adjust to the awareness of Sorcha in the periphery of his senses.

"Good, then." She snatched back her hands and for a moment almost looked like she might wipe them on her trousers. "I see you have your Strop. Is the rest of your kit packed?"

He nodded. "I got it down to the stables last night. I understand the Abbot wants us to leave immediately."

"That's what I heard." And then she turned and strode out of the room, utterly confident that he would follow after.

Fear and anger did a brief battle inside Merrick's head. She might only be of average height, but she moved as quickly as a person twice as tall. He found himself at a near trot to keep up with her. In this way they made smart progress out of the confines of the Abbey, toward the outbuildings. Novices were already in classes but the lay members of the Order were up and about. At this time of the year there was little to do in the gardens, but many were bustling around the stables. Geist activity was not solely limited to manipulating humanity. Locals often brought their livestock in to be freed of unliving influences.

Sorcha was going to ignore him as much as she could. She was colder than the late-autumn day, and the only thing Merrick had to warm himself was his growing anger, so he nurtured it a little.

"Perhaps"—he smiled at her while matching her pace—

"perhaps you could tell me exactly what happened outside the gates two days ago? The whole Abbey is rife with rumor."

Her stride broke for just an instant. "The Abbot will talk about it at Matins when it is appropriate."

"Ah, but you see, we will be gone before that happens; and besides, now I am your partner . . ."

Sorcha stopped completely and spun about. He observed how she held her body in tight, tense lines. "Are you trying to irritate me? You're bringing up things I have no control over, and I don't like having no control. Having no control makes me exceedingly cranky, and when I get cranky, I eat novices for breakfast."

Merrick found himself enjoying the moment. He could actually vaguely sense her discomfort on the edge of his perception. He liked it. "Fair point," he replied with a slight twist in his lips, "but I am no longer a novice and therefore not on the menu. I only want to be the best partner possible." The tinge of humor in his voice was apparent even to himself.

It was also immediately obvious that his gentle dig was not the sort of thing she appreciated. Her mouth opened a couple of times before she finally ground out, "You can do that by being the quietest partner ever."

He made the universal lip-buttoning gesture with one eyebrow cocked. Sorcha stared at him hard for a minute, before turning away and shaking her head. "Unholy Bones, I need a smoke."

Merrick followed her meekly into the stables. The idea of pointing out how the infirmary staff had told him that smoking of any sort was injurious to a person's health popped into his head. However, pushing the point, he sensed, bordered on the dangerous. Many of the Deacons smoked and drank. It was not as if there was any injunction against it, and the life of a Deacon was generally not long.

His would be shorter than most if he crossed his new partner. After what he'd seen as a child, his fear of her wasn't going to go away. But he might have discovered a way to hide it.

Inside, the lay Brothers had saddled up two of the Abbey horses for them. The Breed was almost as ancient as the Order; jet-black, tough as a mountain pony but as beautiful as any from the Emperor's stable. If there was one real perk to doing battle with the forces of the Otherside, it was the chance to ride one of the Deacon Breed.

None of the Deacons actually personally owned any of the Breed, since the only objects any of them kept solely for themselves were the tools of their trade, but particular animals became favored by certain Deacons. Sorcha was examining her stallion, running her hands down his legs and over the withers to check his fitness. She was taking more care doing this than she had in forging the Bond with Merrick. Sometimes being a Sensitive was too much to bear.

"Shedryi?" Merrick cocked his head and examined the stallion. "He was shipped over from the old country, wasn't he? A bit long in the tooth to be relied upon, surely?"

Sorcha glanced up, and her look was pure venom. "And what about me, young Deacon? Would you say I'm a bit long in the tooth as well? Shedryi and I have a real relationship, which is more than can be said for us right now."

Not being that clued up on his horseflesh and also sensing danger in the air, he decided to concentrate on his own mount. As a novice he'd been trained to ride on a variety of lesser horses, and had sat on one of the Breed only in the last few months of training. He'd not settled on a favorite and was happy enough to accept the stablemaster's choice.

Melochi was smaller than Sorcha's stallion, but she seemed well proportioned and more biddable. Her wide dark eye followed him with an expression that might have been resignation, but that was better than the fierce look in Shedryi's. Merrick made a mental note to keep out of the stallion's reach. He had a wicked look about him, as if he had understood the man's aspersions. The pack mule, who he found out was named Horace, was tied to the pommel of Melochi's saddle and looked resigned to his lot in life; following around the superior breed. Merrick wondered if that was to be his lot as well.

Having completed her check of horses, mules and supplies, Sorcha swung up onto Shedryi. Merrick could have sworn she was still glaring at him. "I take it you are a good enough horseman to keep up."

He shrugged. "Winner of the All Novices four-hundred-yard gallop, runner-up in the—"

"A simple yes would suffice," Sorcha grumbled, her bandaged fingers pinching the bridge of her nose as if she were in pain.

"Well, then . . . I suppose so."

"Good, because the fastest way north is going to be the road. The currents around Vermillion are treacherous this time of year, and no ships are leaving until next week at the earliest."

"The Abbot needs us there that urgently?" Merrick had been so long thinking about the ramifications of partnering with Sorcha that he had not really taken much note of their first assignment. "I can catch up on the details when I read the report," he said as smoothly as possible.

This was obviously immensely cheering to his new companion; she actually chuckled. "I'll get you up-to-date with the salient points on the way, lad. You won't have time on the ride to be reading any reports. Keeping your seat on these roads will be enough work."

And with that, Deacon Faris urged Shedryi out of the stable and onto the open road, leaving her fifth and newest partner to once again rush to catch up.

FOUR

No Place for Sanctuary

Raed walked down to the beach with a knot in the pit of his stomach. By the rowboat, five of his crew members waited. Explaining to them the small concession he'd been able to get would be just a taster for explaining to the whole ship.

The title Young Pretender was not one that Raed would have wished on anyone, and yet he had a crew of thirty men and women willing to tie their fates to his. He felt responsible, deeply aware that any decisions he made would affect them. Most followed him in the vague hope that one day he would sit on the Vermillion throne, others because their own families owed allegiance to his. Not one of them wanted him to have the same miserable existence as the Unsung.

So now they traveled the coast, trading and stealing where necessary. Some might call it piracy, yet it was essential for them to keep moving. Even being this long on dry land made Raed a little nervous. He found himself down the cliff path to get to his crew, despite knowing that he bore bad news.

Aachon, his first mate, was watching him with the eagle intensity the older man gave to everything. His clothes were as ragtag as everyone else's, but somehow he pulled it off better than even Raed did. His olive complexion and dark hair could have made rags seem noble. Aachon had been looking after Raed for years, given the care of the Pretender by his father the Unsung. It was a duty that he took incredibly seriously.

"How was your request received, my prince?"

Raed had tried getting Aachon to call him by his given name; the request, or even the order, never seemed to stick for very long. He felt his stomach tense but he tried not to let any of it appear in his stance. "We have been given permission to berth in Ulrich."

"I've never heard of it." Byrd, the youngest member of the rowboat crew, had none of his elder's respect for the name and supposed title. Raed was often glad of it.

Aachon's head, however, jerked in his direction. Byrd took the hint and was silent. "Ulrich, my lord," the first mate whispered under his breath, his expression dark. "Such a place is a deliberate insult."

The rest of the crew looked away, probably as embarrassed at Aachon's feeling of dishonor as Raed was. Sometimes he felt his first mate should have been born the Pretender. He could certainly recite the whole family tree of the Rossin and name all the major battles in their history.

Raed sighed and clapped a hand on his friend's back. "We are starting to run out of sway in this neck of the woods. The new Emperor is gaining support every day. Some are saying he is a better ruler than any in my family ever were."

"But he is a usurper," Aachon spluttered. "He has not the right to the throne that he sits on—they should remember their place!"

"That is not what the Assembly are concerned with, and it was their choice, after all. Let's keep our eye on the positives. For right now, we have to be able to keep on sailing. As long as we do, there is hope."

The two men held each other's gaze for a moment, and it was Aachon who finally looked away. With a shake of his head he seemed to suddenly lose a few inches in height. "You are right, my lord—excuse my rash words. It matters little where we make repairs, as long as we do."

They quickly scrambled into the boat and pushed off. The feeling of water under him was soothing. He was glad to find that the Curse had not activated in the middle of Felstaad's court; that would have put the cat among the pigeons, and would most likely have ended rather badly. He shot a look across at Aachon and guessed the same thought was probably in his head too.

It had been nearly a year since he'd dared set foot on land, but it had been worth the risk. Felstaad would not have dealt with any of his crew, even the charismatic Aachon. Now at least they had a destination.

Raed turned his head toward the mouth of the bay, and there moored in the gentle currents was home. *Dominion* was a small, fast brigantine, with a nice shallow draft that allowed her into shallow harbors that many could not travel. She was the one thing his father had ever given him, apart from an unwanted heritage, and now she was the only vessel in all the seas that still flew the flag of his family; a roaring lion with the tail of a mer-creature, the Rossin. It had once been a creature of magic. Now it made Raed shiver. It was a warning from the Ancients, one that none had believed until his birth.

"My lord." Aachon touched his shoulder, no doubt noticing the direction of his gaze. His first mate had the observational skills of the Sensitive Deacon he'd so nearly become. He lowered his voice and glanced over his shoulder. The rest of the crew were busying pulling for the ship and bantering among themselves. "There was a little trouble while you were gone."

He opened his right hand to reveal the weirstone that had cost almost a chest of gold to obtain. The polished orb was cobalt blue, but every few moments a sheen of white gleamed over the surface. This had nothing to do with the light. Raed knew it was heavy but Aachon carried it as if it were a child's toy—that, it most definitely was not.

Deacons were not the only ones to commune with the unliving; they were just the best trained. Aachon's family had always been seers; hence the Unsung's choice of him as Raed's protector. But Aachon's skill was not of the first order, and it was only with the acquisition of the weirstone that he was able to See into the ether.

Raed dared a glimpse into the orb. The stone thinned the barrier between the beyond and the real world. It was a very dangerous thing, and it made the hair on his arms stand up, but it had saved them all on numerous occasions. "What sort of trouble?" he asked through a dry throat.

"A couple of shades on top of the cliffs. Probably the souls of people lost in a wreck of some sort."

Raed concealed a shudder as best he could. As always the image of his mother's horrified face flashed in his eye, the taste of her blood in his mouth. Not for the first time did he wish that suicide was an option. If only his sister, Fraine, wasn't next in line for the title Pretender and the Curse that went with it.

He just had to do his best by staying on the ocean. It would have almost served Felstaad right if he'd run across a geist in his court . . . almost. That was the danger of dry land: the constant threat of geists. If they had crossed his path on the cliff tops . . . He pulled his mind away from that possibility.

And now they would be sailing toward another port, and with *Dominion* being pulled from her native environment, he would have no choice. "Well, maybe if I just stay on the beach with my feet in the water while we're in Ulrich, everything will be all right." He chuckled.

Aachon frowned, never a connoisseur of Raed's sense of humor at the best of times.

The Pretender shook his head with a little sigh. "What other choice do we have, old friend? *Dominion* needs to be repaired and scraped down. She's slow in the water and we're leaking every time the sea gets rough. We can only survive if we can run."

It was actually possible to hear Aachon grind his teeth in frustration. Most people just used it as an expression; the first mate used it as a method of communication. He nodded reluctantly.

They had reached the heaving sides of their ship. Raed scrambled up the side with the others while the rowboat was tied in close to her stern. He hadn't been born to life on the open seas, but after so many years he was as nimble on deck as those who had been. Aloft in the rigging he might not be the fastest, but he had been known to climb up if an emergency called. He might be captain, but he was all too aware that it was a title he sometimes had to work at.

Up on deck, the rest of the crew waited. They were a collection of every ethnic group on the continent, with a slight majority from the warmer southern climes where the legend of the Unsung still might mean something. Most were male, though several women had also tied their fortunes to the Pretender. Now all were looking at him and waiting for the word on how his petition had gone.

"Well"—he grinned at them—"as I remembered, Felstaad is a bastard."

They snickered at that, but held back the belly laughs until certain of the outcome.

"But I finally convinced him that he might want to at least cover all the angles and give us brief sanctuary. He's allowing us to make use of Ulrich harbor."

As expected, his announcement wasn't greeted with uproars

of delight. Several whispers murmured through the crew as some of the assembled turned to their neighbors with quiet questions about the unfamiliar port. Raed managed not to take it personally. He didn't hold it against them, but he knew it was a reflection of his standing in the world; once, the mere mention of his distant father would have brought a bushel of princes rushing to his aid. Since the Assembly at Briet had brought the Delmaire man over, life had gotten harder and harder. If he thought about it too much, he might just stop running altogether.

Bless them, though; none grumbled about the distance to get there, or the isolation of the place. Raed was just about to express his gratitude in some joke or other, when a call came from above. High in the crow's nest, Aleck called out the one word none of them wanted to hear. "Warship!"

Everyone scattered to their stations. Aachon slapped a spyglass in Raed's hands and he trained it in the direction Aleck was pointing. To the north was indeed an Imperial warship: *Corsair*. They'd had repeated run-ins with that very same vessel for the past three months. It was patrolling the northeast shore with a disturbing new show of interest in the area. They'd made a successful run for it each time that *Corsair* had shown up before. However, they were in a sheltered harbor with light winds, and their anchor was down. Raed didn't like the odds.

Bringing the warship into focus, he tried to make out whether her gunports were open. They weren't, but as he looked he noticed two very odd things: there was no one visible on the deck and, more important, no hand was at the wheel.

"By the Blood," he whispered to himself and swung the spyglass backward and forward over the ship's length before raising the glass toward the rigging. This too was bare of any sign of life, and the sails themselves were tied in as if for running before a high wind, rather than for today's light conditions. Captain Moresh ran a tight ship, from what Raed had heard. A knot of tension began to form in the Pretender's neck.

"She's coming in slow." Aachon, without the benefit of the spyglass, had a hand raised over his eyes as he squinted at *Corsair*.

"Prepare to board," Raed said evenly.

"But, Captain . . ." Aachon protested, until he was handed the spyglass. His argument died on his lips. When he lowered the glass, sweat beaded on his forehead. He wiped it off with the back of one hand and wrapped his other around the hilt of his cutlass. "Mistress Laython, prepare your party to board and offer assistance."

On the lower deck, the battle-scarred quartermaster grinned. They had seen little action lately, and her skills had not been in much demand. She began shouting at the crew in a voice like a foghorn.

"Seems as if you put that weirstone away too early, old friend," Raed said to Aachon under his breath.

Despite the ship's sad condition, *Dominion*'s crew knew her intimately and were quickly under way. With expert ease, Aachon set them to their work getting her out into open waters. Within half an hour, they had turned about and were matching speed with the warship. As they neared, it became apparent to all that she was, in fact, in worse state than their own vessel. Coming up on the port side, they could see that sails were ripped as if from a terrible storm. The hull damage only a little above the waterline looked nothing like the impact of cannon; instead it looked as if something had blown out from inside, though it was nowhere near where the powder room was located. The Pretender's hand clenched on his cutlass.

Even though *Corsair* had pursued her for so long, Raed felt real pity for the once-magnificent warship. She was a sad remnant of the pride of the Imperial Navy.

Their own party was ready; he and Aachon were in the lead with weapons drawn. Laython and her grinning party were at their backs. Yet as they drew up alongside and the boarding hooks were thrown across, Raed knew that there would be no fight.

The deck was covered in bodies, all wearing the dark green of the Imperial Marines or the sky blue of the Navy, though both shades were much darker than they should have been. The sharp smell of blood wafted from *Corsair* in a palpable cloud.

With a glance over his shoulder, Raed saw that most of his crew had turned very pale. They were sailors in the main, not used to battle and blood.

"Aachon, is the weirstone showing anything?" he asked quietly over his shoulder.

His first mate should have protested, perhaps reminding his captain that they were in open water, but with one look at the carnage on board *Corsair*, he mutely removed the heavy orb from his pocket.

Aachon's eyes changed when he looked into the orb, going to a clear milky white as if he were blind. He kept his back to the crew whenever using his Sight; he knew it disturbed them. When he'd been cast from the Order, Aachon's pride had taken a deep beating. Now he cosseted what little talent remained.

After a moment, his eyes cleared. "I see nothing aboard but death and the memory of it."

"Very well." Raed clapped him on the shoulder. "The rest of you, wait here." For once they followed his orders mutely. He and Aachon leapt across to *Corsair*'s deck.

The first step and Raed nearly slipped. Ships were cruel like that: they held on to blood once the scuppers were blocked. And this was very, very fresh blood, and the drainage holes were indeed blocked by masses of bodies.

It was hardly the first time that either he or Aachon had faced such a sight; there had been plenty of battles with princes when he was younger. Many had come to the Unsung's place of exile to kill him, and Raed had fought on his father's behalf. However, this was different.

His senses were only mortal, so he could hardly bear to imagine what his first mate was going through. The stenches of spilled guts, blood and fear were thick over the deck. They both took a moment to steady themselves physically and mentally.

It looked, at first sight, as if every soldier and sailor had died on deck. As Raed and Aachon began to pick their way down toward the quarterdeck where Captain Moresh had presumably once stood, they rolled the occasional body over to see what had caused their death.

Raed quickly realized that they really needed to perform only one such examination. It had been nothing human. No bullet had pierced the sailor he examined, nor had he been stabbed or slashed with any saber or cutlass. The Pretender had hunted wild boar on his father's island and had seen men gored before him. These wounds resembled this more than anything, angry gouges from some great beast with tusks ten times larger than that of any animal he knew.

His fingertips tingled where they grasped the poor dead man's arm. With a gasp Raed jerked upright, shaking his hand and feeling his skin begin to crawl.

"My prince?" Aachon was at his side, weirstone in one fist, cutlass in the other. The orb only reflected blue.

"No, it's all right. It's all right," Raed repeated with a final shake of his hand. The assertion, he knew, was more for his own benefit than for his friend's. The tingling mercifully subsided, but the shock of it had been enough to pull him out of his fear of the dead.

Ignoring the massacre, Raed picked his way through the bodies to the quarterdeck. Here it appeared that some sort of last stand had taken place. Sailors had shoved barrels and coils of ropes down the short steps to the main deck in an effort to block whatever had wreaked havoc there.

Together Raed and Aachon clambered over this makeshift barricade. Whatever had killed *Corsair*'s crew had obviously become enraged at the last few survivors. The remains clustered around the wheel were barely recognizable as human. Both men turned away for a second, sucking in the slightly cleaner air near the gunwales.

Carefully, Raed turned around and tried his best to dispassionately survey the scene for any further clues. He found himself stating the obvious just to get it out of his head. "This was no attack by a man. All the bodies are Imperial, well-trained men. They would have brought down one or two . . . unless the enemy took their dead when they departed . . ."

Aachon raised the orb; through it and milky eyes he surveyed the scene. "There is only their blood." He paused and his breath hissed over his teeth. "My prince, there is no trace of their souls onboard. Such carnage . . . and no souls." His eyes cleared as he lowered the stone, and expressed foreboding. They both knew what that meant.

"A geist of some sort?" Raed whispered, taking in the bloodbath all around them. "But, open water . . . Open water, Aachon . . ." He could feel his precious safety melting away, leaving a chill pit of fear behind. This couldn't be happening.

His friend looked gray at the prospect as well. It was a fact that the Deacons knew—it was a fact that every man, woman and child that breathed knew—geists could not cross a stream, river or ocean. Some of the lesser sorts could even be bested by a full chamber pot.

Raed wondered if this rock-solid, immovable fact had been the last thought on Captain Moresh's mind as he was shredded like a joint of meat. He imagined so. He could see them all screaming it over and over again as they died in agony. And then their souls were gone.

Geists hungered for souls. Most didn't have the strength to take them, though, and were forced to rely on scaring mortals as best they could. Whatever variety of unliving had done all this had more power than any Raed had ever heard of.

He cleared his throat. "You're Deacon-trained, Aachon . . . Did they teach you what kind of geist could wreak this much death?"

His friend shook his head, and Raed noticed that Aachon's grip on the weirstone had become decidedly shaky. "There is nothing—you understand, nothing—that I know of, that can do this. A geist that kills like this . . . Even your—" He stopped suddenly. He'd almost said it; almost crossed the line they had both silently agreed upon. The absolute shock on Aachon's face had nothing to do with the horror around them. "I am sorry, my prince. I . . . I . . ."

"This has got us both knocked back, old friend." He squeezed the other's arm. "Luckily we both know that I wasn't on *Corsair*." His attempt at humor fell flat in very unfertile ground.

"Of course!" Aachon whirled about and began clambering past the ineffectual barricade, back to the main deck.

"What is it?" Raed yelled after him, rushing to follow.

"The ship's weirstone." His friend stood in front of the doors to the cabins, like a man gearing himself up to dive. "Every Imperial warship has a weirstone of the top rank, keyed by the Deacons to warn of geist storms. Stones also remember, just in case humans don't survive to tell."

Raed nodded. Geists might not be known to cross water, but sometimes particularly vindictive ones were known to whip up foul weather near the coastline just for amusement. The Deacons had begun to make life easier for everyone. His grandfather's foolishness in dismissing their native Deacons had been merely the first in the list of bloody stupid mistakes; mistakes they were still paying for.

"Right, then. We find the weirstone." It felt good to have something to do, yet both of them stood at the doors for a second. What horrors lurked back there?

When Raed finally rushed the door, it felt much more appropriate to kick it open rather than merely push it. The sudden bang

in the quietness of the carnage echoed like a thunderclap. Both
men charged in. Despite their weirstone's inactivity, the Pretender considered the possibility that there might still be a geist
in there. After all, if this thing could cross water, what else could
it do?

Inside was as deathly calm as on deck, but the scene was different. They'd been wrong; the captain had not met his death
upstairs. He was in his cabin, and not gored and ripped apart as
his crew had been. Poor Captain Moresh of the Imperial Navy
looked as though he'd been broiled in the desert for months. His
frock coat and hat were still immaculate, but his desiccated body
lay half-slumped across the table on which his valuable charts
and maps were spread. One of his hands was outstretched to the
other object on the table: the ship's weirstone.

"Not possible," Aachon murmured to Raed's right. He raised
his own orb, perhaps to check that it was still intact. It gleamed
back as cobalt blue as ever. "That is simply impossible," he
repeated, as if calling it so would make a difference.

Raed strode up and picked up the ship's orb without any consequences. He shouldn't have been able to touch the thing, but
the weirstone was pitch-black. It was as dead as the men outside,
and their captain.

They stared at each other for a long moment, surrounded by the
stench of death. Somehow, this seemed the worst sign of all.
The talisman crafted by the Deacons, the most powerful force
in the world, was now as broken as a child's toy. The kind of geist
that could do that didn't bear thinking about. As every rule they'd
ever known crumbled, Raed could feel his own security vanish
with them.

FIVE

In Dark Water

Deacon Chambers was, thankfully, silent. Sorcha rode ahead of him and fought the urge to kick Shedryi into a gallop. Sensitives were tricky creatures to get away from. She wanted a smoke badly, but there were only so many cigars in her pocket and she had a feeling if she got trapped in Ulrich, she might need every one of them.

They would have to follow the road north to the calmer port of Irisil, where kinder and warmer currents flowed into the harbor. Sorcha wasn't looking forward to getting on a small ship with her new partner.

Sparing a glance over her shoulder, she was amused to realize that Merrick was actually reading the report. His curly dark head bent while he rode with practiced ease. Maybe he hadn't been joking about winning those events.

She'd realized he would be young; she'd been unprepared for just how young. After reading his file in the records office, she'd noticed that he'd declared a touch of Ancient blood in his line. Though these first peoples had long since been swallowed up by the Otherside, their blood could still be traced in some of the continents' older families. It explained his incredibly high testing in both Active and Sensitive. It wasn't up there with the Abbot's skill, but if he burned out his Sensitivity, he would have been accepted without question into the ranks of the Actives.

She would have to watch this one for sure. Deacons of

near-equal rank in both disciplines could sometimes be tempted to activate when first confronted with a geist. That sort of deadly mistake could leave her looking for yet another partner.

As Sorcha had been thinking about this, Merrick had urged his mare up next to her and offered back the report. "Not many solid details, really." At least he had the good sense to sound concerned about that.

"There seldom are," Sorcha said with a little laugh. "Geists are like that . . . mysterious."

"You know I studied all this, don't you?" he snapped back. "Just like you, I did my training. Difference is I got stuck with the partner no one in the Order wants."

That stung, though Sorcha managed not to let it show. Once upon a time she'd been highly sought—now she wondered what exactly she had done for that to change. Oh, yes . . . all those supposedly private arguments with Kolya.

She glanced at him out of the corner of one eye and measured up exactly how she should play this. They were partners, Bonded and shackled together. They would have to rely on each other in tough situations. The whole setup of this assignment worried Sorcha, and she would need a Sensitive who was not only good, but who cared enough to pull her out of the fire if necessary; so ramming those words back down his throat as she was tempted to do would serve no purpose.

"Sorry you feel that way"—her fingers itched to be holding a cigar right now—"but we've got to make this work for the sake of the assignment."

They traveled in silence for the next few hours. The Bond between them was still fresh and raw, and that was surely why she could feel a tinge of his frustration. It flickered across her awareness and disturbed what might otherwise have been an enjoyable ride.

The countryside on the east coast was beautiful even this late into autumn, and Sorcha looked about with a feeling of real pride. When the Emperor had arrived, this area had been a rabbit warren of unfettered geists and mistwitches. It had been one of her and Kolya's assignments to oversee the clearing of the area from Vermillion to the Turijk Mountains. As they passed through the low-lying areas of marshes and dark water, she was able to look back on those times as simple and rather pleasant. It had been hard work, but satisfying.

Recollection softened the hard knot of displeasure in her stomach. She pointed to a collection of abandoned stone buildings not far from the road they now traveled. "That is the place where my husband and I banished our first geist for the Emperor in his new realm." It was only three years past, but felt a lifetime ago.

Merrick pulled his cloak around him as if he wasn't interested, but she could tell he was. The prickle of frustration subsided a little. "Are the geists of Delmaire the same as the ones here?"

For a second she didn't reply, stunned. If he was asking her that, then he must have been among the new recruits from Arkaym, and if that was true, then he had gotten through the novices faster than anyone since Abbot Hastler. She would definitely have to take care around this one. Sorcha was abruptly conscious of the Bond between them. She'd crafted it so casually, but if she'd joined herself to such a powerful Sensitive, maybe she should have been more cautious.

She cleared her throat. "No, the Delmaire geists have been tamed for centuries. The last attack recorded there was more than fifty years past—that was why so many Deacons jumped at the chance to sign up to this new Abbey: boredom."

"That's one thing we never have to worry about. Sometimes I wonder . . ." The young man's voice trailed off. Flicking his head over his shoulder, he pulled his mare up suddenly.

"What is it?" Sorcha tugged Shedryi to the right, circling her new partner. No matter how useless it was, she too scanned their surroundings. They were in the middle of a narrow stretch of dry ground, with low marshes on each side. Sedge and rushes whispered in the breeze, but she could make out no trace of geist. Certainly there was no scent but the brackish water and the damp earth.

She brought her stallion up tight against Merrick's mare; she wasn't about to let another Sensitive get away on her. Even when she cocked her head and strained her Sensitivity, she could still make out nothing more dangerous than sucking mud. "I don't smell any—"

"Quiet!" The young upstart actually raised his hand as if she were a novice at the back of the class. The tone of his voice, though, and her knowledge of his ranking caused Sorcha to slide her Gauntlets from under her belt and onto her lap.

The marsh to the right, a thinly spread oval of dark water,

was completely quiet. No wading birds disturbed the surface. No frogs chirped from its fringes. Even the expectant resilient midges seemed to have abandoned this patch.

The Deacon Breed horses, male and female, tossed their heads, but unlike lesser mounts did not dance sideways. Trained to stand in the face of supernatural attack, they dropped their heads, blew through their noses, and did not move.

Carefully, Sorcha got down off Shedryi, slid on one Gauntlet and walked to the head of Merrick's mare. He had not shared his Sight. Annoyed, she reached up and placed her bare hand on his.

Sight flared about her, so different from what she had shared with Kolya it was disconcerting. This new partner of hers must be packed full of power; everything was blazing. Behind her she was aware of the gentle slumbering trees, the creatures hiding in the mud and birds winging their way out to the sea. It was the color, though, the sheer brightness and detail, that she reveled in; reveled in, and was definitely overwhelmed by.

This was why new partners usually stayed safely within the Abbey walls, learning each other's strengths and getting used to the sensation of the Bond. After a moment, Sorcha's Center felt like she'd been looking into the sun for too long.

Snatching back her hand, she shot a look up at Merrick. He was glaring down at her. Rated Sensitives didn't need to send their Centers out; they trained to keep both the real world and the ethereal one in focus. What sort of strange double vision that might engender, Sorcha couldn't really imagine. She tugged on her left Gauntlet without looking away.

After a second of playing staring games with each other, Merrick shook his head. "By the Bones, that was uncalled for! Give me a second, and keep your hand off me . . . if you can manage that?"

He too dismounted and wandered a little distance off, looking out over the patch of water. The locals called the little dips in the land *vamma kesi*, or dark water, because no sunlight reflected off the pools that collected there. It was something to do with the earth itself, as Sorcha had read in an indolent moment in the Abbey library. Whatever the reason, they were dire little spots.

Merrick pointed over toward the farthest reaches of the water, where low scrub tumbled down a small rise. "It's not a geist, but there is something lingering there . . . something in pain."

Sorcha snorted. Everything was always in pain or tormented.

She'd trained Kolya not to get involved with every injured kitten or bruised plant, and it looked as though she would have to do the same with Merrick.

"If you haven't noticed, we need to get moving. Those ships are leaving if we are there or not . . ." She looked up and realized that her new partner was already off the road and tromping through the light snow in the direction he had pointed.

"Stubborn," she muttered to herself. "Hastler had to give me a stubborn one." Tucking her fur cloak around her shoulders, she strode after him. He was at least fifteen feet in front of her, not even bothering to look behind him. Basically giving her the same treatment that she'd handed to him at the Abbey. The phrase "too big for his britches" was made for this one. She'd much rather have had a lesser-ranked Sensitive than one who knew he was good.

"You know, if I get wet boots, you'll be riding the pack mule the rest of the way," she barked at him. Merrick had stopped and was actually yanking aside bushes. Whatever he had sensed from the road had probably crawled in there to die. Her only satisfaction was that he was tossing enough snow about to get himself rather damp as well.

Finally reaching his side, Sorcha stood with Gauntleted hands on hips, staring down at her new partner as he fossicked around in the undergrowth. "I'm not carrying any . . ."

She stopped in midsentence as Merrick finally cleared away the snow and branches. A long length of what she assumed was bleached wood was wrapped in the remains of a red skirt. It was a human leg.

Wordlessly she bent and helped her partner yank away the swath of brush that covered the scene; cold and dread were building in her. What she'd thought was merely growing near the water had in fact been deliberately laid down to cover the horror beneath.

When they finally both stood back, panting into the air, the scene had been revealed. It was difficult to count exactly how many bodies there were, but all were frozen into terrible shapes. Merrick clapped a fist to his mouth and turned away.

Sorcha took a deep breath herself. Many of those in the pile of dead were women and children. The jumble of body pieces was not random, however. They were stacked in a pattern, limbs placed like firewood with heads facing upward in an inner circle around what looked like the burnt remains of a wagon. They appeared to have been a family group, probably Tinkers who traveled from village to village repairing items and selling cloth and such. Whatever they had met on the road had been the death of them all.

It was a terrible, half-frozen, macabre display. No doubt it was an exhibit not meant to be seen by mortal eyes.

Merrick, to his credit, wasn't throwing up his breakfast. He turned around and stood at her shoulder. Sorcha felt his Center open, but he didn't share. What he was Seeing, he was best qualified to make sense of.

"They aren't here," he muttered. "The souls are all gone. Such pain and fear should have left terrible marks on the ether—but there is nothing."

"Then how did you . . ."

Merrick cleared his throat. "One of the children didn't die immediately. Whatever it was, it took her soul, but her pain left the smallest whisper."

It must have been tiny, indeed.

"Have you ever seen anything like this?" he asked in a thick voice. "I've read the textbooks, but . . ."

"Not like this." She pointed to the nearest bodies. "This wasn't done by anything human. Think about it for a moment. Geists can usually only operate to kill through humans. These wounds were not made by anything mortal. Something unliving made this circle."

Merrick nodded. "We should at least bury them. Their souls . . ." He stopped and surged upright. Suddenly, he was sharing a portion of his Center with Sorcha.

Through his eyes, the world was tinged with red. Something was coming through the ether toward them; something that she had also never seen before. Leaping to her feet, Sorcha put herself between Merrick and the approaching geist.

In the real world, the *vamma kesi* was bubbling and writhing as if a fire had been lit underneath it. The bubbles were moving toward them at a rapid pace.

"What is it, Chambers?" she hissed. She held the Gauntlets up, as yet unsure which Rune to activate upon them. "By the Bones, what is it?"

Her new partner was scrambling at his belt pouch. "I can't see." There was an edge of real panic in his voice. "I need the Strop to see . . ."

"No time for that," Sorcha yelled. "Give me the damn Sight . . ."

Merrick's Center swept up and filled her just as the geist leapt into the real world. Amid the blaze of light, Sorcha was almost blinded by the detail, but she did finally get a good look at the unliving creature barreling toward them.

Flesh was usually the only container for a geist, yet this one had thrown a body together from what appeared to be mud and dark water. No time to open a door and draw power. It was the height of rudeness, and usually done only after years of being partners, but Sorcha drew from the Bond. As the link between Sensitive and Active was made using Otherside power, it could also be a source of strength for the Deacons.

Sorcha needed strength as she called on Yevah. The shield of fire leapt into existence around them like a bubble, and even Merrick would have a hard time arguing with her use of the Bond to help forge it. The water and debris smashed into the orb as the flame poured from her Gauntlets. The air was full of the smell of earth and charred wood. It made one very spectacular mess. For a moment, steam and flying fragments blinded both Active and Sensitive.

Staggering back, the two mortals almost fell into the strange pattern of bodies. Merrick grabbed her arm, pulling her to the left and away from it. The shield Yevah conjured moved with them, but Sorcha's arms were already beginning to ache from holding it there.

"Name it," she screamed. The howl of wind and water was painful on mortal and Deacon senses. But she could not know how to destroy what Merrick could not name. "Damnation, remember your training!"

"Look," he screamed back. The full power of his Sight flooded into her once more, and only by focusing it on the geist was she able to bear it. Deacons learned all the forms of the unliving: the dukh, the rei, the ghast. Centuries of experience had slotted each shape into categories memorized by every novice. The swirling forms of the vortex and the spinning shapes of the rei were among those familiar to every Deacon.

As Sorcha stood gaping up at the geist that was all around them, she abruptly understood Merrick's indecision. This creature was not in the books. The pattern she could make out in the flickering geist form was like no other; complicated and knitted together like one of those visual puzzles popular at court. The difference was that this one was tightening on them. The shield of fire was actually shrinking under the weight of the dark water. Holding Yevah up within the Gauntlets was keeping Sorcha fully occupied.

"Don't you dare open Teisyat," Merrick bellowed at her while the geist began to squeeze in on the shield of fire.

Did he imagine that she popped that door open every time things got a little hairy? Only Kolya going down in a heap had brought that on. "I don't like you that much," Sorcha screamed in return.

At her back, she could feel Merrick doing something; she could See him doing it. Their shared Sight was unraveling the pattern. He was going deep into it, trying to understand the impossible.

With a grunt, Sorcha took a step back. "It's too much. Yevah is about to pop wide-open. How do you feel about drowning on dry land?"

He pressed his lips right next to her ear to be heard above the howling mass of dark water. "We have to get back into the circle."

That was against everything in the rule books: never step into any sort of summoning circle. Such circles were the base of the geist's power in this realm, and it was actually possible to be drawn into the Otherside from within one.

Sorcha dared a glimpse at Merrick. His face was calm, but his eyes glittered with an intensity shared by fanatics and the faithful. Breathing in over her drawn teeth, she made her decision. Years of training provided her only option: always trust your Sensitive.

Together they stepped backward over the dead and into the ring that had been constructed with such macabre care. They were now in the summoning circle. Yevah had shrunk so much under the assault that Sorcha and Merrick were now breathing against its fiery surface. But, looking up with her partner's vision, she saw something so incredible that their immediate danger paled into insignificance.

They were inside the geist. Craning her neck up, with their shared Sight she could See the pattern of the unliving whirling and spinning around her. It was like being inside a patterned tornado. Teisyat wouldn't help them now; the Otherside would have swallowed them along with the geist.

Sweat was pouring down her back, and her shoulders ached with the effort of keeping her Gauntlets up. "Please tell me that you have a damned plan!"

Nearly there, nearly there. Kebenar will show us. The Sensitive rune bloomed from Merrick to her, and Sorcha could finally see clearly. The pattern flickered around them from red and swirling to white, suddenly revealing itself. It was a braid, as simple as a child's braid. The pattern around them was a combination of three of the most common geist forms: dukh, rei and spokelse. They were the three most innocuous varieties, but it appeared that once they were combined, that was no longer the case.

It was certainly nice to know what she was facing, yet Sorcha was now far beyond any of her training. A geist made out of the essence of three others—such a creation should be impossible. Yet, the last few days had been full of impossible things. It appeared that all bets were off and the rule books might as well be thrown away.

Pyet. The Bond was too strong. She could now hear Merrick echoing in the back of her head. The whole world had gone crazy.

"Explain yourself," she hissed, falling to one knee as the shield buckled. They surely had only a few moments before it collapsed entirely. Merrick put his back to hers, giving her the physical strength to keep her Gauntlets up a little longer.

Keep Yevah, open Pyet. Not so much words leaked across, but understanding. Two runes at the same time? It was a good thing that Merrick hadn't been stuck with an Active fresh out of the Abbey.

"Stay behind me—but not too far." Sorcha clenched her right hand shut, dismissing Yevah. The shield, now held only by the left-hand rune, swayed sickly, sucking down even closer to the Deacons. They were forced to huddle together like two lost children or be exposed to the raw, roaring center of the geist. Sorcha, despite this difficult situation, appreciated that Merrick held the Sight steady and pointed upward, managing to ignore the wobbling shield and concentrate on the patterned geist.

She sought out Pyet. Doing so was like having one fish on a line, and using another hand to balance a rod for another. Her training had covered this tricky ability and she had done it before, but only under controlled circumstances. Had Deacons become so complacent, the thought flashed across her mind, in the way idle thoughts do in moments of stress, as to never expect to need more than one rune at a time?

Her fingers tingled within the Gauntlet, stretching out, while she gritted her teeth. Sweat now slid off her forehead. Finally, Pyet activated, snapping white-hot onto her palm. It was a lesser rune, but still enough to bring down something like a spokelse. These bouncing orbs of light that led people to their deaths had not been seen anywhere near Vermillion for more than a year. Now one was part of this monstrosity.

Her left hand was outstretched, still holding Yevah. Her right contained the undeployed Pyet. She needed a target before this deck of cards collapsed completely. Her muscles ached and her back was howling in protest as she braced herself against her Gauntlets.

Show me. Her shared Sight snapped into focus on one strand of the braid, separating it from the whirling chaos of the others. Sorcha dropped Yevah; no rune power could be transmitted through a shield. The geist was all around them and now they could both feel the raw power of the unliving. It scorched the skin and tore at their hair. Unlike normal mortals, Deacons could stand that power, but not for long.

Sorcha and her partner clung onto each other, holding tightly so as not to be swept away. With Merrick's Sight, she aimed Pyet through narrowed eyes, directly at the rei strand of the geist.

Gleaming fire spun around her Gauntlet and smashed into the unliving creature crushing down on them. The world became a chaos of white fire and dark water, snarling together as if a tornado were tumbling around them. Sorcha's ears and eyes felt like they might explode. She doggedly held on to her young partner as the fierce geist battered them about.

Merrick slipped and fell, but she never let go, shielding his body with her own. She was not about to lose another Sensitive to a contrary geist. Her lungs seemed on the verge of collapse, her eyes burning in her head, and then . . . and then . . . the storm passed, leaving them gasping in the aftermath. Pyet still twinkled on her hands, ready for more action as she pulled herself upright. Merrick was lying there, panting and staring up at her. Certainly for a first real-life battle experience, this one would be hard to beat.

Sorcha found she was smiling. She wiped her forehead, one Gauntlet already inactive. She glanced at the left one, still burning with white fire. With a slight smile she pulled out a cigar from her pocket and lazily raised it to her mouth. Merrick gaped as she used the treasured talisman, still burning with the fires of the rune, to calmly light it. She grinned at him while he continued to stare speechlessly, the smoke curling past her eyes, and took pleasure in his horror. With a mocking smile and a measured shake of her hand, she extinguished the flames. "Ah, white fire." She motioned with her head to the lit cigar. "Preserves the flavor."

On any normal day, the smoke would have calmed her nerves. After all, that was why she enjoyed cigars: guaranteed bliss for an hour, when all that mattered was the smoke and time to do nothing. This had turned out to be anything but another normal day.

As Merrick was still in shock, she turned to one side and began to examine what was left of the summoning circle. She took a good puff and surveyed the damage. It wasn't pretty. What little remained of the circle of bodies was charred almost beyond recognition. Burying them wouldn't take long at all.

At her back she could hear Merrick getting to his feet. Worryingly, even without turning, she could tell he was exhilarated more than terrified. The Bond was never meant to be like this, and certainly not this quickly. Only hours old, and all the rules were quite undone. Still, there was no point talking about it.

"Someone went to a great deal of trouble to create that geist." She traced the outline of the pattern still faintly visible on the ground. "Someone who knows a lot about the unliving."

"Over here." Merrick, whose once-bright-and-new emerald cloak was stained almost completely black, was bent over a clear space among the remains. He was poking something with a stick, like he'd found something distasteful or dangerous.

When she reached him, Sorcha understood why.

"A weirstone," she hissed, chewing grimly on the end of her cigar. "When will people learn?" The cobalt blue sphere was now as dark as pitch.

Merrick, fresh from the novitiate and not having seen the carnage unregistered weirstones could do, glanced up. "People are still frightened. They want reassurance—some of them feel better with a stone around."

"Do you think they feel better?" She gestured to the smoking pile of bones. "Those damned things can draw geists as well as see them."

"We don't know that the Tinkers were carrying one . . ."

Sorcha paused and looked at him askance. "You think whoever made this mess used a weirstone as part of it?"

He reached down and held his hand, fingers spread, inches above the dark orb. "I can feel the geist presence, but also another."

"Human?"

His brow furrowed. "They have covered their tracks somehow, messed with the ether to disguise themselves. I can't see beyond it . . ."

Sorcha bent down next to him and drew in a long mouthful of smoke. "You're the best the Abbey has, Chambers. Are you telling me that there is someone better than you?"

Her new partner glanced up at her, his brown eyes suddenly not at all friendly. "Give me a second." It was actually a growl.

She didn't go far; staying crouched down, looking about and trying to enjoy the taste of the smoke on her tongue. What Sorcha couldn't enjoy was the vague frisson of concentration that was leaking across from Merrick. She hated to think what was leaking in the other direction.

Finally her partner sighed and got up. "Definitely human, and definitely male."

She stood next to him and tried to moderate her tone to something that wasn't disappointment. "Anything else?"

He kicked the remains of the weirstone. "Not after the damage the geist banishment caused. If I had found it when the weirstone was still active, maybe . . ."

"Don't waste time on maybes," Sorcha said. "I have a feeling that we'll be getting another chance at this."

"What makes you say that?"

She pointed to the road. "This isn't a well-traveled spot at this time of year, and the bodies were fresh. They must have only been here overnight."

"So?"

She tapped him lightly on the forehead with one fingertip. "It was a trap for us."

Merrick blinked once in confusion, and then his eyebrows drew together in a frown. "But we only knew last night that we were leaving . . ."

Sorcha puffed contemplatively on of her cigar, let it linger a moment and then breathed it out regretfully. "Indeed, so there are only two options: someone was watching us leave the Abbey, or the perpetrator can somehow see into the future. Take your pick."

Merrick turned pale, quite impressive in this cold. "I don't know which I like less."

Sorcha jerked her head over toward where their packhorse was standing. "How 'bout we get the shovels and bury these poor folk while you think about it?"

SIX

Into the Mouth of the Beast

Two days of riding and Merrick's head was still buzzing with the possibilities of the attack. Even when they rode into the port town of Irisil, he remained shell-shocked. It made sense, yet he almost wished that she hadn't voiced it.

Most novices would have given their eyeteeth to be teamed up with Deacon Sorcha Faris, but now he realized that his nightmare had just begun. Ahead, where she rode, his new partner gave no sign she even knew he was following. However, both were fully aware of each other's presence. The Bond took care of that.

Though neither of them spoke about it, they both knew it was there and very strong, much stronger than it should have been. Merrick worked very hard to keep his thoughts reined in, but was frightened by the possibility that she would hear them again in a moment of stress. The one thing that he did not want was Sorcha running around his brain. The memory of the night that his father died floated to the surface whenever she was about.

As they trotted through the ramshackle buildings and lines of nets hung up to dry, he could feel his anxiety growing at the prospect of being on board a ship with her. How he was going to occupy his mind for that time was a real and growing concern.

"This is the place." Sorcha interrupted his flow of depressing thoughts by pulling up outside a house that more resembled a lean-to.

"This is where we take ship?"

She had slid down from her stallion and was grinning up at him. "Not quite to your standards, my lord?"

It was the limit. He was wracked with fatigue, nerves and the overwhelming desire for a bath, and here she was making fun of him. Merrick opened his mouth to let fly with every expletive he'd learned in the novices' hall, when his eye was caught by a slim form coming down the road toward them, apparently making for the same dreary little building.

His occupational hazard was seeing the inherent beauty in everything. The simplest forms like a petal or the song of a bird could entrance a newly created Sensitive, but he'd thought himself over that stage.

Merrick knew he was agape as the young woman coming toward them glanced up shyly. Her eyes were the most entrancing color, like a woodland doe's, her lips a perfect bow set in a heart-shaped face. As he turned his neck to watch her, she tucked a strand of dark hair behind her ear and entered the building before them. The scent she trailed behind her was light and sweet. Merrick blinked.

It took him a moment to realize that Sorcha was talking to him. He glanced down at her, already feeling a slight warmth in his cheeks.

She might not be a Sensitive, but his new partner wasn't an idiot. Shooting a glance over her shoulder in the direction of the vision, she smirked. "Chambers, you're not going to drop into one of those Sensitive trances over a girl, are you? If so, tell me now so I can have a slap ready." Her fingers were tapping on the edge of her belt pocket, as if she was indeed holding one back.

"Did saving your life not earn me a little respect?" he snapped back. "Just like an Active to forget so quickly."

"Yes, yes, I know . . . Without you I would be blind." Sorcha actually looked away. "You did well, Deacon Chambers. Many newly ordained would have stumbled, faced with something so . . . unexpected."

Merrick decided to take the compliment, and perhaps, in the interests of getting along with his partner, offer one of his own. "You handled Pyet and Yevah expertly. Many Actives would have stumbled at having to manage two runes like that."

Her smile was slow and amused. If Deacons wore hats, she might have tipped hers. "I guess that you and I have been dumped into a maelstrom. The things that have been happening

in the last few days"—she shook her head, as if only beginning
to catalogue them—"we should perhaps turn back and report to
the Arch Abbot."

"You suggested that two days ago, and we decided that we
have our orders." Merrick dismounted as smoothly as possible
and was glad not to collapse immediately. After two days his
thighs still ached. "Think of all those people in Ulrich who are
under attack. If we wait, how many more will die? Besides, with
the Priory weirstone I can contact him from our destination."

Sorcha nodded and handed the reins of her stallion to a stable-
hand who had finally appeared around the corner of the building. "We go on, then." Entering the building, both of them, not
the tallest of Deacons, had to duck their heads. It was just as
cramped inside. Behind a leaning desk sat a tiny old woman who
was coughing so hard Merrick was worried a lung might appear
at any moment. In front of the desk stood the beautiful woman
from outside. When Merrick saw her, he almost straightened
up—though naturally, he realized she would be in here. Without
any subtlety, Sorcha elbowed him in the ribs. Only the Bones
knew what the Bond was telling her about his state.

The young woman glowed to his Sensitive Sight in the dingy
light. She was standing, her head only slightly bent, and her voice
was soft and light when she spoke. "But surely there must be
room on board. My father arranged . . ."

The old woman stopped coughing long enough to wheeze out
a phlegmy reply. "We have an agreement with the Order; they
take precedence."

The young woman pressed her folded hands to her small breasts
and inclined her head toward the hunched one behind the desk.
"But I must get back to my father in Ulrich—he is lost without me."

The older woman, however, had already spotted the two Deacons through her watering eyes and dismissed any further com-
plaints. "Honored guests!" She rang a battered bell until three
young men, presumably her grandsons, appeared. Before either
Deacon could protest at this preferential treatment, their baggage
was taken from them and they were ushered to the desk.

"You are blessed lucky," the old woman croaked. "The tide is
near to turning and my son will have to sail with it."

Sorcha allowed herself to be guided toward the rear door but
Merrick paused and glanced back. The young woman was standing stock-still, arms folded tight around her.

He swung about to face the proprietress. "Surely there is room on the ship for this lady?"

Merrick caught sight of Sorcha's amused expression and raised eyebrow. *Oh really . . .*

The old woman grimaced. "The Abbey specifies that we only carry their people, and they pay very well for the privilege."

His mouth ran away with him before his brain quite caught up. "She is part of our party."

When the old woman glanced at Sorcha, she only shrugged her compliance, but could not quite seem to keep the smirk off her face.

"Makes no difference to me." The crone coughed, and spat into the corner. "If you say she is part of your group, then she is your problem, not mine."

While Sorcha started out of the building and toward the gangway, Merrick turned back to the younger woman. "Please forgive my presumption, but I hope you don't mind being an honorary Deacon if it means getting home?"

"I'm very thankful." From some women it might have sounded common, but she said it so quietly and with such honesty in those brown eyes, he didn't take it at anything but face value.

He held out his hand. "Deacon Merrick Chambers."

"Nynnia Macthcoll." She stared at his offered hand for a minute, before putting her own much smaller one in it with a rather uncertain shake.

Only then did Merrick realize he'd done something very foolish. Dealing with Deacons for years, he'd forgotten that most well-brought-up ladies of any standing found a handshake rather offensive. Quickly he jerked his hand back, though holding hers had been a more-than-pleasant experience.

"Shall we go?" He remembered enough to let her out of the door before him. The scent when she passed was like apples and sweet spring grass; Sensitive observation was certainly a rod to bear at times like this.

Outside a brisk wind had picked up, the slate gray ocean heaving against a stony beach. A set of dark wharves thrust out into the harbor, and their small ship was the only one tied up there.

As Merrick and his new acquaintance walked up the pier toward the ship, he took note of her clothes, trying to judge what they could tell him about her. The sky blue dress she wore was covered with a dark gray cloak, and both seemed somewhat

richer than a farmer's daughter might have worn. The hem of
the dress, however, was roughened and rubbed, indicating exces-
sive wear. He began to surmise that its owner had fallen on hard
times. He imagined this might be her only remaining dress out
of a once-larger wardrobe. The small bag that she would not
relinquish to him also had the look of being well traveled but
seemed rather light for a long sojourn. Her long dark hair was
carefully groomed and modestly plaited at the crown with five
jet pins holding it in place, which, if she was traveling, showed a
dedication to proper appearance.

Merrick ran his hand through his own curly hair, suddenly
aware how uncombed it was. "Are you traveling to meet family
in Ulrich, Miss Macthcoll?" he asked. The pier was slick with
salt spray, and he offered her his arm as she struggled against the
wind to follow the striding Sorcha.

"Yes," she replied, leaning her slight weight against the crook
of his arm, and hitching up her skirt to edge past a stack of barrels. "My father is a physician and works for the Deacons as a lay
healer. I was raised in Ulrich, and now I live there assisting him."

"Then I was not really lying." He chuckled. "You are almost
part of the Order."

Merrick felt her stiffen a little against his side. This close, that
sweet scent was very distracting, but he still caught a glance she
shot him; it was frightened, or possibly angry. Either he wasn't
very good at this chitchat or something else was bothering her.
Even after years of study, he couldn't be that clumsy.

Clearing his throat, he stumbled on. "Did you come from the
south?"

She nodded, pulling her dress slightly up at the hem. "Yes,
from Vermillion. I was visiting a sick relative there. We lived in
the city when I was a child, before—" She paused. "Before my
father lost his position there." He didn't need to be a Sensitive
to know that was a subject she was entirely unhappy with, but it
explained the worn appearance of a once-beautiful dress.

Yet her revelation had finally given him something to say. "It
was lucky you were ahead of us. My partner and I were attacked
on the road. A rather nasty geist."

The look she gave him made him realize the error of it immediately. "You . . . you were attacked?"

"Yes, most likely an ambush." He tried to swallow his words
but they kept tumbling out.

Her eyes dipped away from him. "It was indeed lucky that I was ahead of you, not behind. Anything could have happened."

Merrick felt his face heating up. "Then we would not have been able to assist you with passage. Fate is sometimes kind."

They reached the ship and paused. The Breed horses and Horace the pack mule were being led up the rear gangway and into the hold. Well accustomed to travel, they were providing no problems, and the crew loading them appeared to know what they were doing.

"The Abbey only has two ships stationed at Vermillion"—Merrick decided to try another subject with the silent woman—"and both are to the south with the Imperial Navy. No one thought that they would be needed at this time of year."

She turned and faced him, looking directly up at him, a slight smile curving her bow-shaped lips. "And why exactly is it that you are going to Ulrich this late in the season, Reverend Deacon?"

Merrick was caught by surprise. Most people would not question the movements of any from the Order, but it was perhaps an understandable query considering that they had nearly caused her to be stuck in the South. Still, he couldn't just divulge what he'd read in the report. "The Deacons there are in need of assistance before winter sets in." He hoped she would assume it was a leaky roof, or maybe illness.

"The outpost is small." Nynnia lifted the edge of her skirt and walked up the gangplank unassisted. "I hope you will not be disappointed by what you find there."

Up on deck, his partner was watching the stowing of the mounts with an eagle eye, but she did look up in Merrick's direction when they approached. Luckily, the smirk had gone. "So, who is our newest recruit, Deacon?"

"Miss Nynnia Macthcoll, may I present my partner, Deacon Sorcha Faris." He waited for the fireworks to begin.

"Deacon Faris." The younger woman inclined her head. "You would be the Deacon who expelled the ghast from Baron Leit last summer."

Sorcha's eyebrows shot up, but the corners of her mouth twitched. While the Order did not like its members to be prideful, Merrick could understand a little of the feeling he was sensing across the Bond. Seldom was the work of the Deacons actually discussed in polite society. "My husband and I were involved with that case. I didn't realize that word of it had got out."

"Miss Macthcoll is the daughter of the physician stationed at the outpost in Ulrich."

Across the Bond he felt Sorcha's interest wane. *I'll leave you to deal with the pretty face.* "Well, let us hope we have smooth sailing all the way there." Sorcha gestured to the front of the ship, where a tall man dressed in oilskins and sporting a massive red beard was supervising the securing of the hatch. "The captain seems to think that we may be lucky with the weather."

Without so much as a farewell, she turned and went below, no doubt to see if their accommodation was as good as their horses'. Merrick bit back the urge to apologize for his partner's rudeness. At all times, bonded Deacons were supposed to show solidarity. If Nynnia knew anything about the Order, she would be surprised if he showed any disloyalty.

"Seven days," the young lady said, turning to look where the crew were casting off. "Even one day can be a long time in these oceans. I doubt if the captain is being anything other than reassuring to your partner. No one can tell what the weather will do in these currents."

Then she excused herself most sweetly and went below to find her cabin.

Indeed, this was going to be a long trip. Merrick sighed and idly fingered his belt pocket where the Strop lay curled. He'd feared having to keep his thoughts reined in and away from Sorcha, but now with this new heady distraction he doubted if he would be able to. He imagined that this journey would be full of jabs and jokes of all kinds. Even though he expected Ulrich to be rather bleak, Merrick found he was looking forward to seeing it.

After two days of travel, Sorcha was ready to throw herself over the side and swim for it. Merrick and his cow eyes were only physical symptoms of what leaked across the Bond. It was deeply disturbing to feel his attraction to this girl as intimately as Sorcha felt it.

It would have been bad enough if she'd known him for years, but they had been partnered for only a week. She was standing on the deck on the third morning, smoking a cigar that she had hoped to keep at least until Ulrich. She had needed an excuse to get away from the general foolishness belowdecks. Merrick was too damn Sensitive.

Blowing out a plume of smoke, she watched the umber sun wallow out of the sea. The thought crossed her mind that she was either old and bitter, or old and jealous. Kolya's courting of her had been a lot more measured and a lot less romantic. Partners for a year—it had seemed the logical thing—there had been little in the way of romance.

Certainly there was no injunction against marrying one's partner, nor anyone else, but within the Order, marriages were not common. Life was often short and brutal for Deacons, and Sorcha was honestly surprised every day that neither she nor Kolya had been killed thus far. He had been a good friend and partner—but perhaps she'd been expecting their marriage to end more dramatically than it was—most likely in her own death.

Yet we're both alive. She drew another warm, thick mouthful of smoke. *And we both know it isn't enough anymore.*

This early in the morning, she knew she was prone to maudlin thoughts. She usually enjoyed traveling by water, since the geist danger was limited to only the occasional storm if they passed close to the land. Not today, however. Sorcha found she was as tense as a coiled spring and her hands were actually white-knuckled on the railing. Apparently not even a cigar could relax her.

"Bloody Bones," she muttered to herself. A Deacon's life was short enough, and now she couldn't even enjoy her one vice. The silver hip flask in her cloak pocket downstairs was really only for emergencies.

A startled caw from above made her glance upward. Her brow furrowed. A collection of seabirds, gulls and cormorants circled above the ship. She had traveled the ocean many times, but could not recall having seen so many birds behaving in such a way. A shiver of apprehension ran up her spine. Sometimes the natural world had a strange reaction to the Otherside; animals of all kinds were very aware of fluctuations in the ether. Her jaw clenched as she let her Center flit out, but again there was nothing. In the good old days, she would have been confident that she would have at least been able to sense anything dangerous. These, however, were no longer the good old days.

She was just about to go below and rouse her sleeping partner when something on the horizon caught her eye. Captain Tarce was giving another of his crew an ear bashing and was clearly too busy to notice. She strode over to him and requisitioned his spyglass from his belt while he was distracted. Before he could argue, she was back at the starboard side peering into the swirling mass of red dawn that concealed what she couldn't see with the naked eye. One glance through the scope, and she was yelling at the Captain. "Get my partner up here—now!"

Luckily, familiarity with Deacons had not bred contempt. Merrick was at her shoulder in mercifully quick time. Across the Bond, she could feel his sleepiness evaporating. She handed him the spyglass wordlessly. Once it was to his eye, she remarked, "There are, indeed, no damn rules anymore."

With the naked eye, Sorcha could see the oncoming storm well enough, but with the spyglass Merrick would be able to see what she'd observed: a ship running before it like a fox pursued by hounds.

Now the Captain was in on the game. Pressing his swelling stomach against the rail, he managed to get his spyglass back. When he looked away from it, his face was pale.

"Now, I'm no sailor," Sorcha said to him, "but that looks as if the storm is bearing down on it. Do you recognize the ship?"

"The flag is wrapped around the pole but . . . but . . ." Tarce spluttered. "A geist storm, so far from land? It's . . . it's . . ."

"Impossible?" she snapped. "We know. May I suggest we take the other ship's example and make a run for safe harbor if we can?"

"All hands!" Tarce flew into action that belied his size. Soon crew were scrambling about the rigging, tying it down and preparing to flee before the wind. Cargo ships ran with the bare minimum of crew to increase profits—it was going to be a close call.

In the midst of it, the two Deacons stood and watched the storm. It was no normal phenomenon of weather. The clouds were purple gray, curled on one another like a group of angry fists. In comparison, the ship racing before the storm looked like a paper boat.

Merrick let out a shuddering breath. "A geist storm and no land in sight—is no rule sacred?"

Sorcha had to agree with him. Whoever had cut loose the rules of the unliving seemed to be following the pair of Deacons. If the Tinkers' camp had been an attempt at an ambush, as she suspected, then this might be a frontal assault.

Merrick was silent at her side, peering forward. Sorcha felt his Center snap away and, turning, shared his Sight. The clouds were not geist-drawn, but something of the Otherside was in them.

"A witch," Sorcha spat. "The idiot on that ship has drawn power to give them wind for their sails."

"It seems to be working rather well."

She turned on him. "You're not one of those Deacons, are you, Chambers? The 'let's let everyone have a taste of the Otherside' fools?"

The young man shrugged, and it was confirmed. As far as Sorcha was concerned, witches and warlocks, as those untrained or untrainable by the Abbey called themselves, should still be burned as they had been in the old days. This was supposedly a more enlightened age, but those who meddled with the Otherside still deserved to be punished. Nothing but trouble followed in their wake. Among the younger Deacons and novices, there was a growing movement that felt these untrained were as entitled as Deacons to reach for the power; a belief that they were as worthy of it as any from the Order.

Such foolish ideas. As Sorcha watched the distant ship on the horizon, pushed along by winds of its own making, she felt an angry knot develop in the pit of her stomach. People using Otherside powers made her skin crawl, but to tap into it merely to get your ship ticking along faster was madness.

She was just about to turn around and let the Captain know that they were in no danger from the storm, when Merrick's Sight once more leapt up around her. The world plunged into red, violent patterns.

Merrick cried out, but she didn't quite hear him over the roaring in her ears. The patterns of geist that had erupted from the water were the least of their problems.

The aberrant geist had woken something in the sea below; something massive. The stench of salt and rotting seaweed hit them all like a club in the face, but it was the noise that caused the crew to howl in terror. A high-pitched keen like a thousand rusted gates swinging open made conscious thought, for a moment, impossible.

Sorcha craned her neck up, watching, stunned, as two giant coiled loops, twice the height of the main mast, snapped out of the water. For a moment, her brain struggled with one thought: *A possession—it's possessed a creature of the deep.* A great head, scaled and reptilian, punched out of the water only twenty feet to starboard. The eyes, as big as shields, gleamed pitch-black. The distant storm was, indeed, the least of their worries now.

Flicking her head around, she saw Merrick grabbing up that foolish girl he had been making cow eyes at. Nynnia was only just emerging from belowdecks, but she seemed to be an oasis of ridiculous calm in a tempest of terror. Everywhere, the ship was in chaos; sailors were screaming, the Captain was bellowing, and sails and rigging were snapping.

It was impossible to call to Merrick over the monster's high-pitched keen, the yelling of the sailors and the almighty cracks coming from the dying ship. Instead, she pushed across the Bond. This was no leak; it was a scream.

Follow me. Give me Sight.

Her call must have gotten through, because the air suddenly bloomed. The howl of a falling mast grated at her ears, but now she had the pinpoint accuracy of Sight. The mast seemed to move in slow motion, predictable and easily avoided. She stepped aside nimbly as it crashed to the deck only feet away. Sea spray was flying everywhere, almost blinding her. A huge wave of water, kicked up by the thrashing monster, crashed into her. The taste of salt flooded her senses, enhanced by her shared Sensitivity. At least she had wrapped her cigars up in oilskin. Everything else was soaked. Yet however concerned she might be about her cigars, something else was even more precious.

Over all the noise, Sorcha could hear the neighs of Shedryi and his mare. They were all going to die—that much was obvious as the writhing coils started their downward strike onto the doomed ship—but she was damned if the Breed were going to die in the dimness of a ship's hold.

Gasping and pushing her sodden hair out of her eyes, Sorcha leapt out of the way of sliding ropes and barrels as the ship lurched to starboard. Briefly, her racing mind considered using Voishem, but the rune of phase was one of the most draining; though it would confer on her the ability to walk through walls, it would not help the horses escape this sudden madness.

Again Sorcha could hear her stallion's neighs, sounding more demanding than terrified. Merrick had called Shedryi long in the tooth, and had assumed that he was merely a horse to her. Such attachment to a creature could be considered a weakness. Well, he'd know she cared, once she did this.

Opening herself to the Otherside, Sorcha activated Chityre in her Gauntlets. Bracing herself against the bucking and dying vessel, she raised both hands in the direction of the hold where the horses were trapped. The ship was already being ripped apart; one more hole was not going to make any difference. Her Gauntlets lit up like sparkling fireworks as the explosion ripped from her spread fingers. The rune opened a tiny and split-second gap into the Otherside, a blink-of-an-eye moment that would have been an impressive display at any other time, but at this moment was barely noticeable amid the absolute chaos around her. Chityre blew apart the wood of the hatch and the side of the swaying vessel. Nails and debris flew through the air like blades of grass and disappeared through the momentary rift into the Otherside.

Clenching her fist closed about the rune, Sorcha glanced back. Merrick and the girl were following, drenched and pale but somehow still on their feet despite the thrashing monster and the dying ship.

"Yrikhodit," Sorcha screamed at the Breed. Both of the horses' heads snapped up at the command, and the proud, noble creatures did indeed come. With a surge, both stallion and mare leapt over the remains of the hatch, skidding and sliding on their hooves on the pitching deck. Sorcha scrambled onto the stallion while Merrick pulled Nynnia up behind him on the mare.

"Horace!" the young Deacon howled, but the pack mule was lost in the maelstrom of the sinking ship. The great, seaweed-encrusted head of the monster was dropping down toward them. Its mouth, as large as two rowboats, ripped into the remaining mast.

This was death, then. Sorcha threw her arms around Shedryi. Long in the tooth. Perhaps that was true, but both of them deserved to die in a better place. With her breath coming in broken gasps, the Deacon leaned down to the stallion.

"Kysotu, my love," she whispered into his dark ear.

The ship shifted under them, finally succumbing to the crushing pressure of the monster. Only moments remained. Only heartbeats. The stallion, true to his training, remained steadfast. With a shake of his arched neck, he leapt bravely forward into the waves, his mare following after.

The water was freezing cold, and yet it boiled like a cauldron. She couldn't see Merrick on Melochi. The ocean was full of wreckage and howling sailors. Underneath her, Shedryi was swimming as hard as he could, almost an underwater gallop. His head stretched forward, nostrils flaring. He had no saddle on, only a bridle. Sorcha felt herself sliding off his slick back, and wrapped her arm around his neck.

The waves surged and she let out a scream into the storm as everything tilted. She caught a glimpse of a tangled mass of rigging and mast swinging toward them. There was nothing she could do. Everything crumpled away into darkness and waves.

SEVEN

The Sweet Taste of Intercession

The discovery of *Corsair* had destroyed morale, making every crew member shiver. After Aachon and Raed returned, they cast off from the crippled warship and never said a word about what they had seen there. Silence descended on *Dominion*. Snook, the thin little strip of a woman who was their navigator, had tried to keep the others back from the railing, but the smell of death and the pool of scarlet on the deck had been witnessed by everyone. They were not fools; they too would know that nothing human had wreaked that vengeance on the Imperial Navy. Raed was not the only one to realize the implications of what had happened.

Aachon kept hold of his weirstone, not putting it away as he usually did, as if to reassure himself and the rest of the crew that it was still alive.

"She's a hazard," the Young Pretender whispered to him, jerking his head sideways at the limping warship.

The first mate nodded, understanding immediately. He turned to the gun crew. "Two shots into her, below the water line, if you please, Mr. Eastan."

The report of the cannons made Raed flinch. He didn't turn around to watch the battered ship sink under the waves, though he heard many of his crew rush to the railing to do so. He couldn't blame them for muttering among themselves. It wasn't every day that a blood-soaked Imperial warship went down to the bottom.

He heard Aachon talking to Byrd. "We will send word to

the Imperial Navy when we get to Ulrich. Their families should know." It was a small danger, yet the right thing to do.

Raed swallowed hard. Those relatives would be better off without the knowledge of what had happened to their loved ones. The image of the desiccated Captain, reaching for his dead weir-stone, was burned on the Pretender's brain. He glanced up where the Rossin flag fluttered over *Dominion*. The mer-lion was hanging over him, just like in the ancient Curse.

Every assumption of his life had been blown out of the water, as conclusively as *Corsair* had been, and Raed needed time to pull himself together. He started toward his cabin.

"My prince"—Aachon intercepted him before he could reach the safety of his quarters—"I was thinking . . ." He paused to glance down at the swirling weirstone that he'd still not put away. He cleared his throat. "We need to be away from this area immediately and without delay."

Dominion had been fast once—the fastest in the Northern Sea. Now, with so many barnacles on her hull and with all their running repairs, she wallowed in her native environment. Once a swift runner, she now could barely walk the course. Raed was about to open his mouth to make some quip, yet when he saw the serious look in his first mate's eye, he knew what he was suggesting.

The Pretender glanced down at the weirstone for a moment; then he nodded. "When all the cards turn against you, it is time to stack the deck."

Aachon grinned bleakly and spun about on the deck. "Prepare to run before the wind."

Most of the crew scrambled up into the rigging, but Byrd, as always, was the one to speak his mind. He turned his sun-browned face into the slight breeze. "But sir, we're nearly becalmed."

"My wind, Byrd," Aachon growled and raised the weirstone to his eye line. "Trim the sheets and batten down those hatches!"

As with every Sensitive, there was a touch of Active within the stern first mate. He seldom used it, but they had witnessed exceptional circumstances this day. Raed would normally have been cautious of any use of the Otherside near him, but he was filled with the desire to be away from this part of the sea. Besides, if a geist could cross the ocean, then maybe he needed to recon-sider his options.

As Raed threw his oilskin over his frock coat, he turned and looked to stern. The air was coming alive. He preferred to watch the storm, rather than watch his friend create it. Aachon's slack, white-eyed look was more than disconcerting; it was positively unnerving. To the south, the clouds were already pulling together and darkening. The sunny day slipped into grayness, and the tang in his nostrils filled Raed with heady delight. Despite the nature of the coming storm, he couldn't help but revel in its power.

It had been an unholy day, so it seemed fitting to end it with an almighty thunderstorm. Lightning cracked within the clouds and the crew cheered. It seemed a strange reaction, but Raed understood. After having felt so rudderless for the last few months, it was invigorating to be in control of something.

Naturally, it was a different story once the storm was summoned. The winds began to howl and the reduced sails of *Dominion* whipped in response. Raed turned around to catch Aachon. The tall first mate staggered a step back, his dark complexion pale. There was a decided tremble in his hands as he replaced the weirstone into his pocket. They both looked to stern, into the wind and the clouds that were now coiling on themselves.

"Let's see that thing catch us now," Raed yelled in Aachon's ear. The storm would follow the weirstone that had cast it.

Despite her barnacle-cased hull, *Dominion* leapt away as if she had only been waiting for the signal. Even with her reduced sail, the storm filled her, sending her flying like an ungainly dancer through the waves. It was not quite as dangerous as a natural storm, but still there was hazard in it. Crew scrambled to clear the decks, until only a few held the essential posts.

Raed, however, would not go below. He wanted to experience the storm and to keep an eye on his ship. Aachon, naturally, was at his side, perhaps not quite as excited by what he had wrought; his Deacon training ran very deep indeed.

In the steel gray light, they ran before the clouds for many hours through the night, with only the occasional glimpse of stars and moon to guide them. Wind and water lashed him, but Raed smiled back into it. For this moment, they had control, and it seemed his ship was reveling in it as much as he was. Surely not even a curse could catch them at such a speed. For those blissful hours, storm-tossed and hectic, the Young Pretender was happy again.

The feeling was, however, broken the next day. Aleck, still up the crow's nest, began yelling something, waving his hands before pointing to port. Raed strained his ears to catch the look-out's screams above the roar of the storm. He pulled his spyglass out from underneath his oilskin, and after a moment's difficulty he managed to train it in the direction Aleck was pointing.

It was another ship, some sort of trading vessel by the look of her; not as fast as *Dominion*, even in her current condition, and she was in the clear air, so they were pulling away from her. Whatever she was, she was not an Imperial Man-o'-War. A large collection of seabirds seemed to be circling the vessel. It was certainly curious, but not dangerous. He was losing interest, unsure what Aleck was so concerned about, and Raed was about to look away when he saw something else odd—something he'd seen only once before in his time on the sea. The water all around the other vessel began to churn as if it were boiling. He could see huge clumps of seaweed bubble to the surface, and white foam and bubbles gathered around the other ship's hull.

Every sailor knew that there were creatures in the depths, but they were seldom seen, only whispered about. Raed pulled Aachon around and handed him the spyglass, just to make sure that his eyes weren't deceiving him. They both gaped as the beast, easily twice the size of the boat it preyed upon, wrapped its coils over the masts before bringing them crashing down. The monster had a huge, wedge-shaped head that hung malevolently over the wreck. It reminded Raed of a man crushing a nut in his fist. Dimly, they could make out tiny forms leaping into the ocean in desperation to escape.

It was the law of the sea: *Dominion*'s crew could not sail past such a disaster. Raed squeezed Aachon's shoulder, leaning in closely to bellow his decision. "Dismiss the storm. We've got to help."

Aachon merely nodded. Raising the weirstone once more, he turned to take back the power that was driving the storm. The cobalt blue stone flashed white, but to no immediate effect. Once summoned, a storm was not so easy to dismiss. The first mate braced himself on the deck, prepared for the drain on his strength.

"All hands," Raed bellowed, and Laython leapt forward to ring the bell with incredible vigor. The crew boiled out from below with almost military quickness. "Hard to port," he called, spinning the wheel as nimble hands unfurled the sails. Luckily, the wind was dying a little at his back, or they would have been torn to shreds.

Riding the last of the storm's strength, they tacked toward the thrashing monster and the dying vessel. "Have you got a plan?" Aachon was almost staggering from side to side with weariness. Dismissing a storm was at the very edge of his power.

Raed grinned. He knew a thing or two about sea monsters. "They can't last long at the surface, those scaly demons," he shouted back. "Ripping that ship apart should have exhausted the thing."

"Should?" His first mate shook his head. "You don't sound exactly certain . . ."

"Think of it as an experiment. We'll be able to sell the results to any number of interested scholars."

"And if your supposition is not correct?"

"Then we will at least die with the knowledge that we have been part of the scientific process!" Raed turned the wheel as they came about.

The smell of rotten seaweed and salt was almost overwhelming. As *Dominion* swung around, the other ship's back broke with an almighty crack, the few remaining masts crashing into the water as the monster's coils contracted in a last deadly embrace. The wreckage bobbed on the water for a few seconds, wood entangled with the twisting and scaled form, and then began to slip gradually under.

Raed shot Aachon a satisfied grin as the creature sank out of view. His first mate raised a pointed finger. "Not just yet, my prince."

The Pretender knew better than to tempt fate; somewhere down there, the monster was probably finishing off what it had taken for its enemy. Creatures of the deep were not known for their intelligence.

He dashed to the side and helped to cast out ropes. The water was full of flotsam and jetsam. Barrels and chests bobbed around in the churning waves. *Dominion*'s crew set about pulling people in as quickly as possible. Those they pulled free of the sea were weak and stunned, and they slumped down on the deck. Traders traveled with few crew, as few as they could get away with; every extra person cut into profits, after all. However, when Raed asked the shaking survivors, it seemed that the Captain had gone down with his ship.

"My lord!" Snook was busy pulling in a rotund and puffing man, but she paused and gestured out to the sea. Leaning over,

Raed saw a remarkable sight: a horse swimming for all the world as if it were a dog. The brave animal, black with a star on its forehead, carried a man and a woman, both plastered to its back.

The crew, spurred on by the sheer courage of the beast, whistled and called. "Get the loading nets out," Raed shouted.

It took some maneuvering, but the man on the back of the struggling creature managed to get the horse into the net, and soon, with much grunting and complaining, the crew had it on the deck. It was a beautifully proportioned mare; Raed wasn't so long from land that he couldn't appreciate that.

The man slid from its back and helped the woman down. She stood still and dripping on the deck while he darted to the gunwales, peering down with some level of urgency, before dashing up and down. Raed could also recognize great concern. "What is it, lad?"

The other turned, and with a start the Pretender recognized the silver mark of the Order on his cloak—a cloak that might be emerald green when dry. The young man's hair was plastered to his head and his brown eyes were wide. Deacons did not lose themselves in the Sight like the lesser-trained witches might, but Raed also recognized that the man was Seeing.

"My partner," the Deacon gasped. "She's alive out there somewhere, but very weak. We have to find her."

Raed yanked out his spyglass and trained it on the soup of debris bobbing around among the waves. For a few moments, he could make out nothing but corpses and wreckage, and then, miraculously, he saw movement. They glided a little closer, as if the sea itself was impressed with such survival. By rights any still-living thing out there should have been crushed by all manner of debris, if not snapped up by the monster itself.

"Another horse," Snook whispered. "By the Ancients, what a creature!"

At first it looked like this larger animal was alone, but as the powerful creature drew closer, urged on by the calls of the young Deacon, it was possible to see that it was dragging another form. This one was not on the horse's back; it was being towed through the water, apparently trapped in the bridle. It was hard to make out if it was a living shape or not, but by the Deacon's worried calls, he must have Seen that she still breathed.

With a little more finesse this time, they managed to get the stallion up using the cargo net; another of the Breed, by the look of him. However, this one had more life to him than the mare. As soon as his hooves touched solid ground, he reared up, dropping his charge finally to the deck. The stallion's eyes were wild and froth flew from his lips as he swung about, neighing, snorting and kicking his heels.

The crew dove out of the way as the maddened horse leapt and kicked, but despite the stallion's frenzy he was all the time careful not to trample his rider. Whatever else the Deacons did, they trained their horses well. The young man tried to call out commands, but something seemed to have snapped in the equine's mind. Raed knew all about that.

As he watched the stallion flinging himself about, Raed reached down and touched that cursed bit of himself, the animal part. More nimbly than a mere mortal could, he stepped in and laid his hand against the wet and taut skin of the stallion. For a moment horse and man regarded each other, dark rolling eye to his calm hazel ones. They each recognized something within the other.

"It's all right," Raed whispered. "You have protected her, and now she is safe."

It was like the strings were cut. Blowing hard through his nostrils, the magnificent beast bowed his head, and now could be seen trembling on his feet.

The male Deacon and his pretty young companion ran forward and, together murmuring to the beast, managed to lead it away. Carefully, Raed rolled the still form on the deck over onto its back. It was a woman indeed, near his own age with a mass of damp red hair and a bruise on her pale forehead. Breath, however, was coming through her parted lips, and stirring in her breast. Raed's eyes drifted to her badge of the Order; the upraised fist surmounted by a wide-open eye. That as well as the Gauntlets pinned into her belt and the dark blue cloak all confirmed it; she was an Active Deacon.

Her eyes flicked open so suddenly that it took Raed a moment to realize that he was being examined as thoroughly as he was examining. They were deep blue and there was no confusion in them. Like all Deacons, she was assessing him thoroughly.

One corner of her lips twitched. "The Young Pretender." Her voice had the lilt of someone born in Delmaire. Despite everything, it was a pretty accent.

Raed flinched, hardly expecting to be recognized so quickly—if at all.

"Not quite as young as expected, though." The Deacon, even half-dead, had a sharp tongue. Pushing her hair out of her face, she levered herself up onto her elbow. Raed had been about to offer his hand but pulled it back after a glance at the expression on her face. This was a woman who didn't need help. She climbed carefully to her feet, obviously feeling bruised. Gently, she touched her wounded forehead, winced, and then straightened her cloak about her. She tilted her head toward her partner in acknowledgment that he had also survived, and then patted her pockets.

A smile of relief crossed her face. "Thank the Bones." She pulled out a small package, unwrapped the oilskin from it, and then popped open the tin it revealed. A small sigh escaped her as she took out one of the cigars contained within.

The crew around her was completely silent. Dropping a Deacon into a middle of outlaws was like releasing a wolf into a herd of sheep. Certainly, they were not part of the Imperial Army, but the Order had been brought over by the Emperor and the Deacons owed him allegiance. The crewmen shuffled their feet and looked to Raed for guidance, wondering perhaps if he would order them to tip their new passengers back over the side.

While they contemplated, the woman had managed to get one of her cigars lit and was watching them through the gray-white smoke. The look was measured and predatory. Deacons gave Raed a pause. Aachon had told him a little of their training, which would have been enough to unnerve many, but it was their attachment to the Otherside that particularly worried him—his Curse made that a major concern. Since she knew who he was, she would also have heard the rumors of it. The one disastrous time a more kindly Deacon had tried to "fix" him still loomed in his memory. He wasn't about to allow a repeat.

The woman drew in a long mouthful of smoke, a confident gesture somewhat lessened by the slight tremble in her hands. Apparently a brush with death could give even a Deacon pause. Raed shot a look to his right where the young man was stroking the stallion's neck. His equally assessing gaze was directed at the woman; no question who the dominant partner was.

Finally, the woman removed her cigar, licked her lips and gave a little bow of her head. "Deacon Sorcha Faris. This is my partner, Merrick Chambers."

"And Miss Nynnia Macthcoll," the male Deacon blurted out,

indicating the beautiful, dripping woman who had tucked herself against his side.

Raed did not miss the slight twist of Deacon Faris' lips; it was hard to tell if that was jealousy or something else. But she was now looking around the ship, taking in the set of the sails, the armaments and the huddle of wide-eyed crew. Her neck even craned upward to look at the flapping flag with his family device on it. She raised an eyebrow but did not comment, merely taking another long puff. "Thank you for the timely rescue, Lord Rossin."

She didn't wait for a reply, but walked somewhat gingerly over to the stallion. He raised his exhausted head and blew through his nose in a whicker of greeting. "Hello, my handsome Shed-ryi," she whispered to him in return, before bending to examine his legs gently, and then proceeding to check his flanks. A couple of minor gashes marred the fine black hide, but Raed could see the horse was otherwise in remarkable shape.

Sorcha then proceeded to inspect the mare, her back to the captain and his crew.

"You all right, Merrick?" he heard her ask her partner. The young man nodded mutely, but his clear brown eyes remained fixed on the others. He understood a precarious position when he saw it.

Finally, Raed had had enough. "If you are quite finished, Deacon Faris, perhaps we can discuss what just happened?"

She turned and regarded him with that keen blue gaze. "You mean the monster crushing our vessel, or your use of an illegal weirstone?" She touched her Gauntlets lightly, reminding the Young Pretender of the power a Deacon could wield. He knew a signal when he was handed one. *Watch yourself. You may be a lord, but I can dish out a storm of pain.*

It was one of those few times he actually felt glad for the Curse. Pretender and Deacon locked gazes. Raed heard Aachon shift uncomfortably at his side, but he didn't look. He dared not contemplate what was running through his first mate's head. Being face-to-face with the Order must have been a real shock.

This was not how people were supposed to react after being pulled half-dead from the sea. Raed could feel his blood warming and driving away his concern over the Deacons on his ship. Sorcha's lips were crooked in a slight smile, waiting for him to break. He knew he couldn't match the patience of a Deacon, or comprehend what she was actually thinking. The training they received would have made them excellent and dangerous cardplayers.

"It was your Emperor who made them illegal"—Raed pointed to the flapping Rossin flag—"and as you can see, I am not one of his citizens."

The blasted woman was about to answer back when Merrick stepped between them. "We don't want to seem ungrateful, Captain Rossin. It is just that my partner has had rather a shock. It would be churlish of us to complain." Obviously he was annoyed and worried about his more argumentative Deacon, but he was controlled enough not to give her a look. Raed would have loved to have known what communication was shooting between them. Aachon had never got to the stage of sharing a Bond, but he'd talked about it with some longing. Raed, however, was not sure he'd want to share anything with this prickly, sharp-tongued woman, beautiful as she might be.

Bless Snook—she took a step toward Sorcha, her thin form offering no danger. "We need to sew up the wounds on your horse, and I could take a look at your head as well."

The Deacon glanced around, as if realizing for the first time that there were other people on deck, injured sailors from the cargo ship, exhausted horses and concerned onlookers. Raed wouldn't have said that the wind went out of her, but she let out a little sigh. "Thank you," she said to Snook and allowed herself to be led back to her stallion.

Her partner whispered something to the younger woman, who nodded and hung back as he approached Raed.

"My apologies, once again." This Deacon at least seemed more reasonable. They moved out of the way as the crew hurried to get the injured and horses settled. "We have had a . . . difficult couple of days. This is the third attack in a week that Faris has had to endure."

Even though Raed had been out of the general flow of society, he knew that the Order had been getting on top of geist attacks in the last year. He could not conceal his surprise. "Three?" His mind flew back to the massacre on *Corsair*, and his blood chilled again. "I am sorry to hear that, Deacon Chambers."

A brief smile flitted across the man's pleasant face, and he suddenly looked very young indeed. Was the Abbey now initiating children? "No more than we are, Captain. We were on route

to the town of Ulrich, as our Arch Abbot had received reports
from the Priory there of an upsurge in attacks."

"What?" Raed's hand clenched the hilt of his cutlass. He
swallowed hard. "Geists . . . in Ulrich?"

He knew that he would be unable to conceal anything from
the sharp eyes of a Sensitive Deacon. It was pointless to try. They
would know the details of the family curse. He nodded as calmly
as he could, though. "We also are heading for Ulrich, Deacon
Chambers. They have one of the few safe harbors where we can
make repairs."

A slight frown appeared between the other man's brows, but
disappeared quickly. His smile was just as small. "Call me Merrick, Captain. I'm not one of those Deacons to stand on ceremony."

"Unlike your colleague?" Raed glanced across the deck to
where her tousled red head was bent over the wounds in her stallion's side.

Merrick was a good partner; he did not make any comment.
Instead, he tilted his head. "It strikes me that we may be able to
offer you assistance, since you were kind enough to risk your
ship and crew to rescue us."

"How so?"

"I understand the particular . . . difficulty you labor under,
personally. We, as Deacons, may be able to offer protection."

Aachon was watching from the sidelines, a look of caution
plain on his face, while his fingers kept close to his pockets. He
had never revealed why he'd been cast from the Order, but his
distrust was also evident. Yet, he had never repelled any geists.
He could tell his captain where one was, but lacked the skills a
Deacon could employ to stop it from latching on.

Raed paused, wondering if there was any other way. Could he
not just drop off these troublesome Deacons and sail away? The
answer was, of course, no. *Dominion* had nowhere else to go. She
and her crew were near the end of their tether. It was Ulrich or
nothing. However, the Deacons were part of the machinery of the
Empire—the Empire that had been chasing him and his father for
the past three years.

"I can assure you"—Merrick straightened up—"that the Deacons are not officially part of the Imperial forces. We seek to
keep the Otherside out of this world, and have little concern for
what the military is tasked with."

The Pretender managed to not look shocked. This man must

have been incredibly perceptive. He hoped that was all it was. "And Deacon Faris?"

Merrick rubbed his hand through his hair wearily. "She is the most powerful Active in the Order. You will find no better protection from the unliving. Yet, we are only recently Bonded. I will try my best to convince her, but she . . . Well, she has her ways."

As if Sorcha knew they were talking about her, she raised her head and glanced in their direction. Raed once again felt those blue eyes pinning him down for observation. "I am sure she does," he replied.

The young Deacon was about to turn away when the Pretender grasped his shoulder. He didn't know why, but he found himself asking the question that had haunted him for years, the one that he had been unable to ask that aloof member of the Order. "You would See better than most, Reverend Deacon. How do I look through your Sight?"

Merrick's brown eyes seemed kind. They focused on him, and he flinched back a little.

"Is it hideous?" Raed queried, terrified at the response.

The Deacon actually looked puzzled for a second. "On the contrary, my lord, you blaze in the ether."

"Blaze?"

The other raised his hand as if to sketch a halo around Raed. "You look like silver fire."

"That's a good thing . . . isn't it?"

Merrick sighed and glanced away, once again seeking out his partner. When he turned back, his expression was somber. "It explains many things. You burn so brightly, Prince Rossin, that it is no wonder the unliving are drawn to you."

Raed felt the diagnosis like a hammer blow between the shoulder blades; he swallowed hard.

The Deacon lightly touched his shoulder. "It will be all right. Sorcha and I are very strong, and when we get you to the Priory, there will be others to assist."

The tone of his voice was calming, but Raed now knew the truth. He blazed in the ether, and sooner or later the geist that had killed *Corsair* would be drawn to him. That geist, or something worse.

He watched Merrick return to his partner, and speak in a low voice to her. Sorcha waved her cigar at him, almost jabbing him in the shoulder. She threw her hands up in an exasperated gesture, after which she shook her head for a minute before eventually, grudgingly, nodding. It was impressive, the way that Merrick handled her. Then she was striding over to Raed. Her hair had dried somewhat, and was now a lighter bronze color. If he blazed in the ether, the woman bearing down on him blazed in the real world.

"Captain," she growled, folding her arms and glaring at him. He was slightly taller than she, but somehow it still seemed she was looking down her nose at him. "I understand my partner has made an agreement with you."

"You prefer not to reach your destination? Or perhaps swim?"

Her lips twisted in a smile that had nothing to do with amusement. "No. The people of Ulrich need us, and your ship is the only one currently available. Your agreement with Deacon Chambers stands, but I just want to make one thing clear."

"Yes?"

"When we leave Ulrich, all bets are off. You are not only a fugitive from the Emperor, but you also make use of illegal and dangerous weirstones." Replacing her cigar, she chewed on the end a little.

"Fair enough," Raed replied. Watching her fume seemed to calm him. "But there is one other condition."

Sorcha tilted her head back and looked at him with hooded eyes. "What might that be?"

"I insist that you and your partner take my cabin."

The Young Pretender had enough experience dealing with difficult people to know that giving them what they least expected often sucked the wind out of their sails. It did indeed seem to work on this particular prickly Deacon.

She was stumped for words for a moment, but eventually she pushed back some of her curls and replied. "Thank you, Captain."

With a little bow, Raed turned on his heel and made for the quarterdeck. It was always sweet to get the last word in, and he had a feeling that if he lingered, he would have lost the advantage. The loss of his cabin for a few days was little compared to that victory.

EIGHT

Bringing Judgment

Merrick felt like he was sitting on a powder keg. Sorcha was mortally offended by the Young Pretender's use of the weirstone and seemed unable to realize that their transport, and most likely their life, relied on him.

"He's a danger," Sorcha growled, sucking down the last of her cigar and flicking the remains over the edge. "We're supposed to protect people from loose cannons like this Pretender."

Something about being fished out of the water had really irritated the Deacon. It was almost as if she would have preferred to drown. The Bond between them was no weaker; Merrick could feel her tension in his own bones.

Wearily, he rubbed his head, feeling a headache build behind his eyes. He was unable to tell if it was his or hers. "We're all tired, Sorcha. Can we please just rest and recover a little? Being attacked by two geists in four days has really taken it out of me, and you've had one more than that."

Her eyes locked with his, and there was a strange giddy sensation as for a minute the Bond swallowed them. Both of them felt it, but it was Sorcha who turned pale.

"All right," she whispered. "Yes . . . Yes, that is probably best."

As she went into the cabin, Merrick turned around to find Nynnia at his side. Her dress was torn, but her dark hair had dried in soft curls around her face. Merrick's eyes darted over her, but the tears in her clothing were not matched by any injuries he could see.

None of the crew was nearby; most of those not busy were clustered around the hold hatch where the Breed horses had finally been stowed. Gently, so as not to alarm her, Merrick took Nynnia's arm and guided her farther away.

"I have arranged for you to stay in the Captain's cabin," he started. Her eyebrows shot up and her mouth opened a little. Merrick felt all the blood rush into his face. "Oh, no . . . no . . . The Captain has kindly given up his cabin. You will only be sharing with Deacon Faris."

"Very well." The young woman sighed. His partner had not taken any care to hide her dismissive attitude to the other woman, so it was Merrick who found himself making excuses.

"Faris has had a difficult week; her husband was badly injured and . . ."

"I'm sure she has," Nynnia said quietly. "It's just I don't think she likes me very much."

Merrick looked down into her soft brown eyes. For a woman who had survived both shipwreck and sea monster only to be rescued by what amounted to pirates, she was very calm. She seemed very young and yet there was a cord of strength in her that ran just as deep as in Sorcha. Through his Center, he glanced down at her. She was so vital and lovely it bled into the ether. With the Young Pretender and Nynnia on board, and with the water no longer providing protection from the geists, Merrick feared they were in great peril.

"She is not as bad as she seems, and it would be best if you stayed close to her."

"Why?" Her doe eyes were wide, and with a lurch, Merrick recalled the feeling of her lithe body pressed against him while Melochi swam.

He shifted uncomfortably on his feet. On the whole, the Order frowned on discussing the Otherside with the ungifted; mostly, they believed it only inspired people to dabble with things they knew nothing of. Yet Nynnia was in as much danger as the rest of them and she deserved to know. Merrick cleared his throat, glancing around one more time just to be sure. "Have you heard of the Curse of the Rossin?" He made a subtle gesture up to where the flag of the beast flapped.

Nynnia looked at the flag with the mer-lion creature. Her brows drew together in a frown, still pretty but perhaps more human. "Everyone knows the Rossin is just a story, the creature that gave the ruling family their name . . ."

"And strength to rise to High King over all the other princes. We studied it in the Abbey; the most famous case of geist familial attachment in the book. This ancient unliving creature made a deal with the family, giving them its name and power to rule. In return they agreed that their heir would belong to the Rossin, and could never be born anywhere but Vermillion."

Up on the quarterdeck, Raed the Young Pretender was giving orders to his crew. Nynnia followed Merrick's gaze. To her the Captain would appear nothing more than a slightly rakish, bearded man, but when Merrick looked through his Center, he was almost blinded by the man. The halo of silver fire that burned through him was like a glimpse into the raging core of the Otherside.

Merrick could not look at him long through his Center. "The Unsung's son was not born in Vermillion and he has inherited the Curse. The unliving are drawn to him . . . and when they touch him . . . the Rossin is unleashed."

"Unleashed?" Nynnia smiled slowly. "But being a mer-creature . . ."

"The Rossin has many shapes, not all of them as pretty as the one on the flag, and all of them uncontrollable."

"But they cannot cross water . . ." she whispered. "Everyone knows . . ."

"All the rules are being rewritten, Nynnia—even that one. We are not safe."

She bit her lip and glanced down at her toes, swaying slightly. "What—what do you want me to do?"

"Stay close to Deacon Faris." Merrick pressed her shoulder lightly. "She may be prickly as a desert cactus, but she is also the most powerful weapon against the geist."

"Very well."

With real relief he turned toward the quarterdeck himself.

"Merrick." The tremble in her voice made him pause, as did her use of his name. "What are you going to do?"

"The thing I do best." He smiled broadly and went up the first step. "Watch."

* * *

Sorcha did not like the guard dog Merrick had set upon her. Those wide brown eyes followed her as she paced the Pretender's cabin. Being closeted with nothing more than a girl, let alone a girl who was obviously made nervous by her, was demeaning. Sorcha realized that she had misjudged Merrick; he was a schemer. Making a deal with the Pretender was surely just the beginning of the end. Sensitives, if you didn't watch them, could easily believe they were the boss in a partnership. Actives, they said, were nothing more than weapons to be used.

Sorcha strode to the window and looked out into the darkening sky. Night was sinking over the ship and, despite everything, she thought of the sea monster with a shudder. Surely that particular individual had had enough of life on the surface, but if the unliving could possess one, then they could possess others. That realization was deeply disquieting—enough to make her glad of her sharp-eyed partner above. Yet there was nothing for Sorcha to do but pace and feel uncomfortable under scrutiny.

She stalked the decks for a while, feeling more helpless than she had in years. On her return to the cabin she realized why.

In all her time as a member of the Order Sorcha had never let her Gauntlets be anything more than an arm's reach away. But they had never been soaked in seawater, and so she had left them drying by the little range. The door was open a fraction and through it she saw something that made her freeze in place.

Nynnia wasn't actually touching the talismans—that would have been dangerous—but her fingertips flickered over the tops of them. Curiosity was perhaps understandable—her words, however, were not. She was reciting the Litany of Dominion. Her voice was soft as she repeated the words an initiate learned in their first years in the Order.

Aydien, holds my foes as bay.
Yevah, my mighty shield of fire.
Tryrei, a peephole to the Otherside.
Chityre, the power of lightning in my fist.
Pyet, the cleansing flame consume them all.
Shayst, my enemies' strength is mine.
Seym, makes me more than I am.

Voishem, no wall can hold me.
Deiyant, everything moves to my will.
Teisayt, the door to their world I dare not open.

The Deacon could not abide the travesty any longer. "You know the words, child." Sorcha strode over and snatched up her Gauntlets. "But you should not meddle in the Order's affairs."

Nynnia flushed scarlet and scampered back to her side of the cabin. "Forgive me. I just heard the chant around the Priory." She picked up some socks she was darning for the Captain and remained silent for the rest of the night.

Though the explanation made sense, it also disturbed the Deacon. What if Nynnia was more than just a stranger they'd encountered by chance? Sorcha shook her head. No—if anything was amiss with Nynnia, she trusted Merrick would have seen it. The world was already full of enough complications.

Trying her best to ignore her silent young companion, she decided that if the Pretender had given up his room, it was her golden opportunity to do some snooping. On the table were spread various sea charts that she could not see much of interest about, and the rest of the cabin was sparsely decorated. The only items that were intriguing were an old sea chest and a large leather-bound journal that she found rammed down the back of a battered chair.

Head on one side, she considered. One hand strayed to her Gauntlets while the other traced the outline of the embossed cover. She drew out one of the fine pins that held up her hair and set to work on the large brass lock of the journal. While the sea chest might contain treasures, the pages of a journal would reveal even more.

The little brown-eyed mouse in the corner squeaked. "I don't think you should—"

Sorcha glanced over her shoulder. The woman was barely out of girlhood, sitting with her hands folded ever so properly. Undoubtedly she had some moral objection to Sorcha's little piece of thievery, but then, maybe she'd never had to live in the real world. With a snort, Sorcha focused on the lock once more.

"No, I really think you should—" Nynnia ventured again.

"Don't you dare—" Sorcha rounded on the other woman and then stopped. Standing in the doorway was the owner of the book she was trying to pry open.

For a moment, all three of them stared at one another like

some comic tableau. In this light the Captain's eyes were hard
and green. Sorcha's mind scrabbled for a witty excuse. In the
intervening silence, the Pretender's voice was flinty. "May you
excuse us, Miss Macthcoll?"

The girl exited the room without so much as a whimper. Yet
she shot Sorcha a strangely triumphant look, the expression of a
far older woman.

Sorcha straightened and as calmly as possible slid the pin
back into her hair. "I wasn't aware that we had anything to say to
each other, Captain Rossin."

He carefully closed his own door and walked over to the table,
his lips pressed together in a thin line above his neatly trimmed
beard. Sorcha was not much of a Sensitive, but she was enough
of one to sense something strange about the man. This close and
all alone, he had a faint attractive scent: leather and sea salt. She
couldn't help it; she let her Center fall toward him.

Merrick was right. In the normal world Raed was a handsome man, but through geist-Sight this man blazed, and not
just visually. Her partner had not mentioned the scent, but that
was probably because he was a male. Raed's was like a heady
perfume. Sorcha's Center enhanced all her usual senses, which
could produce some rather uncomfortable chemical and physical reactions. With a little gasp, Sorcha put away her Center and
dropped back into her body. She shook her head to try to get past
the effect.

"Are you all right?" Raed leaned forward, his hand resting on
the top of the charts. "Or just trying to apologize?"

Sorcha tried to still her racing heart. The unliving had many
aspects, many ways to tempt mortals to bend to their will, and
few were more primitive than sex. The possessed often displayed
aggressive sexual behavior or urges. This man, this cursed man,
had a flame in his core, a flame that was designed to draw people
to him. Even those who weren't Deacons would be unconsciously
attracted to him; would find him good-looking, charming and
very, very sexy.

Sorcha knew of nobles who would kill for such effects. But
she was damned if she was going to tell him this. "I don't know
what you mean," she snapped, feeling her body respond to the
unliving effect.

The flicker of concern slipped from his features and was
replaced by the kind of dark scowl that should have thrown ice

over her. It didn't. "Well, then maybe you can explain why you are taking advantage of my good nature by breaking into private property?"

She felt a pang of guilt, but didn't let it show. Shoving the book toward its owner, she tried to act flippant. "As a Deacon, I have the right to examine any item I think may contain information on the unliving."

His jaw clenched. "Again, we are back to that." He leaned forward once more, both hands now on the table. "I am not—repeat, not—a citizen of the Empire, so your foolish rules do not apply."

Sorcha laughed shortly. Spinning on her heel, she threw herself onto the chair in a studied example of indifference. "I would think our agreement gives me the right. After all, I may have to throw myself between you and a raging geist at any point."

His mouth opened and she was sure there was a bitter retort ready to come, yet he bit it back. Sorcha swung her leg over the arm of the chair and tried not to inhale his scent.

Instead of replying, he made a grunt of displeasure and turned his back on her to open the sea chest. She tried to crane her head as subtly as possible, but it appeared all he was taking out was a clean shirt. Ignoring her completely, he stripped down to the waist.

If Sorcha didn't know better, she would have sworn that he was deliberately trying to distract her. Admiring the shifting planes of the muscles in his back was certainly diverting, but the fact remained: this man was the burning light, and the places they were going would be full of very large, very dangerous moths. She clenched her fingers in the arm of the chair and reminded herself that her reaction was all related to the Curse.

When he turned around suddenly, Sorcha quickly flicked her eyes away—hopefully, quickly enough. "I appreciate your talents, Deacon Faris"—his voice was softer—"but I am still captain of this ship. And, while on my ship, I would be grateful if you at least showed me the common courtesy of a houseguest to a host."

Sorcha's mouth twisted. "A host that could turn into a raging beast at any moment."

For a moment, his hazel eyes reflected the light of the waning sun. "Yes, and you'd do well to remember that in the future," he growled, his body tense like a coiled spring.

Sorcha's heartbeat leapt up two levels and her skin prickled as if in the presence of a geist. Every instinct screamed to her to leap out of the chair and wrench on her Gauntlets, but a quick flick of her Center revealed nothing but the flaming presence of the Pretender.

She forced herself to remain still, though her mouth was dry and her hands trembled with their yearning to be wielding power. Instead, she let him get away with something she rarely allowed: having the last word. He stormed out of his own cabin, taking his disturbing presence, thankfully, away.

For the next two days, Sorcha took Merrick's advice and stayed in the cabin. Even Nynnia was better company than the Captain. Merrick, however, seldom ventured below. Her partner had taken it on himself to watch the seas for more unliving activity. Across the Bond, Sorcha could feel his guilt at not having spotted the sea monster that had brought them to this. He ran himself hard, napping on the quarterdeck when exhaustion claimed him.

While he slept, Sorcha would venture above decks, drape her cloak over him and take up his duties as best she could with her Sight. The crew seemed to take comfort in the fact that two Deacons were on board. After their initial fright, they began to see the advantages and show some proper respect for their passengers.

They also seemed intrigued by the Breed horses. The stallion and mare were in the small confines of the cargo hold, along with two goats and a crate of chickens. Sorcha visited, but found two crew members tending to them, one carefully grooming the mare while a slight young girl fed Shedryi lumps of sugar. The old devil rolled one eye at her as if in embarrassment but snuffled up the remaining sugar like a child's pony.

Apart from watching over Merrick, Sorcha found herself next to useless on the ship, and while the same had been true on the first vessel, somehow this was different. The Pretender watched her but did not approach, probably still annoyed about her little slipup. She was very glad when the coastline moved from ragged cliffs to undulating tundra and Ulrich itself came into view.

Joining the throng on the deck, Sorcha discovered Ulrich was just as bleak as she feared. She'd seen many little towns just like it, huddled on the edge of the Empire, scraping an existence out of the sea. It was low-lying and gray, and the only thing to recommend it was the deep harbor and wharf jutting out into the sullen ocean. To the right of the jetty, a long stretch of sandy beach continued the half-moon shape of the bay.

The relief of the crew around her was palpable. Merrick wriggled his way past them to stand at her side. "I've never been so glad to see dry land." He rubbed his darkly circled eyes wearily and leaned on the gunwales.

A twinge of sympathy disturbed her own dark thoughts. "You'll be able to rest in the Priory." She pointed to the one hill that looked above the town. "I suppose that will be it."

Priories were usually ramshackle affairs, yet this one looked to be the proudest building in the town; with its white stone and parapets, it almost resembled a fortification.

Both Deacons glanced at each other with raised eyebrows.

Nynnia had followed in Merrick's wake and, seeing their confused expression, laughed. "Everybody is surprised at Ulrich Priory. It was built as part of the defenses of Felstaad, hundreds of years ago when this area was being fought over."

"Who would war over this place?" Merrick wondered aloud.

Sorcha knew enough of her history to answer that one, before Nynnia could impress him. "This area used to be rich with minerals, gold and silver in particular. But those were mined out over a hundred years ago."

"Now there is only the fishing"—Nynnia tucked a strand of her dark hair behind her ear—"and no one is prepared to go to war over herring."

"Not even good herring." The Pretender's voice made Sorcha jump a little. She didn't turn her head to acknowledge him as he continued. "But it will suit us well enough to beach *Dominion* and get her careened and repaired."

"Careened?" Nynnia asked.

"It means scraping all the barnacles off the ship's arse." Sorcha turned and beamed at the girl. "Useful if you want to keep out of the way of the Imperial Navy."

She could feel Merrick tensing at her side. Diplomacy wasn't her best skill—she'd never really needed it before. She let the Sensitives deal with all of that.

Dominion docked easily enough at the jetty, with local harbor workers rushing up to tether the ship. No other vessel could be seen, and at this time of year the workers would be grateful of the fee.

Raed grinned as his first mate handed him papers. Sorcha glanced at them, but one look at the Captain's face told her that he wasn't about to explain. He leapt lightly off the ship, before the gangplank could be added, and strode in the direction of the harbormaster's building at the end of the quay.

"You'd better go after him, Chambers." Sorcha could feel her lips settling into an unhappy line. "You made the deal, so go and make sure no little geist creeps up on him."

Not as limber on board as the Pretender, her partner scrambled to obey.

"You could be nicer to Merrick," Nynnia said at her side, and her voice seemed stronger somehow. "He is trying very hard to be a good partner."

"Oh, really?" Sorcha gave her a wicked grin. "And how can he do that, pray tell, when he is also trying very hard to please you? Or have you not noticed his attentions?"

The girl turned bright red for an instant, and then straightened up, tucking her shawl around her and trying to look calm. "You, Deacon Faris, are a very uncomfortable person to spend time with."

She gave a short laugh, thinking of partners past and present. "That's what they say."

Merrick and the Captain returned in short order. Raed looked very pleased with himself. He stood at the end of the gangplank. "Everything is arranged. Let's start unloading."

The tension seemed to go immediately out of the crew.

"All passengers"—Aachon's stress on that word was hardly friendly—"should now disembark."

It felt good to be on dry land. Merrick stood at her side while the Breed were carefully led out of the hold and onto the quay. Shedryi and Melochi looked as well-groomed as they would have been back at the Abbey, but they would need rest and care to recover their strength. The mare seemed to have fared better than the stallion. Shedryi would bear scars on his fine black hide for the rest of his life. Even if there had been saddles available, Sorcha would not have advised they be ridden.

Merrick had taken Melochi from the quay worker, and was talking in a low voice to Nynnia on the other side of the horse. He was not that far away, yet he was using some Sensitive trick to conceal his words. Feeling along the Bond brought Sorcha a sensation like a slap. That boy was getting decidedly uppity, considering how long they had known each other. One rescue and suddenly he was in charge. She clenched her teeth on a growl of displeasure.

"We should get to the Priory," Sorcha snapped, taking hold of the stallion's bridle and patting his tall, arched neck. Raed was standing a few feet away, shouting directions up to his crew as they bustled about like ants. "That means you too, Your Highness."

A muscle twitched under the narrow strip of his short beard. "I have duties to attend."

"Certainly. But we need to report in," she replied sweetly. "And as such, your geist protection will be out of range. Is that all right with you?"

She found something very satisfying in the angry look he shot her. However, there was nothing he could do; either resist and be open to the unliving, or follow along like the horses.

Sorcha turned Shedryi's head up the hill toward the impressive Priory and led the way through the town, ignoring the Pretender's glare. Merrick hung back, still jawing away with Nynnia. Apart from the looming castle above, it was an unimpressive place. Little gray stone buildings low to the ground indicated that in winter this was a dire town. Nets were strung everywhere, and presumably the fishing fleet was out today, which explained the lack of other ships in the harbor. A few citizens were about, wrapped up tightly in wool or, in some cases, oilskin.

Their cloaks and the Breed horses marked Sorcha and Merrick out as Deacons, so eyes did follow them, but there was something very strange about that. She'd been to towns with plagues of unliving, and in every single one of them the Order was greeted like delivering heroes. Naturally, people rejoiced in the arrival of Deacons to clear up their pesky unliving problems.

Not the residents of Ulrich, however—they actually seemed to flinch away. No one ran up to the Deacons and thrust a squalling child at them, begging for them to protect it. Not a single person clutched at their cloaks howling for salvation. One old man, sitting in front of his house mending a net, actually frowned at Sorcha, dropped his needle and hurried inside.

"I'm beginning to feel we are not the most popular new arrivals," Sorcha whispered back to her partner. "Do you See anything?"

Merrick caught up with her, so that the horses were between them and prying eyes. He was impressive; even she was not able to tell just by looking at him when he was using his Center.

"Nothing," he whispered back after a moment. "Nothing unliving, that is. This place reeks of anger, not fear. And it is directed at us."

"Ungrateful idiots," Sorcha muttered.

"And I thought Deacons were usually greeted with more fanfare." The Pretender had pressed his way to the front, and the smug note in his voice made Sorcha even less happy with the situation. Walking between them, he actually threw an arm over each of their shoulders as if they were comrades. "Whatever have you folk of the Order been up to?"

Sorcha tried to shrug his arm off, rather unsuccessfully, as Shedryi had recovered some vigor and was prancing about. The touch of his arm only increased her sensitivity to that strange geist charisma that infected him. "They are probably just annoyed that their local Deacons haven't been able to help. Once we sort this situation out, they'll give us a parade."

Raed glanced around with a skeptical tilt to his eyebrow. "That, I wouldn't bet on." He cleared his throat, as if pleased with his own wit. "Or don't Deacons gamble?"

Sorcha glanced at him, feeling his immovable damn arm tickling her neck. "Deacons gamble. Deacons can do anything they want to; drink, whore around, smoke. We gave up those inhibitions centuries ago, along with religion."

"Oh, really?" Raed's grin widened. "Decided the gods don't exist, then?"

Sorcha really wasn't up to giving a history lesson. "There are plenty of religious orders back in Delmaire. Ours chose to refocus on protecting the world from the unliving." She flicked his hand off her shoulder, and her glare indicated that he'd better not replace it. "I notice your native pantheon of gods didn't exactly help you out."

A full-blown argument was brewing, and Merrick, like all Sensitives, tried to act as peacemaker. "We're nearly at the Priory." He pointed to where the town faded away and the raw rock slope led up to the looming castle. It was certainly impressive.

The first thing that Sorcha noticed as they climbed the hill was that the Priory had a portcullis and it was lowered. The place was presenting formidable defenses, as if it was expecting an army rather than ragtag travelers. She idly fingered the edges of her Gauntlets and glanced over her shoulder. The stares of the townspeople suddenly felt more ominous.

"Keep an eye out." She nudged Merrick.

"Already doing so," he replied. "Want me to share?"

Recalling his blinding strength, she shook her head. "No, just give me a warning if something is about to happen."

"Nothing, so far . . ." But his voice held a waver of concern. She couldn't blame him; after the week they'd had, pretty much anything was possible.

The Pretender at their side drew his breath in over his teeth. Raed, that blazing silver fire in the ether, had his hand on his cutlass, as if he too could sense the malice in the air.

This was just a Priory. It was perhaps not as safe as an Abbey, but it was still a place of the Order. Sorcha kept telling herself that as the four humans and two horses approached the gatehouse to stand before the gate and the lowered portcullis.

"This isn't right," Nynnia whispered to Merrick. "The portcullis is never lowered like this."

"It'll be all right," he replied to her, the assurance not tripping easily off his tongue. "The Arch Abbot must have sent word by weirstone that we were coming," he hissed to Sorcha.

The sharp edge of his concern felt through the Bond only added to Sorcha's own worry. At her side, Shedryi gave a sharp whinny and pranced as if jabbed by something. Yet nothing appeared from the air, and Merrick was silent.

Finally, after a few inexplicably tense moments, Sorcha managed to move her hand from the Gauntlets to the rope hanging by the gate. The clanking of the bell in such silence made them all even edgier. She was so tense that her grip on Shedryi's bridle actually hurt. Merrick shifted closer to Nynnia, and Raed's breathing went up a notch. She was well aware that her own was doing similar.

When the crooked figure of a young man hobbled to the portcullis, she let out a long breath. Wearing the brown of a lay Brother, he was at least a sign of normality. He looked at them through the bars with unveiled caution, and her ire started rising to replace her concern.

Handing Shedryi's bridle to Raed, she walked forward to confront the man, her hand on her cloak, the badge of the Order standing out bright silver. Even though he glanced at it, he didn't rush to raise the barrier.

"Who are you?" He spoke slowly through malformed lips.

"Deacons Sorcha Faris and Merrick Chambers. The Abbot should have weirstoned the Prior that we were coming."

The answer that the young Brother gave made her start. "Our Priory stone was destroyed four nights ago."

The wrongness of this place was now impossible to ignore. "Quickly, then . . . We must speak to your Prior."

"She's busy, and I'm not allowed to admit anyone."

Her anger was about to boil over, and her fingers itched to be in the Gauntlets and blasting the damn portcullis out of its footings. Once again, it was Merrick who found the right words.

Standing next to her, he took out the long, decorated leather Strop and held it before him. "Do you know what this is?"

The young Brother's eyes lit up. "The Strop of the Sensitives."

"Good." Merrick pointed to the Gauntlets tucked into Sorcha's belt. "And those?"

"Gauntlets of the Active."

"And you know only Deacons can wear them?"

"Yes." The Brother nodded so hard it seemed his head might fly off.

"Then you can let us in. Your Prior wouldn't want you to keep out Deacons."

After a moment's deep contemplation, the Brother finally scampered off to turn the wheel and raise the portcullis. Once they ventured inside he seemed incredibly excited, capering around them and barraging them with questions. Eventually Sorcha gave Shedryi and Melochi into his care just to get him out from under their feet. He grew quite solemn with the responsibility, and led the horses off toward the far corner of the courtyard.

"Prior Aulis is over there." He jerked his head toward the main doors of the keep, before turning back to the horses and the stable.

The large yard was the place in which Felstaad's knights would have assembled in olden times, but it made a very poor showing in the current one. Sorcha had read the file before it had been lost with their first ship; Ulrich Priory had only a compliment of a dozen Deacons and twice that of lay Brothers. This place could have housed a hundred times more.

Abruptly, she remembered something. "You live here?"

Nynnia nodded mutely.

"Then, is it usually like this?" Sorcha gestured to the quiet stone expanse that looked as deserted as a grave.

The girl shook her head, foolish brown eyes wide like those of a spooked deer.

Sorcha gritted her teeth and then took a deep breath. "So where does your father practice his craft, then?"

"In there." Nynnia pointed timidly toward the main keep.

The Deacon realized there was not going to be much sense coming from that particular quarter.

"You know"—Raed still hadn't let go of his cutlass—"this has the feeling of a trap."

"Here?" Merrick's brown eyes were still scanning the area, and his voice had a note of real concern. He didn't want to believe that such a thing was possible in a house of the Order, but some deeper instinct was kicking in.

Bunched up together, they climbed the short flight of stairs and opened the doors. Immediately, the smell of charcoal and smoke forced Sorcha back a step. Glancing to her left, she got a little shake of the head from Merrick, and she went in.

Sorcha found herself wishing very hard that there might be some rules that still remained sacrosanct. A week of strangeness—geists crossing water, geists laying traps and geists summoning sea monsters—was still nothing to this. The inside of the keep's great hall had been laid out to mimic the form of an Abbey, as all Priories were, yet it was burnt to a cinder. The white stone was charred and, when she cautiously laid a finger to it, she realized that it had actually melted on the surface. Remains of wooden pews were scattered about, some disintegrated into ash, while others lay discarded at the edges of the room as if flung there by fleeing Deacons. Debris crackled under their boots as they cautiously moved up what had once been the central aisle, but Sorcha did not bend to examine it.

Nynnia let out a muffled sob, her hand up to her mouth. Merrick put an arm around her, but his other hand still held his Strop ready. Reaching the pulpit where the Prior would have given her daily lesson, Sorcha turned to examine the scene. The front of the hall was relatively undamaged. The hanging above the pulpit was not even singed.

"Whatever happened"—she swallowed hard to regain a measure of her professionalism—"it happened right in the center of the room." Glancing down, she realized that the Prior's notes were still on the lectern. "And it happened suddenly."

Raed, the pirate and the Pretender, obviously thought he knew more than a Deacon. "But the Brother outside, why did he let us in? If they are under attack . . ."

"We were under attack." A steely voice to the right made them all jump. A neat little woman in the blue cloak of an Active, pinned closed by the grand flourish of a Prior's insignia, stood watching them with bright green eyes. "But it was not the total devastation you see here."

"Prior Aulis." Sorcha gave the appropriate bow to a superior, and felt a little warmth return to her bones. She'd imagined all of the Deacons dead, so the relief made her actually smile.

"Enough of that." The woman turned and gestured them to follow. "I have no time to spare. We need your help immediately."

That much was obvious; yet the sight of a living Prior was still a good sign.

As he brushed past her, Raed raised one eyebrow. "This deal about you protecting me . . . I think I got the raw end of the bargain."

Sorcha resisted the urge to slap him and followed after, moving deeper into the Priory to see what further horrors awaited.

NINE

The Thunder of Destruction

Merrick held tight to Nynnia's hand, or maybe she was holding tight to his—whichever the case, he was glad of it. He had not pulled his Center back, from the moment they had entered this place. Ahead, Sorcha was a smoldering scarlet ember, the Bond running back to him twisting like living lava, while Raed flickered like hot silver flame. Prior Aulis was also scarlet, but flecked through with blue fire: the mark of a Sensitive.

This confused Merrick. While he knew that Sensitives were usually in high positions in the Order, he had never thought to find one so high in both Active and Sensitive in such a remote outpost. Deacons like the Abbot, with such high ratings in both, warranted positions in larger Priories or Abbeys. To find Aulis tucked away here was rather strange.

These concerns were shoved to one side when she led them into what had to be the infirmary. Merrick immediately yanked his Center back; too much human pain could overload his senses. This, then, was where the remaining Deacons were.

The room reeked of so much sweat, urine and fear that it was like a blow between his eyes. If he had been viewing this with his Center, it would have been unbearable. All four of them stood in the middle of the chaos, while the Prior watched their reactions. Doing a quick head count, Merrick reckoned that pretty much every Deacon and lay Brother was in the infirmary, apart from three or four. After the destruction out in the Hall, it wasn't difficult to imagine what had happened to them.

Several lay Brothers, also bearing wounds, were trying to hold down a young man wearing the blue of an Active, yet he seemed to have no physical injury. His eyes were bulging from their sockets, and with a start Merrick realized that the Brothers had gagged the struggling man. Froth was starting to leak from the corner of his mouth and stain the leather bit.

"Father!" Nynnia let go of the Deacon's hand and dashed over to a bulky older man sewing up a gash on a lay Brother's head. Merrick was relieved that she had not traveled so far only to face grief at the end of her journey. He watched as the old man tenderly pressed his daughter to him and kissed the top of her head. She smiled at him so broadly that it was like the sun had dawned in the small infirmary. "Father, this is Deacon Merrick Chambers—he is responsible for me being able to get back to you—and this is my father, Kyrix Macthcoll."

The stout man's hands were covered in blood, so he did not offer a hand for Merrick to shake, but his smile was a smaller reflection of his daughter's. "Then I thank you, Deacon Chambers—I need my girl home." He turned and looked over his shoulder. "Now more than ever."

Nynnia was rolling up the sleeves on her dress. "Who can still be saved, Father?"

"There are several Brothers in the other room who could use your talents." He patted her on the shoulder and then gave a slight bow to Merrick. "Excuse our rudeness—but as you can see we are both needed here."

The Deacon, who was feeling particularly useless, tucked his hands under his cloak. "Please don't stand on ceremony on my account."

The girl's eyes darted to Merrick, soft brown and—he wasn't imagining it—warm. She turned away with a swirl of her dress.

He hated to leave her, but it was obvious that Prior Aulis needed him, for there was one thing he had noticed: all of the Deacons here were Actives. Not one Sensitive remained; had any been alive, they would have been here watching over their brethren.

Sorcha was voicing the very question that buzzed in his head. "What the hell happened here?" She moderated her tone slightly since they were in a heaving infirmary, but still, the edge of panic was audible.

The short gray haircut that Priors often favored made the older woman look somewhat masculine, Merrick noted as he took in the deep wrinkles on her forehead. This woman's life had been hard to begin with, and it looked like it hadn't been any easier in the last few days. "What do you think happened?" she snapped, her tone belying her grandmotherly looks. "We were attacked by the unliving!"

It was the one thing no one wanted to hear. Even with all the evidence out in the main hall, it was not a pleasant thing to have confirmed. An attack on a sacred building of the Order had not happened since the dark ages. Not in Arkaym, not in Delmaire. Powerful runes were carved into Priory and Abbey foundations and walls—kept active by constant reworking by the Deacons. Their protection was immutable, more so than water. A huge chasm opened up in front of Merrick as he realized the training he had so recently completed was not proving as useful as he'd imagined.

"Why is no deal I make ever simple?" Raed muttered grimly.

Prior Aulis' attention turned swiftly on him. "Who is . . ." Her voice trailed off. "Raed Rossin!"

The Pretender threw his hands up in the air. "Is there no such thing as anonymity anymore?"

"We were also attacked." Merrick stepped forward in front of their rescuer. "Captain Rossin saved our lives when a possessed sea monster attacked and destroyed our ship. We made a deal with him, or we wouldn't have been able to get here at all."

He expected surprise from the Prior, but perhaps her experiences of the last few weeks had softened her attitude to the impossible. "I see," she said, without any sign of emotion in her tone.

The chaos of the infirmary swirled around them while all three of the Deacons silently contemplated what to do next. Merrick wondered what the point of those years of study had been, if none of the rules held true any longer.

It was Raed who broke the stalemate. "Is there somewhere else we can discuss this?" He jerked his head toward the Deacons around them.

Prior Aulis nodded mutely and led them through the stone corridors deeper into the keep, away from the smells of charred flesh and blood. Her second-story chambers were small and modest, looking out over the windblown courtyard. Without needing to be asked, Merrick opened his Center to see if there was any threat around them.

Through that double vision, he let his perception stretch out as wide as it would go. The three people in the room with him, the mad scramble in the infirmary, the damaged silhouette of the lay Brother with the horses out in the stable, even the chickens in the yard, all became immediately obvious to him—but no taint of the unliving. He was becoming less and less sure of his own abilities, but his search did confirm that one disturbing fact he had already guessed.

"You really don't have any Sensitives left within the Priory."

Aulis folded her hands, the tension apparent in the set of her shoulders. "They were the very first target of this attack."

"Start from the beginning." Sorcha stood next to Merrick at the window, almost as if she was lending him some sort of support.

"At first, there were only small attacks," the Prior said, rubbing one hand wearily over her mouth before continuing. "Shades seen in the graveyard, farm animals shocked out of milking."

"All low-grade incidents." Merrick nodded, feeling like he should at least be taking notes, but Sorcha kept her arms folded and he couldn't write properly while using his Center. He knew which was more important at this moment.

"They increased, more and more, until we were drowning in them; that was when we sent word to the Mother Abbey for help." She opened a drawer in her desk and pulled out a sheaf of papers. "Read some of the reports if you like."

Sorcha made no move toward them, instead dipping into her pocket and removing a cigar. She was polite enough not to light it, but seemed to gain some calmness merely from rolling it in her fingertips. "I think what happened after you sent that weirstone message is more important."

The Prior's lips tightened, and her frown deepened.

"The townspeople lost faith in you." Raed took a seat and shot Sorcha a sharp look. "After all, they must have been disappointed when their protectors weren't up to the task."

Aulis half rose out of her chair, her face glowing red under her cap of gray hair. "They did more than lose faith—they turned on us! Why do you think we have the gates barred? That isn't against anything unliving!"

Merrick narrowed his Center on the Prior, feeling her rage flare up to strangely high levels. Aulis cleared her throat, regaining her composure slightly before taking her seat once more. Many of the Order were a little arrogant; the sad fact was that it often came with power.

The cigar in Sorcha's fingertips stilled as she too concentrated on the riled Prior. "And what happened after that?" she asked softly. Along the Bond, Merrick felt her own Center reach out to him. It was a strangely comforting, and yet frightening, gesture. She trusted him enough to give it to him, but felt in enough danger that she thought it might be needed. The situation felt as desperate to her as it did to him.

"Morning Matins." Aulis' hands were clenched tight on each other, her eyes unable to meet anyone else's. "It came for us at morning Matins."

"In what form?" Sorcha's voice was flat and expressionless, but Merrick felt her tension in the Bond, and observed the way her fingers unconsciously arched toward where her Gauntlets lay at her side.

"None I know of."

Merrick felt his mouth go dry. The geist by the roadside, the one summoned from the bodies of the Tinkers; that too had been a new form. He licked his lips. "Could the Sensitives identify it—"

"They had no time," Aulis replied shortly. "They were the first to burn. You saw what was left of them in the center of the Hall."

"Sensitives being attacked, unliving forms we've never seen before . . ." Sorcha took a long, slow breath.

"And don't forget, ones that can travel over water," Raed offered, his jaw tightening under his narrow beard. "I take it, Prior, that you have a plan to survive all this?"

Her eyes flitted to Merrick and Sorcha seated in the stone window. The glance was almost embarrassed.

"Oh, now I know you are joking!" Raed kicked the chair away and jerked to his feet. "Those two? I had to pull them out of the sea myself."

Merrick clamped his arm down hard on his partner's shoulder, fearing she would beat ten kinds of revenge into the Pretender. But, strangely, she attempted no such thing. Her body was tense, but she was not even looking at Raed.

Out in the courtyard, the crippled lay Brother was running toward the sound of a bell once more at the gate. Through his

Center Merrick could sense nothing unliving, but something very human and very angry.

All three members of the Order leapt to their feet, sensing a conflagration of rage from beyond the walls. Together they bolted for the door, Raed shouting after them, "What? What is it?"

Neither of the women was going to enlighten him, so Merrick barked what they'd all sensed. "The locals are at the gate, and they are very unhappy."

As he raced down the stairs, Merrick heard Sorcha ask the Prior how many of her lay Brothers and Actives were ready to defend the Priory. Another first for the Order, he thought miserably.

"We have five Actives uninjured, and maybe seven lay Brothers, all in the infirmary."

"No time for that." Sorcha ran ahead of them and he noticed that her Gauntlets were already in her hand. Merrick had to remind himself that she was an experienced Deacon, with years of dealing with people in a crowd situation, thanks to her time seconded to the Imperial Guard—at least, that was what he hoped.

He and Raed followed the Prior and Sorcha. The terrified lay Brother was racing back to them, his hair flying loose about his shoulders, and his eyes were wide circles in a pale face. "Prior, Prior!" A thin trail of spit ran down his cheek. The poor man was probably used to a very quiet life in this remote corner of the world; the shock looked like it might kill him. "I shut the gate as you told me to . . . I did . . . but they want to talk to you. They're shouting so loud!"

Indeed they were, jumbled words and threats that made for an animalistic roar. The lay Brother had managed to get the huge oak gates and the thick iron bar down, so most likely the portcullis was still secure.

"Quickly." The Prior gathered her habit around her knees and scrambled most inelegantly up the walls to the parapets. Night was drawing on and, as they reached the top of the walls, the raw air wrapped itself tight around them. Snow could not be far off, but the cold had done nothing to cool the anger of the crowd below.

It seemed every citizen of the town had climbed the hill. Many were carrying lit torches and shouting up to the Prior. The crowd's words were mostly blended together into a primitive growl, but he heard many of them screaming for Aulis to come down to them. She stood there staring, her lips pursed in real anger, and looked ill moved to do so.

"I've never seen a person pulled apart by a crowd." Raed put one foot on the parapet and tilted his head down. "Exactly how many of them have died thanks to your inability to protect what you are supposed to?"

Merrick could understand that the Pretender had no love for those who worked for the Emperor, but he found himself defending the old Prior. "We've all been surprised by the events of the last week or so. It's unprecedented—the Prior Aulis can't be held responsible for that."

"Watch out!" Sorcha slammed into Merrick just as he was getting into full diplomatic flow. Together they smashed into the stone of the parapet and tumbled away, just as fire burst right where he'd been standing.

He dimly heard Raed's shocked oath, while Sorcha helped him to his feet. A portion of the parapet was now a puddle of flame, almost like a geist attack of some sort . . . yet he had sensed nothing.

Raed was shielding Prior Aulis. "Felstaad fire." She darted closer to the Deacons. "The local alcohol is deadly stuff. It makes for excellent missiles."

They heard the clatter of other incendiaries smashing and burning against the wall. Obviously the first had been the best aimed. Cautiously, Merrick dared a glance over the edge. The locals did look very well armed, and in the flickering light of the torches they could be seen lighting rag wicks on small pottery jars. Most of these they hurled at the gate, but they also sent a fair number flying in toward where they'd last seen the Prior.

"Let them see how they like Chityre," Aulis growled, yanking her Gauntlets out of her belt.

"What do you mean?" Sorcha actually grabbed hold of her superior, stopping her before she could put them on. "You cannot use the runes against civilians!"

Turning the power of the Order on the locals could ruin all the work the Mother Abbey had done. In the falling dark, the Deacon and the Prior stayed locked in a tableau of tension. Merrick knew what his partner meant; the powers were never to be used against people, only against the unliving. Aulis must have been half-maddened by her terrible situation to even contemplate it. Sorcha's fingers stayed locked around the Prior's wrists.

Shots rang out now. Wealthier townspeople often had guns, for hunting and protection. Merrick, for one, had hoped Ulrich was a poor town. The snaps of bullets reported off the stone, while Aulis and Sorcha went through their silent battle of wills. If either of them managed to get her hands on her Gauntlets, bullets would be the least of anyone's worries.

If it came down to it, Merrick realized with surprising calm, he would give his Center to Sorcha. Then they would be battling a Prior in her own jurisdiction. Another first for the Order, one that would rock its very foundations. Merrick held his breath.

"Venerable Aulis," Sorcha hissed in a voice that had not an ounce of deference in it, "let me deal with this." A long moment passed, and Merrick was not sure which he was more afraid of: the two women or the mob screaming for blood outside.

Finally, Aulis let out a ragged sigh and gave a short nod to the tense Deacon. Sorcha rose cautiously to her feet and slid on her Gauntlets.

Still crouched on the parapet, Merrick touched her leg, afraid of the sudden expressionless glaze over his partner's features. "Sorcha?" It was a personal address that he hoped might snap her back.

She looked down at him, and he recognized the gleam of something in those vivid blue eyes; he'd seen it on the stairs in his father's castle, just before everything had gone mad.

"Trust me," Sorcha said through a grim smile. "You have to trust me."

Slowly, Merrick let his hand slide away from her. Despite everything—or maybe because of it—at this moment, he did.

Thrusting on her Gauntlets, Sorcha opened a tiny pinprick to the Otherside and summoned Chityre. Her hands lit up like popping fireworks in the half-light, flashing and burning like embers snapping from a brilliant fire. Stepping to the very edge of the parapet, Sorcha held up her hands as they writhed with power. Against the dying sun, her form was dark with only her Gauntlets burning. Glancing to his right, Merrick saw Raed's face outlined by the light. He could tell by expression alone that the Pretender had not seen an unveiled Active up close like this. The air prickled with heat, as if a storm was coming. In a way, one was.

With a jerk of her hands, Sorcha let a surge of power break from Chityre into the sky. It ripped through the air like the boom of a cannon, accompanied by a flurry of bright fire. It was a

display that would not have been out of place at one of the Imperial celebrations, and it had the desired effect.

Below, the crowd was suddenly silent. Merrick wanted to
stand up and see the expressions on their faces, but he made do
with reaching out with his Center. The waves of anger washing
off the mob were fluctuating, replaced with eddies of fear.

Sorcha let another explosion flow through her Gauntlets; this
one was louder and seemed to rock the wall. Merrick's ears rang
and through his Center it was like a pulse of light that momentarily blinded him. When he recovered, he feverishly checked;
still no sign of the unliving.

"I hope you get my point!" Sorcha yelled from the parapet,
her Gauntlets still pulsing with Chityre.

The crowd below muttered, but at least they weren't screaming.

"You may have a couple of guns," Sorcha continued, the air
around her warm and smelling faintly of almonds, "but you are
attacking a Priory full of Active Deacons. How many different
ways do you think we have of killing you?" She gestured with
one burning Gauntlet.

The night sizzled, warm now despite the wintry chill only
minutes before. And just as suddenly, the mood of the crowd also
changed, its rage dissipating into the night. A mob, Merrick considered, was an ethereal thing that could turn on a heartbeat, and
the unveiled power that Sorcha was displaying was enough of a
catalyst.

"We'll be back," one last brave soul screamed at them, and
then they turned and descended back down the road. Merrick got
to his feet, while at his side Sorcha stifled Chityre.

"They're only retreating," he observed. "They'll take some
time to get their bravery back, but at some point they will."

His partner stripped off her Gauntlets with a terribly grim
expression. He felt through the Bond that even this empty display
had cost her. It had cost him too. It seemed that there wasn't a
rule that couldn't be broken.

Aulis was still crumpled against the wall, perhaps waiting for
someone to help her up. After a second, realizing that no one was
going to, she started to get to her feet. "You see now," she said in
a low, angry voice, "what we have had to deal with these last few
weeks. Unconscionable."

No one answered.

It was the Pretender who found his voice first. "I don't care about your impotent Deacons—my crew are in danger." Raed's expression dipped away from rakish, toward deep concern. Merrick could understand; no one could see the harbor clearly from up here.

"The townspeople won't let you leave the Priory." It was now Aulis' turn to grin; a hard, bitter expression. She pointed to the road and it did indeed seem that the mob had retreated only to the bottom of the hill. The Prior gave a short laugh. "It won't matter to them one little bit that you aren't a Deacon. You've been in here; our taint has rubbed off on you."

Raed let out a sharp oath, took a half pace and then jerked around. "I will get back to them, you know—whatever it takes."

Sorcha ran a hand through her hair. "This is an old castle, no doubt with many secrets. No self-respecting lord would let himself be trapped up here."

The Prior tucked her hands into her long sleeves. She remained silent for a moment, as if she wanted to hold on to something. Finally she let out an annoyed sigh. "There is an underground passage—an escape route that the Felstaads built."

"That's all I need." Raed turned and took the stairs down into the yard once more.

"I will go with him," Sorcha said bluntly, tucking her Gauntlets away.

Merrick couldn't believe what his partner was saying. "You can't!"

Her blue eyes were pools of darkness in the drawing night. "You were the one who made the bargain, Chambers. The Order does not go back on its word."

"Deacon Faris is right," Aulis chimed in, apparently having recovered some of her commanding nature. "Much as I dislike your companion, he should not be abandoned to those evil townspeople, or to the unliving."

Merrick was glad at least to hear something like compassion from his superior. "Well, then, we should get after—"

"Not we." Sorcha caught his arm before he could follow Raed. "Just me."

"But we're partners—we shouldn't get separated."

"Would you leave the Prior undefended?" Aulis snapped. "You are the sole Sensitive left!"

"Deacon Faris could run across this geist that attacked you—"

"I will manage on my own Sight. By the sounds of it, even

I should be able to See the cursed thing." Her eyes locked with his, a hint of a smile playing on her lips. She knew she had him beaten.

Merrick's mouth worked, but the two women pinned him with their stares.

Sorcha gave him a nod. "It won't take us long to get the Pretender's crew to safety. Keep your Center wide-open, and you can still reach me." She clapped him on the shoulder.

She was the senior partner, more experienced than he—this time he would have to trust her instincts. The Priory could not be left blinded. However, Merrick could not let her get the last word. He leaned over the wall and called after Sorcha. "Just remember, Deacon Faris—no Teisyat. Absolutely no Teisyat!"

TEN

Rites of Passage

Deacon Sorcha Faris looked down the ladder that disappeared under the floor. She held the lantern in her right hand while her gaze clouded over. Raed stood to her left and watched with interest. Aulis and a very unhappy-looking Merrick had gone back into the main keep. The distressed lay Brother had lifted the hatchway for them under instruction from his Prior, and was now lurking in the shadows behind them; he too had seen Sorcha's impressive display.

The clouds faded from her blue eyes as she stood, and she sighed. "It seems clear." She made to swing herself down the ladder.

Raed caught her elbow, so that her movement turned her around to face him. "I need to know one thing: why exactly are you doing this?"

Her lips crooked in a wry smile. "You saved my life, Captain Rossin, and I believe in repaying all debts."

Raed knew he was playing with fire, but he said it anyway. "Are you sure that there isn't any other reason?" His raised eyebrow and broad grin were deliberately goading.

Sorcha favored him with a long look and then sighed. "You do enjoy testing my patience, Captain Rossin. Now, let us go." She clambered down into the cool tunnel.

He joined her below, and the Brother dropped the hatch above them with a loud clang. Now it was just the two of them, standing in a rough hewn stone chamber lit only by the flickering light. It was cold and slightly damp.

Sorcha handed the lantern to him. "If I am here to protect you, then you'd better carry this."

And the woman accused him of trying to irritate her. Raed snorted, but took their illumination into his care.

"How long do you think this tunnel is?" he asked, suddenly aware that he'd spent a long time avoiding dry land. Now here he was, surrounded by it.

"Not frightened of enclosed spaces, are you?" Sorcha asked, pulling her dark blue cloak tighter about her against the cold. "If you become hysterical, I may have to slap you." It was hard to tell if she was serious or not.

"I think you would like that," he whispered to himself as she peered down the tunnel once more, her clouded eyes indicating the use of her Center.

Sorcha did not laugh. "Considering your . . . problem, I shall go first." Her voice bounced commandingly off the walls.

Aachon was the only person whom Raed was used to having keep an eye on him, and even that rankled. Still, it was impossible to argue with logic. With a mocking bow, he swept his arm before him. "By all means, my lady."

She brushed past him in the narrow confines, the faintest scent of jasmine tickling his senses. Did Deacons wear perfume, or was it his own tormented imagination? He'd been a long time at sea, after all.

The tunnel was very tight, and at certain points it ran with water. Raed and Sorcha had to bend low in several portions, and gained a few bruises at tight bends. "Whoever this was built for, was obviously not a tall man," the Pretender commented with a wince after knocking his head on the ceiling.

"Don't worry. I can give you a kick if you get stuck," Sorcha quipped, glancing over her shoulder. In the glow of the lantern he could tell she was definitely smiling.

He'd not expected a Deacon to be so witty, so prickly, or so pretty, and he was very glad Sorcha Faris was not much of a Sensitive. He would not have liked her to know that he was watching the fiery glint in her hair, or the sway of her hips ahead.

She'd mentioned to one of the crew and gossip had brought it to his ears: she had a husband. Thinking disreputable thoughts of a happily wed Deacon . . . That was a complication he did not need. One curse was more than enough for him.

Raed was so busy contemplating that he almost stepped on Sorcha. The Deacon had stopped suddenly, and his heart began to race; luckily, it had nothing to do with the closeness of the lovely woman. They had come to a slightly wider portion of the tunnel. They were actually standing side by side and perfectly straight. Raed's back appreciated that last bit.

"Do you think there are rats in this tunnel?" she asked, taking the lantern from him and swinging it around. As Sorcha turned her head back the way they came, her eyes were as milky as cataracts. This, combined with the weird tilt to her head, poured ice down his spine.

"Why?" he asked, his mouth dry as drought.

She raised a finger to her lips. "I hear scampering," she whispered after a moment.

"And do . . ." He cleared his throat. "Do the unliving scamper?"

The film on her eyes cleared, until they were that clear blue that he'd first been struck by. Her little laugh eased the clenching feeling in his stomach. "Generally, no. They tend not to have any feet. I do believe, however, that we are about to have some company."

Raed stood stock-still, and now he could hear them tumbling nearer; a wave of chattering rodents pouring down from the direction of the Priory. He saw Sorcha slam her eyes and mouth shut before bracing herself against the wall, so he did the same. The bodies streamed about them, squeezing past and over the motionless humans. Certainly the sensation was shudder-inducing, and the flow of bodies was horrifying, but it was over quickly. The feeling of furry bodies sliding over him would give his nightmares plenty of ammunition, yet none had even paused to bite him.

Finally, when they had passed, Raed shook himself. "Well, that was unpleasant."

"Not just unpleasant," Sorcha whispered. "Confusing. Why would—"

They both felt it, an unsettling breath of cold air pouring down on them from the same direction as the rats. The Deacon's eyes were once again covered and white. "Not unliving . . ." she assured him. "Just water. They must be flushing something up there—explains the rats."

She might have just thought it was sewage, but Raed knew

otherwise; not because he could See as she could, but because he could feel it in his bones. The water was from deep in the earth, ice-cold and shocking when it smashed into them. If that had been all it was, Raed would have been delighted. But something lived in that water, something geist that stirred what lived in him.

The Curse was uncoiling itself from his core, wrapping its dark tentacles through bone, blood and flesh. Light flared in the back of his brain, blinding him for an instant. His worst fears were being realized and yet he managed a gasp from his tormented throat. "Run Sorcha—run now."

Then his body was drowning under the Curse. It sucked away logic and control, and yet Raed clawed desperately at it, trying to at least slow the Change so that the Deacon could escape. Trapped in the tunnel with the Rossin, she would have no chance. Swinging his head around felt like a monumental task, and he was horrified to realize that she was still there. She'd put the lantern into a niche and was shoving on her Gauntlets. The Order had tried once to tame the Rossin, and those deaths were still deeply etched into his conscience. However, his human voice was gone, so his attempt at a shout came out as a primal howl. He managed to get his Changing body to turn and run a little. In his heart he knew he wouldn't get far, and sure enough, after a few staggering steps he collapsed. The Change was now wrapped all around him.

That was the worst of it: he was well aware and conscious, trapped in the body of the growing animal. Primitive function took over, and he could only watch in disgust as he was wracked by the demands of the shift.

It should have been painful; muscle and sinew dancing into new forms, skin rippling as fur punctured it from within. However, the Change felt very, very good; shamefully good. The ripple of his own Changing flesh was as sensual as any feeling he'd had in bed with a woman. The howl from the Rossin's mouth was not one of pain.

The clothes on his back ripped and the lacings on his boots snapped and broke apart as Raed's form doubled in size. His body gained the bulk of the Beast while hands became paws and his head twisted into a jaguarlike snarl. The Rossin's earth form, the great cat with patterned fur and long mane; he'd seen it as a young boy, painted on the ceiling of his bedroom. It was a beautiful thing. It was also a thing that the artist had never seen, only read of.

The Rossin was indeed a great patterned cat, but what a painter could never capture, what no one understood, was the hunger. The flame of it burned so deep in Raed that it consumed all. The Rossin had to feed, had to live on the blood and fear of others.

In this tight corridor, there was only one person that the hungering Beast could feed on. With a snarl, the Rossin turned and crept toward where Sorcha still stood. The closeness of the corridor meant that its shoulders were constricted slightly, but in the wider portion of the passage it could still pounce upon her.

Through the golden eyes of the beast, the Deacon burned like warm embers just stirring to flame. While it would take many normal humans to sate the urges of the Rossin, a Deacon would drown them for a while. Raed, buried deep within, tried to halt the great cat's advances on her, but it was like trying to claw his way out of a sand trap. The Rossin had him, and now it would have her too. He could only watch. In these close confines and against the Beast, her sword would be nigh on useless. Even gunshot had no effect on the creature. She had to know that.

The Rossin liked fear—that too fed it—but there was little of that coming from the woman. As a Deacon, she must have seen many horrors, so the great cat stalking toward her couldn't have been the most dreadful. However, unlike a geist, the cursed Rossin was more than capable of ripping her body apart to feast on the fire within.

"Hello, kitty." Sorcha was actually taunting the creature a little, but green light was dancing on her Gauntlets, throwing her features into eerie angles.

The Rossin snarled, making the tunnel shake with its rage. It did the taunting, not any foolish mortal. Raed screamed inside, but the Beast was utterly in control now. He could feel the muscles of its great legs bunching. Sorcha was going to be shredded and he could do nothing about it but watch in horror. The feeding would be the worst bit, the sensual joy of it that he would be unable to avoid. Raed remembered everything from the previous nightmare, when it had been his mother beneath the beast's claws.

No need for stealth in this corridor. The Rossin snarled again and leapt at her. Claws skittered and found marginal purchase on the steel and leather of her armor, but the weight of the Rossin bore her backward. Tumbling onto the ground, the Beast tightened its grip on Sorcha and lunged toward her throat.

The Deacon was strong. She managed to hold the Rossin off with one hand, though her angry cursing belied the ease of it. The beast pressed harder, snarling and snapping, eager to taste her blood.

Sorcha brought up her other Gauntlet, still streaming eerie green light that almost burned the Rossin's eyes. The great cat flinched, caught in midsnarl, and the Deacon thrust her hand, Gauntleted power and all, into its throat. Raed heard the Deacon grunt, "Enjoy the taste of Shayst, kitty cat."

The pain was immediate and exquisite. Green fire bloomed in the snapping jaws of the Rossin. Sorcha was screaming, and her cries mingled with the howls of the Beast. Raed felt what the great cat did; a pulling sensation as if his soul were being sucked away from him. Surely his body couldn't take that much pain.

Something snapped and broke—something had to. The Rossin struggled, but the power it lived on was being yanked away from it into the Void that the Deacon controlled. As swiftly as it had come, the Beast disappeared.

The abruptness of it left Raed gasping, awash in the emotions of the Rossin: rage and anger. It had to have an outlet, and with Sorcha still pinned to the ground beneath him, he shook her hard and screamed in frustration.

"Holy Bones," she swore and slapped him hard. "Get a grip on yourself!"

His head rang with pain and his blood still raced with the power of the Rossin. Beneath him, Sorcha was gasping in shock as well, her armor clawed and marked.

She jerked upward just as Raed bent. Their kiss was rough and hungry, more a struggle than a display of affection. Brutal desires still swirled in the Pretender, mixing with his own barely contained lusts. Raed heard Sorcha moan, just as the tingle in his body subsided from anger to something else just as primitive.

They struggled on the floor of the tunnel, a tussle rather than an embrace. Her lips were soft and hot on his—it had been a long time since he had kissed anyone like that. Yet it was Raed who pulled back. The Rossin had always ruled him, and he wouldn't let it take him down a path that he hadn't chosen for himself, as enjoyable as it might be.

With a shuddering breath, he scrambled backward, suddenly aware that he was completely naked. In the flickering light Sorcha's eyes were wide and feral, just as he imagined his own were. She licked her lips and he could see her heartbeat racing in the corner of her neck. His eyes couldn't seem to stop watching that.

The Deacon cleared her throat, then unhooked her dripping cloak to hand it to him. "Put—put this on."

It was very cold down here—Raed remembered that—yet his body was burning from the flood of the Change and from something else closely linked: desire. The cloak, wet as it was, would help cool him. He put it on, unable to look directly at her. She wasn't going to mention what had just happened—she was just going to ignore it. That was what he would do, as well.

"I see Merrick was wrong," he muttered, trying to reclaim his dignity. "You didn't spot that geist at all."

A frown darkened her brow. "I am not sure that was even a geist . . ."

That made him snap. He held up hands that had only just reverted back from claws. "Not sure! Not sure . . . Well, I can tell you that I am!"

Sorcha shook her head, looking more confused than he'd ever known a Deacon to be. "I need to talk with Merrick."

"We're not going back," he growled, turning and stalking away down the tunnel. Stooping, he picked up the remains of his clothes. Everything was destroyed. "By the Blood, this was my favorite shirt."

"The boots are still usable," Sorcha pointed out. "I have some spare lacings. Put them on so at least you won't be hobbling."

He frowned. The Deacon's tone was almost gentle. He wondered if it was guilt or desire that moderated it. Nevertheless, he was surprised when she dropped to one knee and laced up his boots for him. Surely that was to save his modesty—the cloak was not offering that much to protect it—but he felt another rush of warmth travel his spine.

As she worked on getting his boots secure, Raed cleared his throat. "No one has ever managed to dismiss the Rossin. How did you do it, exactly?"

Sorcha glanced up. "It was Shayst, the rune of drawing, usually used against geists to take away their power."

"There was a Deacon who tried that rune before." Raed clenched his teeth shut, lest he tell her how that had ended.

It would have been in the textbooks, however. From the way Sorcha nodded, but did not look up at him, she probably knew. "I would hazard he wasn't quite close enough."

Raed let out a muffled laugh, but the image that flashed into his head of exactly how close they had just been made him deeply aware of her nearness now.

"There you are." Sorcha patted his foot, and it must have been his imagination that her hand lingered there a moment. He would much rather have had her slide her hand up his leg . . .

Those thoughts were dangerous and foolish. The Pretender cleared his throat. "Thank you. It will make the going that much easier."

Rising to her feet, Sorcha wrung out her damp hair and examined the deep scores in her armor. "It was certainly interesting to see the Rossin close up; I studied the Beast as a novice. Quite something to tell them about in the Abbey."

"But can you explain what just happened?" Raed clenched the damp cloak around him. "Aulis is, after all, the only one who knows we are down here . . ."

Her face clouded over, those blue eyes seeming almost capable of shooting him dead where he stood. "I don't like your implication, Pretender. The Order is under attack; that much is obvious. Now, do you want to save your crew, or shall we continue arguing?"

Standing in a wet cloak, with nothing but a pair of boots on, he was hardly in a position to break into an argument with the Deacon, especially with the frisson of desire still tugging away on him. He gave a small bow. "By all means, let's get on."

The rest of their progress through the tunnel was thankfully both uneventful and silent. The initial warmth from the Change wore off very quickly, and Raed was soon shivering underneath the cloak. When they emerged in the hills just to the south of the town, his teeth were actually chattering. A strong wind was gusting from the sea.

Sorcha glanced across at him, and while her expression was hard to read in the moonlight, he guessed she was smiling. "Not enough clothing for you, Pretender? Would you like some more of mine?"

One comment was enough to send a jolt of physical reaction through him. Raed drew the cloak closer around him. It was one thing to have the Deacon at a disadvantage, as he'd had when she'd been plucked from the sea. It was another altogether to be on the receiving end of it. "I'll be fine," he replied stiffly.

"Don't be an idiot." She jerked her head toward the faint lights of the town. "We still have a long walk to go. You'll be frozen solid before we get there."

"What do you suggest?" Now his limbs were trembling with the cold.

Before he knew it, she'd found a little cave a few yards away. Settling him there, she strode off, and returned a few minutes

later with arms full of both dry wood and fresh fernery. While
he sat silently, feeling utterly miserable, she built a fire. He found
that most interesting, since they had no tinder. He'd always
imagined the Deacons using their runes only for things of great
importance, but she used her Gauntlets without any fanfare.
"Pyet," she whispered. A fingerling of flame leapt out to catch
the dried wood. To extinguish the flame she simply clenched her
fists around the Gauntlets before taking them off.

Then she built a bed of the fresh greenery, and held out her
hand. "Give me the cloak and I'll dry it."

Her tone was anything but erotic, yet Raed felt curiously
reluctant to give it back to her. She rolled her eyes. "Your virtue
is safe with me, pirate Prince, but a night in that wet clothing and
your ship will need a new captain."

The smirk on her face said she knew she was right, and the
worst thing was that he knew it as well. With as much dignity as
he could muster, Raed handed her the cloak, and hoped his body
wouldn't betray him. He quickly did as she bid, and lay down
close to the fire. Carefully, she covered him with more of the ferns.

Then he gulped, because she was taking her own advice. A
better man would have looked away, but Raed was unable to. Sorcha used a framework of sticks to hang her cloak close to the fire,
and then she too stripped off her clothes. Raed swallowed hard
as she unbuckled her armor. Then Sorcha peeled off her sodden
underclothes, and draped them over the sticks to dry along with
the cloak.

He was going to say something about being suddenly grateful to the Rossin, but as she shook out her hair and revealed her
nakedness, all without the slightest sign of embarrassment, his
mouth went dry. Her body would not have been proper in the
court of Felstaad or probably the Empire, with scars and muscles
that spoke of a hard life, but it was certainly beautiful. He was
entranced by the flicker of the firelight over the soft curves and
harder planes of her form.

Padding over to where Raed lay curled in the greenery, Sorcha dropped her Gauntlets to the ground nearby and slipped in
behind him under the ferns. Raed felt his body spring to life at
the press of her against him. The sharp line of her hip and the soft
swell of her breast made him draw a ragged breath.

"By the Ancients," he whispered, completely unsure what to
do or what the protocol of having a nude member of the Order

right next to him was. What was the Deacon thinking? Should he turn around and kiss her or would she blast him into charcoal? All these thoughts raced through his mind as his body screamed in favor of action. Against his back, he could feel that she was tense too.

"It won't take long for our clothes to dry," she whispered, her tone uncomfortable. "As soon as they are, we can get going." The way her breath tickled the back of his neck was incredible torture. If it had been any other woman, he would have rolled over and let those chips fall where they might. But this was a Deacon, a married Deacon, and one that he was relying on to keep the Rossin from taking hold. It was taking every ounce of his willpower not to turn around. The world narrowed down to simple and torturous sensations: the smell of her skin and the feeling of her breasts pressed into the small of his back. Raed let out a long breath as every muscle in his body clenched. He tried to keep the memory of the Rossin and the Change in his head, tried to drive away the surging blood he could feel everywhere.

It seemed, however, that the same could not be said of Sorcha. After a minute, he was able to tell by her breathing that she'd actually fallen asleep. His male ego was more than a little pricked by that. It had been a long while since he'd had a naked woman anywhere near him. Raed was sure that she had kissed him back in their tussle in the tunnel.

With a groan, Raed curled tighter. He really shouldn't have recalled that memory. The next hour or so was spent miserably as he suffered the tides of desire. Just when he thought he had conquered his body and mind, Sorcha would murmur in her sleep and brush differently against him.

Finally, some sort of internal clock must have gone off, because she got up and stretched. When she dressed, she was thankfully quick. "Nice and dry," Sorcha said, tossing her cloak to Raed. "Now, let's get down this hill and find that reprobate crew of yours."

Every supposition that the Pretender had about Deacons had been blown out of the water. He'd had only one miserable experience with one to go on, of course; yet he'd always imagined they lived staid, boring lives; ascetics who only studied and never actually experienced life. When Sorcha had told him that there was nothing they couldn't do, apparently she hadn't been joking.

ELEVEN

The Martyr, the Pretender

Sorcha couldn't stop smiling to herself as she led the silent Pretender down the hill. He was shocked by her behavior, and truthfully, so was she. On one hand, it had been only practical to dry their clothes after getting them soaked, and they had needed to keep warm while waiting for the garments to dry. On the other hand, she still wasn't sure why she had deliberately tormented Raed.

Pretending to sleep was the first thing novices learned in the Abbey; when the Presbyter came to check on the students after lights out, it paid to be good at it. She could have lain still, but part of her—a part of her that she had thought long dead—had deliberately moved against the Pretender's back. What exactly she would have done if he had succumbed to her goading, Sorcha didn't know.

It had been nearly two years since Sorcha had made love with Kolya. Their partnership might still exist, but their marriage had been dead for a long time. Whatever safe harbor she had thought he might offer, she had made the wrong choice. It didn't make her feel good about herself, but there it was . . . the truth.

With a little flush, she acknowledged that she'd enjoyed seeing the naked man more than she expected to. And that kiss . . .

Sorcha stumbled a little on the rocky slope, catching herself only at the last minute. It could have been a nasty and embarrassing tumble. In truth, the kiss had felt like an awakening. How long had it been since she'd been kissed like that?

With a curse, she shook her head. She was far too old for this idiocy—it had been only a kiss, and it was behind her now. There were enough complications to her life already. "Catch up," she found herself snapping in Raed's direction. He made no comment, and for the next two hours they scrambled silently through the broken landscape toward Ulrich proper.

She looked through her Center before they got down to street level, but found no evidence of the unliving. After the last few encounters, however, that was no longer a reassurance. Hearing Raed come up behind her, she let out a sigh. "Looks nice and quiet."

"So did that tunnel," he growled.

His bluntness brought a bitter smile to Sorcha's lips. "Fair enough. So let's not just walk straight up to that ship of yours."

He nodded in agreement. Keeping to the shadows of the houses, they reached the ship in short order. The quay was more open, with only small stacks of cargo offering any cover. Sorcha could feel her skin prickle with a heat that was at odds with the season.

"Plenty of lights on," Raed whispered over her shoulder, "and it looks like Aachon has posted guards."

Two crewmen were indeed sitting huddled around a lantern on the deck, though their usefulness as lookouts was limited by the playing cards in their hands. She raised an eyebrow in the Pretender's direction. "And these are the people you trust your life to?"

"Most of the trouble they run into is due to their captain's presence; with me on dry land, they don't need to be vigilant."

Sorcha snorted. This was why everyone always thought the Deacons so efficient—the rest of the world was just terminally incompetent. She was tempted to slide on her Gauntlets and deal a hand of her own. Raed had, however, slipped away from her and was striding toward his ship, obviously not too happy about her assessment of his crew.

She heard the cardplayers greet their captain, and their greeting turned to laughter just as she walked up. The men had just realized their captain was stark naked under his borrowed cloak. When she climbed aboard, the laughter stopped abruptly. Many things weren't so funny when face-to-face with a Deacon.

Dominion's first mate appeared, and he did not share in the crew's amusement. He took in the Pretender's state of dress and made the logical leap.

"My lord—the Rossin?" At Raed's curt nod, he sent the so-bered crew to fetch spare clothing from the cabin.

The Pretender gave a spare gesture toward Sorcha. "Were it not for the assistance of the Deacon, who knows what would have happened."

"Well, since I would have been his first victim, I can't say it was a totally selfless act." Sorcha's lips twisted wryly.

Aachon's stern face reminded her of Presbyter Rictun. "But you were with the Deacons at the Priory—how could this have happened?"

This truth stung more than the other she'd discovered. "Truth-fully, I don't know. The unliving have conformed to the same set of behaviors for hundreds of years; but these past few days their actions have defied the historical record."

Raed recovered some of his old confidence as he slipped on his pants. "We had ample demonstration of how the people of Ulrich feel about the Deacons. Have any made a move against *Dominion*?"

Aachon shook his head. "We haven't seen many of them apart from the harbormaster, and he seemed friendly enough."

"Maybe we should cast off and make for another anchorage." The Pretender's voice was awash with exhaustion; the Change had sucked a lot of energy from his mortal form. Sorcha knew he would need sleep, and soon.

"I'm afraid we don't have that choice, my prince." Aachon led them over to the stern and pointed out to the entrance of the harbor. The faint moonlight glinted strangely off the water, and it took a moment for Sorcha to process what she was seeing: sea ice sealed the headlands as completely as any stone wall.

"By the blessed Ancients!" Raed thumped the gunwales in frustration. "How on earth did that happen? Ulrich's deep-sea currents keep it open for months—that's one of the reasons we came here."

Sorcha knew the explanation. She considered not voicing it. If they were to be stuck in this cursed town together, though, then they really had only each other to rely on.

"Geist storms have been known to drag in sea ice before." She took a deep breath. "In the siege of Eygene, in fact, we used it to crush the Prince's fleet . . ."

The men were staring at her hard now. People usually looked at Deacons with a great deal of trust and expectation, so she wasn't used to this expression of wariness. She only hoped that they weren't catching whatever had infected the townspeople.

Infected. The word bounced around in Sorcha's head. Out from under the horror of the Priory, her mind was beginning to work; maybe the Otherside had infected Ulrich. In the textbooks, there were old cases of such things.

It was a consideration that required a cigar. Perching on the gunwales, she took out one of her precious supply and opened the storm lantern to light one. Her companions seemed to expect some further explanation, but she was not yet ready to give voice to her thoughts. Instead, Sorcha drew in a mouthful of smoke and blew smoke rings into the night air.

"Wonderful!" Raed glared at her from under lowered brows. "So, are you suggesting someone has deliberately sealed us in here?"

"Not necessarily." The Pretender hadn't taken her hint. "I have a few theories, but I would prefer not to voice them until I've spoken with Aulis and Chambers. For now my suggestion is this: we all get a good night's sleep, and then we get your crew to safety up at the Priory. I have a few ideas that I'll need to discuss with Aulis and Chambers."

Raed looked for a second as if he might grab her cigar and flick it over the side. If that happened, he would be following soon after.

"Very well." He and Aachon turned to take her sensible advice, but he stopped as he realized she wasn't moving from her spot. "What about you, Deacon Faris?"

Sorcha grinned back. "Remember, Deacons need very little sleep. I'll keep watch tonight."

A rakish smile pulled at the corner of his lips, perhaps recalling how little sleep he had gotten up on the hillside. Sketching a little bow, the Pretender left her to her vigil and her cigar.

Things had calmed down in the infirmary, but Merrick could not relax. The Active he'd been restraining earlier had subsided into a hazy serenity after receiving a tincture from Nynnia's father. Still, Merrick felt very much at a loose end.

"Prior Aulis, what exactly can I do to help?"

She waved a hand at him without even looking up. "What you Sensitives do: watch. Let me know if any of those damnable townspeople come back to the gate."

The tone in her voice was not one that Merrick was used to having directed at him. To the outside world, it might indeed seem that the Sensitives were the subordinate partners, the ones with less flash and not much to do. But they were the cool hand on the hot mind of the Actives and, if necessary, there were things that only they could do to restrain their partners. For this they were valued, elevated to high positions, and never, ever talked to as if they were servants or dogs.

His back stiffened, but Aulis didn't see it; she'd already gathered her group of uninjured Actives around her. Merrick had never felt so dismissed in his life. He could have eavesdropped on their conversation, but that would have broken several rules of the Order, and there'd been enough of those destroyed lately.

"Deacon Merrick." Nynnia emerged from one of the side rooms where the most critical of the injured had been placed. She smelled of sage and soap. Her beautiful brown eyes locked onto him and a wide smile parted her soft lips. It took the Deacon a while to notice that her stern-eyed father was at her side.

Even that made no difference—Merrick realized he was melting and had no idea how to stop it. The logical, trained part of his mind knew it was ridiculous to be entranced by a woman after so short an acquaintance, but other, less ordered parts were shouting at him more forcefully.

"Is everything all right?" he asked in a low voice, knowing that the question was a foolish one as soon as it was out of his mouth; everything was patently not well around them.

"The injured are at least comfortable now." She glanced at Kyrix. "Father has them well sedated."

"Much good it will do some of them," Kyrix muttered. He looked over his shoulder as if he expected someone to come up behind him. Merrick felt the stirrings of unease.

"Do you know anything more about the attack, sir?" Merrick decided to err on the side of diplomacy, even though he was technically the superior in this situation.

The old healer's face folded into a dark frown. "Things have not been right at the Priory for months." He touched his daughter's shoulder. "That is partly why I sent Nynnia away to my sister's home in Vermillion. I am sorry to say that there has been no improvement."

The concern in his voice was palpable, but Sensitive senses also picked up an edge of real fear. "Things?" Merrick pressed.

Kyrix shared a glanced with Nynnia, but after she took his hand and squeezed it he seemed to gain strength. "Prior Aulis." He kept his voice to a low whisper. "Ever since her arrival the Priory has felt . . . different."

"And not in a good way," Nynnia added.

The healer guided them over into a corner. "As soon as she was assigned here she cast out most of the lay Brothers."

That was different, indeed. Deacons depended on lay Brothers to handle the practical tasks necessary to keep the Order running smoothly. But as much as he wanted to rush to judgment, Merrick knew that the feelings of two people he had just met were not enough evidence. The attraction he felt toward Nynnia was something he could absolutely not allow to sway him.

And perhaps the Prior had wanted to bring in her own lay Brothers, or had purged those she thought below her own standards. Such things, while rare, were not unheard of and would be in keeping with Aulis' evident arrogance.

"Thank you, sir. The information you've given me is very valuable," he replied. Then he turned to Nynnia. "I know that neither of us has slept since we've arrived, but I am eager to begin my investigation. Care to join me?"

Kyrix looked sternly at Merrick, so that the Deacon quickly added, "I'll absolutely look after her."

"You can trust him, Father." Her tone was insistent, and she squeezed his hand. "And who knows? Perhaps Merrick will need me to watch after him." She gave an odd little laugh.

Kyrix stared at them a moment before grumbling, "I really should sit watch on my patient. Mind you do take care of Nynnia." With that the old man stalked off back to the infirmary.

Merrick wanted a closer look at the main Hall first. Sorcha had cast a cursory look over it but they'd all been in a state of shock. Nynnia watched quietly from the pulpit area as he walked to the place where the geist had appeared. The scorch marks blasted into the stone were indeed impressive, but not quite as Sorcha had said. They were not in the exact center. Though they were in the middle of the length of the Hall, they were slightly to the right in the width. He knew well enough that the Sensitives always sat to the right of the pulpit.

He took a long, slow breath and glanced over at the woman

at his back. She wasn't smiling any longer, but her gaze was unflinching. Despite her slender form and doe eyes, there was real strength beneath—he liked that about Nynnia. *Distractions, distractions,* he told himself firmly. Turning once more to the scorched stone, Merrick stepped into the blackest and most deeply pitted part of the floor.

His Center had been open for hours, and like an eye that had stared too long at the sun, it was tender. He knew that when he moved into the place where so many had died, it would not be easy or pleasant. It wasn't. It was like stepping into a tornado. When the ungifted died suddenly, there was a rend in the ether— a brief moment when the Otherside could be glimpsed. When Sensitives died, their deaths stained everything.

Merrick had walked into the moment of their destruction. The horror and disbelief of nine Sensitives engulfed him. He felt their fiery deaths burning on his own skin and howled as they had for a brief moment. Yet his training held firm. Even while he relived their experiences, he tried to see what they had been too busy dying to observe. The geist.

It was indeed like nothing he'd read about or seen. The geist that had smashed down on the Deacons was more like a being of fire than the typical power vortex. It even seemed to have material form and, obviously, the intent that went along with it, which was also unheard of. The unliving acted through mortals. Of course, they also never attacked Sensitives. Merrick trembled at even this secondhand view of it. His sight blurred with tears— looking upon it burned both his eyes and his Center. And the geist looked back.

Little Deacon Chambers. The eyes of burning light bored into him, saw him standing in the black ring where others of his kind had died. It was merciless and ancient and reaching down to him . . .

"Merrick!" Nynnia jerked him from the place of death. Her hands, digging into his forearm, were shaking.

He staggered a little, taking a long time to shake his head loose of that vision. Nothing remained here but the still silence and the smell of charred death. The thing he had seen, the entity or whatever it was, had no name in any of the books he'd learned from. Nor had he heard of anything like it from the older Sensitives.

What if this wasn't a geist? Surely if it was like no known form, it might be something else entirely? That idea was worse by far than any uncertainty. If it were so, then they were unprepared for dealing with this new threat.

He pressed a hand to his mouth and swayed slightly. Catching himself against an upturned pew, Merrick happened to glance up. The hammered-beam ceiling was made of oak and almost as badly charred as the floor. If the stone flagstones were where the being had landed, then the towering ceiling was burnt for a reason. "Look, Nynnia. I think the thing entered this world from there."

"Through the roof?"

It was a common misconception that a summoning circle was the only way a geist could be purposefully called into the world. Sometimes a certain person or thing, a nursery rhyme or a pattern of music, could also summon them. However, as he concentrated his Center upward, Merrick realized that there had been something carved on the ceiling. The words had been blasted clear away, but visible under the charcoal was a heraldic figure, and one that he knew very well. The Rossin.

Without thinking twice, Merrick reached out across the Bond, feeling with dread for Sorcha. She was there. He let out a ragged breath. "Thank the Bones, she's alive."

"Deacon Faris?" Nynnia's mouth twitched in an unconscious bitter smile. "Why would you think she'd be dead? If anyone can look after themselves, she can."

Merrick let out a short laugh, but he did not mention the Rossin. It could just be coincidence, and the Pretender had been with them for the past week. He couldn't shake the feeling that there was more.

Putting away his own fears and concerns, he went back in his head to the basic training of his kind. Terrible as it was, the only clues were in those dreadful moments he'd glimpsed before death took the Deacons. Letting his head droop a little, he shut away all physical sensation, relying totally on his Center; replaying those moments as slowly as possible. Then, through the confusion, he began to count the screaming faces he had seen.

"How many Sensitives did the Priory have?" he demanded of Nynnia.

"Ten," she replied quickly.

A look of hope spread across his face. "I only saw nine die here. And yet . . ." His Center darted once more around the

Priory. "I can feel no other in the area." He paused and cocked his head. He could feel all the little embers of people inside and out, townsfolk, Deacons and lay Brothers. Even the smallest animal could not escape his notice: the tiniest of insects flowed through his awareness like bright motes. However, what he could not feel was anything, anything at all, living below his feet. It was as if the sphere of his awareness had been cut in half.

"Nynnia"—Merrick felt his heart begin to race with dawning realization—"are there tunnels and chambers underneath the Priory, apart from the one to the town?"

She felt the seriousness of his question, but couldn't possibly know why it was important. "Yes," she said hesitantly. "When this place was a fortress, the Felstaads built many."

He could not feel even the smallest beast down there, and surely there could be only one explanation: something or someone was blocking his perception. He took her hand. "Show me."

Nynnia was used to the strangeness of Deacons, and led him to the farthest end of the keep without further question. An iron-bound door was set into the wall and swung soundlessly when she pulled it open. Merrick frowned, his Deacon observational skills already burning with curiosity. It looked ancient and seldom used, yet when he ran his fingertip over the hinges he could see they were new.

He hesitated a moment, feeling along the Bond with the distant Sorcha to reassure himself that she was all right. Training told him that he should wait until his Active returned, yet he couldn't afford to. If there was a Sensitive somehow miraculously still alive, then they might not be safe. If that being came back . . .

Merrick swallowed and adjusted his saber at his hip. If it came down to that, he was surely done for. "Stay here," he said to Nynnia.

"Shouldn't I go tell the Prior?" she asked.

He paused and thought about it. Somehow he didn't trust that the Priory Actives would be able to protect him. After all, they had failed to save their own Sensitives right in the middle of Matins. Merrick shook his head. "If I'm not back in half an hour, then yes, but I should be fine."

He looked at Nynnia then, and though he hadn't even thought about kissing her before, the possibilities of what might be down there spurred him to action. The soft touch of his lips on hers was almost gentlemanly, but he was proud of himself for having taken that step. It had been a good few years since he'd kissed anyone in such a manner. Then, while she was still looking at him in surprise, he turned and strode down the stairs. If this was to be his final impression, he wanted it to last.

TWELVE

A Deacon and Her Rites

The sunrise was flickering off the ice, and Sorcha was still huddled at the stern in her fur cloak, a dark shadow except for the
copper blaze of her hair. Raed paused as he came up the stairs
of the quarterdeck. She had to be aware of his presence, but she
did not turn.

As he watched, Sorcha flicked the remains of her cigar over
the side. "Well, that was the last one of those." She sighed the-
atrically.

"I have some in my cabin," he offered, walking over to stand
at her back. "I acquired them off a pirate captain."

Sorcha glanced up at him. "No honor among thieves, then?"

Raed laughed despite himself. This Deacon was as prickly
as a desert cactus. Leaning on the gunwales, he stared over the
ice. It was beautiful in a threatening kind of way, like shattered
gleaming glass as far as the eye could see.

"I don't suppose you are going to be able to careen your ship
now." Sorcha pulled her legs up close to her on the bench in a
curiously childlike gesture.

"Now, that would be rather foolish under the circumstances."

She shrugged. "You could. After all, it doesn't look like anyone is going anywhere for a while."

"Which leaves us with another problem. What do we do about
these annoyed townsfolk? They outnumber us by quite a bit, and
not all of my crew are fighters."

They were both silent a moment. The sun was finally free of
the ice, but Deacon Sorcha Faris was not looking at it. She was
looking at him with an expression he interpreted as trust. Something had definitely changed between them back in the tunnel.

Both of them glanced up at the sudden creak of a step. Aachon,
his weirstone clenched in one hand, had managed to walk up on
them unnoticed. The Pretender knew by his expression that he
did not like the look of the situation he thought he'd stumbled
into. His first mate knew him better than even his own father, and
he felt incredibly uncomfortable under that dark gaze.

Still, on the surface Raed managed not to reveal that, keeping
his voice level when he spoke. "What is it, Aachon?"

"I thought you'd like to see this," the older man replied and
gestured toward the quay. Quickly, Raed and Sorcha scrambled
down to where a group of the crew was leaning over the side.

Jocryn, with his shock of balding red hair, was yelling something down to someone on the dock. For a second Raed thought
that a battle was about to break out. That was, until he heard,
"No, I need more fresh kale, my friend. These mouths need feeding, you know, and sharpish." As *Dominion*'s cook, Jocryn was
in a constant battle to keep the vessel provisioned, ideally with
supplies that wouldn't be—literally—thrown back in his face.

Sorcha yanked at Raed's sleeve. "Townsfolk." Her look was
still feral, and he remembered her display on the walls of the Priory with sudden vividness. Quickly, he looked her over. The tell-
tale blue cloak was in his cabin, and nothing about her screamed
Deacon . . . except for one thing. When he reached out and took
her badge of office from her shoulder, he thought he was about to
get another slap. Perhaps even a punch.

"Wait." He held up one hand. "You've just discovered the Priory is not what it seems. Maybe the townspeople aren't, either."

"Your point—and quickly?"

"The Deacons are not exactly popular here." Raed pressed
the badge into her hand. "So perhaps a little discretion would be
sensible right now."

Sorcha's fingers tightened on her badge but she gave a little
nod. "Very well, then, but I think these might also be a bit of a
giveaway." The Gauntlets.

Raed snorted. "I was not about to try and take those off you."

"Sensible." A ghost of a smile tugged at the corner of her
mouth as she loosened her shirt and tucked them underneath,

against her skin; his eyes followed the Gauntlets' progress. Ancients, he had been naked next to her only hours ago.

The crew were now yelling at Jocryn, while he continued to negotiate with the unseen person down on the dock. Food was the only thing that crew ever argued about. A long time at sea had only sharpened their desire for decent rations, and their confinement on *Dominion* had made them somewhat cranky.

Sorcha and Raed managed to get through to the crowd to see what was going on below. The person standing on the dock was a young man, his face just bursting with its first hair. Around him were several baskets stuffed with fresh food, making the crew go almost insane with delight. Aachon had ordered the gangway pulled up and no one allowed on board, so how exactly this youngster was going to deliver his produce to Jocryn was an interesting question.

"Lad," Raed called down, "are you the only grocer in Ulrich?"

The boy looked down at his baskets, realizing that their small contents were not going be to able to feed the entire crew. "No, sir," he replied after a minute. "These are a sample. My father will bring more this afternoon."

"Why not this morning?" Sorcha leaned down over the side, her unbound bronze hair falling off one shoulder. Without her cloak, badge or Gauntlets, she was simply a beautiful woman, and the way the grocer's lad was blushing, he'd not been questioned by many of those in his life. "Is he up at the Priory with the others?"

Even from this distance the boy looked shocked. "No, ma'am . . . He . . . he is with my sister." This last part was muttered.

Sorcha stiffened. "The lad has a strange aura," she said to Raed softly. "Touched by a geist."

Before he could stop her, the Deacon had swung her legs over the side and dropped down next to the boy. Being on the high tide, it was quite a distance and an impressive physical feat. The lad leapt back in shock and knocked over several of his baskets. Leaning over the side, Raed watched cautiously. He doubted that one grocer was going to be much danger to the Deacon, but if he broke and ran for his kin, there could be a mob surrounding *Dominion* in very short order.

From this distance he couldn't hear what Sorcha was saying. At their captain's gesture, the crew scrambled to thrust out the gangway. She was talking to the lad earnestly with one hand

resting lightly on his shoulder. At first he looked very tense,
ready to make a dash for it, but as Sorcha continued he began
to nod and relax. By the time Raed and Aachon had lowered
the gangway and jogged down to where they were, the lad was
positively calm. The Pretender was surprised. He'd never seen
any sign of diplomacy from the Deacon before, but perhaps the
danger her partner was in had tempered her mood.

Sorcha turned to them. "I've told Wailace here that my partner and I are not from the Priory. You can vouch for that, Captain
Rossin?"

The lad's wide eyes focused intently on him. "Indeed. We
brought Deacon Sorcha from the South, direct from the Arch
Abbey itself."

The grocer's lad let out a sigh and then abruptly grabbed
hold of Sorcha. "You must come back to our house, then. My
sister . . ."

"No need to explain." Sorcha shoved her hand once more into
her shirt and pulled out her Gauntlets. The appearance of these
talismans made the lad's eyes light up, or maybe it had been the
glimpse of the top of her pale breast.

The Deacon and the stunned lad turned and trotted back up
the street. He'd not been invited, but Raed was certainly not
about to let Sorcha go anywhere without him. He told himself it
was because of her ability to dismiss the Rossin.

"Look after the crew." He squeezed Aachon's upper arm.
"Keep them on the ship a bit longer, just in case."

His first mate fingered his weirstone's bag and nodded som-
berly. They both knew that nowhere was safe. "Be careful, my
prince," was all he said.

Raed, as he turned and raced after Sorcha, only wished that
he could promise such a thing.

After the strangeness of the last day, Sorcha had been reassured
to see something familiar in Wailace's eyes—at last, something
normal. Relief. After she'd told him the story, he had willingly
grasped it. Whatever the Priory had done, they had not quite
eroded the built-in faith in the Order.

This time, as she followed him into the town, there were even
fewer signs of life.

"Tell me when the first attacks came." She actually had to tug the young man back to slow him down. "I need to have information if I am to help your sister."

He gulped a minute, clearing his throat and shaking his head. "They—they began slowly at first, a month ago. We thought our Deacons would protect us."

"A month." Sorcha wished Merrick was here. He would perhaps see the significance of that more than she could.

"Where are we going?" Raed had caught up with them at a jog, neither out of breath nor put off by the glare she shot him.

She waved at Wailace to lead on, while whispering at the Pretender out of the corner of her mouth. It was never good to expose frailty in front of a distressed next of kin. "What are you doing here?"

"You don't have a partner at the moment"—he grinned—"so I am standing in for Merrick. He would want me to keep an eye on you."

"By the Bones," Sorcha hissed, "you are more useless in this than a fifth leg on a dog."

"Now you're just hurting my feelings."

The lilt of his voice, charming and roguish at the same time, should have irritated her, but instead her mind treated her to a recollection of his nakedness and the feeling of his mouth on hers. Ridiculous.

"Since you insist on being here," she asked as evenly as possible through gritted teeth, "may we just concentrate on helping this boy and his family?"

He was mercifully silent for a bit, though she was still painfully aware of his presence. It was almost a relief to get to the grocer's house.

Wailace stood by the door, talking to a man who sat slumped on the ground, leaning against the wall of the house with his head in his hands. Sorcha walked up slowly and stopped to look down at him. His eyes were red-rimmed and haunted, his hand trembling. "Can you—" He cleared his throat. "Can you help my daughter?"

She knew better than to offer any definitives. "I promise to try."

"She—" The father looked away, shame burning on his face. "She says things that . . ."

Sorcha had seen plenty of distraught relatives who had been forced to do terrible things, so she was partly ready for what lay within. "I understand." She gave his shoulder a light squeeze, and asked the one question she needed to have answered. "What's her name?"

"Anai," he whispered, clutching his son's hand.

Sorcha let him nurse his shame and distress. It wasn't her job to comfort the kin, and now at least she had a familiar task at hand.

The door creaked open; the door always creaked. It was a given. Inside, there was an incredible plunge in temperature, enough to make her wish that she'd stopped to gather her cloak. Accompanying it was a smell, a pungent odor that assailed her mortal senses.

"Ancients, what is that stench?" Raed, who had probably experienced plenty of vile odors in his time on board ship, held his arm up over his nose.

It was certainly one of the stronger ones she'd encountered in her time in the Order. The unliving were fond of odor because it was one of the most evocative senses. This one was, appropriately enough, very like ripe fish heads—ones that had been out in the sun for a few days. But there was something else; the scent of shit—a sure sign of the unliving.

Sorcha already knew what she would find when she followed her nose to the locked door leading down into a root cellar. She turned about and warned Raed. "Whatever you do, Pretender, keep quiet."

"Is there anything more useful I can do?" he gasped through his mouth.

She gave a little shrug. She wasn't about to tell him that she was grateful not to be alone. "You can watch my back, for what good it will do."

Sorcha knocked the lock open and stepped inside. It was as expected. The cellar had been cleared of everything; drag marks in the ground showed where the grocer's stock had been quickly shifted. The small window at the far end had been barricaded from the outside, and the light was consequently gray and limited. Against the far wall was where they had chosen to shackle their daughter.

She could only have been about eight or nine years old, curled up on the bare floor sniffling to herself, her head hanging down with tangled copper hair obscuring her features. Her clothing was stained and torn, as if she had been at the center of some violent storm. It was a sight to soften the hardest heart.

Sorcha, however, was not fooled, even though the few maternal instincts she possessed kicked in every time a child was involved. Instead, she jerked her head at Raed, indicating that he could come in. When he made to go to the girl, she stopped him with one hand on his chest; a silent gesture that reminded him to be quiet.

The troublesome pirate frowned, but thankfully remained still by the door.

Together they stood there for a few minutes, breathing in the fetid odor and waiting for the child to stop crying. Finally she drew in a ragged hiccupping breath and looked up at them. Her eyes gleamed like a cat's in the dimness of the cellar, but the light they were reflecting was not from this world.

Sorcha did not put on her Gauntlets, but instead went over to the girl and knelt down. The child's lips drew back in a feral snarl while her head tilted at a knowing angle. The Deacon and the unliving creature inside the girl regarded each other; she with cool professionalism and it with undisguised hatred.

Finally, the Pretender couldn't contain himself any longer. "What is it?"

The girl's eye fell on Raed and she snarled, surging upward only to be brought back to the ground with a jerk as her chains snapped taut. It was good that her parents had been vigilant.

"A poltern, I think." Sorcha, having stepped back smartly, now sat down on the ground two feet away from the thrashing girl.

"Then why . . ." He cleared his throat. "What about the Rossin?"

"This particular geist is buried very deep inside, barely any of it is actually in this world. Very much like a parasitic worm. You should be safe enough."

He came to stand behind her, obviously taking her request to watch her back seriously. "And what about the girl?"

Anai's lips stretched wide, but no words came out; polterns were not the most verbose of the geists. Instead the air grew even colder, an attempt to drive them out without expending too much of its energy or giving away its location.

The Deacon flicked a sharp gaze at Raed. "Remember the bit where I told you to be quiet?"

He took the hint and stepped back into the shadows. She had to have the geist's entire attention. Letting her Center drop away from her, she concentrated her vision on the creature. Seeing into a possessed being was hard. The geist could hide deep within the psyche of a person, and a child was more complicated still.

The changing facets of a still-forming personality made an ideal hiding place, so children were favored victims of the pol-tern. Sorcha knew immediately that she was ill equipped to judge the strength of this one with her Sight. The hollow space where Merrick should have been felt even more gaping now.

Finally, she retrieved her Center and sagged back with a sigh of annoyance. The geist, meanwhile, danced in the eyes of the child and looked smugger than a cat with a mouse in its mouth.

"What's the matter?" Raed was pacing, showing that being this close to a geist was unnerving him. Sorcha could understand that.

Without stopping to explain, she got up and went out of the ripe cellar into the house; a welcome if slight respite from the strength of the odor. Everything lay in disorder out here. The family had been forced to keep their supplies in the rooms where they lived. The mother was coping with a possessed child and a house she could barely move about in.

Scrambling over boxes, Sorcha went into the kitchen to find something heavy but innocuous. The drawer of knives and cut-lery was immediately discarded as something she didn't want to arm a geist with. Anything breakable, like the stoneware dishes, could also be deadly, and they were not nearly heavy enough. Finally, she settled on an iron cooking pot that had probably been used for making jams in better times.

Spotting Raed as he stood watching her made her chuckle. "Afraid to be alone with a little girl?" she asked, struggling with the cooking pot. It was big enough, even, to boil the child in it.

"Not at all," he replied. "I'm just enjoying watching you." She gave him a look that could have melted lead, until he took the hint and strode over to help shift the large pot back into the cellar.

The gleaming eyes of the poltern stared at them with visible delight. Nothing pleased a geist as much as the ability to stymie a Deacon.

"What on earth is this for?" Raed grumbled as they posi-tioned the pot to her liking, only a few feet away from the cellar's occupant. "Planning to whip up some jam while we're here?"

"You'll see." She jerked her head toward the girl, hopefully reminding him that they were not alone.

She slid on her Gauntlets, just in case this all went horribly wrong. For the sake of the girl and the structural integrity of the house, Sorcha hoped that everything would go smoothly. She prepared to use Aydien just in case.

Unlike Merrick, her Sight was a blunt object. The Deacon had no way of judging the strength of the poltern, hiding within the girl as it was. It would be an important thing for her to know. If she tried to remove a powerful geist from within the soul of a child, she could rip the girl's psyche into nothing, but if it was a small one, she might be able to manage it.

First things first. "Whatever you do"—she glanced over her shoulder at the Pretender—"do not move unless something comes at you."

He opened his mouth, ready with some smart remark no doubt, but closed it when he saw her stern look. Sorcha flicked her head back and activated Shayst. At the flare of green fire, the girl's eyes grew impossibly large in her head, glittering like dark jewels. Sorcha felt the Otherside's presence as an ice-cold breeze on her skin.

"Time for you to leave," Sorcha growled between blue lips. The stench crashed about her, filling her nostrils and her enhanced senses in repulsive waves. At her back, she heard Raed choke back an oath. Every vile ounce of air was ordering her primitive brain to run, to flee before the horror of the geist. But training and experience were a stalwart defense against this assault.

With a flick of her wrist she brought one Gauntlet, burning with barely contained green light, up in the direction of the girl. The reaction was instantaneous. Dust whirled up around them and the air was suddenly full of tiny spinning debris. Little pebbles bounced off her exposed skin, but there was nothing much else in the room for the geist to use as a weapon. Except for one thing.

The huge cast iron pot wobbled in its place as the poltern screamed through the throat of the girl. The wind grew louder. The walls themselves seemed to swell like sails on a ship and the stench made Sorcha's stomach churn like the worst kind of sea-sickness. And the pot, that pot that she and Raed had only been able to move together, swung upward in the grip of the geist. It flew at Sorcha, clanging and spinning, end over end.

She'd hoped the poltern was a small one, but had been prepared for the worst. As the pot tumbled through the air toward her, she seamlessly closed her right fist around Shayst, and with the other hand summoned Aydien. The pot smashed into the blue shield she'd summoned and bounced off, like some toy thrown by a child in the grip of a tantrum. The warmth of the rune filled the room, momentarily driving off the freezing miasma surrounding the geist; the unliving creature she had now convincingly identified as at least a level six poltern.

Little Anai was thrashing about in her chains like one dog being worried by another. Spittle and phlegm flew from her snarling mouth, while her eyes of reflecting darkness burned with utter hatred at Sorcha.

The Deacon had no choice now. As quickly as possible, she closed her fist on Aydien and once more summoned Shayst, the green light flashing from her left hand. The ripping of power from the geist was abrupt and unforgiving, but if she did not deny the poltern its strength as quickly as she could, the geist would turn on its foci. The rush of the Otherside into her was heady and delightful as ever, sending her pulse racing and blood surging through her veins.

"Ancients," Raed whispered, going to where the thick cast iron pot lay upended on the floor. "It's dented!"

The state of the cookware was the least of Sorcha's worries. Anai was slumped on her side, tangled copper hair falling over a face slackened by unconsciousness.

"But you got the thing out of her?"

Slowly the Deacon shook her head. "No. There is a good reason why we work in pairs. Without Merrick, that is quite impossible. I cannot see where it is hiding to root it out."

"Then it will be back?" The tone in the Pretender's voice was sad. He could undoubtedly comprehend what the girl was going through.

"Yes, I am afraid so." Sorcha bent and with the corner of her shirt wiped the spittle from Anai's mouth and pushed her hair back behind her ear. "She must be incredibly strong to hold out so long against such a powerful poltern. If she survives, she would make a fine Deacon."

"What?"

"The poltern are attracted to those children with talent. If the Order find such little ones, they are often brought into the Abbey for protection—most later become Deacons." She glanced up at him in the half-light, and despite herself her voice was a little shaky. "It was how I became a member of the Order."

"But if she is so powerful, why did the Prior not take her in?" His question was deliberately pointed.

"I think Aulis had other plans for her, or even"—Sorcha paused before being able to give voice to her darker fears—"or may have even caused this to happen." She stood up and looked down at the girl. "Please do not give Aulis the title she doesn't deserve. She is no Prior of the Order."

"And the girl . . . Can you do anything for her?"

She was sick of feeling powerless; it was not the natural state for a Deacon. "No. She will wake with the poltern still in control. I have only given her some rest—hopefully enough to hold out a little longer."

As Merrick descended the steps beneath the Priory, he felt the cold envelop him, banishing the warmth that had flooded him when he was near Nynnia. Writing decorated the walls to each side of him. Taking a deep breath, Merrick stopped at the last step to look at the scrawls. It was a protection cantrip, one that Sensitives were taught in those final months of training, and it was made in blood. This explained the blind spot in his awareness.

Once beyond the ring of the cantrip's protection, his Sight flickered down the corridors, and it didn't take long to find the body. The cellar was at the end of the corridor. The Deacon jogged toward it, his throat already dry. The door was locked, but Merrick carried his tiny toolkit everywhere out of habit so it took only a few moments with the brass implements to flick the mechanism open. The Sensitive must have been truly terrified because she had also barricaded herself in.

Merrick had to shove hard against it to get past the barrels she'd used. He knew that she was dead long before he actually saw her. Yet, the moment he burst in, for a blink of an eye, he considered that he'd been wrong. A pale shape flickered in the corner, the face turned toward Merrick in abject misery. The glimpse of her shade lasted only a moment, a full apparition that blinked back to the Otherside as soon as she had been seen. Whatever her name, she'd waited to be discovered.

The young Deacon was curled up in the dusty corner of the cellar. One of her hands, lying limp and red by her side, showed where she'd taken her own blood to write the cantrip. Her eyes were wide and bulging under cropped blond hair, while the Strop she'd been using hung slack and askew around her neck. It was charred as if it had been held over a flame.

Merrick shifted aside his cloak and glanced down at his own Strop, still firmly in its case. Until now there had been no call to use it, but as this whole mess was unraveling he was certain that would change.

Kneeling next to her, Merrick carefully slid her eyelids shut, avoiding touching the Strop. Only an Abbot could touch another's talisman without repercussions. His attempt at dignity made no difference to a corpse, but not having to look into her ruined eyes made him feel a little more comfortable. He examined the scene as his training had taught him. She was wearing the emerald cloak, but underneath she was dressed in a light shift, the kind of thing a Deacon might well sleep in. Therefore she'd obviously got up hurriedly, stopping only to grab her cloak and Strop.

Cautiously he opened her curled, bloody left hand. The tips of four fingers were sliced almost down the bone in ragged cuts that indicated she'd been in a hurry—desperate for her own blood to save her. A small knife was discarded only a few feet away, its dull blade darkened with blood. It was not much of a weapon, more like something used at the dinner table than for eldritch spells. He could see no other wounds immediately visible.

Merrick pressed his own finger to her flesh. She was cold, but it was clear she hadn't died in the initial attack. She could have come upstairs at any time for help—and yet she hadn't.

Sitting back on his heels, the living Deacon ran his eyes once more over the scene to seek out anything he may have missed, but the body before him seemed to have already revealed all it could. The Strop was another matter. Such an intimate item, so personally connected with another Sensitive, and she had actually died wearing it. Merrick was not foolish enough to pick it up, even though it looked destroyed.

A noise, the slightest noise in the ether, made him spin around on his heels and reach for his saber. It was nothing mortal. Some other part of the dead Sensitive still lingered in the dimness of the cellar. Carefully Merrick rose to his feet.

The unliving thing was scuttling among the barrels like an ill-proportioned rat. He knew it instantly—a darkling. Mortals, when touched at the moment of death by the Otherside, usually passed through into it. But some, those touched by the unliving, became shades. The darkling was a form of shade, one created specifically from Sensitives. If they were killed while their Center was away from their body, it would shatter and the pieces could become darklings.

Merrick quickly brought his Center back to him. He didn't want to risk the same thing happening to him; even death was preferable to that. He knew he should lay down some light cantrips of his own, go back upstairs and get one of the Actives to exorcise the darkling as quickly as possible.

It was only the smallest of geists, a slice of pure blackness that seemed unable to find its way out of the room. It had no physical presence, but as it stumbled around the barrels rolled sideways and the dust from the floor kicked up. He actually felt sorry for it.

Caught in a moment of indecision, he glanced over at his dead fellow Sensitive. If the Actives came down here, they would kick the darkling back to the Otherside within moments, and it was the only portion of the nameless Deacon left.

"Bones," he swore at his own recklessness. His tutors back in the Abbey would have a fit at what he was about to do.

Merrick held out his hand to the darkling—more than that, he stretched out his Center to it. The shade spun around, sensing warmth and Sensitivity; it was drawn to it like a mad magnet.

The portion of the dead woman rushed into Merrick, locking itself into his Center. To take a piece of the Otherside in like that was prohibited by everything the Abbey taught, but the time to obey prohibitions was long past. If the unliving had stopped following the rules, then so would he.

The darkling merged with him, becoming part of his own soul; a tiny sliver like a scar that he would bear forever. But it brought with it memories, flashes of what the young female Deacon had seen.

Sweat broke out on Merrick's forehead. Shakily he got up and went to the body. "Illas," he named her softly. "Poor brave Illas."

Gently he rolled her over. Thanks to the darkling, he knew what would be under there, but still he had to see.

The Deacon's corpse made a gentle sighing noise as the final air was squeezed from her lungs. Beneath were the marks he'd known would be there, but that he feared.

Five deep gouges had wrecked the stone, tearing it as easily as cloth. They had passed through the Deacon's body, destroying her but leaving not a mark on her. Only the stone revealed what had actually killed her.

Merrick let out a ragged breath and slumped to his haunches, staring at those five marks. They were so familiar and had haunted his nightmares since he was seven. Five gouges in stone, just the same as had been carved above the stairs where his father had stood on that terrible night. They'd summoned a Deacon all the way from Delmaire to try to help him, and it had ended in disaster. Distantly, he heard himself let out a strangled gasp.

He delved suddenly and dangerously into the darkling's memory. It was not the moment of her death that Deacon Illas had desperately tried to preserve; it was not even the memory of the night she had died.

Through the eyes of his compatriot, Merrick watched the Prior Aulis give the command—the command that Illas could not obey. It was this command that had sent her fleeing in terror in the dead of night, rather than join the rest of the Priory at morning Matins.

The attack on the Sensitives had not been a surprise. It had been deliberate, arranged by the Prior as a way of summoning a being from the Otherside.

Merrick came to himself, choking on disbelief and shock. This was why Illas had risked creating a darkling; her darkling was a bottle cast adrift on the sea, seeking a home and someone to believe her story.

He was shaking, terrified of what he had found. This was a cursed way for him to get an introduction to the life of a working Deacon. Struggling to his feet, Merrick felt the cellar spinning around him. He'd grab Nynnia and find Sorcha. Only together could they decide what to do with this rebellious and corrupted Priory.

"Well, aren't you the little investigator?" The sound of Aulis' voice behind him made Merrick jerk straight. Wheeling around, he saw Aulis and three of her Actives framed in the doorway. He moved to draw his saber, an instinct that seemed justified even if it was against his own kind.

The room shimmered with heat and the air cracked with power. Merrick didn't have his Center open, but he caught a glimpse of one of the Actives raising a Gauntleted hand even as Merrick was slammed back against the wall and held there like an insect. It was Deiyant, the ninth Rune of Dominion, and they had used it against him. Merrick screamed out in shock more than pain.

Knowing it was useless, Merrick struggled nevertheless, furious and raging. His fingers arched, desperate to reach his Strop and invoke the final solution taught to every Sensitive.

Aulis, the Prior who had seemed impassive but honest, now grinned at him, crossing the distance and ripping the box containing his talisman from his belt. "You won't be needing that."

"Abomination," Merrick yelled fruitlessly. "Fallen into the clutches of the unliving, you sacrificed your own Sensitives. Kill me if you like. It will make no difference . . ."

"Ah, but it will." She smiled up at him. "It will most certainly make a difference. Our task is not done here, and you, young Deacon, will help us complete it."

Merrick would have denied it, but a sickening realization was growing in him. Whatever this corrupted Prior was planning for him, it did not require his permission. His only chance was to reach Sorcha across the Bond, warn her if he could . . .

The rune Deiyant tightened around his throat. He was choking and twitching. His Sight twisted and blurred; the one thing every Sensitive relied on was suddenly being taken away. He reached out desperately for his partner, hoping despite it all that they couldn't stop him. *Sorcha, be careful, Sorcha. They are . . .* And then all was silent.

THIRTEEN

The Congregation Will Speak

If the sight of a poltern-possessed little girl had not sickened Raed enough, he was treated that very morning to a tour of Ulrich's misery. The grocer and his lad had not seemed very surprised that Sorcha had been unable to save the girl. Apparently the Priory had fostered fairly low expectations among the population of the town.

Wailace showed them more; much more than Raed had wanted to see. It was no wonder that the townsfolk had assaulted the Priory. Twelve children were possessed by poltern in a similar manner to the first. Sorcha did not repeat her experiment with the pot again, but her face grew sterner with each visit. Raed did not get any more accustomed to the stench and the horror.

After the first five, he waited outside. Sorcha, however, insisted on seeing all of them. When she came out of the last house, she looked gray. Leaning against the wall, she wearily rubbed her face.

He knew enough about her to realize that she was craving a cigar and a quiet place to smoke it. If he'd had his choice, he would have sailed *Dominion* out of the cursed place. Since that wasn't an option, he had to make do.

Raed was not used to following another's lead; he'd always been the heir to his father's Curse, and that meant he had a small retinue to obey his orders. When the time had come, it had been these soldiers whom he had led into battle. Then, after the first onset of the Curse, when he'd taken to the sea, he'd been captain of a whole crew.

Yet now he was watching this woman—this Deacon, what was more—and hoping that she had some answers. Apparently there wasn't a worse place in the world for him and his Curse to be.

Sorcha pushed herself away from the wall and walked over to him. The moment of exhaustion had obviously passed, for there was a real spark in her eye.

"So." He stroked his beard and glanced warily at her out of the corner of his eye. "Just how bad is it?"

The Deacon chewed on the edge of her lower lip, for a moment looking as though she might be choosing her words with care. "Let's just say that I have been a working member of the Order for nearly twenty years, and this is the worst outbreak of poltern possession I have ever seen. Bar none."

"And you can't help any of these children?"

"Not without Merrick, and not without identifying the foci." At his blank look she sighed.

Raed felt a little flare of resentment. "Look, I am not your partner—I know that—but I am the best resource you have right now. I'm sorry you have to explain things to me, but please do."

She unfolded her arms. "For a cluster of attacks like this, something so consistent and so particular, there must be something holding a gateway open. Not a large opening, or we'd be seeing a full-on invasion of geists, but one concentrated on particular levels of the Otherside."

"So, some sort of object?"

Sorcha nodded.

"And any idea what it would look like?"

The Deacon began tying back her bronze curls, reclaiming the severity that didn't do her beauty justice. "That's the bad news. It could look like anything." She pushed one stubborn strand back out of her eyes.

"Then how are we expected to find it?"

The Deacon opened her mouth to reply, but all that came out was a strangled whimper. Grabbing her throat, she slumped backward, and only Raed flinging himself forward and catching her prevented her fall to the ground. A fine bead of sweat had broken out on her forehead while she clawed frantically at her neck.

He loosened her collar, wondering if she was choking on something or being strangled by some sort of invisible foe. After a second she let out a great gasp and stiffened in his arms, her blue eyes wide. Raed was sure she was dying, but then she shook herself like a cat emerging from a dunking.

Jerking free of him, Sorcha leapt to her feet. "Merrick—Holy Bones, something has happened to Merrick!" Her face was as pale as milk and her lips, drained of blood, were a straight line of anger.

Raed knew of the Bond between partners; the kind of connection that was both a strength and a weakness to the Deacons. Fearing that she would leap over the side and start racing back up toward the Priory, the Pretender put his hand on her shoulder; partly in reassurance, but also partly in restraint.

"Calm down," he said as reasonably as possible. "He's alive, isn't he?"

She pressed a hand to her forehead, her breath still coming in little gasps. "Yes. He's alive. You'll have to excuse me, pirate Prince. This Bond Chambers and I share, well, it's surprisingly strong. I have never felt anything like it before with any other partner."

Was that a twinge of jealousy niggling at his core? Raed stuffed that strange emotion down as best he could, and tried instead to understand what Sorcha was going through. "Can you See where he is, what has happened?"

She gave him a quizzical look, as if he were a child. "The Bond does not allow me to See through his eyes. I heard his voice, like a muttering in another room. I could hear his tone, but not the words."

"And then?"

She pulled out her Gauntlets and stared down at them in some concentration. "I recognized something, the taste of . . ." She shook her head. "No. No, that is impossible!"

"What is it?" Raed watched her fist clench tightly on the Gauntlets. "Come on, Deacon, we're all in this nasty little affair together—like it or not."

"Unholy, cursed Bones." She spun away, pushing her hands through her hair. When she turned back, he could see the rage in her eyes. "I recognized Deiyant, the ninth rune." She waved her Gauntlets at him. "Do you understand? A rune from these!"

Saying, "I told you so," at this point would probably have earned him more than a slap. He was not that foolish, but he had to mention the thoughts that had been running through his sleepless mind. "They meant to kill you."

The anger drained out of her face and now she looked very vulnerable. Having people that you trusted turn on you—he could sympathize with that easily enough; he and his family had been living with the consequences of that for years.

"Do you think so?" She remained staring at her Gauntlets as if they had the answers. "Unholy and damned Bones, I think you're right."

"What now, then?" He put a hand on her shoulder.

"Now?" Sorcha said, not shaking off his touch. "We go and get my partner back—by whatever means it takes."

Together they glanced up the hill to where the Priory dominated the ridgeline. She smiled at him, a weary, bitter little smile that brought no warmth with it.

Merrick awoke adrift in his own Center, falling into it rather than letting it go ahead of him. All of his normal sensations were denied him, and now vibrant hues of his Sight were all he could see. The Prior and her Actives burned like recently raked fires as they clustered around him. He couldn't hear what they were saying—yet the ether was turning a distinctly indigo shade and the smell of burning invaded his brain.

They were going to do something terrible to him, and it would not just involve death. His senses let him drift higher, and from his height he could make out the faint blue glow of a Sensitive below—it was his own body.

Around it he could see flickering designs that he recognized from his training—the training that had warned of dark things that could be done with cantrips. If he'd been capable of it, he would have recoiled.

A hissing roar enveloped Merrick, a pulling tug that he did not want to give in to. The Center was a more pleasant place, and now he wanted to stay—down below, pain waited for him. The Deacon struggled, but he could feel awareness of his body coming back to him. It was reeling him in, and despite his training, he couldn't resist.

The first sensation to return was a bruised and sore windpipe. The Actives had surely been within moments of killing him. He retched and gagged on the sharp taste in his mouth. So far, Aulis had not noticed he was conscious again, so he took the chance to try to see exactly what they had done to him.

The smell of damp earth filled his nostrils, so he knew he was somewhere underground—maybe another cellar. He was pinned to the bare earth, his arms and legs spread.

Merrick tried to reach out along the Bond; the powerful nature of their partnership, unexpected and annoying as it had been up until this point, might prove to be useful. The pain that flared through his body gave Merrick a more complete understanding of Aulis' methods. It was impossible to break a Bond, but it could be rendered poisonous to a Sensitive by overloading his talent.

The ragged scream he let out alerted them to his consciousness. When the blaze of agony subsided, he opened his eyes to see Aulis crouching over him. Her face had become positively evil.

"By all means, test the limits." She smiled. "Our use for you does not require you to be awake."

"What are you planning, Traitor?" he croaked through his damaged throat.

Her eyes gleamed in the dim light, but she ignored his question. "You know you only have your partner to blame for this pain. We planned to have her here, not you."

"She's going to come back, and then you'll be—"

"Sorry?" She smiled again. "One Deacon is of no consequence to us." She waved her hand as if batting a midge, then stood up again and pointed above him to the ceiling. "Perhaps you have missed that."

With a chill, Merrick followed where she was pointing. The floor might have been dirt, but someone had taken a lot of time with the ceiling. The curve of the brickwork had been whitewashed and decorated with the swirls of more cantrips than he had ever seen in one place. He did indeed recognize many of them, but there was one whose swoops and spirals occupied the middle of the circle and hovered directly over the center of his body.

It was written in the language of the Ancients; a language that had been dead a thousand years. Only Deacons ever bothered to learn it, and they did so only because Ancients had been the first experts on the Otherside and the unliving. He had never seen the swirling script used in a cantrip, but there it was; a huge scarlet letter that could only have been made in blood, and outlined in something he instinctively knew was the charcoal remains of the Sensitives. The word was "First." Why exactly it would be written so large and importantly above him, he had no idea; however, he imagined that it meant nothing good.

Merrick struggled against his bonds, but they were iron, solid and tight. Desperately he reached for his Active strength, a feat that he had not attempted in years. The flame burned all the way down every nerve and muscle. Thought blew away in the searing agony. He thrashed about, more terribly aware of his body than he had ever been in his life.

"Foolish, but amusing." When he finally was able to think enough to let go of his attempt at Activity, Aulis was above him once more. Her grin was a sickening parody of grandmotherly concern. "Every time you reach for your power, no matter which one, the fire will enter you. Open yourself wide enough, and it will burn out your eyes and your mind. Go ahead—neither is what we require."

She turned back to her Actives, having apparently gotten her fill of amusement from Merrick's pain. "The Pretender must be found before tomorrow evening and the Third Pass."

They bowed, tucked their hands into their sleeves and left the room. The Third Pass. Merrick's head swam, but he had heard correctly.

"You can't be serious," he managed to say, his voice sounding a dry squeak in his own ears. "The theory of pass was discounted three centuries ago; there are no cycles to the closeness of the Otherside."

"Oh, really?" Aulis' curiously green eyes hardened beneath the line of her gray hair.

Merrick blinked, trying hard to focus his eyes.

"The theory did not fall accidentally from grace. It was discredited for fear that common folk would make use of it. Just like the use of weirstones. The Order has always tried to smother the use of power. They seek to control the knowledge of the unliving and keep it all for themselves."

Good: he had her talking. He might be powerless at this instant, but maybe there would be an instant when he would not be. Knowledge was the only thing he could gather at this moment.

"But you're one of us," he gasped. "A Prior, a confidant of the Arch Abbot . . ."

Her smile showed a lot of yellow, sharp teeth. "I am so much more than that, lad, and tomorrow night all shall be revealed."

The cold knot in the pit of his stomach began to resolve itself into boulder-sized apprehension. She did not linger to elaborate. He was left alone, manacled to the floor and looking up at that word hanging ominously above him. The Deacon couldn't tell how long he lay there with his own bitter thoughts.

"Merrick." The familiar voice to his left made him both incredibly glad and incredibly worried.

"Nynnia." He lifted his head off the ground and flicked it from side to side, trying to find her. Finally, he saw her standing in the dancing shadows cast by the torches on the wall. Her sweet face was pale and folded in concern, but she did not come closer. She was looking up at the cantrips above him.

"It's all right," he whispered, terrified that Aulis and her Actives would return. "They are only meant to hold me here and stifle the Bond between Faris and myself. Maybe you can find the key for the manacles?"

She stayed where she was, huddled next to a pillar, and her brown eyes focused upward with the sort of dread horror he would have thought reserved for geists or murderers. "I . . . I can't." Her voice was very soft, so soft, in fact, that he almost feared that he was hallucinating and she was only a wishful figment of his brain.

"Please, you have to help, Nynnia. They're going to kill Sorcha and do something worse to Captain Rossin." He hated to put her in danger, but what other choice did he have? It wasn't just his life at risk. Every person in Ulrich was in danger—or maybe even further. Aulis had a plan, and lordship of one remote township didn't seem worth the risk of bringing the Arch Abbey down on herself.

"I wish I could." She paused, and he could hear the honesty in her voice. It sounded as though she was really torn. "My father, Merrick . . . What will they do to him if I help you?" Nynnia still did not come out of the shadows.

He slumped back against the floor with a sigh, and gradually it dawned on him; there was only one real choice. He stared up at the cantrips for a minute, and then spoke. "What about my Strop, Nynnia? Did you see where they took that?"

Out of the corner of his eye, he saw her give a quick nod.

"Then can you get it—can you bring it to me?" Stripped of his Sight and afraid, it was very hard for Merrick to judge anything. The rapid trip of her pulse in her throat indicated she was indeed frightened, yet her expression was hard to fathom.

"I can try." She sounded like she was very close to tears. "I will try, Merrick. But I am afraid of the Actives. If they could do this to you . . ."

He knew was asking a lot of the young woman, but if she didn't bring him what he needed, Sorcha would be only the first to die. He didn't need to know the Prior's plan to be sure of that.

Merrick tried to keep his voice low and even, like he was talking to a very nervous animal. "Just the Strop, Nynnia. Just bring me the Strop and I will do the rest." His next words remained locked inside him . . . *If I have the courage for it.*

As they climbed the rise for the second time in as many days, Raed noticed that she tested the pull of her sword in its scabbard. Deacons seldom bothered with physical weapons, but he heard they trained hard with them. The Pretender had no need to check his saber.

As they neared the top, almost within sight of where they knew the townspeople were gathered, she stopped him with a hand on the crook of his elbow. "Your crew, Captain Rossin— how many of them know how to fight?"

Perhaps he should have said something like, "It won't come to that," or, "You're not making cannon fodder out of my men," but one look at her deadly serious face and he knew that more was at stake than she would admit to him. He guessed that it was not just about a dozen possessed children, but something much darker. Anything that could scare a Deacon, let alone this one, was not something he could ignore. If he was honest with himself, he considered this still his kingdom.

"About half are well-seasoned warriors," he replied. "The others are brave enough but have not trained. We tend to avoid conflict rather than take it on full tilt."

Her nod was thoughtful, as if she was quietly making the mental calculations of what was stacked against them. Her head jerked up, and those sharp blue eyes met his. "We'd best see what other resources we have available, then." With that, she turned and strode in the direction of the encampment.

Raed wondered how the citizens of Ulrich would respond to being described in such a way.

It was certainly a good thing that Sorcha was not wearing the immediately recognizable cloak of an Active, because they would probably have been peppered with gunfire before they got within thirty yards of the group. It helped that the citizens were all watching the Priory rather than the approach from the town.

Even if they'd not just come through the empty streets of Ulrich, it would have been apparent that this was nearly the entire population. The crowd included men and women, all carrying makeshift weapons; fishermen with long gaffes, farmers with their scythes and pitchforks, and bakers with their long wooden paddles. Everyone was focused on the grim building that hung over their town. After doing a quick head count, Raed judged there to be more than a hundred people, all waiting for something to happen on the ridge.

He pointed to the middle of a group on the left. "There's the mayor—see his chain of office?" It was a small insignia, to go with a small town, but he'd caught a glint off it from the noon sun.

Sorcha straightened her Order badge on her left shoulder and indicated he should go first. If she had expected that the Young Pretender would get a better reception here than she would, she was sadly mistaken.

The Mayor turned to Raed and gave him a somewhat withering look; either he recognized him and was not impressed, or he didn't and was annoyed at the interruption. His face was young but his eyes were hard in their sockets and his face was grim. Raed knew the look. Very well, he judged, a man who appreciates straight talk.

He held out his hand. "I am Captain Raed Rossin, of the ship *Dominion*. I've come to offer my assistance."

"I am Mayor Erasmus Locke." The Mayor's face relaxed slightly, but then his gaze drifted to the woman who stood behind the Pretender. His eyes dropped to the sigil she had replaced on her chest and his mouth flew open in shock. Raed decided quick action was called for, before either the Mayor or, indeed, Sorcha could say anything.

"This is Deacon Faris, whom I myself transported on my ship, and who was sent by the Arch Abbot to aid you against these transgressors."

The Mayor's gaze flitted between the two of them. His voice was gruff, almost that of an old man. "We have no need of more Deacons here."

Raed took hold of Sorcha's arm, giving it a slight squeeze as he drew her forward. She glared at him, but leapt into the breach he had created. "I can assure you that I am no friend of the woman calling herself Prior—in fact, she is holding my partner prisoner."

Mayor Locke's lips twisted. "And now I suppose you want our help to get him back?" The tone of his voice was bitter. The citizens around him shifted, muttering to themselves.

The moment hung on a knife's edge. Raed wondered if they might not have to make a run for it, but once again Sorcha surprised him. "I have examined your children and I know you have good reason to be angry." She ducked her head and then glanced up at the Mayor with a grim smile. "However, I am here to set things right." Her bright blue eyes sparkled with determination through the strands of her copper hair.

The Pretender realized that Sorcha was not beyond using her beauty to manipulate those around her if necessary. It might not be her weapon of preference, but she was aware of it—and Erasmus Locke was not immune. His shoulders relaxed. The people, those who should have been Raed's people, had learned to trust the Deacons in the last years, and it was easy to fall back into that habit under the steady stare of Sorcha Faris.

"We can't get in." A tall woman tightened her grip on a baling spike and shook it in the direction of the locked Priory. "They stood and did nothing while my Lyith suffered." Her voice cracked. "They actually turned us away."

Sorcha exchanged a glance with Raed. Her face was flushed with anger, but her eyes were glassy with something that might have been a tear. "We shall make everything as it should be. That is what the Arch Abbot sent us here to do, and when I have my partner back, we can help."

"How can you do anything against a Priory full of Deacons?" A sharp voice rang out from the huddle of the crowd, and Raed knew it for a very valid question. He was wondering the very same thing.

"There is one thing we have that they cannot stand against." Raed felt her eyes focus once more on him; her expression was both calculating and sad.

Surely, she was mad. Surely she couldn't possibly be contemplating what he imagined?

Sorcha made a slight gesture, asking for his silence for a moment. "Mayor Locke, could you send someone down to the Captain's ship? Ask for Aachon, and get him to send up all those who are ready for a fight."

A boy was dispatched, and Raed watched from the sidelines as Sorcha conversed with the Mayor and his councilors in a low voice. He didn't take much notice of what they were saying, because his mind was spinning. He knew what she was going to say, so after a few minutes when she strode toward him, his jaw was clenched and he was ready to argue.

Behind her, the people of Ulrich were newly invigorated, snapping into action and organizing themselves into something resembling forms. Whatever she had said to them had brought positive results.

He glared at Sorcha, feeling every muscle in his body rigid with rage. It was much easier to be angry than to be scared.

"So you've guessed," she began. "The only advantage we have right now is you, and the Rossin."

"You cannot use the creature as a weapon!"

"Listen," she hissed, shooting a glance over her shoulder at the townspeople, "they are right; there is no way I can possibly stand up against the dozen other Actives waiting for us in there."

Raed shook his head. He didn't want to hear anything, let alone something that might make sense.

"Aside from the fact these people need us"—she stepped closer to him, so close that he could feel her warmth—"we are trapped here, and I am sure that Aulis has a plan of her own. It won't be good for us. I can tell you that now, for free."

All of his choices were whittled away. Raed felt as trapped as sheep in a farmer's pen, ready for the butcher's knife. He took a slow deep breath; it never hurt to hear what people had to say. "All right—what do you propose? How can you possibly control the Rossin?"

Sorcha smiled, a flash of wry amusement. "Control him? I have no desire to control the Rossin. But I believe I can possibly give him something productive to do."

The Priory looked as impregnable as any fortress he'd ever seen. He thought about surrendering to the Curse, about how he had feared it since his own mother's blood had filled his mouth. It seemed unlikely that anything good could come from the Rossin. Then he thought of the children chained in their own homes, his own crew trapped on the ship, and the Deacon whom they'd unknowingly left to his fate.

Raed, the Young Pretender, cleared his throat. "If you think you can stop me from killing the innocent—if you can promise me that—then yes. Do it."

Sorcha's hands wrapped around his; soft, warm and strong,

while her vivid blue eyes remained steady with his. "Trust me, Raed. I won't let the Beast have you for any longer than necessary, or let you slay anyone needlessly."

Aachon would have tried to talk him out of it, but something in Raed felt her honesty and strength. "There is no other way," he found himself replying steadily, "and I trust you to do as you promise."

"Good, then." Sorcha held his hands a little longer than strictly necessary. "Because I make none I cannot keep."

FOURTEEN

A Use for Blood and Bone

Aulis' voice penetrated the fog that Merrick had fallen into—exhaustion and near death could do that to a person. He levered his eyes open. The woman who so falsely called herself Prior was again staring down at him as if he were a piece of meat, head on one side. He wondered what she was seeing with her obviously limited Sight. Trapped, he longed to be able to stretch forth his Center, but he'd learned from his earlier attempt. It would have to be reserved for the final moment of desperation.

"He's ready. Bring him." She gestured to the Actives lurking in the shadows. One of them brought forth a set of keys and unlocked the shackles around his wrists. Merrick left himself limp until they had unshackled all his limbs; then with a surge of energy he went at them. Unfortunately, after getting strangled into unconsciousness and spending many hours lying on the cold, damp floor, he was not in the best condition. Still, he surged up at them, swinging his arms, trying to remember all that he had been taught as a novice. He managed to get a few punches in, but his body felt sodden, wrung out. He was moving too slowly.

The Actives laughed, their voices grating on ears that felt raw. Merrick shook his head and swayed while they yanked his arms behind his back and tied them firmly. As they pushed him ahead of them, he tried one last time to reach Aulis.

"Think of your vows." His voice sounded slurred even to his

own ears, his tongue too large for his mouth. Yet he had to try. "Think of all the Order stands for!"

Her graying eyebrows drew together in a sharp line. "Oh, but I am thinking of it, young fool. You should have studied history more closely."

The Actives dragged him upstairs, and he realized he had no chance of calling on their compassion. Yet, he tried.

The one to the right, with deep-set eyes, looked as though he must have been with the Order a long time. "You can still stop this," Merrick managed to whisper out of the corner of his mouth, though his lips had gone slightly slack. He could only hope it was some effect of lying under those cantrips for hours and not some kind of palsy.

The man snorted his derision.

"Surely your partner who died—surely they . . ." Merrick called on the one thing that all Deacons shared.

"There are no Bonds that mean anything between us and the Sensitives," the younger-looking Active to his left growled. "They are sheep and we are wolves."

"Shut up, Falkirk," the other snapped. "Let's just get him upstairs as ordered."

Merrick was not capable of any more questions anyway; shock had driven him to silence. The Bond between partners was the most sacred thing to any Deacon. It was not to be mocked and used so callously. Even if Actives and Sensitives did rib each other in the confines of the Abbey, they would never say such terrible things as had just issued from the mouths of these men.

Whatever this place called itself, it was not a Priory. They might wear cloaks the same color as Deacons, but they were not of the Order.

Any further contemplation was cut short when they reached the ground level of the keep. The numbness in Merrick's body turned suddenly to ice. They were once more in the main Hall. It had, however, been cleansed. The charcoal patch was scrubbed clean; the benches were pushed to the outer edges, and when he managed to turn his eyes upward he also saw that they had somehow repaired the scorches in the ceiling. The Rossin was there, glaring down at him.

The Beast was not just some fanciful myth Raed's family had decided to use for their family crest. It was tied to the land here; a geist of the highest order, around which legends had been built. It had never truly been tamed; its submission had been the result of a negotiation between it and the greatest Deacon in the mythology of the Order. Myrilian, who had been able to use his Active and Sensitive powers jointly—a feat never since achieved. It was this Deacon who was Raed's ancestor.

All these thoughts ran through Merrick's fevered head as he was dragged on his heels to the front of the Hall. They'd given up all pretense of interest in him. Merrick scrambled weakly, unable to find any power in his own legs.

A stone had been set in the spot where the lectern had once stood. Merrick shook his head groggily as he suddenly recognized the device from books—a draining board. They shoved him back roughly against it, the lines of razors slicing into his back. He lurched forward with a howl, but the two men were already lashing him against the device with merciless efficiency.

His mind scurried to make sense of it, trying to call on his memory and his training. Blood, bone and flesh made any summoning stronger. The blood of a Deacon already steeped in the midst of the Otherside would be best of all: it would be not only his power that could be drawn, but that of his partner, as well. Sorcha Faris, the strongest of the Actives.

To his right, Aulis appeared once more. She had discarded the blue cloak of an Active and was dressed in bright red robes. He'd never seen or heard of the like among the Order. The sleeves were embroidered with symbols and cantrips. "You see, young Deacon? All your training, all your talent—they shall not go to waste."

Merrick turned his head away with a sick realization burning in his head. They had weakened him enough to enter his mind; normally, of course, a Sensitive was too powerful to be broken into in such a way.

Aulis leaned in close to him, so that he could smell sage and a whiff of smoke in her hair. "Thank you for your donation to our cause."

The sharp little knives dug deeper into his body with every breath. The blood slid down the channels into the brass bowl the woman bent and placed at the base of the rock. They were draining him of life, as if he were an especially ripe fruit.

At Aulis' gesture, the two Actives who had brought him in loomed into view. "We are nearly ready. Go and get the royal.

He is right outside the gates." She glanced upward once at the image of the Rossin on the ceiling, and her smile was dreadful and happy.

Merrick's vision was darkening around the edges, shadows creeping in from around the lit torches to feast on his fear; shades and memory. The only mercy was that he felt so little pain, but he was sure that this was not a deliberate kindness. The Otherside was pulling at him—he knew the symptoms. Aulis and her Actives needed his blood for something, and he would probably never live to see it.

Don't give up . . . Hold on.

"Sorcha?" he whispered, shaking his head, trying to clear it. Reaching desperately for the Bond, he tried to open his mind to his partner.

And then he felt soft fingertips on his forehead. He had to be dreaming, for now he heard Nynnia's whisper. "I can't get these shackles off." The tiniest tug on them awakened coils of pain through his back. Merrick managed not to moan.

He licked his lips, desperate for moisture to make his mouth work. "Don't . . . They'll hear."

At the far end of the Hall, they were still waiting for his blood to drain out of him, chatting among themselves as calmly as if this were a marketplace. He surely couldn't be far from passing out. "Have you got it, Nynnia?"

His own heartbeat was slowing in his ears. The room began to waver. She had to be careful handling the Strop.

"Yes." Her voice was muffled and distant, but he felt the smooth warmth of the talisman glide over his eyes. Suddenly everything was clear, and Merrick Chambers slipped into the Otherside.

The pain in Sorcha's head was not going away—a hollow space in her mind where awareness of Merrick should have been. Her protective instincts told her to race up the hill back to the Priory, blast the doors off with Chityre and demand her partner back. However, she had not reached seniority in the Order by giving in to pure impulse.

Sorcha could feel Aachon's glare like a knife in her back. She didn't turn about until she had explained the last of her plan to the Mayor and the citizens of Ulrich. She kept it simple; the fewer people running about with complicated instructions, the better.

"As soon as you see the light, retreat back as quickly as you can. Aachon will do the rest." Only when the crowd had nodded and shuffled away with something that looked like hope in their eyes did she turn around to face the wrath of the first mate.

Raed was enjoying this moment; he had a grin that threatened to split his face. If he was afraid of her plan, there was no sign of it.

Sorcha gave him a glare, but wasn't about to get into a fight. Over the Pretender's shoulder, the sun was sinking into the sea. The days here were incredibly short and they had little time to pull this off.

Taking out her Gauntlets, she thrust them onto her hands in a couple of short gestures. "Aachon, you understand how important timing is? You must choose your moment and wait until the Actives are on the wall—all of them."

The man's brow furrowed and he glanced down into his right hand, tightly clenched around the weirstone. "It feels wrong . . ."

"That's because it *is* wrong," Sorcha snapped. "Imagine how it is for me—this goes against everything a Deacon is ever taught!" She readjusted the slim pack on her back and watched him out of the corner of her eye.

Perhaps those had not been the right words, for he actually flinched as if struck. The native Order had fallen apart under the weight of the politics of so many fractured kingdoms. That they had rejected a man with such excellent Sensitive potential was only a symptom of that internal rot.

"Old friend," Raed broke the stalemate, "we are all risking much here, but I know this is the right thing. I cannot always be hiding, and this is what a proper prince would do for his people."

Aachon glanced down at the brilliant blue orb in his hand, staring into its depths as if the answer could be found there. Finally when he spoke, his deep voice vibrated with emotion. "I was given care of you by the Unsung, but you are my leader, my prince. I know you are also a good man, and if you say this is the way—then this is the way."

With that, he took his place among the crew and waited for the sun to finish sinking. Sorcha led Raed away, far enough so that they could choose their moment, concealed among the rubble of rock to the right of the road. A quick glance at the Pretender brought her some reassurance; despite their plan hinging on releasing his inner beast, *Dominion*'s captain looked remarkably calm. His eyes darted to where his crew stood loading their weapons and preparing to assist the citizens. Two rickety old rifles wouldn't bring every heretic Deacon to the wall, hence the full firepower of his crew. By the slight frown on his forehead, she knew his concern was all for them. Good; she didn't want him thinking too much on his part in this hasty plan.

His hazel eyes were green in the torchlight when they turned on her. "A lot of people are counting on you knowing what you're doing."

Sorcha clenched and stretched her fingers in her Gauntlets; the well-used leather made not a creak. Command often fell to a Deacon in similarly volatile situations, yet her heart was pounding and a tingle ran down her spine. She told herself it was just because Merrick was in danger and she didn't want to lose her partner.

"I am aware of that, Raed," she replied, keeping her eyes on the citizens advancing toward the gates. "Believe me, I am fully aware of that."

With the addition of the crew members, the mob did seem larger and imbued with a newfound enthusiasm. As before, they charged toward the gates, but this time they carried a sturdy length of oak offered up by the local carpenter. It made an excellent battering ram. For effect, the raiding party from *Dominion* began shooting at the crenellations of the Priory, creating lots of noise and dislodging flying fragments of stone. The booming sounds of the battering ram and the angry mob's roar were quite impressive.

And so too were the imposter Deacons. Sorcha tugged Raed down into a crouch next to her as hooded forms appeared on the battlements. It was immediately apparent that Aulis' initial restraint had been all for show, because these newcomers were already reaching for runes. Sorcha's hand tightened on the Pretender's shoulder. "Here's hoping the Mayor remembers what I told him, or this could get very messy."

The words had barely left her mouth when Mayor Locke, standing right near the front, called out. The speed with which the citizens dropped the battering ram and scattered was impressive. They might not hold formation liked trained men, but they at least took orders—or maybe they simply had a good, healthy dose of fear.

Aachon now stood alone at the foot of the wall, the swirling

weirstone held up. In the dark, he needed no torch; the orb's light
flared blue, making him look like an actor on some eerie stage.

"He's a bloody beacon." Raed made to get up.

"And he knows what he's doing." Sorcha grabbed his arm.
"Give him a second."

She hadn't been wrong—if she had, it would have been the
end of this whole crazy endeavor. Through her limited Sight, she
watched Aachon summon shades. Of all the geists, they were
the best choice, being common, hungry and incredibly mindless. Stripped of all humanity, they were drawn like magnets to
Actives since they had no power of their own.

Raed and the rest of the citizens would see only twists of mist,
like strands of thrown scarves floating up to the battlements, but
through her Sight they had shape and form. The stretched and
screaming wraiths might seem exactly as a child would draw a
geist on paper, but their effects when they reached the Actives
would be far from infantile. She wondered if the punishment
dished out to Deacons for calling geists into the world applied to
instructing someone else to do so.

"Is that mist going to be able to hold them?" Raed asked
doubtfully.

Sorcha could feel a cruel grin forming on her face. "Without
Sensitives? Oh yes, they'll be occupied for a while." A couple
gave out screams, batting at the circling geists. It was most satisfying. For what they had done to their partners, they deserved
every moment of it.

The first mate had chosen his moment perfectly. Aachon
turned and jogged back to the mob, but he did glance in their
direction. Sorcha got the message. Raed gave a little reassuring
salute in the direction of his crew, while she took a deep breath—
ready to break every lesson of her training.

She was doing the right thing. Raed would never know what
she'd done, and once it was over, she would break the Bond. The
Pretender frowned when she grasped his hands, but he didn't
look away when she looked into his eyes. It was too late now to
go back, yet as the Bond snapped into existence Sorcha already
regretted her choice. Raed Rossin, the Young Pretender to the
Imperial throne, had been a very bad choice of Bond partner.

Merrick had told her about the silver fire he'd seen around
the Captain. She'd glimpsed it herself, but it was a very different
story when it was in her. Naturally, being untrained, Raed could

not feel the Bond—it was a one-sided joining. Sorcha held back a curse.

"Let's go," she whispered as lights began to flash and burn on the battlements. It might take a long time for those heretic Deacons to find the right rune to fight off the shades, but then again, they could stumble upon it by accident at any moment. Crouched over, the two of them ran toward the rear of the Priory, where there was nothing but wall and tumbled rock. It was as impregnable as any Imperial fortress.

"Are you ready?" Sorcha asked. In the darkness, she could make out little but his form. It would have been good to see his eyes; to glimpse his thoughts.

"Say it one more time." The Captain's voice was calm but insistent. "Tell me you are sure."

"I can hold the Rossin." They taught classes in lying in the Abbey—it was sometimes a very useful skill for a Deacon. Still, this lie felt very wrong on her tongue. "I can control you."

"I don't know why"—the Pretender let out a long breath like a man about to dive—"but I trust you."

She should have been relieved, but instead a sick knot was beginning to develop in her stomach. To cut it off before she could betray her fears, she concentrated on this plan of hers; a plan that could go horribly wrong at many various junctures. Sorcha reached down deep inside her, calling on her Active Center to open every door.

The two rogue Deacons couldn't have chosen a better moment to attack. The world was burning white in Sorcha's eyes as her body shuddered with the rush of power. The gate flickered open, for an instant outlining the two shapes against the swirling mists of the Otherside. She had no time for shock. *Holy Bones*, was her only thought. They were traveling *through* that realm—the implications would have to be considered another time.

The Pretender was facing her, his back to the wall and the silent arrival of the two hooded men. Her enhanced senses noticed that the dark eyes of the other Deacons were not locked on her—they were focused on Raed. One had a dark coil in his hands, something that looked suspiciously like a collar.

The Rossin. Her mind leapt ahead; Aulis might have meant to kill her, but Raed and the Beast within him had never been in danger. They wanted the Captain, Curse and all—no. *Because* of the Curse. Why, she couldn't say, but Sorcha knew she had to stop them.

She grabbed hold of Raed, who was still unaware, and yanked him behind her. Though she had her hands on his skin for only a moment, the warmth of his power licked against her. With the gate to Otherside so near, the Rossin was very close to surfacing.

Deacon had never fought Deacon, but ever since she'd felt the attack on Merrick, she'd known this moment would come sooner or later. Better it be over with. Already full of power, Sorcha whirled Raed away, shielding him with her body while thrusting out a hand that burned with the blue fire of Aydien. The rune of repulsion made a noise like a cannon firing, smashing into the rebel Deacons just as they stepped out of the gateway.

One was flung backward in a most satisfactory manner, but the second was a little more observant. He managed to get Yevah up quickly enough to repulse her casting. All of them were fighting without Sensitives, so it was going to be a rapid-fire and dirty fight.

The first Deacon was lying, groaning, on the broken ground, but she couldn't rule him out. Full of the power of the Otherside, sometimes physical injury meant little. Sorcha's ears were sharp, and she heard Raed draw his saber.

"Stay behind me," she gasped, closing her fist around the blue fire, and reaching at the same instant for another rune. "They want you." She couldn't spare the concentration to see if he was obeying her; she could only hope he knew better than to get in her way.

Pyet. She opened her palm and poured scorching flames at the shield of the rogue Deacon. The sensation of it tore through her—there was a limit to how much even one of the Order could channel. Sorcha knew that she was perilously close to that point.

The one scrambling to his feet didn't have enough time to raise Yevah. The flames of Pyet wrapped themselves hungrily around him. The screaming began. While Sorcha had used this rune on the irretrievably possessed, never—*never*—had she thought to use it on one sworn into the Order. Her stomach rolled as the man burned like a candle, howling and beating uselessly at himself. It took all of her training to hold Pyet on the other man, the flames battering at his shield. Something had to break.

In the corner of her eye, Sorcha saw the flaming man fall mercifully to the ground, consumed like dried kindling. The smell of roasted flesh and bone was an awful thing, and she heard Raed swear. Behind Yevah, the remaining rogue Deacon's eyes narrowed, lit up by the shield and the raging fire smothering it.

She saw it in his expression; the dawning realization that she was the stronger. Without Sensitives, it was indeed coming down to raw power, and Sorcha knew there was none in the Order anywhere that could match her. Her smile of victory froze on her face as she realized just what she would do if the tables were turned.

He did it. He reached for Teisyat. With the raw power of the Otherside streaming through him, all bets would be off. Yet he was trying to do it while holding up Yevah the Shield. Sorcha yelled to him, wrapping her fist around Pyet in an attempt to get him to stop. Summoning Teisyat while holding another rune was insanity. He would be destroyed and the gateway would be wedged open. Anything could come through. Anything.

But the fool didn't care. His Gauntlet streamed lava, smashing a hole into the reality of the world. Sorcha bellowed at him to stop, darting forward and throwing herself against Yevah in a futile effort to reach him before he carved out the gateway. Too late.

A growl pierced the madness. Deep and loud, like a rumble from the earth itself. Sorcha felt it travel through her legs, and she knew instantly that there was only one thing capable of such elemental force.

Slowly she turned and backed away from the shifting sphere of Yevah. The Rossin crouched atop a rock; its form different from that last time in the tunnel. The shape was still feline, but larger and more muscular—almost twice as big as any Breed stallion. The Beast was not a shapeshifter—he was the lord of shapeshifters, varying his preferred form to meet any situation. His intent now was massive destruction, if this shape was anything to go by. Sorcha wondered for an instant how it felt for Raed to be inside this thing. Intoxicating and terrifying at the same time—the answer came dimly along their newly formed Bond.

With a snarl that shook the air, the Beast leapt from the rock and through the fire of Yevah, shaking off the remains of Raed's clothes. Both rune and Rossin were of the Otherside; it was small impediment to one of the great geists. The Beast fell upon the rogue Deacon like a dark storm. So huge were its jaws that it tore

him in half with one bone-shattering snap. The man had time
for only a single horrified howl. Sorcha flinched but did not look
away. The man had been a fool, a dangerous fool.

Now she was alone with the Beast that she held by the slim-
mest of leashes. A newly formed Bond seemed a very fragile
thing to hang her entire life on. Pushing her hair out of her eyes,
she fought her instinct to run. If she did, her life would definitely
be over—probably before she got more than a yard. Slowly, she
bent and took up Raed's dropped saber, feeling its weight nestle
into her palm. It was an insubstantial kind of reassurance.

The great Beast turned and looked over one dark shoulder
at her. Fitful flames from the remains of Pyet reflected in those
eyes. Muscles were bunched and ready under its thick fur. The
Beast was primed and the gaze seemed to suggest she had better
find it a target very quickly.

Sorcha took a long deep breath, called on her runes and raised
both hands. The power of Chityre smashed into the walls with
the strength of twenty battering rams. Stone and mortar blew
apart, creating a cloud of sudden debris. The rattle of masonry
raining down around her was earsplitting.

Yet she could still hear the roar of the Beast, the satisfaction
of a creature ready to act on its only instinct. The Rossin was
now unleashed. The dust had not even settled before it bounded
into the Priory.

FIFTEEN

A Sacrifice to the Darkness

The Rossin was free. Almost. The fire-haired Deacon, the one that had bound him, followed in his wake. He could hear her behind him, running to catch up. As it should be. As it had once been—with humans serving the Rossin, as they did on the Otherside. He did not know her name yet, but once he did, there would be a different kind of tethering, for her pitiful Bond could surely not be enough to hold him. Let her think that her puny link to the foci spared her. For now she served her purpose.

Deep down, the Rossin could feel the struggles of the human foci. The ancient foe, the family that had stolen his name and power and tethered him, was now suffering. But the Rossin had more immediate concerns. He scented prey in the immediate area; hot and warm and full of blood. The great imperative drove him as always—to feed and grow strong. The great teeth bared in a snarl that was an almost-smile as he leapt clear of the destruction.

Once beyond the tumble of broken walls and clouds of dust, the Rossin's exceptional senses made out the racing of human hearts and the coursing of human blood more fully. Deacons— but not the sort of Deacon that followed him. These stank of the Otherside and desperation. Centuries before, there had been many such kind; before the coming of the Order.

The humans came running out, slamming on their Gauntlets, preparing to meet any attack. They weren't expecting a geistlord.

The Rossin tore into them even as they threw their puny runes at him; mere shadows of the real power of the Otherside.

He gorged himself on more than their flesh; he chased them around the compound, relishing their terror. Their screams delighted him as he broke them so easily, sending their shades in shattered shards into the Otherside, the realm that he was denied. Their pain was delicious to him, but no recompense for what their kind had taken from him. The recollection made the Rossin howl again, rending and tearing every morsel of flesh he could reach. Weak humans did not deserve breath. He threw their pieces around the compound like scattered chaff.

The female Deacon was behind him, closer now, and he could feel the Bond. It was not as weak as he'd thought. It was as fragile as a spiderweb—gossamer thin, but strong as steel. The Rossin threw himself harder against it. By the deep shadows—it was tightening!

How dare this woman presume to put bonds on a geistlord? The image of the first Deacon, the one who had bound him to this fate, flashed in his ancient memory. The ignominy of that event still burned the Rossin. Now these people would pay. No punishment was enough. The great muscles in his body bunched and exploded as he turned toward her, fast as thought. She would learn the lesson he'd been unable to lay upon the first of the Deacons. Spinning around, the Beast was ready to rend, but something held him back.

There was one trait in the human world that the Rossin admired: beauty. It was not the kind of beauty of the flesh that tethered men—but the beauty of power. When he turned those blazing eyes on this female, he saw it, gleaming like a gem in a pit of darkness. Perhaps it was the faint influence of his foci—though the Beast would never admit to such a thing—that stopped him from pouncing. Instead he crouched inches from her face, breathing destruction and the smell of blood on her. He saw the Deacon flinch slightly, her blue eyes watering from the nearness of his power. She had dismissed him with her rune Gauntlets before, when he was weak from the transformation. Even if she managed to wedge open his jaws and do the same right now, there would be no repeat. The Rossin had feasted and grown strong. She knew it. He knew it.

Deacon and geistlord were eye to eye. She was frightened, but did not move. He was transfixed by the thing that only he could see. For now, he would let her live.

The stalemate was broken when three lay Brothers emerged from the stables and made a break for the gate. With a great shake of his dark mane, the Beast let out a snarl and whirled about to give chase. It was glorious to release himself upon them and he could not contain himself long enough to enjoy the chase this time. Blood, hot and sweet, flooded into his throat, momentarily sating the thirst that never seemed to end. Bones snapped in his mouth and he heard the wail of souls ripped free of their meaty cages. The fizzle of power and blood in the Rossin's veins was heady bliss.

He roared again, full of power and delight, before looking around the courtyard. It was clear of anything living apart from the tethering Deacon. Her great power and beauty saved her for now, but would not restrain him forever. He would keep her for last. Once he had taken his fill of energy from the Priory's humans, no pitiful Bond could possibly hold him. The Rossin looked forward to seeing those blue eyes widen in horror just before he fell on her. He wondered what her soul would taste like.

Now it was time to find more flesh. He sprang away, his hide the color of angry clouds rippling under the torchlight. Magnificent, he knew. Great paws with their retracted claws moved silently over the stones of the courtyard toward the keep. The doors smashed most satisfactorily as the Rossin landed against them, his great bulk ripping them free of their mounts and scattering their broken fragments on the scarred floor.

Within, the keep was lit with torches and the moonlit glow of cantrips. Seven large weirstones described a space encompassing the back and the center of the room. The Rossin's ears lay flat against his neck and the white lengths of his fangs gleamed as he snarled in terrible rage.

The smell of the Otherside was overwhelming, bringing him to a stop for a moment as he inhaled the remembrance of home. His huge head swung about, emerald green eyes sweeping like searchlights, scouting out the next to die. To the side were the glowing forms of those who were performing the summoning. These whelps were delving deeply into the Otherside—looking for more than the garden-variety shade or spook.

Then his gaze fell on two forms toward the rear of the room. One female was supporting and clinging to a male strapped to a drainage slab. It was not an unfamiliar sight; human blood was a valuable commodity. Yet, it was not the blood that gave the Rossin pause on the very threshold of further feeding.

The geistlord, in his great feline form, growled low and slow. He recognized the bubbling energy in this room. One of his own kind was here, and one not chained to a form as the Rossin was. Hackles rose on his bunched dark shoulders and his tail began to lash.

The gray-haired human female snatched up the cup of the foci blood and spun around with it, splashing a wide scarlet arch around her to paint the floor in that ancient pattern. It wouldn't have held him. He could still have ripped her apart, and yet, and yet . . .

It was looking at him. One of them at the end of the hall was more than it seemed. He knew its name; he knew where it came from and its nature: ancient enemy and utterly dangerous to geist and geistlord alike. So few of them now, and yet here was one staring at him with eyes full of power. The Rossin knew no fear on the Otherside, yet here he was corporeal, trapped by the Curse. No pitiful human could touch him, but he was still considerably weaker than he would have been in full unbound form. From the end of the hallway, the being smiled. They both knew which of them held the upper hand for now. The beast was filled with hatred, intense and bitter in the back of his mouth. He wanted to destroy, to rend, and yet could not cross that threshold.

Not you. Not yet, he thought in terrible rage.

Instead, the Rossin did what he had never before done in this realm. He fled.

Never work with children or animals. That was what the thespians said, and now Sorcha was beginning to understand what they meant. The Rossin might not be a true animal, but he proved just as unreliable. She had put her trust in a geistlord and now she was paying the consequences.

"Unholy Bones," she growled as the massive bulk of the Rossin dwindled and fractured into the male form of the sea captain. She threw her cloak once more about the shivering naked Raed and slid the pack from her back, dropping it at his feet. They were better prepared this time.

Her heart was hammering in her chest like a jackrabbit's, and her whole body tingled. Taming the Rossin had been exhilarating and mad; every moment a victory against destruction and death. The beast was magnificent, a force of nature that none of the rogue Deacons had been able to stand against. She knew of no Deacon who could claim to have stared into the eyes of the Rossin and lived.

It was ironic, then, that by the looks of things, she was instead going to be killed by two of her own. Aulis held the bloodstained bowl in one hand and grinned maniacally. All semblance of sanity had vanished; the cool Prior had been replaced by a scarlet-robed madwoman.

"Thank you for bringing us what we wanted," she hissed, flinging the bowl into the far corner of the room. "The Pretender's blood will finish the summoning." An odd triangular stone hung about her neck, and Sorcha knew it immediately for a foci—the one that was drawing the polterns. It was going to be tricky to get it away from Aulis.

The Deacon judged the odds. To her left, Raed was struggling to his feet, shaking his head like a man concussed. Behind Aulis, Merrick looked gray. Though he was not quite dead, he was near enough to it as to make no difference. Nynnia, the fool with the wide doe eyes, could be seen peeking around the draining slab. No help there. And now, advancing on Sorcha, two remaining Actives. If all this wasn't enough, the air was alive, humming with power that made her skin tingle and the hair on her head leap away from her skull. A summoning; one hell of a summoning was under way.

Sorcha took a careful step backward, watching the Actives advance on her while darting a glance upward. There, in the vaulted ceiling, she could see the Otherside pulling closer to the living world; she could feel it like an angry dog preparing to spring. A gathering storm was being born. And for it, they needed Raed, the Young Pretender. Deacon Faris had fought many battles for souls, yet this one was the first one where she doubted victory.

Perhaps sensing her hesitation, the enemies clustering around them straightened and smiled to one another. However, they did not summon any runes. Instead they drew their swords, and she understood why. The atmosphere here was very finely balanced. Whatever they were doing was dangerous and delicate work. One rune, one summoning of the wrong sort of power, and there would be consequences. Sorcha didn't think that killing everyone in the room was a good idea just yet, so she was prepared to follow their lead. The sound of her own blade being drawn was like a snake hiss.

Obviously, with the amount of blood they had taken from

her partner, the usual injunctions against spilling it were not in force. It remained to be seen how much of what was about to flow would belong to her and the Young Pretender. Raed, who had recovered from the change far more quickly than Sorcha could have hoped, drew his saber and staggered upright at her side; a noble and impressive gesture, considering he was nearly naked.

"So"—his breathing was ragged, yet his usual bravado was still in place—"are we going to die?"

The cocky tone in his voice, despite this rather awkward situation, made Sorcha smile wryly. "I don't know—I think they just want a gallon or so of your blood."

"Well, that is damned unfriendly," he replied, and then, in between his gasps, the Actives attacked.

Sorcha was under no illusions about her sword-fighting skill; it was what might be called adequate. Raed Rossin, on the other hand, was a master. While she hacked and parried as best she could, the Captain was a flurry of speed and sweet footwork. Despite the rigors of the Change, he was beating his opponents while she struggled to hold her own. It irked Sorcha to know that. Some competitive streak in her flared at the realization. Her eyes narrowed and she concentrated on her attacks, hearing the Pretender's grunts of exertion as her admonishment to do better.

If she survived today, she promised herself more time in the practice yards—that was for certain. For now, she wished she had a pistol instead of a blade. Or a dozen loyal Deacons at her back.

Her attacker was grinning, his crooked teeth flashing in the half-light; damn it, he knew he was winning. With a half growl, she caught a riposte aimed at her head just in time. An edge of steel sliced through her guard and nicked the shoulder of her armor. That hadn't happened. It had been a while since Sorcha had been forced to resort to hand-to-hand, not since the bad old days of the Order's first landing with the Emperor.

While the swordfight raged, there was no one to stop Aulis. She held her arms spread in the universal gesture of supplication, and the seven weirstones flared. Warmth beat down on the top of Sorcha's head as she struggled to hold her own. She couldn't afford to look up to see the cause, yet it made her opponent laugh. That could not be a good thing.

To her right, a man grunted, followed by the clatter of a body falling to the ground. A quick glance ascertained that it had not been Raed. He was turning to aid her, but suddenly Sorcha had a more pressing concern. Her eyes were drawn to the writhing space above them.

Something was now rending apart the very air. Her attacker, and indeed everyone capable of movement in the Hall, clapped their hands to their ears. The noise was visceral, felt more than heard, echoing all the way down to the bone. It set muscles to twitching and eyes to watering. Somewhere deep inside Deacon Sorcha Faris, fear bloomed.

Sorcha had felt this once before, on a staircase in an ancient castle. That memory was one she seldom touched—yet now it reached for her with a great five-clawed hand. Through streaming eyes, she looked up. Aulis was also standing with her hands to her ears, but her face was stretched in a grimace of delight. It was bound to be a short-lived victory—nothing good ever came through from the land of the dead. The rogue Deacons had reached far indeed. No Active had a rune to stop it.

Sorcha reached out and grabbed hold of Raed. It was an instinctual gesture—a final one. A need to feel human skin one final time.

Merrick was wide-open to the Otherside. Having slipped loose of his body, he was perilously close to losing sight of it altogether. He had to be near death—surely he had been drained of enough blood for that. None of the books had ever covered what would happen when a Sensitive wearing the Strop stepped out of life— none had ever made one of his kind such a target before. In the calm of his Center, he could feel the bonds of flesh and bone still tying him to something. Could it be the Strop that held him in place?

He heard the Rossin smash through the keep doors, witnessed the mysterious retreat of the geistlord. Then he saw Sorcha, not as blazing as the Pretender Raed, but still gloriously beautiful through the Strop.

The books spoke of detachment at the very edge of death. Yet one thing penetrated his calm: a heat from above. It could not have been purely physical; he was beyond the physical now. Merrick did not want to look up. He did not want to see what was coming; what his blood had helped allow through.

See deep; fear nothing. A voice, light and near, repeated the Sensitives' mantra, reminding him of his purpose. Even as he was dying he clung to it. It had to be Sorcha. Their Bond, their inconvenient connection, leapt into life.

Through the Runes of Sight, Merrick tilted his vision upward. Cantrips, weirstones, blood and runes; all the power of this world had been turned to one purpose—to reach deep into the Otherside. He did not know which level Aulis had tapped into, but one glance at the huge five-taloned hand ripping itself into the real world told him all he needed to know.

Calmness fled in the face of remembrance. The five deep gouges in ancient stone; he'd traced them with his young hands, memorizing the spot where his father had died. He had never been able to find out what had killed him, no matter how many books he read or how many Deacons he quizzed. And now here it was. He wanted to flee. He wanted to fly to the Otherside and quit life. However, the voice was once more in his head. *You are stronger than that. Remember your training. Remember your own power.*

The Bond must have been intensified while he wore the Strop. The Strop—of course!

Merrick bent his mind to the rune carved on it, no lesser than those on Sorcha's Gauntlets. Mennyt, the rune that could take him to the Otherside. It was not the last Rune of Sight, but it was enough. Through it he could see his connection with the real world. The Bond was not the only link. Many things tethered him to this side: hopes, words and dreams. These were the things that made a person's spirit into a shade. He had complete knowledge of his fate. He wouldn't allow it.

The being was moving toward reality, pushing its head against the natural boundaries of the world like a nightmare child pressing its face against a shop window. It wasn't meant for this world, though Merrick could feel its siren song tugging at him, promising him much. A deep part of him wanted to give everything to it; bone, flesh and sinew. His blood pulsed in his temples, drowning out all other sounds.

The weirstones, the cantrips, the blood, Sorcha, Raed and himself; Merrick could feel them like chess pieces in his Sight. Everything was so finely balanced. All it required was one little push. One little nudge and the stack of cards Aulis had so carefully constructed would tumble down.

However, this was not something he could do. As always his role was to See—Sorcha had to take her place in this drama. He reached out to her. *The stones,* he whispered into her head. Her eyes narrowed and he knew she was Seeing as he did. The Bond was growing stronger; he could feel it like ivy scurrying up a wall, tying them closer and closer.

The weakest point. Her Active thoughts followed his lead. She was like lightning, burning, acting without thought. He admired that—he now relied on it. Pyet. Naturally she chose Pyet. He could have guessed that.

Fire bloomed from her Gauntlets, bright and beautiful. Sorcha's power smashed out at the weirstone positioned right below the trembling arch of the hall, under the vaulted ceiling. The noise of the marble imploding was like a thousand souls screaming from beyond, calling out in horror and loss. The world burned and swirled with runes, a tangle of power that flared brightly for one moment. It was too much for anything but destruction to follow.

Above, the being from the Otherside howled, wrapped in shreds of white light and anger. However much it bucked and heaved, struggling against the natural order, it could not quite overcome it. The Otherside pulled it back, though it did not go easily. The Priory shuddered right down to its bones, as if it was clawing at itself to be free of the creature's touch.

Now Merrick knew he was going to die. The real world was peeling back, breaking apart in a tumble of rock, mortar and dust. Something had to be sacrificed, and if it was himself and the Priory—then so be it. This was the end, but at least there would be no intrusion from the Otherside. His blood had caused the rift, and yet he had pointed the way to stop it. He could leave now. *Take me.* He opened up himself to the world, letting it do with him as it willed.

The ringing in his ears was distracting. It hurt. It shouldn't hurt. The world spun, and then sensation snapped back to him. Someone was holding his face in a viselike grip and calling his name in a very demanding tone. It took a heartbeat for him to realize just who it was.

"Wake up, Merrick. You're lying down on the job." It sounded like a cruel collection of words, but he could detect the hint of real concern.

He came around with a smile on his face just as Raed managed to free him from the draining table. He slipped down and Sorcha caught him around the shoulder, holding him up against her. His body felt as though it had been flayed—which, of course, it had. Merrick licked his lips experimentally and then croaked, "Where—where's Nynnia?"

"Oh, by the Bones," Sorcha snapped. "Back from the brink of death and you're still all doe-eyed over that—"

He didn't let his partner finish the sentence. "She was here; she brought me the Strop." He realized Sorcha was holding it naked in her hands. He snatched it back in horror and the effort nearly knocked him over his feet. Even she shouldn't have been able to touch his talisman.

Looking dazedly around, he realized why his partner was so irascible. The Hall was destroyed; not just damaged but reduced to a tumble of stones as if leveled by cannon fire. Only the places where his body had lain and the portion by the west wall where Raed and Sorcha had fought for their lives remained. He could see the bodies of their opponents lying among the stones.

Sorcha was grinning at him. "I don't know what you did, Merrick, but remind me not to annoy you anytime soon."

He looked at the back of his hand with horror; it was pink and warm and full of blood. And yet . . . and yet . . . His brain tried to process it. "It wasn't me," he mumbled. "It was you—your Active power. I just showed you where to attack."

"Pardon?" He felt his partner stiffen against him. "What do you mean?"

"Through the Bond." He felt real strength returning to his limbs, but from where, he would not hazard to guess.

Sorcha was looking at him now through wide blue eyes. "I couldn't feel the Bond, Merrick. Aulis did something to dampen it." And she was right. He could feel it returning now; warmth and awareness, and a glimpse into her thoughts. She was not lying.

He had not been communing with Sorcha, and if it had not been Sorcha, then it begged the question of who exactly it had been. Managing to get his own feet under him, he looked around, but there was no sign of Nynnia.

"Impossible," he muttered. "It must have been you . . . You must have just not felt it." Sometimes Actives were so blind to the reality of things that it was almost reassuring.

SIXTEEN

After the Tribulation
Comes Realization

Raed watched Sorcha and Merrick together out of the corner of one eye. Deacons were always so damn secretive.

The Pretender let out a long breath, one that felt like he'd been holding it in for hours. His nerves were still twitching erratically with the remnants of the Change—and also with relief. Sorcha had not let him down—his trust in her had not been misplaced. No one had ever been able to control the Rossin before, yet Sorcha had done it twice in less than a day.

He glanced over at the woman as he slipped on his breeches and shirt. Her bronze hair had come loose and was full of dust; some of it flew in the air as she argued animatedly with her partner. Sorcha looked tired but unbent. By the Ancients, she was beautiful. Beautiful, powerful . . . and married, he reminded himself, as the faint moonlight glinted off the runes on her Gauntlets.

A very salient point. He was used to postbattle shock, and even the aftereffect of the Beast was familiar; what he wasn't used to was having a building narrowly avoid falling on him. The rumble of that event was still affecting his ears. Raed shook his head, like a diver trying to remove water from his ears. Hopefully, the ringing would clear eventually.

While the Deacons conferred with each other, he decided to make absolutely certain that the Prior and her remaining minions were, in fact, dead. In too many battles, he'd seen men cut down by foes that they assumed had been dealt with. The human body

was remarkable; a man could still pull the trigger of a pistol, even
if he was destined to cough out his last breath a second later.
What a Deacon could do in their final moments, he really didn't
want to find out.

Strapping on his saber, and thankful to once more be in
clothes, Raed turned to this mundane task. Dust and smoke
clawed at the back of his throat as he struggled to locate their
enemies among the debris. Whatever Sorcha and Merrick would
finally determine had protected them from the destruction was
immaterial to him; it was a good turn by someone, and that was
enough.

Unfortunately for the Prior's Deacons, that same someone
had not been so kindly inclined toward them. He found their two
initial attackers beneath a massive column that had managed to
crush both of them, like some giant skilled hand. One glance
was all that was required; they were well and truly dead. Bugs
crushed against a window had a better chance of stirring than
these two poor fellows. Victory allowed Raed to be somewhat
charitable in his assessment of them now. For the one who still
had a face, he even bent and closed the dead eyes. The Pretender
muttered a prayer to the little gods, though he had no way of
knowing if they had been believers.

Now he had to find Aulis. Just as the whole building had come
apart, he'd caught a glimpse of her making a run for the rear
exit, and this was indeed where Raed found her. A buttress had
given way, flinging rocks down on the Prior just before she would
have reached the relative safety of the door. However, there was
still life in the old girl. She might have been pinned beneath the
rocks, undoubtedly dying, but her bone-white fingers were reaching out for the shredded Gauntlets that lay tantalizingly close.

Raed was taking no chances; he kicked the remains of the
cursed things out of the way and crouched down next to the dying
woman. The pain had to be significant, yet her eyes were clear
and full of rage when they locked on him. "Traitor," she spat,
blood giving extra emphasis to her spittle.

He'd seen this sort of final vigor from many dying men, but
he didn't know how to treat a dying Deacon. Her fine red robes
were torn and a silver disc around her neck glowed in a way that
froze Raed's blood. He knew that he had found the foci Sorcha
had mentioned. Quickly, as if it burned, he jerked it off Aulis'
neck and threw it away into the rubble.

The fading Prior grinned at him crookedly. Raed might have called Sorcha or Merrick over, but something about her stare stopped him in his tracks.

"Traitor to the Emperor?" His laugh was short. "I am no more his—"

That grin was turning his skin to ice. "Not the Emperor, fool—to that great gift you carry."

A thundercloud of a frown crossed his forehead. "You have no idea what you speak of—if you had any idea what it is like—"

Looming death had obviously devoured her manners, because Aulis cut him off again. "But I do . . . I do have an idea." Her smile flickered beatific for a moment, as if she could see something he could not. Raed nervously glanced behind him as he realized that she was looking through him. He felt a sudden, strong urge to pick up a rock and finish her off then and there. Anyone who worshipped the Rossin had to be both mad and dangerous.

She stretched out one arm, bent and twisted as it was, toward him. "The pocket prince sent you, and our lord supplied the rest." Scarlet boiled up from between her stretched lips. Her last words were, "So close . . ."

Raed crouched still for a moment, processing what she'd said. She may be mad, but he knew truth when he'd seen it in her smile. No further confirmation was needed—Felstaad had deliberately sent him here. But the Pretender doubted very much that the Prince had been able to predict that Raed would pay a visit to his court. No Diviner had been known for four generations. A far more likely scenario was an informant in his own crew—that idea was one he hated to contemplate.

"By the Blood." He pushed his hand through his hair and stared down at the dead Prior. "Another complication I don't need."

"We seem to have found nothing but complications." Sorcha was standing above the newly minted corpse, her Gauntlets twinkling with green light. "Perhaps we can still wring some answers out of this traitorous bitch." She gestured, and a very pale-looking Merrick came to stand at her shoulder under the moonlight.

Raed was silent but his skin prickled. The mythical Deacon Bond was obviously working hard, because the glance the two of them shared was loaded with significance.

"She's dead." The Pretender rose to his feet, feeling a wave of exhaustion pass through him. "The only answers she will be giving are to the gods."

Merrick shook his head. "No . . . Not yet, she won't." His tone was flat and colder than this winter night. "If we use necromatic cantrips and I use Kebenar to its fullest extent . . ."

"Necromancy?" Raed's stomach churned and he glanced at Sorcha with a concerned frown.

She brushed away his concern. "We are trained. We are not some peasants foolishly playing with what they cannot understand."

Raed glanced at her partner, expecting his support, but Merrick shook his head sharply. "We must find out what they are planning. This is only the beginning of the skein."

"Move," Sorcha barked, "before the shade escapes." A wan light was flickering over Aulis' remains. Sorcha snorted as if something amused her, and green fire leapt to life on her fingertips. Drawing a pattern over the corpse, she seemed satisfied.

"Now," Sorcha said, her voice ripe with delight, "you shall answer our questions, Aulis."

Raed had heard of such rituals, but had never witnessed one. Necromancy, the ungifted called it, and despite all his study and reading, the Pretender had to agree with them; it went against the natural order.

Merrick slipped the leather Strop over his eyes and the dark symbols writhed like poked snakes; the effect was both entrancing and disturbing. The younger Deacon inhaled, drawing a great deep breath that seemed to go on forever. The weakened shade wavered, struggled, but could not resist; it was drawn into the Deacon. Most sane people wouldn't have taken a shade into their body willingly, yet Merrick had the demeanor of confidence that made Raed more curious than worried for his safety. Certainly there was a beautiful irony in the lad sucking down the shade of the person who had meant to kill him.

The twisting symbols on the surface of the leather flared blue-white for a second, and then the light flared again, but this time behind the Strop as if something was looking out on the world. Raed was glad that Merrick did not remove the Strop—he had a sinking suspicion that if he did, Aulis would be looking back.

It was disconcerting enough when Merrick spoke in her voice. For a good minute the only thing the recently departed woman was capable of saying was, "Fool, fool, fool . . ." Though whether this was directed at herself or any of them was hard to tell.

Eventually she ran out of steam, and Merrick's voice took control. "Name the creature you were trying to summon." His tone was amazingly commanding and Raed was strangely sure that if the young man asked him a question in that tone, he would automatically answer it. This lad had untapped depths.

Sorcha moved to stand at her partner's back and rested her hand lightly on his shoulder. Her expression was concerned rather than grim.

"Can't." Aulis' voice was pleading and desperate in a way none of them had ever heard it in life. Obviously death had robbed her of some of her confidence.

"Name it!" Merrick's voice cracked like a whip.

"Don't know. We didn't know. We only took instruction."

Behind the Strop, blue-white light flickered fitfully as if blown by a distant wind, and Merrick's body tightened; apparently he was holding Aulis' shade together by sheer willpower. "Who gave you instruction, then?"

Now his shoulders twitched and swayed, his top half trying to escape the spot his feet were rooted to. However, Aulis couldn't get away. Raed almost felt sorry for her . . . almost.

"The Unending Knot." The words were torn from Merrick's throat like a curse.

Sorcha glanced at Raed blankly, but he only shrugged—the name meant nothing to him either.

"Let me go, let me go," Aulis' voice wheezed through the young Deacon's throat.

Yet now it was Sorcha's turn to ask a question, and she made it a good one. "Why did the Emperor tell Hastler to only send two Deacons?" She cleared her throat, looking down at her boots for a moment as she wrestled command of her next words. "Is he part of this?"

Merrick's body heaved with the dry, wracking sobs of an old woman—a truly strange sight. It was even worse when they became a laugh that didn't seem to stop.

"Can't hold her much longer," the young Deacon gasped, pressing his hands over the top of the Strop. The gesture struck Raed as a curiously childlike one. "Answer. Answer or I will swallow you."

Raed had never heard of such a thing, but it seemed to have the required effect.

"No," Aulis howled.

"One answer and you can go. The right answer!"

A deadly grin spread on Merrick's face, a grin that Raed had only just seen on Aulis. The effect was chilling. "You should ask the Grand Duchess Zofiya that question."

Sorcha jerked back as if hit.

The laughter went on, and the final words were gasped out in terrible dead delight. "You think you've won the war? Foolish Deacons—this is just a skirmish. The war will make you wish to be back here . . . with me."

A long gurgling gasp, a strangled choke from Merrick, and he coughed the smallest hint of white mist back into the air; a slight breeze rose suddenly and dispersed it. Raed didn't want to know if the spirit was gone to the Otherside or destroyed. That was Deacon business.

Merrick wiped a thin bead of sweat from his forehead. The lad still looked shaky and Raed would have offered the Deacon a shoulder, but he knew fragile pride when he saw it in another man. Instead he gave him a little nod of respect.

"That is what I hate about damn shades." Sorcha kicked a rock out of her path with ill-concealed rage. "Always with the cryptic answers! What does the Grand Duchess have to do with any of this?"

"I think we can help with that." Nynnia appeared in the shattered doorway, her father tight under one arm. For such a slight girl she looked like she was holding up much of Kyrix's weight. The old man had bruises on his face and held his arms half-curled around his belly. Raed recognized the signs of someone who had received a good beating—he'd seen enough of his crew return from shore leave in similar condition.

The expression on Sorcha's face was priceless; she had no time for the girl and wasn't afraid to let it show. Maybe she hadn't wished Nynnia dead under the rubble, but undoubtedly she'd hoped the other had run off. Yet when Raed looked into the woman's deep brown eyes, he saw nothing like fear. Her mouth was as determinedly set as Sorcha's.

Merrick darted over to Nynnia and kissed her on the cheek, forgoing her lips in deference to her father's presence. "Where'd you go?" he asked, lightly touching her hair. "The Hall came down, and—"

Her voice was so soft that Raed strained to hear her answer. "I had to find my father. I'm sorry."

"It was incredible," Merrick said, glancing back over his shoulder to where his partner was still glaring at them. "I don't know what happened. I mean, I should be dead—"

"We should all be dead." Kyrix brushed blood out of the corner of his mouth and looked through dark eyes at them. "For months I knew something was wrong with Prior Aulis."

"Well, we've taken care of that," Sorcha snapped. "Merrick here stopped whatever that mad old bat was trying to do. Your daughter would have seen that if she—"

"You are the type of arrogant Deacon that allowed Aulis to prosper." The old man's words cut through even the stalwart Sorcha. He raised a trembling hand and patted his daughter's arm. "You were lucky that Nynnia was here to save your partner."

Sorcha blinked, her forehead darkening, a dangerous storm drawing in. Raed hoped that the old codger was going to explain himself very quickly.

"It was you?" Merrick was the first to realize, and then he smiled; a broad grin that flashed as bright as his partner's was dark. "You saved me!"

"A healer, just like her father." Kyrix straightened with a little wince, though pride beamed from his bruised face.

Raed had seen few miracles in his life, and Nynnia had no weirstone. He could not imagine how the girl had accomplished the feat. "I didn't think anyone who had lost that much blood could still be walking around." He glanced at Sorcha and caught the tail end of her own furrowed brow.

The girl glanced away. "I did only what I had to. The important thing is that Father heard more of their plans."

"And they are much, much wider than this." Kyrix waved his hands weakly. "This . . . Well, I am afraid this is just the beginning."

Raed glanced down at the broken form of the former Prior. "Why can't anything just be simple in my life?" Realizing that everyone was staring at him, he let out a sigh. "Do go on."

"Come here." The old man pulled out a sheaf of papers from inside his cloak. "I found Aulis burning these, and I managed to snatch them from the flames—but one of her minions took exception to my actions." He gestured to his battered face, almost apologetically.

"You shouldn't have done such a thing." Nynnia bit her lip.

"Nonsense, child." Kyrix looked at her sternly. He spread the

largest piece of paper out on a fallen column. It was a map showing the countryside immediately around Vermillion.

"In six other locations, six other Priories, the same has happened." Nynnia's father pointed. "Seven pairs of Deacons were
meant to die tonight, but you did not go quietly." He bent over
and picked up the foci Raed had kicked aside. When he turned
it over in his hand, six scorched marks could be seen around the
edge of the silver disc.

"Durnis," Raed heard Sorcha whisper, and saw her face twist
in something that could have been anger or despair.

"The Emperor would not let such a thing happen!" Merrick
was quick to leap to the defense of his sovereign.

Raed noticed, however, that Sorcha was not. She chewed
on the corner of one full lip and stared down at the Gauntlets
tucked at her waist. "Presbyter Rictun hands out assignments,
Merrick—but it was not he who gave us this one. The dispatch
box was from the Emperor himself."

Despite what that meant for the Empire, Raed felt a warm
glow in the pit of his stomach. At last, Kaleva had shown his
true colors. Consorting with creatures from the Otherside was
not likely to be forgiven by the common folk.

Her partner must have felt some of her doubt across the Bond
because he spun around. "Not the Emperor—he's a great man,
Sorcha. Think of all the good he has done!"

"Then why . . ." Sorcha cleared her throat and looked up at
him with steel in her eyes. "Why did he instruct the Arch Abbot
to send us here alone, Merrick, when he could have sent a Conclave? Can you answer that?"

Merrick pressed a hand into his hair as if his head were going
to explode, and Raed's sympathy forced him to throw him a life-
line. "Let's not jump to conclusions without any evidence." By
the Bones, defending the Emperor felt very wrong.

Sorcha drummed her fingertips against her thigh. "Indeed. We
will need to consult with the Arch Abbot—find some answers if
we can, like what part the Emperor's sister has to play in all of
this."

Nynnia raised her chin and looked the Deacon squarely in the
eye—an impressive feat as far as Raed was concerned. Sorcha's
expression was brittle and dangerous, yet the smaller woman
spoke with conviction. Raed again found himself wondering at
this change in the girl.

"Royal blood is good for many things." Nynnia's voice was flinty.

Her words stopped the conversation dead.

"Damned and Holy Bones." Sorcha turned her back on them and looked up to the newly revealed night sky.

Royal blood is good for many things. Those words. Raed had heard them before, years ago. The wreck of a deposed Abbot had whispered them to him in that room he'd wanted so desperately to get out of. The smell of stale old man and musty clothes flooded his nostrils, mixed with the scent of his young boy's fear.

Raed shook his head to clear the memory and realized that Merrick was looking at him. The muttering in his head was still there. That was it; he'd been injured and many things had been shaken loose.

"There is one thing more." Kyrix pulled out another piece of paper. This one was a mere scrap, the fire had consumed nearly all of it, but just legible was one word: "Murashev."

It was the younger Deacon who let out a gasp. "A geistlord . . . Sorcha, they are planning to release a geistlord."

Sorcha's fists clenched at her sides before she turned back to them. "No—not a geistlord, Merrick. *The* Geistlord."

All of them stared at one another, and even Raed knew what they meant. The Murashev was the boogeyman under every child's bed: the mythical creature that lived in the depths of the Otherside, feeding on not just the souls of the living but on other geists as well.

"They wrote 'first.'" Merrick was the first to speak. "But there are other meanings to it—it can also mean 'family.' They wrote it in Ancient above me, soaked it into me. The Murashev cannot just come into our world; he needs other geistlords to bring him."

"Well, you stopped one here." Raed let out a breath he'd been unconsciously holding in. "So we don't need to . . ."

Kyrix let out a sound that was more a wheeze than a real breath. "They did not need all seven geistlords."

Nynnia squeezed his shoulder when he faltered. "If they had all seven, it would have been easier for them to bring through the Murashev, but there are other ways."

Merrick and Sorcha exchanged another glance. One look at their pale faces told Raed all he needed to know, but he asked anyway. "What 'other ways'?"

The younger Deacon licked his lips nervously before replying. "Many, many deaths."

"I overheard her." Kyrix swayed where he stood, near the end of his waning endurance. "She spoke of a grand event in three days—in Vermillion itself."

"We can't get back to the city in three days, and the Priory weirstones are burnt out, so we can't alert anyone." Merrick was looking at Sorcha with all the intensity of a young boy looking to his older sister for guidance.

"Even if the ice broke with sunrise, I couldn't get *Dominion* near Vermillion in so short a time." Somewhere along the way, Raed discovered he had given up caring about his Curse and the geists that might bring it on. If the Murashev became real, those things would matter very little. The last words of the decrepit deposed Abbot still echoed in his head—his last ones before he tried to best the Rossin inside him: *You're their tool, foolish boy. The geists will use you like a lever to open the way.* He hadn't known what those words had meant back then, though they had frightened him a great deal all his life. But now he realized that the Prior had wanted him for more than his connections to royalty.

"There is another way," Sorcha was looking at him, the bleak expression fading from her like a sea mist. The Pretender did not know if he liked it at all, and when she spoke, it was confirmed. He didn't.

"The Imperial Dirigible depot is four miles from here." The Deacon beamed. "We fly back to Vermillion."

"You can't be serious?" Raed couldn't help a little laugh escape him. "You want me to load not only my crew, but myself, onto an Imperial dirigible and fly with you to Vermillion?"

"No." She raised one eyebrow. "Not all your crew. Bring Aachon and five people you can trust."

Raed glanced at Merrick, but the younger man was going to offer no support. He was talking in a low voice to Nynnia, effectively leaving his partner and the Pretender to sort it out for themselves.

"In case you hadn't forgotten," Raed said, shooting a raised eyebrow right back at her, "I am a wanted man—and not just by the ladies of the Imperial Court."

She gave a short laugh, but her expression remained set. "This cult—or whatever they are—want you for some reason." She smiled slowly. "To keep you safe, we need to keep an eye on you."

"You'll be able to do that admirably as they take me up to the gallows," Raed muttered. He stroked his narrow beard for a second and glanced at her speculatively. "Are you sure this isn't just an attempt to take the bounty yourself?"

"At times like this, I wonder about your education." She sighed. "Whatever are they teaching at Pretender school these days? Have you not heard of the concept of sanctuary?"

A tremor of fear ran through his belly. "You plan on holing me up inside the Abbey?"

He watched as she slipped on one Gauntlet. She whispered, presumably for his benefit, "Seym." When he took a step backward, she held it up. The rune was colorless but the air around her fingers moved as if with heat. "The rune of flesh, and I promise this won't hurt."

He'd already trusted her with everything he had, so when she placed her index finger against his forehead, Raed managed not to flinch. It was, in fact, cool on his skin, like a touch of an ocean breeze. A clean, sharp scent filled his nostrils. The rune of flesh. It made him think about what that word meant. A memory of all he'd seen last night up on the hilltop made him twitch, abruptly aware of how close the Deacon was to him.

"There." She stripped off her Gauntlet, and he wasn't sure if he imagined it, but her look was somewhat proprietary. "You are now officially held under the Sanctuary of the Order—not even the Emperor can break the seal without risk of losing the Arch Abbey's support."

Raed frowned at her particular choice of words. "So I am effectively your property?"

Sorcha looked smug, like a cat that had finally caught a pesky mouse. "Basically . . . yes."

It was most definitely the *wrong* thing to say, and she had to have known it; when his jaw tightened enough to nearly break a tooth, she responded with a grin. For a moment the Pretender considered doing something foolish just to see that look wiped from her face. He was surprised when he felt her hand take his. Its warmth and strength was a shock, even more so when she gave his fingers a light squeeze. He wondered if she was resorting to using her feminine wiles on him, until she looked into the utter honesty of her blue eyes. "Until we find out why they want you, Raed, it is imperative we stick together. The sea is no longer safe for you."

He looked down at her hand in his, and for a moment neither of them pulled back. His heart was beating fast, and this time it had nothing to do with the Rossin or the swordplay. Out of the corner of one eye, Raed glimpsed Merrick striding over to them, a sudden cold bucket of reality on their quiet moment. Their hands fell away from each other.

Raed could wait for the geist-driven ice to melt away, take *Dominion* out of Ulrich harbor and sail away, but really, there was nowhere to hide. All of his life had been spent facing up to uncomfortable realities; and besides, this realm was still his by right. He wanted to protect and serve it, even if his father did not. "I've been running all my life, Sorcha—I shouldn't trust anyone, and yet I have already given my life into your hands twice this week."

Sorcha's lips twitched upward in a beautiful and cruel smile. "I'm just that sort of woman, my lord Pretender."

→ SEVENTEEN ←

Creature of the Air

The Imperial Dirigible outpost was unimpressive next to the large transports themselves. Two long cigar shapes twice the length of the building, with large boat-shaped quarters hanging beneath them, were tethered by thick cables into the rocks of the headland. They were both painted with the Emperor's device, a green fist holding a skein of ribbons. A sharp wind had come up from the sea and they shifted like hunting dogs impatient to be let off the leash.

Shedryi tossed his mane, gave a whinny and then a little buck that Sorcha had to pull in quickly. He might be of the Breed, but horses were never overly fond of looming shapes that seemed to defy the laws of nature.

"Having a little trouble there?" Raed kicked his borrowed mount up next to hers with skilled ease.

She made a face at him and replied shortly, "You're riding a nag. The Breed are somewhat more of a challenge."

"Excuses, excuses," he chided, then rose in his stirrups and called back to his men and Aachon. "Who wants to be last there?"

With a whoop of delight, the pirates galloped past. After being cooped up in a ship for years, undoubtedly there was a certain freedom in it—yet Sorcha couldn't help but feel a little put upon. Shedryi clenched underneath her, upset that she wasn't letting him have his head and show the inferior horses his heels. But there was certain decorum a Deacon had to maintain, and

Merrick was taking the rear with Nynnia and her father. It would look bad if Sorcha took off chasing the scruffy pirates.

The mare Melochi must have felt it too, for she was chomping at the bit as Merrick held her to a trot. Their two tag-along guests were mounted on the shaggy ponies and were going as fast as they could.

Kyrix was pale, but remarkably his bruises were already fading. His daughter too seemed to have undergone a change. She'd followed them and actually watched as the Deacons performed the exorcisms on the affected children. It was relatively easy, but it was not a sight for those with a weak constitution. She hadn't objected to them cleansing the girls, but neither did she allow them any but minimal time to prepare themselves. Raed had only a short moment to choose his men and give orders to those who were to remain in Ulrich with the ship.

Sorcha had observed that while the Pretender seemed to trust the Deacons, he had still instructed the remaining crew to careen *Dominion*—just in case it was needed.

She nursed the thought that they'd be lucky if any of them survived. Raed might have heard of the Murashev like all children had, but he had not read the thick tomes held in the Arch Abbey's library. Her novice thesis, the requirement before gaining her Gauntlets, had been on this very thing: the dark threat that lurked in the farthest reaches of the Otherside.

It was not the numbing wind that made her shudder.

When they reached the dirigible base, she had another situation to deal with. A handful of shouting pirates descending on an Imperial outpost had caused some issues with the local guard. Sorcha kicked Shedryi into the gallop he'd been so desperate for.

The garrison commander, the type of seasoned old battler that the Emperor favored, was standing behind a rank of his troops—probably his *only* rank of troops. And yes indeed, as she neared, she could see that there were rifles raised.

At the sight of a Deacon among these reprobates, the commander called out, "Identify yourself!"

Sorcha heard the beat of Melochi's hooves behind her and felt the reassuring warmth of Merrick's presence at her back. "Deacon Sorcha Faris and Deacon Merrick Chambers," she called, kneeing Shedryi up so that she was between the soldiers and the sailors. The troopers were unlikely to fire upon a member of the Order, unless things had gone very wrong here too.

They might not have recognized Merrick's name, but at hers a flash of relief crossed the old commander's face. He told his men to stand down and strode across to them, with only the barest of limps discernable. After they had dismounted, he took Sorcha's hand in a warm shake. "Commander Boras Llyrich," he said gruffly. "Apologies, Sister, but there has been some trouble from the town these last weeks."

Sorcha's lips quirked in a bitter smile. "No need to explain; we have come from there. Your caution is completely understandable."

After shaking Merrick's hand in turn, Llyrich studied the leader of those he had just considered assailants. His gray brows drew together and Sorcha knew immediately that there could be trouble; this didn't look like a man who forgot to read dispatches when they came.

She flicked her hands and the cantrip of concealment blazed in white light on the foreheads of the pirates. It was not a rune, so would not last more than one night—but at least it would get them away from here. The rest would just have to look after itself.

Llyrich shook his head, shot her a glance and then snapped off a salute. "What can the Imperial Legion do for you, Deacon Faris?"

"We need to get to Vermillion immediately." She gestured to the dirigibles. "One of these will be adequate. I trust an hour should be enough to get ready."

The commander's jaw tightened, his white beard fluttering in the wind against his dark blue uniform, but this was a man well used to taking orders, and the Deacons had carte blanche with any and all Imperial assets. "Captain Revele is the best we have. She commands *Summer Hawk*."

"Then pray tell her she has a new course."

Llyrich answered with another salute and hurried off to inform the Captain and crew that they would have to abandon their breakfasts.

Sorcha had flown several times with the Imperial Air Fleet, but it would be everyone else's first time. She looked forward to their expressions once they took off. They boarded with brisk military efficiency. The Breed horses, their eyes covered, were loaded into the large hold of the dirigible, while troopers had been assigned to return the borrowed horses to their owners.

Captain Revele appeared from the depot, buttoning her flight jacket and hurrying over. She looked a smart woman, young and probably overly confident as most air captains were, but the gleam of real intelligence was in her green eyes, and she actually smiled at Sorcha as if she recognized her. The Deacon could be sure that they had never met.

"Captain Vyra Revele." She snapped to attention before the assembled pirates, Deacons and various hangers-on. Even though it was necessary for a member of the Imperial forces to salute one of the Order, Sorcha appreciated the genuine nature of the gesture. "Pleased to meet you, Captain. This is my partner, Deacon Merrick Chambers." She didn't bother to introduce the rest and hopefully the Captain wouldn't ask.

Thankfully the Abbey had a reputation for mystery. "Well"—Revele cleared her throat and led her way toward her vessel—"*Summer Hawk* is at your disposal, Deacon. We've been tied up here for a week after a trip from the Usul Mountains, and the crew have been itching to get moving. We were scheduled for reconnaissance farther north, but south works just as well."

Summer Hawk was new, as were all of the fleet, but she had the sleek look of a seagoing frigate. Sorcha caught Raed skimming his eye professionally along the keel as if she were just that. The usual complement was twenty crew, and Imperial marines in the order of a further eighty.

Sorcha liked the looks of both the ship and the Captain. She gave the latter a nod. "We will need you to run on a bare minimum of crew and marines. Speed is of the utmost essence. We have to get to Vermillion within three days."

Revele's frown was present, but not deep. A run to the capital was not fraught with much danger. "I'll make arrangements." She stepped aside. "If you'd like to board now."

They walked up the gangplank laid out for passengers; horses and landlubbers needed special attention. Raed looked confident right up until the moment he set foot on the deck of the *Hawk*. He'd probably been expecting it to be the same as a ship, but though a dirigible might share a similar shape, it was a different beast. He glanced over the side and muttered something that sounded like, "How safe is this damn thing," as the rest of his crewmates climbed aboard just as gingerly.

"Having a little trouble?" Sorcha asked sweetly, knowing her lips were giving the game away.

"Laugh all you want," he shot back, "but this thing is a travesty of a vessel."

The air Captain shot Sorcha a wide grin. "Many people say that before we cast off—amazing how quickly they change their mind."

Raed looked skeptical and Sorcha found she felt a little sorry for him. Although these past weeks had been tough on her, she couldn't imagine how it was for him. One moment a captain of his own ship, albeit with a curse hanging over his head, the next at the center of a geistlord conspiracy of unknown dimensions.

Revele was perceptive. "Well, I'll get one of my men to show you to your cabins. With a reduced crew, you should all travel comfortably."

After seeing his men settled, Raed asked to see the operation of the ship, and Sorcha tagged along just to watch his face. A small cabin boy called Hoise showed them around, even taking them down the length of the dirigible to where the propulsion system was housed.

"Weirstones." Raed let out a little laugh. "Priceless! You lecture us on the use of them—and yet here the Imperial Fleet is powered by them!"

"There is a difference." Sorcha patted the swirling blue sphere. The orb was smooth and cool under her hand. "These have been constructed by the Arch Abbey for this purpose. They can only be used by trained engineers, and they only provide propulsion."

As if on cue, a gust caught the ship and bounced it around, even though they were still tethered. Raed grabbed onto her— half instinctually, but half for comic effect as well, she suspected. The touch of his hand on her body sent her blood racing, and Sorcha didn't move it away.

Raed smelled of leather and sea salt, as if the ocean had invaded every piece of his being, and underlying it was a faint sweet smell, almost like honeysuckle. Unwittingly Sorcha drew in a breath, though her heart was definitely running faster than usual. The Bond she'd created was now a web for her, for she could feel his heart racing too, like a counterpoint to her own.

The Pretender did not move, but he smiled; his teeth flashed white against his suntanned face. On her arm, his fingers tightened slightly.

"The Captain asked me to show you to your cabin." The young lad, Hoise, appeared around the edge of the weirstone array, and Raed let go of Sorcha and stepped back a little. "I think that would be an excellent idea."

"It has been"—Sorcha cleared her throat, knowing that she was, of all things, blushing—"a long few days." She couldn't believe the warmth in her cheeks. What was she—eighteen again?

Hoise glanced between them as if suddenly catching wind of a current. "Well, we will be casting off very shortly. The cabins are back here."

Raed gave a little bow and gestured for her to follow after the boy. Sorcha was glad to do so, sure that he could tell the effect his closeness was having on her. Stupid.

The rest of their companions were exhausted and had retreated to their own cabins to rest. Only Merrick remained, leaning against the side. Sorcha thought he looked like he'd aged several years in two weeks. That was normal for those fresh out of the novices, but Sorcha found she was sorry for the strain in her partner's face.

Wordlessly, all three of them waited at the gunwales as the *Summer Hawk* crew scrambled to cast off. She might have seen it all before, but it still was impressive. Once the ropes were cast off, the dirigible rose upward like a child's balloon—a balloon that could carry more than a hundred troops. The only sounds were from the crew and the creaking of the hull. The weirstone power system was silent and Sorcha had to admit that it was eerie.

Raed and Merrick watched the ground recede from under the hull. Not many got a chance to fly in the Emperor's fleet, and many would not want to.

"Everything's so small," Merrick said as they climbed higher. The line of hills and the sea spread out before them.

"There's Ulrich." Raed's discomfort appeared to have given way to awe as he pointed to the cluster of gray and brown. He whipped out his little spyglass and trained it on the town. "And I can see *Dominion*. Amazing!"

Merrick yawned. "Yes, absolutely. But I feel like a horse ran over me."

"There's no need for you to stay up." Sorcha could feel his exhaustion leaking through to her. She wasn't as tired as all that, so the sooner he got rest, the better for her.

He glanced across and smiled slightly, knowing exactly what she meant. "Very well." He turned away, stopped, and Sorcha could feel him opening his Center. It was just for a moment, like a dog raising its nose to sniff the breeze. She caught the faintest impression of a laugh as he entered his cabin and shut the door. Very strange. But then, it had been a long few days for her partner.

She shook her head, aware of her own growing heat. Raed was looking at her now, and in a totally different way. Along the Bond there was no escaping the knowledge of what he was thinking, and she was perfectly aware that he was unconsciously tasting her own thoughts. She had not mentioned the Bond, she would not mention the Bond, and yet it was wrapping them both up in desire; like a snake eating its tail.

"A handful of people against the greatest monster of legend." Raed stroked his beard and looked at her askance. "This could end very badly."

Her hands, where they rested on the edge of the railing, were trembling slightly. She looked down at them and wondered when that had happened last. She was the strong Deacon, the most powerful Active in the Abbey. She certainly didn't feel strong or powerful right now.

"We should rest." The Pretender's voice was loaded with meaning in those few words. He held out his hand to her, and without thinking she took it.

Inside, the cabin smelled of well-oiled wood. A wide bed, perhaps the Captain's own, dominated the center of the room. She noticed it was strung on chains, so that the swaying of the wind would rock it rather than tilt it. Raed touched the corner of her cheek, the lightest of caresses, but in her chest her heart began to race.

"Deacon Sorcha Faris," he whispered, and her name on his lips sounded incredibly erotic. "I want you so."

Those eyes, which she had noted could be green one minute and blue the next, held hers steady—honest in their desire. He had spread his cards on the table and his look said the decision was hers. At this point Sorcha might have expected to at least hesitate, to remember who she was, and her marriage; but it had been so long since she had felt this rush of desire and emotion. Too long.

She couldn't pause to consider. She had to experience what she had glimpsed. He mustn't have been expecting her to, though, because in the half darkness she saw his eyes widen a little in shock. She meant only to taste his lips, to sample a slice of forbidden fruit, but when they kissed, everything changed.

It was no simple kiss, not the soft, gentle kind Sorcha had

become used to; this was teeth and tongue and gasps. This was a kiss that was felt everywhere. And soon, merely to kiss was not enough; skin needed to be against skin. Raed slid his hand under her tunic, grasping her breast and sending jolts of desire down her spine. Sorcha should have pulled away, but instead she arched her back, inviting him to take more. He bent, and his teeth tightened on her nipple. She cried out—a gasp of pleasure and pain. Then she was pulling her tunic off, while his mouth traced every curve of her body he could reach.

Sorcha helped him with his shirt, tugging it apart and then reaching for his pants. She had thought she wanted Raed, but now it was a need, a requirement. When they were finally naked she let out a long, satisfied sigh. His body felt like warm satin on hers. Consumed by pleasure, Sorcha slid herself up and down against him, relishing the sensation. Raed groaned, and then laughed a little. "I never guessed Deacons were quite like this. If I'd known, I might have risked a visit to the Abbey."

Sorcha felt a satisfied grin on her face. Years with Kolya had almost made her forget her own power, her own sexuality. It was heady stuff to be naked with someone who appreciated it. So she took the compliment and pressed her lips back to his. Raed's hands slid over her body gently at first, and then suddenly pulled her tight against him.

Frantic for more, they staggered back together onto the swaying bed. With surprise, Sorcha realized she was shaking. She couldn't recall her body ever reacting like this before. It was like she didn't even know it, as it obeyed more primal instincts. Raed curled his hands around her hair, trapping her against him. His strength was intoxicating, and for once Sorcha did not feel the need to fight another's power. Instead she bent under it, giving way with a satisfied sigh.

Sliding her hands down Raed's back, reveling in the texture of his skin and the faintest beginnings of sweat between them, Sorcha knew that she was being wanton. Yet even this realization was curiously satisfying. She groaned deeply as his tongue ran the length of her neck.

He didn't deny either of their needs. They rolled slightly on the bed, as the airship thrummed around them, climbing higher. Sorcha giggled, quite undone by desire and awareness of her own mad folly. Pressing her down against the bed, his lips never leaving her, Raed thrust himself inside the gasping Deacon Sorcha Faris.

The sensation was so intense that all of her remaining control dropped away. "Raed." Her voice came out as a half moan as she dug her fingers into his back. Sorcha's thighs locked around him tightly when he moved in her, while every other muscle clenched to draw him closer. Pleasure fanned through her body from the places where they joined, until that was all there was.

They ate up hours with each other. Laughing in the between moments at their own passionate madness, drowning in the sensation. Sorcha let herself be carried away, for once forgetting the control that had been taught to her and enjoying their moments together. Finally they lay against each other, sweat drying on their bodies and drowsy exhaustion lying over them like a blanket. Even though Sorcha had thought herself a fit person, her body ached pleasantly in places she didn't know it could. She made a mental count of them; tongue, thighs and back cried out.

And also unexpected. Sorcha took what felt like her first real breath in hours. Raed rolled over and kissed the damp spot at the base of her neck. "You, Mistress Deacon, are quite the minx, and quite the surprise."

"As are you." She trailed her fingers over the outline of his lip and brushed against his teeth; those teeth that always flashed in that smile that had caused this whole thing. Even now she wanted to be kissing him, bruised and battered as she might be.

They stared at each other a moment, smiling in disregard of the storms that loomed ahead. His voice broke through the silence they shared, and he surprised her yet again.

"And if I said I am falling under your spell, Mistress Deacon, would that get you to leap from this bed and run back to your Abbey?"

He was smiling, but behind his eyes, green in the candlelight, was something serious. Slowly she shook her head. "No—strangely, no." It was the truth.

Raed kissed her lightly and pulled back. "I should not seek out more complications in my life, but you are a delightful one." His honesty once again completely disarmed her. Used to dealing with men in a controlled void, where emotion and circumstance were never really discussed, she had no experience to fall back on. She floundered a bit in this new environment.

Sorcha had to rely, for the first time, on her own feelings. With a lazy smile and a sigh, she replied, "I certainly thought all this behind me—that makes you dangerous, Captain Rossin."

His hazel eyes widened but the glint of teeth in his smile made her deepest core twitch. "It is the situation that is dangerous, and frighteningly good."

"Frighteningly good," she whispered back in agreement. "But I love it when reality exceeds expectation—that rarely happens."

She'd laughed, before, at people who told her, "I couldn't keep my hands off him," but now at the receiving end, she understood. Raed was a need that was impossible to deny. She felt overcome with sex and pleasure. The experience could prove dangerously addictive. Stroking Raed's dirty blond hair, she tried to file away the sensation of it; surely this much pleasure couldn't last. The realization was bittersweet.

His eyes narrowed on her and she feared what was coming. "And your husband, Sorcha—what of him?"

So this was not to be more than sex, then—not for him. The Deacon sighed, her gaze dropping to Raed's chest. "I don't suppose you can imagine how it is to be in a dead marriage? How it is to realize you made a huge mistake?"

Raed's breathing slowed, but she wouldn't yet meet his eyes. "Is it really that bad?"

"If it was good, you and I would not be in this cabin." Sorcha said it lightly, hoping he knew she wasn't sorry. It was the truth, though, and for some reason she wanted to tell him the truth.

Raed tipped her chin up to meet his eyes. "I'm sorry, Sorcha."

The Deacon frowned. "He shut me out of everything: our love life, our friendship—even our work." The hollow pit inside her, the one she had been ignoring for so long, was opening up at her feet. "I married him because I loved him, and then I watched him slip away from me."

By the Bones, she had not wanted to talk about this with him, but it also felt good to finally confide in someone. Yet Sorcha was also fully aware they did not have much time until they reached Vermillion—and there her problems would be waiting for her.

"Don't let's talk about Kolya . . . please." She reached out for him to drive away those moments yet to come.

Raed smiled slightly, the kind of melancholy smile that she knew was on her own lips. He let his fingers trail down her hip, and despite her exhaustion Sorcha was shocked to feel her body stir to life. She should be hungry—she hadn't eaten since breakfast—but her body still wanted only him. Certainly, there couldn't be many more moments left to them.

"So, Sorcha," Raed whispered, "have you finished with your interrogation of this dangerous fugitive?" His tone was husky and teasing, as if he knew what he'd awoken in her. His fingertips traced patterns on her skin, writing his name or trailing cantrips she didn't know. If only there were a rune to make time stop outside the cabin. If only she could order the Captain to circle the City of Vermillion instead of landing.

Now should be the time for guilt, but that was not the emotion that filled her. Instead, it was something Sorcha had experienced before, in the face of a geist—exhilaration. She stroked his thick hair before curling her fist tightly in it. "Fortunately, for both of us . . . no. I haven't."

He laughed as she pulled him back to her mouth; for now, there were still moments left to them. They would enjoy every one.

EIGHTEEN

Epiphany at the Scarlet City

Sorcha and Raed had barely left their cabin for two days. Everyone was uncomfortably aware of this, but none more so than Merrick.

He'd heard the rumors of his partner's marriage, the whispers that it was now nothing more than a convenience, but in their short time together he had not been able to get the details. Now, however, he was getting much more than he had ever wanted to.

"Are you all right, Merrick?" Nynnia squeezed his arm.

The ripples of pleasure along the Bond were doing very uncomfortable things to his anatomy, especially with the young woman at his side standing so very close. Merrick tugged his cloak tighter about him as quickly as he could. "Yes. Yes, fine. It's just cold."

She turned and looked out over the rolling clouds and bright blue sky. "It is a little cold, I suppose, but the view makes up for it."

Merrick gritted his teeth as spasms of reflected delight ran down his spine. Whatever the young Pretender was doing, he was doing it very well. Knowing these things about another man was awkward, and it was something that had not been covered in any novice class he could remember.

He should have been thinking about the task ahead: what they were going to say to the Arch Abbot, how exactly they were going to find the Grand Duchess—anything at all but the physical pleasures his partner was indulging in. However, the only thoughts Merrick could muster were along a similar vein. The curve of Nynnia's soft neck, the swell of her breasts beneath her bodice, the long, tapered length of her fingers, the . . .

He swayed sideways and smacked his knee into the wood of the halyards; it was not entirely accidental.

"Merrick." Nynnia clutched him to her, completely negating any advantages from the momentary pain.

He wanted to turn and kiss her—certainly he had already, but he knew if he felt her soft lips beneath his, there would be no going back. He wasn't about to satiate desires based on Sorcha's—that felt wrong, and a disservice to Nynnia.

Merrick jerked away as Kyrix hobbled toward them. The old man was slowly recovering from the beating he'd received at the hands of the Prior, but his eyes were still weary.

He nodded to the Deacon, but clasped Nynnia's hand in his own. His fingers on hers were white and almost shaking. "Daughter, I would speak to you." His gaze darted almost resentfully to Merrick. "Alone."

"Father, I—"

"Please, Nynnia."

The woman straightened, kissed the back of his hand and allowed herself to be led forward beyond the range of everyday ears. The expression on Kyrix's face tempted Merrick to strain his trained senses further, but he heard the snap of boots on the wood behind him.

Captain Revele was striding along the gangway toward him. With Sorcha occupied, the officer turned to Merrick for instruction—not that there had been much required. The young fleet officer's short dark hair ruffled in the winds that drove her ship, and her lips were slightly pursed. Beautiful, full lips that—

Merrick cursed the Bond, and tried once again to concentrate on his throbbing knee. "Captain," he managed to mutter, "is there a problem?"

"No, not at all," Revele tucked her hands behind her back. "In fact, we are drawing up on Vermillion."

"Two days?" Merrick glanced over the edge of the dirigible. "Very impressive."

"*Summer Hawk* is one of the fastest in the fleet, and we have encountered fortunate wind . . ." Her voice trailed off

"Is there a problem, Captain?" Merrick pushed his hair out of his eyes with one hand.

"Well"—Revele glanced down at her boots—"I was wondering which dock you wanted us to make for—there are several in Vermillion we can choose." She leveled a knowing look at Merrick. "Depending on how . . . obvious you want to make your arrival."

Most captains of the fleet were not known for their tact, yet Revele had obviously recognized Raed as the Young Pretender. She was as subtle as possible, but was letting Merrick know that she knew.

The Deacon cleared his throat, wishing that Sorcha were standing at his side. She might not be diplomatic, but she had a certain commanding presence. "Our mission is . . . sensitive." He smiled a little at this choice of words. "So the less obvious, the better. In fact, if you could possibly—"

"Make an excuse for diverting from Flight Central?" Revele asked him directly. She tapped her finger on the top button of her uniform. "*Summer Hawk* is due for a ballast refit. It wouldn't be a lie, and it doesn't directly affect my orders."

"The Order would appreciate your tact." Merrick leaned forward, adding in a conspiratorial whisper, "And if you could talk to your crew as well."

The Captain let out a long sigh and looked at him through narrowed eyes. "My crew know how to keep secrets, but you won't have very long, even if I do all these things. The outpost commanders submit their logs at the end of the month, a few days from now. Once they reach Vermillion, the General will be informed of your"—she shot a glance in the direction of the cabins—"traveling companions."

The old commander at Ulrich had undoubtedly recognized Raed, and that could make things very tricky. The Emperor would be very interested to know that the Pretender to his throne was in Vermillion. If what Sorcha said was true, then the man that they had all put their trust in was corrupt beyond any understanding. Merrick's fists clenched unconsciously at his sides as he contemplated what that would mean for the Empire.

Revele was watching the clouds, sensing a change in wind; perhaps like the namesake of her ship. "We'll land at the Imperial Air Fleet repair facilities, then—not many troops or officers about. They're not likely to want to get their hands dirty."

"We understand, Captain. Thank you for all you have done for us." He gave a little bow, the most a Deacon was permitted to give to any not of the Order. "Now I must go and inform my partner that we are nearly at our destination."

A tight knot was growing in his belly, even as he watched Nynnia kiss her father on the cheek and walk back toward him, alone. When they'd set off for the dirigible depot, she had insisted on coming along with them, and no one—not even Sorcha—had been able to deny her. Taking her hand in his, Merrick pressed it. She was wearing gloves against the cold, and he would have loved to feel her skin; flesh-to-flesh contact was always best.

Flesh. A warmth began to spread from the base of his spine, fanning out through nerve endings that weren't his own.

"Merrick," Nynnia asked softly, "are you quite all right?"

He was more than all right, more than any normal person could possibly understand. He nodded shortly, not willing to risk opening his mouth, just in case a groan came out instead of anything sensible.

"Well," she began, pulling him further in the direction of the cabins, "we should go immediately and let Deacon Faris know we're about to land. Father told me we are close." Seeing her expression, Merrick wondered if that was the only thing her father had told her, but he refused to pry.

Nynnia was quite possibly the only one who did *not* know how his partner had been spending the last few days. Merrick stayed her hand, contemplating the reflected waves of enjoyment racing along the Bond. He cleared his throat. "In a minute. I think we should wait just a few minutes."

Raed heard the knock on the door, lifted his head with a sigh and glanced across at Sorcha. The Deacon, out of her armor and cloak—in fact, completely naked—looked incredibly beautiful and uncharacteristically vulnerable. She was curled in the bed, bronze curls in a tangled mass against her white back, still glistening with a sheen of sweat. Her lips, even asleep, were curved in a faintly satisfied smile. An artist could not have painted a better picture of a woman relaxed and satiated. She did not look like a woman who could challenge geists and dare the Otherside, yet it gave him a curious thrill to know that was exactly what she was capable of.

His thoughts ran to the past two days—the most enjoyable of his life. Even a Pretender had a chance at a throne, and there had been plenty of nobles who had thrown their daughters at him—at least, before the onset of the Curse. As a young man, he had enjoyed his fill of them. He could find no memory, however, to match the Deacon. The situation was filled with complications, and yet he had no regrets—save that she could not be his. But that was the truth of it.

The knock came again, more insistent this time. Snapping away from the tinge of melancholy that had snuck up on him, he slid out of the bed. Wrapping the sheet around his waist, he walked to the door, twisting his neck slightly to alleviate a crick.

Merrick was standing there, knuckles raised, deciding whether to give another knock. The two men stared at each other for a second, caught in an embarrassing moment that would have made a good story at any inn. However, it was the young Deacon who blushed, a deep, deep red. Surely the young pup wasn't a prude. "What is it, Merrick?" Raed grinned.

The Deacon looked up at him but his eyes refused to meet the Pretender's. "We've got lucky, caught some good winds, and the Captain says we should be descending to Vermillion in about an hour or so."

Raed's stomach contracted as if they had just dropped from the sky. He cleared his throat. "Thank you . . . We'll . . . I'll . . ." He stopped. "Meet you by the helm?"

Closing the door, he heard Sorcha stirring, and when he turned around he saw the same disappointment on her face that he could feel upon his. Her blue eyes, which had only recently been clouded with pleasure, were now as sharp as beams of light. He could begin to see the Deacon take hold in her once more.

She scrambled out of the swaying bed and smiled widely at him. Even as tired as he was, Raed still wanted her, and if Merrick and his ill news had not intruded, they would have spent another day in each other's arms.

Sorcha did not move to cover her nakedness, as if to do so was to spell the end. She crossed to him and embraced him with a little sigh. He hugged her tight, stooping slightly to press as much of her against himself as possible. He didn't know what to say to her. Neither of them wanted to step outside and face the real world; a world where he was a fugitive and she was a married Deacon of the Order, but there was no other choice.

It was the Deacon who spoke first. "Thank you," she whispered into his ear.

They dressed in silence. Raed shared a pitcher of water and a cloth with her, taking the opportunity to memorize the planes and curves of her body while he still could. There was no tension—just sadness. Then he held the door open and let her go out first. Raed wanted to say something, but he knew she was not the type of woman to take comfort in empty promises.

Merrick was not outside, but the slender form of Nynnia was waiting on the promenade, lightly holding on to one of the guy ropes. She turned, and it was as if a different creature was looking out at them. Raed was suddenly constricted with tension. He'd seen such expressions on assassins' faces more than once. His mind flashed with how little they knew about this woman. She'd charmed Merrick and wound Sorcha up so tightly that she was effectively blinded. Deep down, the Beast stirred slightly, recognizing something about her.

"I believe Merrick is waiting for you in the helm. I must attend to my father." She turned on her heel and stalked off. The farther she got away from them, Raed noticed, the more her walk altered from an aggressive stride to the gentle scamper he had observed in her previously. It was as if she was adjusting a mask back into place.

Sorcha must have noticed something as well. "Do you really think we can trust her?" she asked. "These last two weeks have been so beyond my training, I wonder if my judgment is impaired."

Raed considered the question. The Beast was not waking within him. Whatever lurked behind Nynnia's sweet face was not a geist—powerful yes, but not one of their kind. "She did save Merrick's life." It was a platitude; he had plenty of experience to tell him that preserving a life was not always done out of love or concern.

Sorcha appeared not to detect his lie, perhaps too deep in her own concerns. Stroking his fingertips, she nodded. "I hope so. We have enough troubles ahead without adding to them." He knew she was not just referring to the Murashev. They walked together to the tiny command deck. It seemed ridiculous, but Raed felt a little of his queasiness return. Sorcha might have managed to distract him from it for a good few days, but standing in the exposed cabin brought back his nervousness. Most especially because the vast spread of the City of Vermillion was laid out before them like an intricate map. The buffeting didn't help either.

Two chairs outfitted the tiny cabin, and Merrick was standing behind the Captain's, bracing himself against an abrupt onslaught of wind that shifted and shook the airship. The young man was actually grinning. "We've hit a bit of—what did you call it, Captain?"

"Turbulence and crosswinds," Revele replied distractedly as she worked the levers set in a gleaming wooden console before her. With the other hand, she held the small wheel as easily as if it were a child's toy and not the only means of direction for a vast, fragile vessel.

"Turbulence." Merrick laughed. "Isn't that just like your swells in the ocean, Raed?"

"No," he grumbled. "It is absolutely nothing like it." His insides were still churning from the unnatural motion of this vessel—but he was not about to tell anyone that. He'd already suffered enough ribbing about that particular issue.

Revele let out a muffled snort, spinning the wheel about and turning the nose of the ship into the wind. It was an enviable maneuver; the weirstone propulsion system allowed the dirigible to navigate against the vagaries of the weather. For a moment Raed forgot his own tumbling stomach, his sea captain's mind wondering if the same methods could be provided for proper ships. As soon as he had the thought, he realized that the Emperor must have considered the possibility. Who knew what projects the nimble mind of his pursuer was having constructed in his naval bases. The idea of a fleet of Imperial ships powered with the speed and maneuverability of a dirigible made him shudder.

"You all right?" Sorcha touched the back of his hand, murmuring her concern under her breath.

He looked down at the center of Vermillion. The city was laid out in a star formation, with all the spokes of the main street draining into the Civic Center and eventually the palace, while a crosshatch of side streets filled out the spaces between. "This is the city where my father was born; now the city of my enemy. How should I be feeling?"

"Concerned?" she ventured.

He squeezed her fingertips and laughed. "Exhilarated. I plan on seeing the sights." Both of the Deacons looked at him in horror, and he laughed. "Oh, well, if you think it is a bad plan . . ."

"There's the repair facility." Revele pointed out the window to the right. Unlike the majority of the Imperial forces, the air fleet was not housed in the neat lines of streets that made up the center. Instead, the fleet and the combustible gases needed for the dirigibles were housed on the outskirts of the great city.

Raed might never have been to Vermillion, but that did not mean he was unfamiliar with it. When his father had decided he would never seek to reclaim his throne, all the attention of his advisors had fallen on the Young Pretender. Raed knew every curve of the city by heart; the town houses of the nobility, the public fountains, the marketplaces, every statue on every corner and the history to go with them all. He was, however, not so familiar with the Edge.

The area that had not been built on top of the shallow lagoon, but instead on the soft marshes of the mainland, was called the Edge. It had been so named after one particularly jocular ancestor of Raed's had referred to it as "the edge of humanity." It was also much larger than the center, and was separated from it by a circle of canals.

Now, looking over it in the gathering evening, he realized his training wouldn't help him there. The streets were narrow, some disappearing almost completely under the eaves of houses from up here, and they meandered around on themselves. City planning had long ago given up on the Edge.

As they dropped lower, following the edge of the lagoon, he gestured out to an area that was not covered with houses. Certainly there were signs of rebuilding, but it looked as if fire had swept through the area.

He was just about to ask, when Revele cut him off. "That," she said grimly, "was our depot up until three months ago."

"A geist attack?" he asked.

The look his fellow captain shot him over her shoulder matched her tone. "No—an explosion in the gas refilling station. These dirigibles are like your ships . . . not without their risk."

By the size of the devastation, the Emperor's fleet must have suffered considerable losses. It was in his mind to make a quip about sea vessels at least not exploding—but it seemed in far too poor taste. He had wondered why he had not seen Sorcha lighting her cigars for the last few days. It had not just been his sweet attentions, then.

The new repair facility was not built far from the scene of the previous one, but space in this ancient city was obviously at a premium. The lowering sun bounced off the shapes of several dirigibles tied up in the facility, and to Raed they looked very menacing. He suddenly wanted to get off this floating exploding death trap, and he was very glad that he hadn't known of this danger when he'd set foot on it. It would have considerably dampened his ardor for Sorcha. And yet, he shot her a wicked look. *Maybe not.*

"You have to come in slow, so the watchtowers have enough time to alert the ground crew," Revele explained. "We're lucky there seem to be several moorings."

She yanked on a cord hanging beneath her console, and somewhere a bell began to ring. Leaning out, curious despite it all, he watched her crew scurry to drop the ropes from the gunwales. *Summer Hawk* began to slow, the kind of gliding entry into port that any sea captain would have been proud to achieve. Below, more men could be seen pouring out of the huge buildings.

"What are they?" Raed asked. "Those are the biggest buildings I've ever seen."

"Hangars for the dirigible repair," Merrick replied, before the busy air Captain could. "One of the Emperor's greatest achievements."

Raed bit his lip on the comment that surged forward. *Summer Hawk* was gradually pulled downward; a combination of the Captain venting some of the dangerous gas, and the ground crew cranking the ship closer with their winches.

"Captain." Sorcha stood stiffly at the portal, not meeting anyone's gaze. "If I can trouble you to keep the Breed horses in your hold for as long as you are able, and then return them to the Mother Abbey?"

Merrick wasn't fooled. His partner had risked her life to save Shedryi and Melochi, and the tautness of her back said this request cost her more than she would admit.

"Certainly." Revele snapped a salute, which might not have been necessary at this point. They circled lower in stiff silence.

When they were only a few minutes from the ground, Captain Revele pointed to a locker in the rear of the cabin.

"There are uniform coat jackets in there. If you get your people into them, you should blend in with my crew. They are usually quick to head for the attractions of Vermillion after I have dismissed them. After that, you are on your own."

Raed grinned at her. "That's just the way we like it."

NINETEEN

The Price of Redemption

It was one thing to return home covertly—it was another altogether to find yourself already a fugitive.

Merrick held the poster up so that she couldn't avoid it seeing it. His eyes were wide in utter disbelief. "Rogue? Sorcha, what in the Bones have we done?"

Understandable. Certainly, it had to be a shock to be declared a rogue Deacon only two weeks out of the novitiate. He had a right to be upset. She wasn't feeling that good about it either.

Taking the poster in her hand, she stared at her own features on it with a deep sense of unreality. Both her face and that of her partner were on it, and the headline above screamed, WANTED. Beneath was an account of their "crimes" in Ulrich, which included the slaughter of a peaceful Priory and the summoning of geists to torment the population.

She hastily screwed up the poster and threw it into the shadows. "Obviously we missed one traitor back there, and one weirstone. Once we explain to the Arch Abbot, it will be fine."

"We better move quickly." Raed touched her shoulder, making Sorcha jump. "We can't rely on Captain Revele not to report us once she sees that."

Merrick's distress was flooding across the Bond. "The posters are everywhere," he muttered. "Come daybreak, we'll be in real trouble."

"Come, now." Raed glanced at Aachon, while trying to ignore

his dark look. "We've all been fugitives for years and managed just fine."

If only there were time to stop for a cigar in a corner, time to stop and consider how this was all going to fall. Instead, Sorcha had only moments. "You think the Empire has really been trying hard to find you?" She smiled slightly.

"I'm the Young Pretender," he replied, tucking his thumbs into his belt. "I have a sizable sum on my head."

"If they really wanted you dead, you would be dead." The slight droop of his expression might have been amusing in a less dangerous situation. "But a rogue Deacon—let alone two? Now, those get people's attention."

Aachon made an unconscious growl in his chest. He knew well enough that was true.

"They will send out a Conclave to hunt us," Merrick whispered, as if he couldn't quite bring himself to voice it fully.

The Young Pretender could not have any idea what that meant. Even for him, there had never been a Conclave formed—it was something only Deacons gone mad warranted.

"I say we go straight to the top while we can." Sorcha felt strength flood into her, despite the situation. This was what a partnership was supposed to be. She remembered it from before Kolya. Trust, belief and a well of power. She'd missed that. "Once we have explained ourselves, finding the Grand Duchess will be much easier."

"My prince!" Aachon shouldered himself between the Pretender and Sorcha, as if by physicality he could sever the power he thought she had over him. "I gave my word to your father that I would protect you; going to the Mother Abbey is neither sane nor safe. I cannot allow it."

Raed's hazel eyes never left Sorcha's face. "We are in Vermillion, my friend—nothing is safe. The time for caution is past—we must needs be daring."

Aachon folded his arms and glared at the Pretender without a word. Sorcha wondered how difficult it would be to tie the big man up and leave him in a corner somewhere. Tough, was the conclusion she came to.

"What has running got me, old friend?" Raed said, gesturing around him. "This is my first time in Vermillion—the city that should have been mine. I have been running for years. It is time for something new."

Sorcha guessed his protective first mate would blame her. Two days locked in their cabin; everyone knew about it. They would think she was some witch who had thrown a spell around their captain. If only they knew that the opposite was much closer to the truth.

That was the Young Pretender's gift; she'd seen it before but never really appreciated it until this moment. Many tried to manipulate others with lies or pretty stories—Raed, however, offered up the truth so completely that it took people by surprise. An honest man in a dishonest world could be a very powerful thing.

While Raed presented his argument to Aachon, Sorcha contemplated the real problem: how to get inside the Mother Abbey. Phasing and using Voishem would have been her first choice if it had been any other building—but like all Order structures it was well protected against such powers. It would not be easy to use other methods either. Even in winter, with many Deacons settled into outlying Abbeys, there would still be more than a hundred staying within the confines of the complex. Not all of them were of Merrick's rank, of course, but they would still be Sensitive enough to spot two rogue Deacons clambering over the wall.

Sorcha was slightly distracted by Nynnia whispering to her father. Kyrix had made a miraculous recovery. A prickle in the back of the Deacon's mind was disturbed by that, but if the two of them were using weirstones or some other proscribed magic, Sorcha did not have the time to investigate it.

Nynnia moved over to Sorcha's side. "My father and I will wait here while you attempt this madness."

The Deacon felt a heat kindle in her stomach. "Just what I was about to say. We wouldn't want you to get in the way." She arched her eyebrow as a warning that she was prepared to say so much more.

The young woman glared back. "Indeed. If you do not return, we will need to take on the Murashev instead."

Merrick reached across and squeezed her hand. "We will be fine. It won't come to that."

It was quite impressive, really, how completely Nynnia had enamored the young man. That was the problem with the novitiate; too many young people coming out of it with no real world experience.

She glanced at Raed for a second. Whatever they had was

different. The level of physical passion was unexpected but not
dangerous—what gave her pause were the gentler feelings that
she dared not examine right now. The Pretender whispered to
Aachon, instructing him to stay with Nynnia. The first mate,
whose dark eyes bored into Sorcha's, nodded as if completely
compliant, but she wasn't fooled. Like Kolya, he was the type to
give way and then flow back like water.

The Pretender came over to their little huddle. "Aachon has
agreed to take the crew—and you and your father, Nynnia—to
a bolt-hole he knows here in Vermillion. A little pub in Dyer's
Lane called the Red Flag. But if we're not back by morning, I
can't guarantee what he will do."

"It won't matter." Merrick took a deep breath and turned in
that subconscious way that all Deacons had, in the direction of
the Mother Abbey. "Trying to enter the Abbey as outlaws—if
we're not back by morning, we're dead anyway."

Sorcha let out a little laugh. "Entering the Abbey as rogues,
indeed. Dead might be the best we can hope for."

Across the Bond she felt Merrick's surge of interest. He was
fingering his Strop and looking at her with something better than
fear and excitement. The boy had an idea, and by the look of
it . . . it wasn't going to be the type she'd enjoy. He hugged Nynnia tight, even dropping a kiss on her lips.

Sorcha grimaced, but said nothing. It was strange for her to
feel such dislike and have it tinged with the overflow of his emotions. It was enough to give a person a stomach complaint.

Still, once the little band had left them on the street corner,
she was impressed with her partner's ability to snap back to the
matter at hand. When it was just the three of them, she was much
more comfortable.

"So, you have an idea, Merrick," Sorcha whispered. "Some
brilliant plan to break into our own damn Abbey—full of Sensitives who will pick us up the moment we set foot in it?"

"You're really not going to like it at all. I thought of it, and
I don't like it."

Once he had explained it, she knew that he was, in fact, under-
estimating how little she would like it. Even Raed turned pale at
what Merrick suggested. "I . . . I can't do that, Sorcha."

Her partner coughed a little and withdrew around the corner.
She touched the Pretender's face, running her thumb along his lip
line. He kissed her fingertips, and the sensation ran down deep

inside her. Beautiful man, even in this dire moment, she couldn't help reacting to him. "You gave your life into my hands, Raed—now I am giving you mine. I trust you too, you know."

The Pretender pulled her in close and kissed her. "I won't let you down," he whispered against her lips.

It was he who found them the donkey and the cart in a quiet knackers' yard, and liberated the poor creature. The Abbey was in the final deepest curl of the city; only a mile from the gates to the castle, yet a small town to itself. It had no defenses like the Emperor's residence. It needed none. However, there was still a lay clergy guard. Raed pulled up his hood, smeared mud on his face and hid his saber in the hay on the back of the small cart.

Sorcha and Merrick, meanwhile, prepared themselves. Taking her Gauntlets from her belt, she shoved them inside her shirt and buckled the belt tight around them. Her partner, however, held his Strop in one hand. Light was already flickering in the deeply etched runes.

She knew what he was thinking; not just because her thoughts ran across a similar vein, but because his were actually echoing in her own. *I'm afraid. By the Bones.*

Her own throat was tight. The white walls that surrounded the Abbey had once been protective, but now they seemed so very similar to those that she had been forced to breach at the Priory. Everyone within had to be considered an enemy, at least until she and Merrick could explain themselves to Hastler.

"Do we really need to do this, Sorcha?" Raed whispered. She understood what remained unsaid. *Do you really need me to do this to you?*

A knot of tension cramped her neck while her stomach clenched like it had been punched. "Yes . . . When the Conclave begins hunting us, there will be no other choice. We need to see the Arch Abbot—he is the only one with enough influence to sort this mess out." She looked up into his hazel eyes and let her admission out. "And I need you to help me." The word "need" was not one she was familiar with.

Raed nodded but his voice was rough. "By the Blood, this feels very, very wrong."

"This whole thing has been wrong." She kissed the palm of his hand. "Except for you."

Merrick coughed. "We better get this done, before I lose my nerve altogether."

"Of course." Sorcha nodded and scrambled up into the back of the cart among the straw. Merrick took his place next to her, looking young, vulnerable and frightened—yet he was more than that.

Sorcha looked him full in the face, not letting a single ounce of fear or doubt reflect in hers. "I'm not just trusting Raed, you know."

"But I have only read about this," he said quietly, looking at the Strop resting in his hands. "I can't be sure—"

"Yes, you can be."

The Bond sang, determination ringing along it from each of them, amplifying and building like an infinity knot. This was the pinnacle of partnership, the type of strength that she had never felt with Kolya. Merrick trusted in her more completely in two weeks than her husband had done in all their years. With a little smile, Sorcha lay back in the straw.

Merrick put on the Strop, tying it around his eyes quickly and summoning up the Rune of Sight. Through the Bond, the world grew more beautiful than she could have ever imagined; the circling wheel of stars directly over Sorcha's head flared like a thousand multicolored fireworks. The silent street filled with a siren sound of distant bells that at this hour certainly couldn't be real. The scent, honeysuckle and jasmine, flooded every portion of her brain. It was also the last thing she was aware of.

Merrick claimed his power, and pulled them into the Otherside.

Raed felt the racing of his own heart as the Deacons' stopped. Merrick had dropped inelegantly, but Sorcha—as she did with everything—had taken control; choosing how she lay, hands resting lightly against her thighs with her head tilted slightly upward toward the sky. Her face was soft and had a gentle smile on it as if she'd fallen asleep in his arms. The Strop over her partner's eyes had gone dark. Raed took it off gingerly and tucked it into his own pouch, pushing the young man's eyelids shut. Merrick looked even younger than he had a right to be—almost a child. Raed draped Sorcha's cloak over the two of them. It was easier to pretend there was something else in the cart that way.

He let a ragged breath escape him. "How very odd—now I get to collect someone else's bounty."

As he led the donkey toward the gates of the Mother Abbey, he felt like he was in some weird nightmare; striding toward the institution that not only supported his enemy but housed the husband of his lover. These were two things that should have had him racing in the opposite direction. However, considering he was the living one right now, it would have been worse than rude to walk away.

The guardsman shook himself awake at the sound of hooves approaching. "Who goes there?" The man might be a lay Brother, but he was large enough to have been a bare-fisted boxer and he carried a polearm long enough to skewer twenty Pretenders. The Mother Abbey, despite all her otherworldly protection, still maintained a front of physical dominance as well. A quick glance upward showed that there were plenty more where this one came from. He glimpsed another group of guards patrolling the walls. With the number of Sensitives living within the walls of the complex, it seemed like overkill. Except—the Pretender felt his throat constrict—the guard striding toward him was wearing a green cloak. He was a Sensitive.

The Rossin was buried very deep now; so deep that even Raed could not feel him. As long as the Young Pretender did nothing foolish to arouse the guard's suspicion and inspire him to look a little closer with a Rune of Sight—this might actually work.

Raed took a breath, summoned up his very best Southern accent and held aloft another of those dreaded posters. "You the one with the reward?"

The guardsman's brow furrowed. "Not personally, but yes, the Mother Abbey is looking for the two rogue—"

"Then look no damn further." Raed flung back the dark blue cloak to reveal the still shapes beneath.

When the guardsman swore, the Pretender was reminded of Sorcha's comments about the Order's lack of real decorum. It was a good thing that the situation was so serious or he might have laughed; watching the hefty soldier look down at the two cooling forms, he felt anything but jovial.

"Both of them!" The guard's mouth twisted in an impressed knot. "How'd you manage that?"

"The old favorite." He shrugged. "Poison. I have an inn on the road south and when I saw the reward"—he sniffed loudly—"I saw a chance to get in before anyone else."

The guardsman laughed. "Good idea—the reward was posted

only this morning, and there's already been plenty rushing to offer 'information.' Still, this could be the quickest bounty in the Order's history." He moved to take hold of the donkey's bridle. "I'll just get this to the Presbyter of—"

Raed's chest tightened and he lurched forward. "Now, hold on, there! I ain't letting those two out of my sight . . . at least not until I have my palm crossed with some honest gold."

The guardsman glared at him. "Are you saying you can't trust me, friend?" His voice was laced with nothing like friendliness.

There were times to be affable and there were times to hold firm; this was one of those latter times. Raed had a decent grasp of the character he was meant to be playing—and this man would not let another take his bounty from him . . . not for that amount of coin particularly. "Trust is one thing, 'friend,' but when gold is involved I wouldn't even trust my own brother."

He held the sharp gaze of the guardsman, as if they were two dogs sizing up just how full of teeth the other was. Finally, it was the guardsman who gave way. With a snort he threw the cloak back on the dead bodies. "Very well." He waved into the Abbey. "Follow the path until you see the three-story white building with a red roof, on the right. That's the Presbyter of the Actives' building; there'll be a guard outside who'll get the right person to hand out the reward."

Raed led the donkey away, feeling his heart thundering in his head like a rapid drumbeat, and walked deeper into enemy territory. He followed the path as directed until he was out of sight of the guard tower. He had only a little time; there was every chance some insomniac Deacon would blunder into him, and then—well, then he guessed he would end up on the cart right next to the other two.

Carefully, praying that the donkey wouldn't remember its natural heritage and bray or kick up a fuss, Raed turned left to a smaller building than the one he'd been instructed to. In the half-light it was impossible to tell if it was the *right* building on the left, but Sorcha had given him instructions and there had to be a way in. He just hoped that she'd been right about the Sensitives at the gate being the lower-ranked ones, directing their lesser powers only at those entering the complex.

He also hoped she was right about this small building being occupied by only one other. Leaving the cart, he opened the door cautiously; but he needn't have. The old man sitting by the fireplace was looking right at him, with not the faintest hint of surprise. He unfolded his tall form awkwardly from the chair and smiled. "Ah, the Young Pretender. You're late—now, where did you leave Little Red?"

Raed blinked. Deacons always put him at a disadvantage, but this one had literally rocked him back on his heels. "You"—he cleared his throat—"you were expecting me?"

The man, who Sorcha had told him was called Garil, had gray eyes and the sort of face that radiated charm like a favorite uncle or grandfather. The Pretender had known neither of these, but despite all that, he found himself smiling back. "Lucky for you, she is dead, or you'd be in real trouble."

"Dead, you say?" Garil cocked his head. "Not dead . . . just gone over. Still, a perilous thing to do." He waved Raed back to the door. "Well, bring them in quickly. The longer they are there, the less likely they are to come back."

Raed ducked outside and carried first Sorcha, and then Merrick, laying them side by side in front of the fire. The soft light reflected on their still faces. Garil gently touched her cheek. "Good, there is still warmth in them. Give me his Strop."

The Pretender fished it from his pocket and handed it carefully over to the Deacon. Even dark, the thing made his skin crawl, so he was only too happy to relinquish it.

"If you don't mind me asking," Raed said as Garil sat once more in the chair, with some difficulty, "how long have you known Sorcha?"

The old man's head whipped up and he fixed the Pretender with a steely gaze. "Sorcha, now, is it?" His thick eyebrows shot up. "I have known *Sorcha* ever since she was a child—when her family first brought her to the Order."

These were the details Raed craved to have. She might have lain in his arms, but she had spoken so little of herself. It might have been their combined breathlessness or it could have been that she didn't want to say. "How—"

"Quiet now," Garil snapped. "Sorry to be abrupt, young man, but if I don't have silence, then there won't be a Sorcha to be curious about."

Raed could feel a chill descending into the room and realized that whatever the elderly Deacon was doing, it had already begun. "Is there anything I can do?"

"Hold her down." Garil was now withdrawing his own Strop.

"The return is never easy, but particularly hard for the Actives. She is physically stronger than she looks."

Raed crouched down over Sorcha, trapping her legs under his, while leaning over to pinion her arms. They were cold, and he found this strangely sexual position very uncomfortable given the situation. The old Deacon seemed to be taking no notice, however. He was busy laying his Strop on top of Merrick's with some care, matching the edges so that there was no overlap.

"Never thought I would be doing this again," he muttered under his breath as if to himself. "Here's hoping there's enough strength in these old senses to do the job."

With a sigh he placed both Strops over his eyes and secured them behind his head. The hairs on the back of Raed's head began to tremble, while the rolling sensation in the pit of his stomach made him regret eating. Otherside power made the air wintry, and the flames in the fireplace spluttered and died low as if there was not enough fuel around them. Raed's short, sharp gasps of breath were actually coming out white, even though he was only feet from the wavering fire.

Garil's hands tightened on the arms of his chair convulsively, and his head, burdened with two Strops, flicked backward to connect sharply with the chair's back. The runes in the topmost leather sparked with blue fire, tracing the shape of the rune— though which one it was, the Pretender could not have said.

The cold was now a scent as well, harsh in his nostrils, as on the morning of a new snowfall, and every breath stung. Then, beneath his hands, Raed felt Sorcha's body move. It felt nothing at all like the feeling of her body under him early today. It felt . . . inhuman. Her body rippled as if something was stirring. It elicited no desire in Raed—in fact, he wanted to leap up and flee the room. But when he looked across at Garil, he realized that he had the least of their problems.

Sweat was running down from under the Strops, and the old man's mouth was set in a mask of agony, the like of which even the battle-experienced Pretender had not seen before. Whatever power the Deacon was drawing was taking a lot from him. Merrick moved, but lethargically, as if waking from a relaxing nap. He turned his head and let out a long, soft breath.

Beneath Raed, Sorcha was not so lucky. Abruptly she began jerking violently, almost catching the Pretender unaware. Her back arched and she twisted in his grip like a wild creature. He had to bend all of his strength to her, and give no heed to bruises he might inflict.

"Hold her, tight," the old Deacon by the fire nearly screamed, his fingers turning red where they were buried into the arm of the chair. "By the Bones, hold her tight."

It was like trying to restrain a thrashing snake of the Western Wilds. Sorcha's skin was slick with sweat despite the fact that she was as cold as ice. Raed howled, determined to keep her from harm, leaning down as hard as he could, every muscle in his body straining against hers.

Sorcha's eyes flicked open, and they were no longer blue—they no longer had a color at all. Beyond those pits he could see the Otherside: a sucking maelstrom in which forms could be seen moving; the ultimate end for the spirit, and the most dangerous of realms. This was what Merrick and Sorcha had cast themselves into to avoid detection. That made them either heroes or fools. This close to the realm of its birth, the Rossin within him shifted, uncoiling to sniff the air.

That would have been the ultimate nightmare. "Come back," Raed screamed. "By the Blood—come back, Sorcha."

He didn't know if his voice made any difference, but for a moment all was still. He was looking straight through into the Otherside and it was looking right back at him. Over there were spirits, geists and the geistlords—the ultimate answer to everything he had ever wondered. Raed had never been so frightened in his life, and yet he could not look away.

And then . . . and then the cold blew away and Sorcha's eyes reverted to blue, like a shade being pulled down on an awful scene. He scanned her face, desperate to see if any trace of the geist world remained, but when she smiled he knew it was her—undoubtedly, unequivocally, Deacon Sorcha Faris.

"I'd love to have the time to enjoy this"—she laughed weakly—"but . . ." At her raised eyebrow, he let out a relieved laugh of his own, and got off her. At her side, Merrick was stretching. The look he shot Raed was confused, angry almost—but the Pretender couldn't fathom why he would be deserving of that. He had done his job pretty damn well, as far as he could tell.

"How was it?" Raed asked as he helped Sorcha to her feet.

She looked at him askance. "How did it look?" Her voice was rough, as if she'd been screaming, even though he had heard no noise at all from her.

"Bad."

"Then enough said." Sorcha took Merrick's arm and helped him up. Behind her, Garil was slowly removing the Strops, with the kind of care Raed had only seen a sapper use when handling gunpowder. He handed Merrick back his Strop and let out a long breath.

Then the old Deacon smiled at Sorcha with real warmth, and they hugged tightly. When he pulled away after a lingering hug and looked straight into her eyes, his expression had changed. "Why did you come back, Little Red? Why, when there is only death here for you?" It was hardly the greeting Raed had expected, and the words stung him.

TWENTY

Accepting Kenosis

The memory of the Otherside was fading, even as Sorcha felt warmth return to her fingertips. She had, mercifully, not felt a thing after the initial flash of white. Her throat was raw as though she'd been howling, but whatever pain she'd encountered on the brief trip into the world of the geist, she couldn't remember. As far as she was concerned, if she couldn't remember it, then it didn't matter. For Merrick it would be very, very different.

The Bond sang with his distress. Only his strength had held them back from real death; quivering on the very edge of falling over and into the Otherside. It was the kind of trick that only partners of many years would have usually dared. Sorcha grinned at him with lips that were rough. "You were brilliant, Merrick—just bloody brilliant."

The young man let out a ragged sigh and staggered. Raed took his elbow and led him over to the chair on the left hand side of the fireplace. "Thank you, Sorcha," he managed with a gasp. "Glad you approve. But if Deacon Reeceson had not been able to call us back—"

"But he did." Raed squeezed Merrick's shoulder, his eyes locking with Sorcha's. "He did."

"Enough of this," Garil barked, his voice now sharp with an edge she had seldom heard. "There are far more important things to consider."

Some things were never spoken of in the Order, certain gifts that fell outside the comfortable bounds set by the Mother Abbey. As Sorcha stood, still reeling from her icy trip to the Otherside, she looked into Garil's eyes and saw that he was finally ready to acknowledge his gift.

She'd had hints of Garil's abilities, but had never talked of them with him. Whatever glimpses he got into the future always seemed to frighten him—even if they had been useful in their work.

"What did you see?" she murmured under her breath, though there was no way Merrick and Raed could avoid hearing what she was saying. She caught at her old partner's hand as he sat shaking in the chair by the fire. "Was this what you wanted to talk to me about before?"

She knew her fingers were icy, but his were just as cold. "What did you see on the Otherside, Sorcha?" he asked wearily.

"Nothing." She gave a laugh, even though her stomach was suddenly full of bile.

"What about you, young Deacon?" The piercing gray eyes of the elder swung toward Merrick. "You must have Seen!"

Her partner turned his head away, and the Bond flooded with real fear—not the kind of fear that she might expect from a trained Deacon, one who had proven himself up to any task. It was the fear of a child; unreasoning fear that clawed its way up from the most primitive part of his subconscious.

Sorcha could still remember her own flood of this kind of panic. Just a lonely child left in the care of the Order, she could have been no more than five, and yet the memory was as fresh to her as any other. Pareth, the Presbyter of the Young, a beautiful dark-haired woman who smelled of honey and warmth, was the only person she had ever known as a mother. Early one morning, Sorcha had overheard two novices in the garden talking about the Otherside, death and geists. Though she had been seeing shades all her life, she had never connected them with death before. When she slept that night, the realization had crept up on her— of her own mortality, and that of her caretaker. She'd woken screaming and had rushed to Pareth, seated at a fire much like this one. Sorcha had sobbed into her skirts, begging her to deny the existence of death; deny that one day, both of them would be no more. All Pareth had been able to say was, "Not yet, Sorcha. Not for a long time."

That ultimate realization haunted every living thing. She let her thoughts play out along the Bond, letting Merrick into that terrible memory, reaching out to him.

Slowly, he turned his head and looked at her, his back straightening. "I saw you that time, the time you went to the Castle Starlyche. You fought the five-clawed geist on the stairs."

Now he was opening the Bond to his own memories in return. The image flashed against the back of her eye, a curious double recollection of what he had seen and what she had. He had been the child hiding and observing when he should not. She had been the young novice still hitting her stride, but asked to do the impossible when other older heads were unavailable. It was the nightmare that chased her harder than any other.

Lord Starlyche had been a good man, and she had been unable to save him. Her breath seemed frozen in her chest as she recalled the creature she had glimpsed briefly on the stairs of the castle; a vast five-clawed hand reaching out from the Otherside, awash in a tide of swirling geists like moths clustered around a bright flame. Starlyche had been the foci of the attack, but even so, she could have saved him. Her inexperience had caught up with her, reaching for the wrong rune, just a heartbeat mistake, and the backlash had alerted the creature to her attack. In its fury it had tried to reach her through any means possible, and had killed its physical link in the process. The Lord had died, and not quickly or cleanly.

And her partner that day—he had seen it too. Probably more.

"Garil?" Her voice broke, as if she were once more standing on the stairs, covered in the blood of the man she'd been sent to save. The remembered taste of iron and bile flooded into her mouth.

"It waits." The old man would not meet her gaze, instead staring into the fire, his expression like soft clay. She recognized it too—somehow the old man's talents had extended beyond the strictures of the Order and were now venturing into the future. "It and many like it have been growing in the depths of the Otherside. So alone, and ready to return. They hunger for the light." He turned and looked at all three of them through eyes that burned white. "And they need you. Together."

"The Body." His finger lanced out in her direction.

"The Beast"—toward Raed now.

"The Blood." Merrick flinched as if he'd been struck.

The image of her partner strapped to the draining table

flashed in her memory. Sorcha began to feel sweat on her brow, a sick knot clenching deep in her belly. "Holy Bones!" She clapped a hand to her mouth. "What have I done?" she muttered past her fingers.

Realization was sliding into place, the pieces tumbling into recognizable shapes in her head. The Bond she'd forged with all three of them—she'd thought it had been her idea, a convenience to harness the power of the Rossin.

"Sorcha"—Merrick's face was bone pale—"you gave them what they wanted."

"Would you both have a conversation normal people can follow?" Raed, leaning against the mantel, was not Deacon-trained; he could no more feel the Bond she had woven around him than he could feel moonlight on his skin. She hadn't thought it would matter; Sorcha could dismiss it quickly enough once he no longer needed to fear the Curse. He would never need to know. How many times had she said that to herself?

"Tell him!" Merrick rose to his feet, a deep frown etched on skin that had seldom known such an expression. "By the Bones, Sorcha!" He seldom cursed either.

She struggled. Raed was looking between the Deacons, puzzled but not yet angry—there was still time for that. The Bond was still fresh. It could be undone, and then everything would be all right. Reaching out, she clasped Raed's hand as if in a loving gesture, but at the same time desperately reached for the tendrils of the Bond. It should be easy to dispel a Bond formed only days ago—a simple matter that he wouldn't even feel.

Her power yanked at the strands of empathy and awareness, and Raed fell to the floor howling in agony. Dropping to her knees beside the writhing Pretender, Sorcha knew that there was no chance he was still ignorant, but the Bond—she had to get rid of the Bond or he would never forgive her. She pulled harder at the coil of connection between them.

It was now hurting her. Thousands of little flames burst to life in her muscle and sinew as her body reacted to the power. It was like having barbed wire wrapped around her bones, and *pulling*. Dimly, Sorcha heard Merrick's indrawn breath as it burned him too. But Raed would never understand; he would never . . .

The icy thrust of Merrick's control stopped her like a slap to the face. *Stop it—stop it now! You're ripping us apart!* His voice—his actual voice—thrust into her mind like a knife of steel.

She fell back with a yelp. Sorcha might have thought that was the worst of it, Merrick yelling directly into her mind like a man possessed, but it wasn't. The worst was the look on Raed's face.

It should not have mattered. The look of betrayal in his eyes, hard and glittering like a dread stone, should have made not one iota of difference to a Deacon. She'd used plenty of people before—the Order's work sometimes required toughness. However, this was different. Her breath caught in her dry throat and her hands clenched tight. *Raed, tell me I have not ruined what we have.*

"What we had?" he snapped, giving his head a firm shake and glaring at all of the Deacons with equal vigor. "What have you done to me?"

"It is the Bond," Merrick answered for Sorcha, who could not find the words. "She managed to forge a Bond with you as well as with any Deacon. It should not be possible with a normal person, but you are hardly normal—"

Sorcha fell back on her defenses, and sharply cut in, "You wanted the Rossin controlled. He is controlled."

Raed swore and turned away to glare into the fire. "He may be, for the moment, but if you think he can be used as your weapon, you may find him more wily than you think. I have lived with him inside me . . . I know him better than you."

His voice was full of such contempt, Sorcha had to try to reach him. "You don't understand. They manipulated me to do this," she replied desperately. "I think the whole situation was all about getting you there; the sea monster, the Priory, even the possession of the children."

"Then why did they try and kill us in the tunnel?"

"I think they hoped it would drive me to make the Bond—and they were right."

"But the Rossin could have killed you." Raed looked at her from under drawn brows. "How could they know you would do any such thing?"

Her natural instincts were to hug him, kiss him—but they were long past that point. She stiffened. "They must have studied me." She shook her head. "I don't know how else . . ."

"You have no idea what you are dealing with, Little Red," Garil whispered, "but young Merrick does. He knows, like I do—like all Sensitives do . . ."

This was what Actives whispered about Sensitives. When

Actives went off to learn of their runes, they wondered what the
Sensitives were learning of theirs. While everyone could see
exactly what the ten Active runes were, the Sensitives kept theirs
to themselves, never discussing them—even with their partners.
Most Actives dismissed whatever their partners could do as
merely different versions of their own lesser Sight, but Sorcha
had always been curious about the Strop. It was much more seldom used than the Gauntlets. Unlike her gloves, it was dangerous
for anyone but another Sensitive to touch a Strop while its user
was still alive.

"Do you know why they want us Bonded, Merrick?" she
asked quietly.

His jaw clenched and he looked up at her through his brown
hair, almost feral for an instant. "Yes."

Across the Bond she felt nothing but blankness, as if he had
slammed a door shut on her. She needed a smoke. She needed a
strong drink. What she didn't need was to find this out just when
the Murashev was looming on the horizon.

She wanted to smash something, hurt someone, let some of
this building frustration and upset out. Unfortunately, Garil's
retired quarters were only lightly furnished; she kicked the fire
grate instead, sending burning wood embers scattering along the
length of the fireplace and bouncing logs out of their orderly stack.

"Everything since that damn geist in the mob has been madness." Her mind suddenly knew that too had been planned, to get
Kolya out of the way and make room for Merrick.

"Are you going to finish what you started, or have yourself a
temper tantrum on the floor?" Garil asked mildly. "Merrick is
no more able to tell you these things than you can tell us how to
control the Gauntlets. *He* is not the one who can explain."

"The Arch Abbot," Raed growled. "It's about time we went
and got some bloody answers—and he must have them if any-
body does!"

With a start, Sorcha realized a tremble was growing in her
hands. She had known Hastler all her life, traveled with him from
Delmaire hot with the fervor of her convictions. To all of the
Deacons, he had been a hero, someone ready to lead them to
glory and victory. She recalled him serving her hot tea, the calm
smile on his face—she'd thought it meant he knew something she
did not. She hoped it was not true in the worst sense.

Straightening, she looked at Garil, who was watching her

with hooded eyes. "If you cannot tell us what lies ahead, what is the use of your gift?"

His old eyes watered slightly. "I have often asked myself that question. I can only see pathways, Little Red—possibilities. If you get your answers from the Arch Abbot, then I may be able to point you in a direction. However"—he reached out and grabbed her hand—"I can tell you one thing: I am not the only one with these gifts."

She chewed the inside of her cheek, her lips yearning to be clamped around a cigar. "Come on, then . . . We came here for a reason. Let's go get this whole mess sorted out." The clench of her innards, however, told her she might not like the answers when they finally came.

Merrick watched Sorcha slide on her Gauntlets, and then shot a glance across at Garil. The older man would not meet his eyes. All Sensitives prepared for the day when their final training might be needed—and every one of them hoped never to use it.

Raed wouldn't look at anyone either. The Pretender stood glaring into the fire, his fists clenched on the mantel.

"She meant well," Merrick muttered to the other man. "She meant to protect you from the Rossin."

Raed grinned, but it was a bleak expression with no comfort in it. "Who knows what she was trying to do, Merrick, but now we are all stuck. Not much else we can do but go on."

The three of them did, indeed, have no choice. Garil would tell them no more, though Merrick was sure that the elder Sensitive had Seen paths of both success and devastation ahead of them. He had brought them back from the Otherside, and his part for now had apparently been played as he had Seen.

"So, what is the plan?" Raed asked, his hand curling around the hilt of his saber. "Are we just charging in?"

"Hopefully, just walking," Sorcha replied mildly, though she sang with tension through the Bond. Unlike Merrick, she might not remember the glimpse of the geist realm, but the body and soul did.

"With all these Sensitives around?" the Pretender asked.

Sorcha's lips twitched. "In the history of the Order, no one has ever breached a Mother Abbey. Those few on watch will have their Sight fixed on the walls."

"And the others?"

She raised a finger to her lips. "I strongly suggest silence."

They slipped out into the frosty night air where their cart stood. The donkey was mercifully quiet, his head drooping slightly as he chewed on scruffy lavender that grew against the wall. Avoiding the loud white gravel of the paths, they followed alongside them farther into the complex, toward the Abbey itself.

It had been only a few short weeks since the two Deacons had walked here with all the possession of belonging. Now every tiny noise made Merrick's heart leap. He could, of course, send his Center out, but then their chances of being detected would be even greater. To any Sensitive, another's Center would be a bright beacon, and would be bound to invite investigation in the quiet of night.

Instead, they had to rely on soft footsteps and low breath to get them deeper in. They kept to the shadows of the gardens and worked their way toward the side entrances. Above them towered the shape of the Devotional, the tallest building in Vermillion— not even the magnificent Imperial Palace stood as high and proud. The great spire blocked out sections of the stars like some ancient giant; that which had been so comforting to Merrick now seemed to loom over him like a disapproving parent.

The cool feel of the wall cut like ice against his back as they took their bearings before entering.

"Guards within?" Raed's whisper sounded loud in the still silence.

Sorcha shook her head mutely, unable to meet the Pretender's eyes. They might have been manipulated into this Bond, but Merrick could feel the strength in it. She had woven the Bond with Raed as casually as she had with Merrick, but it was as deep and as powerful as any he had studied. If he concentrated, he could actually feel the Rossin hidden with Raed, like a coiled darkness waiting to be set loose among them.

For a second, the Beast looked back at him, with ancient eyes that surveyed him as if he were an insect. Merrick broke away with a little gasp.

The Pretender, with no trained senses, was already moving toward the door. Merrick had to hurry to catch up with the other two as they lifted the bar and slipped into the Abbey. It was colder inside than outside. Merrick's breath fluttered white in front of his eyes.

Hunched low, they ran up the nave toward the rear of the Devotional, where a series of doors led to the living quarters of the Arch Abbot and the Presbyters. Out of the corner of his eye, Merrick saw something twist like a glimpse of ash blowing through the air, and instinct made him grab hold of both his companions. He yanked hard, since yelling would have only echoed down the stone Devotional like a gunshot.

No one ever expected Sensitives to be physical—but like the Actives they had their own training regime. Geists were supposed to ignore Sensitives, but that didn't mean that humans always would, and geists were not the only threats a Deacon faced. The other two jerked to a halt, and he pressed them down among the pews with a hand on each of their backs.

Something white was indeed floating in the opposite direction from them, only a few feet away. He could barely believe it—there had not been any geists, any shades, in the Abbey, since the first few days after their arrival. And yet there it was; a shade in the deepest sanctuary of the Order. The pale, flickering form lit up a corner of the vast building with a shifting blue-white light, a shimmering flutter to normal eyes. But when Merrick used his Sight, he could make out far more detail. What he Saw took his breath away.

The face, tilted slightly upward toward the rose window, was bone-white and skeletal, so the victim was long dead. But it was the robes it wore—the cloak of a Deacon—that appalled him. He could make out the hint of blue about the clothing, through the Sight, and when it turned, even the glimpse of gold could be made out at the shade's shoulder. It was the mark of an Order, indeed, but a graceful circle encompassed the five bright stars, rather than the fist and eye of the newcomers from Delmaire. The stars were the symbol of the native Order, the one that had destroyed itself nearly seventy years before the Emperor and his Arch Abbot had come across the water.

Raed's eyes widened and Merrick knew why. The Rossin twitched, stirring with that hidden part of the Pretender. The thought of the Beast loose in the Abbey was a nightmare that Merrick couldn't let become real.

The younger man called not on his training, but on his past. He whispered across the Bond, words of comfort and calm—the words of a mother to a restless child; soothing balm to a creature not even human. And they worked. Sorcha might not have known what she was doing when she made that Bond, but there was no doubting the strength of her work.

The geist was so close they could have reached out for it. Merrick's partner, crouched at his side, twisted under his grip. The Active training was kicking in, and she reached for her Gauntlets. Grabbing her hand, Merrick shook his head firmly. *This is not the place.* Words were getting easier to send.

This was the type of Bond that Deacons dreamed of; a true symbiotic partnership, and yet Merrick was scared by the reality of what it could mean. He recalled dark tales of such closeness, taught to Sensitives in those special history lessons no Active was ever allowed to attend. History could well be repeating itself.

He couldn't think of those possibilities now. Merrick flicked his head upward and risked opening his Center. The geist was moving away from them. He found he was squeezing Sorcha's hand tightly—half to keep her from reaching her Gauntlets and half to steady himself. It was strange what a couple of weeks could do. The man terrified of his own partner was long gone. He'd seen enough in the intervening time to give him far more to worry about than Sorcha.

He probed gently toward the geist with as little Sight as he could open. This one had no sign of self-awareness and was merely operating on a single track, probably a repeat of its living habits. It might not belong here, but it was not inherently evil. He gestured his two companions on, toward the Arch Abbot's quarters. They could not dare a cleansing until things were clearer.

The hallways were still deserted, but they had only a few scant hours until novices would be about. Some kinds of training required darkness, and the moments before the sun rose were often the best times for new recruits to glimpse a little of the Otherside, the boundary being at its weakest.

Together, the three of them padded through the corridors to the door. It looked just as it had last time Merrick had been here. He recalled standing nervously outside this very portal, waiting to go in and find out if he had passed the test to be accepted into the Order. However, it had been nothing like the nerves he was feeling at this moment. The pounding in his chest and the sweat on his brow were matched only by the tremble in his hand as he reached out for the door handle.

Inside was the small antechamber where the Arch Abbot's secretary slept. Their entry was quiet, until Sorcha managed to

trip over a small stool in the half-light. And then she swore.
The clattering and the exclamation broke the silence like a rock
dropped into a still pool. Merrick winced, sure that they were
about to be discovered.

All that came from the niche by the window was a gentle
snore. Sorcha straightened as the three of them shared a cautiously hopeful glance. She stepped over the stool and walked
to the sleeping secretary. Merrick joined her. It was easy enough
to see, even without Sight. A silver pattern gleamed on the lay
Brother's forehead.

A cantrip! Merrick couldn't quite believe what he was seeing.
A cantrip used on a Deacon, even a lay one, seemed impossible.

Sorcha shrugged in his direction and he saw a wry smile on
her lips. Cantrips, like many of the lesser magics, were only
barely taught to novices. If they wanted to learn them, it was
generally done in their own time, and yet here was one blatantly
used in the very hallowed halls of the Arch Abbot. Merrick bent
to look it at a little closer. It was indeed the curled spiral of the
cantrip for sleep.

What that could mean, he couldn't say. "Are you ready for
this?" Sorcha's words were flat and void of emotion. He wanted
to say no. He wanted to tell her that this was a mad idea, and
they should turn around and go back. Yet what other choice did
they have? They were hunted, and come morning there would be
nowhere for them to hide. Without the Arch Abbot clearing their
names, they wouldn't stand a chance.

Sorcha read these thoughts in him. He read her thoughts
reading his. For a moment, they were seamless. One creature
reflected in itself. That creature felt its own power. That creature
wanted answers.

TWENTY-ONE

All Is But Mere Flesh

Merrick pressed his ear to the door, cocking his head and listening to something that the Pretender could not hear. Sorcha's blue eyes were turned toward him, gleaming and unnaturally bright in the half-light.

Part of Raed wanted to touch her, reach out and reclaim some of that heady magic that had grown between them on the dirigible. The other part of him, the royal rebel, was still seething with anger.

He'd been chained his whole life to a curse that he hadn't had any part in causing. The knowledge that he was responsible for his own mother's death was a nightmare he also could never escape. To be tied unwillingly to anyone, let alone the woman he found himself falling in love with, was a terrible blow. He had yet to decide if he could forgive her.

He wondered if she knew how close she had come to waking the Rossin when she'd tried to break that unsanctioned Bond. The Beast was not far away; that much he could feel. Sorcha's attempt at un-Binding, and then the hint of geist presence, had enflamed the Rossin. It yearned to rampage through the Mother Abbey—nothing would have given it more pleasure. The image of ripping Deacons limb from limb as they slumbered tasted delicious to the stirring Beast.

"Sorcha." He touched her shoulder, and the gesture, meant as nothing more than a warning, flared into something more. His body responded to her nearness even as the Rossin howled for her blood. "What is your plan, exactly?"

Her smile was a ghostly flicker of a happier one. "This is my Arch Abbot, Raed. He will set things right."

Could the Arch Abbot negate the bounty on the Pretender's head? Unlikely. But he was here now, and they had to find out what the conspirators had in mind for the people of Vermillion. His capital, even if he might never claim it.

Raed straightened as if he were one of his father's soldiers. "Then after you, milady." He gestured to the open door as if it were the portal to a throne room.

She drew in a little, shaky breath, a combination of what she was no doubt sensing across the Bond and the weight of the terrible situation. He followed on her heels. Inside was even more deathly quiet.

Raed might have thought a lot of things about the Arch Abbot from across the sea, but after seeing his bedchamber, he would not think him ostentatious. The cell was as bare as a sunbaked rock. The domed roof gave the impression of one of those isolated cells that communing Deacons sometimes took to in the wilds, and the furnishings were nearly as sparse as a hermit's. One niche contained two hard-backed chairs, a tapestry-covered stool and a carved wooden table; the other niche on the far side looked to serve as a sleeping area. Merrick was already there, standing above the rumpled blankets. It was obvious that the Arch Abbot wasn't in.

Sorcha was frowning and turning about slowly, as if she expected the man to emerge out of the shadows—but there was no one else present. Nor were there any doors apart from the one they had come in through.

"Looks like he is not receiving guests right now," Raed muttered, folding his arms and trying to calm the yammering of his chest; he knew it was related to the Beast's desire for chaos.

Sorcha pushed back the thin blankets as if she expected to find him curled up in there somewhere. "Something must have happened to him," she muttered with real concern in her tone.

"Not prone to nighttime wanderings, is he?" Raed couldn't help the sharp tone in his voice. The Deacons had been so sure that coming here would solve everything.

"Not at all," Merrick whispered, leaning back against the cool stone with a ragged sigh. "The Arch Abbot is always supposed to be available, should the realm ever need him."

"Someone put that cantrip on the secretary," Sorcha hissed back. "I think he's been kidnapped."

Raed was about to ask who would have the power to do such a thing, but then he thought of what they had faced back in Ulrich—and swallowed the question.

"What's that?" Merrick raised himself off the wall by his elbows, his chin pointed up toward the ceiling. Raed strode over to stand next to him, determined not to be left out of any further discoveries—he had a real stake in all of this now. Sorcha and Merrick scrambled onto the Arch Abbot's bed so that they could trace the strange shapes.

Indecipherable letters were scrawled on the ceiling of the alcove. Raed was no expert, but they did seem familiar. He'd spent many years in exile as a child, being schooled by the aristocrats who had chosen to go with their king, and he had learned many languages and many stories. These words seemed on the very edge of his understanding. They looked similar in construction to the Brytsling tribesmen's language of the far north, but also similar to the Edgic letters of the warm swamps of the south. He was just beginning to figure out the pronunciation when Merrick, closer in years to his scholarship, whispered the sounds that had been forming in the Pretender's mouth.

"Taouilt." He blinked hard. "Isn't that the word for—"

The grating of stone against stone bought the words to a halt in his mouth. The raised dais of the bed was beginning to shift. The two Deacons leapt down hastily.

"Hidden." Merrick finished his sentence softly as the stairs leading downward slotted neatly into formation.

Sorcha grinned brightly. "Arch Abbot Hastler is trying to help us—he must have been able to scrawl that before they got him away."

Raed ran his fingers across his beard and considered. He did not like the idea of blindly going down those stairs. They seemed a little too convenient for his liking. But they had come this far, and it wasn't as though they could just go back the way they had passed. He would have said something but he knew it would matter little; if there was one person Sorcha Faris believed in, it was Arch Abbot Hastler. Instead he swallowed his suspicions and determined to be on his guard, even if his companions were not.

He placed his foot on the topmost step and turned to look back at the Deacons. "Well, let's find the old man."

He wanted to hold out his hand to Sorcha, and in fact half raised it toward her, but then remembered his anger. He tucked the hand instead into his belt as smoothly as possible. This was going to make a difficult situation even worse. Everything about this was wrong. He wasn't meant to be on land. He wasn't meant to be falling in love with a Deacon who had betrayed him. Vermillion should have been his city.

Raed let out a little sigh. They'd whispered that into his ear since his birth, but he'd never really believed it. Still, others had, and he felt responsible for them and their hopes. What would happen if he died here, though? The vision of his green-eyed sister, so fragile and happy, flashed in his memory. He knew the answer—she would be the heir, and the Curse would fall on her.

Raed disliked the atmosphere. As they descended, it filled his lungs like buckets of ice. The steps were wetter the deeper they went, and in Vermillion they surely couldn't go very far down. The lagoon couldn't be too far below them. He wiped moisture off the back of his neck. The lantern Merrick had taken from above cast orange light about them as they reached the bottom.

If the Abbey above was huge, below was just as vast; it was a cathedral of the earth. Soaring limestone walls leapt above them to meet in smooth vaulted arches, while great caramel-colored decorations swooped down at some points, almost resembling gargoyles. Merrick's small lantern was not the only light now. Vast patches of glowing blue lichens covered the swells of limestone like fine tapestries, filling the intricate crevices with a soft light. Everywhere was the sound of water and the feeling of moisture on the face. For a second, the Pretender stood still in the unexpected beauty of it. A secret world that a man of the sea could never have dreamed existed.

"Did you know this was down here?" Raed asked softly as they looked about.

"No." Sorcha's whispered reply did not go far, swallowed up by the vastness and not returned.

The more scholarly Merrick looked just as surprised. "I've never even heard a rumor of it, but this place must have been known by the native Order; the stair mechanism would never have been put in easily by the Arch Abbot. Not in complete secrecy."

Somehow the way he said "native" sounded ominous to Raed's ears. He knew as much, if not more, than they could know about the Order that had once occupied the halls above their heads. His

family and Arkaym's native Order had been as intertwined as
two snakes, sometimes mating and other times fighting. Those
Deacons had originally claimed to be benefiting the people of the
continent, just like these new ones. However, they had fallen into
corruption, and not all of it political.

It was true they had meddled in the affairs of his family—the
royal line—but they had also wanted more than that. Few knew
the truth of how far that native Order had fallen, yet he was wary
of telling Sorcha and Merrick. Would it make any difference to
them to know that their predecessors had reached for the ultimate power? Perhaps these newest Deacons were no different
from the previous set.

While Raed was considering this, Sorcha was leading them
farther in, her dark form visible only as an absence of light
among the gleaming lichen. At his side, Merrick shuttered the
lantern. "We will need to be quiet, I fear. If the Arch Abbot's
kidnappers hear—" Merrick did not finish the thought.

Raed was not entirely convinced about these "kidnappers."
He'd seen no sign of struggle above, and his gut told him it was
nigh on impossible to spirit the most powerful Deacon on the
continent away from his own Mother Abbey.

While the Deacons ahead of him quietly followed the damp
path forward, his heart began to race with fear and excitement.
The Rossin was very close to the surface now—not yet capable
of emerging, but so close that he could do the one very disturbing
thing Raed hated: he whispered into the Pretender's mind.

*We should kill her. Her blood would taste as sweet as her
sweat did. She betrayed you.*

The Rossin's intense hatred for the Deacons engendered in
Raed a physical reaction that was only a few steps away from
desire. These primitive reflexes were the ones easiest for the
Beast to reach. He tried to ignore the hardening in his breeches
and the dark whisperings that went with them.

*Tear her, play with her a little, perhaps, if we like. She de-
serves it, after all.*

The images began, flashing in his head like vivid tapestries
of what the Rossin would do. Suddenly, Raed's skin burned like
lava in the freezing cavern.

She will burn for real when you touch her this time. The Rossin laughed seductively, showing him an accompanying image
that was both terrifying and erotic. Sorcha's red hair would be

made of flame as she caught alight with what was within him. When he entered her, she would scream . . .

"Raed?" He almost ran into Merrick, who had stopped, concerned, near an upward curve in the path. Merrick's brow was furrowed and for an instant the Pretender was sure the Deacon could actually see the Rossin lurking nearby—after all, he was a Sensitive. He was surprised when Merrick glanced almost guiltily ahead toward Sorcha.

Pitching his voice low, the Deacon ducked his head. "If things go badly, Raed, Sorcha has two choices . . . She can open Teisyat, or she can unleash the Rossin."

Oh, the Beast liked these words. He twisted in near-orgiastic delight at the thought, but he did not like the next words from Merrick's lips.

"She must not do either."

Oh, she can; she will. Let me loose, let me feed on her sweet charms, or open the Great Door and I will take us all there.

Raed shifted uncomfortably, choking down a groan. "Why not?"

"I have been thinking. The only people who could take the Arch Abbot"—Merrick pressed his lips together for a second before going on—"would be Deacons. And if they are that powerful—they could perhaps control the Rossin."

The Beast was suddenly silent, turning inward and hiding its thoughts from its foci with uncharacteristic subtlety.

"And if she opened the Great Door?"

Merrick's sharp look caught him by surprise, but then he realized—he had used the Rossin's words. They'd just slipped out. The Deacon didn't make any comment, though. Instead, his voice dropped lower. "She has opened Teisyat once before, and such things . . ." He paused and his expression hardened, making him look a lot older than his years. "They can affect a Deacon . . . weaken them."

"So if it comes to a confrontation, what's your suggestion?" Raed instinctively checked his saber in its sheath.

In a similar fashion, he noticed Merrick tuck his hand within his cloak, touching the one talisman that all Sensitives relied on. "I'll take care of it, but you may have to restrain Sorcha. Stop her from going for the Gauntlets."

"I can't touch—"

"Thanks to the Bond . . . yes, you can," Merrick said sternly, and then he turned and trotted after the very person they'd been discussing.

You can touch her. All of her, with fangs or hands or . . .

"Shut up," Raed hissed, pulling his own cloak around him.

Up ahead, the blue light of the lichen was giving way to an orange glow that reminded him of a large fire. When he crested the rise, at first he didn't know what to make of what he saw. Neither, apparently, did Sorcha, for she was still standing there, looking down into the odd grotto.

A great ceiling of daggerlike rocks hovered over what looked at first glance like a floor covered in tiny streams and honeycomb-shaped pools of water. The red light was coming from the rocks above, not from another form of lichen but a brighter, deeper light that seemed to well up from inside the stone itself.

The air was even colder here, penetrating through the Rossin-induced heat. He shivered wildly, trying not to let his teeth chatter. A quick glance at the others revealed that they were having the same problem. Raed closed his eyes and swayed slightly, feeling through the Bond. Apart from the usual surge of fear so close to the Change, he could sense other strengths. Merrick's presence in his head was like a light seen through winter trees, cool but entrancing. Sorcha was a hot sun against his side, reminding him of their time aboard the airship.

Caught between these two presences, now fully aware of the Bond, the Rossin struggled briefly; but they were trained, and they held against him. They were, in fact, as deeply ingrained within the Young Pretender's psyche as the Beast.

Damn crowded in here, Raed thought with little rancor. It was good to be sharing the load of the geistlord in his head. With a sigh, he opened his eyes. Sorcha's bright blue gaze and Merrick's steady brown one were only inches away; her hand wrapped around Raed's waist, while the younger Deacon had one hand on her shoulder. It should have been uncomfortable, and he should have still been angry, but they had literally just saved his skin.

Instinctively, he felt for the Rossin. The Beast had gone deep, hidden further down so that it would be unable to speak directly into his head. Another relief.

"We have to go down there and see what that is," Merrick finally said softly, though they were all feeling the same desire to run in the other direction.

Sorcha took a deep breath and nodded. "You tell us what to do. You lead us."

The young Deacon turned his eyes toward the still-glowing red rocks. "The Otherside is near, but I think we should be all right as long as we don't trigger anything."

"Fine, then." Raed clambered out of the stalactite grotto and made his way down the path toward the carpet of pools and rivulets, ignoring the urge in every fiber of his being to flee from it.

Each little depression was filled with water and interconnected to the others by a web of streams. It was a large area; he couldn't actually see the end of it under the ruddy light cast by the rocks. What he did see gave him the shivers. Instead of reflecting the rough cave surface above them, each showed an image. The three of them stood and looked out over an ocean of possibilities.

He saw his own face: at the court of Felstaad; standing beside Aachon at the helm of *Dominion*; fishing out Merrick and the fiery Deacon. He recognized all those, but there were others, just as disturbing, nearby: the Rossin running, raging, through Felstaad's mirrored halls, *Corsair* sailing with a possessed crew and chasing down *Dominion*, and finally the chilling image of himself, fishing out the dead body of a red-haired Deacon.

"By the Blood, what is it?"

"This," Merrick said in a voice that verged on reverence, "is a Possibility Matrix."

"A what?"

"The Scholar Abbot Horris, two generations back, speculated that some of the wild powers that crop up in Deacons, such as foresight, could be replicated by the physical construction—models to aid those without the gift."

"What my learned friend is saying"—Sorcha tucked her hands into her belt—"is that this is why we have been dogged from the very beginning."

Merrick, who only moments before had been pale with worry, was now scrambling around the edges of the cells and rivulets like a boy who had just discovered rock pools for the first time. He peered into them with great enthusiasm, and Sorcha shot Raed the ghost of a smile.

"Horris theorized the creation of a matrix, but he reckoned the background activity in the human world would make it far too difficult to accurately use it predict the future." Merrick's gesture swept out over the cavern floor. "I wonder—" He darted over to the edge where the cave wall began its impressive swoop upward. The young Deacon's head cocked.

"Is he going to start writing his own thesis?" Raed asked, not feeling nearly the same level of excitement. In fact, the sooner they got out of here, the better he would feel.

"Give him a minute," Sorcha said softly.

"It's the rock itself," Merrick called. Raed winced at the loudness of it. The echo seemed to go on forever, and the chances of hundreds of enraged Deacons descending on them seemed not too far off. But the young man came darting over to them, and his hands were covered in white dust from the rock.

"The natural color is white"—he rubbed it between his fingers—"but the glow is from another kind of lichen. Can you guess what it does?"

Raed opened his mouth for a rather snappy reply, but Sorcha tugged on his hand. "Haven't a clue. Why don't you tell us?" Surprisingly, there was not a trace of irony in her voice.

"It's a barrier; a barrier against geist power." He waved his hand excitedly. "It shields this place from detection. After all, we are sitting on the largest repository of Sensitives on the continent. Even if they were all part of a conspiracy to keep the matrix a secret . . ." Merrick paused to consider that dread statement. "Even if they are, I should have been able to sense something."

"I'm feeling something myself now." Raed was sure the shadows were deeper now. The spot between his shoulder blades was twitching.

Sorcha took a sample of the rock dust from her partner's fingertips, ignoring the Pretender's grumbles. "Well, that explains it . . . but that is an awful lot of trouble for just this matrix." She dropped to her haunches and looked more closely at the pools.

Raed wanted nothing at all to do with them, but they had come this far. Sorcha was leaning so close to them that strands of her copper hair, which had come loose, almost threatened to break the tensioned surface.

"Careful!" Merrick crouched down next to her. "The power here is very finely balanced, and Horris never defined what would happen if it were broken."

With a slight clearing of her throat, Sorcha straightened up.

"So, who built this thing?" Raed asked, averting his eyes from the disturbing images.

Merrick was so intent that he didn't answer, instead muttering under his breath, "The answer is here somewhere." Sorcha and he spread out, staring down into the fractured possibilities with an interest that quite unnerved the Pretender. This wasn't finding the Arch Abbot, he felt like reminding them.

It was Sorcha who let out the first gasp.

Merrick darted to her side. "Have you found—by the Bones!" Sorcha spun on Raed. "You need to see this."

The look on her face brooked no argument. At her side, looking down, he understood.

He had no love of the Emperor or his kin, but the shimmering pool that reflected the Grand Duchess' assassination showed not just her death; the City of Vermillion was in flames behind her. The scenes around that one showed her being gunned down: all showed the city burning, though the method of her murder varied. All these possibilities seemed to show death and disaster for the citizens of the city—the city that Raed had been brought up to believe was his.

"Whatever they are planning," Merrick said, "it must need a great deal of death and the blood of the Grand Duchess Zofiya."

"That is one hell of a summoning," Sorcha chimed in grimly. "It will make the Ulrich Priory look like a summer picnic."

"Is there no other possibility?" Raed said, feeling his pulse race. If they were not trying to bring on the end times, it—it was damn close.

They scrambled about, desperately looking for any other sort of outcome. And then by sheer chance he found it. A small pool reflected something he would never have guessed in dream or nightmare. He was standing in place of the Grand Duchess, pulling her out of harm's way; the bullet missing its target and burying itself into his own chest.

Raed cleared his throat while the others looked on in silence. "Just how accurate are these things?"

"Truthfully, I don't know." Merrick didn't sugarcoat his answer. "Too many variables . . ."

"But in this one, the city isn't burning." Raed took a deep breath, like before plunging into an icy ocean. "In this one, Vermillion survives. Do you know where it is?"

Sorcha was grinding her teeth a little, and he hoped it was concern warring with common sense.

She meant well. She had always meant well, despite everything.

He didn't care that Merrick was only feet away and watching with steady brown eyes. Raed cupped her head in his hands. She tried to pull loose, but he wouldn't let her go. "Tell me where this is, Sorcha!"

Her blue eyes, like chips of ice in the red light of the cavern, finally were able to meet his. He felt her swallow hard. "Brick-maker's Lane." The words came out as if choked.

"Then we know where we have to go."

TWENTY-TWO

The Danger of Vespers

They followed the water out of the caverns. Merrick came up with that idea, and Sorcha was only too grateful to let her younger partner take the lead. She trailed at the rear as Raed followed Merrick. The cave grew narrower and the red light dimmed as they got out from under the baleful presence of the Possibility Matrix.

Raed caught her arm just as Merrick disappeared from view around a corner. The Pretender's lips against her ear were for a moment warm and distracting, until he whispered into it, "Did you notice the one person who was not shown in that contraption?"

He pulled back, and in the light of the lantern his eyes were stern. Comprehension flooded across her mind: Nynnia. The slip of a girl should have been in many of those scenes, but she had not been; what exactly that meant, Sorcha couldn't grasp.

Raed tilted his head and shrugged, indicating he too was at a loss. Neither of them asked Merrick, though; he was too busy trying to get them out without going back up through the Mother Abbey.

They went on, wrapped in silence and contemplation. Sorcha couldn't get the images she had seen in the Possibility Matrix out of her mind. Fire was one of the true elements of the geistlords, and were Vermillion to burn, it could mean only one thing: someone wanted to release a hell of a lot of them.

History was littered with plenty of crazed people's attempts to reach the deepest parts of the Otherside. All had ended in disaster for the summoner and usually a fair proportion of the innocents around them.

Sorcha was so concentrated on these dire thoughts that she nearly crawled into Raed. "Not right now," he quipped as she brushed against his breeches. "Merrick says there is a large pool of water ahead. Shall we risk swimming under it?"

"Not much choice, unless we want to go back through the Abbey," she said, suddenly feeling the walls closing in on her.

They swam, diving down beneath the rock and into the frigid water of the lagoon. Sorcha ducked under, feeling her chest constrict as if a person were sitting on it. Her muscles tensed as she concentrated on not taking a disastrous gulp of water. For a moment it felt as though her arms and legs were made of lead and she might just sink to the bottom of the lagoon. Then the Bond clicked over in her head, guiding her like a compass, swinging reliably north, if north were the two men. Though her skin was stinging uncomfortably, she was able to kick out and swim alongside Raed and Merrick as they popped up in the predawn grayness of the city.

Together they swam to an empty pier. It looked like they were only a few streets away from the Abbey at the Prince's Canal. The boats bobbing nearby were painted the bright orange that said they were available for hire, but there was no sign of any ferrymen just yet. This deep into Vermillion, trade was nonexistent until the daylight hours. Activities that required darkness were carried out farther away on the fringes—places that these city-sanctioned ferries would not go.

As they hauled themselves onto the pier, Merrick gasped through chattering teeth, "We—we are lucky the lagoon isn't—isn't frozen."

"Yes," Raed choked, wringing out his cloak in a vain attempt to get dry. "Very damn lucky."

Sorcha did the same to her hair before tying it back up against the nape of her neck. The important thing here was to think only one step ahead at a time. If she tried to take in the big picture, she might just seize up. If they were to change the possibilities they had seen in the matrix, then they would need to work at the top of their efficiency—they couldn't afford to begin doubting. "Now we need to find the others at this tavern and get to Brickmaker's Lane. No way of telling when those events may happen."

Raed nodded, and then smiled wickedly. "If I know the habits of aristocrats at all, it won't be early. Not much of a reputation for early risers." He craned his head over the tops of the boats and voiced the one issue that was now bothering Sorcha. "The question is—how do we get to the tavern? Normal observers I can handle, but this Sight thing—"

"I have an idea," Merrick chimed in, and raised a leather pouch with the shape of a tin inside. It was a very familiar shape.

Sorcha's hand flew to her pockets. It was indeed the very same container she kept her cigars in. "How did you—"

"Now, now." The young man's eyes gleamed with delight at his having managed to fool her. "Some of us weren't brought up by the Abbey—some of us learned a thing or two beforehand."

He pulled the tin out of the pouch and opened it. Inside were not the two remaining cigars Sorcha had gratefully accepted as gifts from the citizens of Ulrich, but a mound of the white rock dust from the cavern.

Despite their dire situation, she felt rage fill her. "Where are my cigars, Merrick?"

"I needed to keep this dry, and believe me, this could save—"

She snatched the tin off him and stared hopelessly at the pile of dust. "Where—where are the cigars?" she choked out. She'd been planning to grab a moment, even just a short one, before heading to Brickmaker's Lane. Facing imminent death, it was the least she deserved.

When Merrick pulled the sad, wet remnants out of his pocket she almost sobbed. It was too bitter an end for such a fine smoke as a Nythrumi gold. A crime. Among all the danger, this was the last straw.

"You better have an explanation, Chambers!"

At her back, she could hear Raed break into laughter. She understood it was faintly ridiculous to be worrying about her cigars at this point, but damn it, they were the only part of her old life that she had left.

The young Deacon smiled at her, a reaction that only a few weeks before would have provoked a damn slap in the face. "The rock blocks magic . . . My thinking was, if it could do that, what might it do if used in a cantrip?"

Through her dismay, Sorcha's brain clicked over on that concept. The design *ylvavita* could hide people in plain sight well enough for the ungifted, but wasn't even worth the bother against

Deacons. However, if Merrick was right, then maybe it was. Her cigars would have at least been sacrificed for a worthy cause.

"I'll buy you two fine new cigars," Raed whispered to her in a voice that made her heart pick up its pace. She turned and smiled at him, glad that he'd been able to forgive her the Bond—or at least put it out of his head enough to go on.

In the end Raed very skillfully jimmied open the ferrymen's silent building, and they were able to find some clothes there. It felt wrong to stuff their cloaks, Order emblems and talismans into rough sacking bags. Stripped of clothing she'd been wearing since a child, Sorcha felt weakened somehow.

It was silly, but there it was. Raed was also the expert in disguise, and before she knew it he had them cloaked and looking nothing like two powerful Deacons. Merrick's hair was twisted at odd angles, his face smeared with dirt, and, at the Pretender's direction, he even dragged his foot a little.

He concealed Sorcha's femininity with extra clothes, and tied the bundle of sacks on her back. It wasn't heavy, but it was still slightly galling. It was with some grim humor that she cleaned the first cantrip off Raed's forehead. "All right, let's see if this works." Dipping her finger in the dust, she drew the new design, all curls and flourishes on his warm skin, and then turned to Merrick.

The younger Deacon let his Center fall away; she could feel it like it was her own. He cast his head from side to side. "I think it works. If I'm not looking specifically for you, my Sight slides off you."

"As long as he doesn't do anything to draw attention," Sorcha commented wryly, to which Raed let out a little chuckle. "If I can sacrifice my cigars, then you can sacrifice your pirate swagger. Now, Merrick, try the cantrip on me."

He did so and then stood back to examine the effect. "Not quite as effective, but in a crowd of people I think it would hold."

It wasn't exactly a ringing endorsement, but it was all they had. Readjusting their disguises, they went out into the street. Luckily away from the Prince's Canal, trade was beginning to pick up; three more disheveled porters made not one jot of difference. They worked their way, dodging carts and streams of pedestrians, to Dyer's Lane and the little tavern called the Red Flag. The street reeked of the trade it was named for, but at least it was a stench of this world.

Raed had a quiet word with the craggy-faced proprietor and they were led out to a back room where Aachon and the crew, as well as Nynnia and her father, were waiting. Their faces showed the feral looks of the hunted. Sorcha guessed the same expression was on her face.

"What did you find out, my prince?" Aachon cut straight to the point, his dark eyes lingering only momentarily on their garb.

"The Arch Abbot has been taken and the Grand Duchess will be sacrificed, most likely by day's end." Raed took a seat next to his first mate and poured himself a tankard of ale. No one said a word until he had drunk his fill. He let out a satisfied gasp and dropped the tumbler back to the table. "And what's more, forces unknown have something called a Possibility Matrix, in which they can see the future."

The crew members' eyes widened at that. Frith swore, "By the Ancients, Captain—if they can do that, how can we beat them?"

Nynnia sat staring into her cup of ale. Almost too quietly to be heard, she said, "The future is a very fragile thing. The possibilities are always changing. If we move quickly enough and act unpredictably enough, it is not impossible to beat."

Sorcha gave her a startled look as the feeling in the back of her head changed from a niggle of little importance into something far more concerning. "What can you possibly know of such things?" she barked.

"I know much, Deacon Faris." She raised her eyes until they met Sorcha's. Suddenly the world contracted around the slim young woman's form. None but the Deacons in the room could feel it, but whatever cunning mask she had fashioned for herself had now slipped.

Sorcha pushed back from the table and leapt to her feet. "What are you?" she demanded.

Merrick's Center flared as he too surged upright. "Nynnia?" His voice cracked even as he stood at Sorcha's side.

Nynnia remained seated, calm, but her father leapt up. "Foolish Deacons! You only ever see what you want to." The old man's eyes bulged and his fists clenched at his side. If his relationship with Nynnia was an act, it was a damn good one.

She is not a geist. Merrick's voice in Sorcha's head was steady, despite what was being revealed. *I cannot tell what she is, but she is not one of their kind.* Dazzled as he was by Nynnia, Sorcha still did not doubt his skill.

Nynnia spoke but did not look directly at Merrick. "You know something of the Murashev." No expression touched her young features, but her eyes were swimming with power. "Therefore you cannot be ignorant of what it could do in this world. We have very little time. Do you want to stay and argue or save this world?"

For a moment they stood there, frozen in a tableau: the Deacons poised, Kyrix glaring, the crew looking about in confusion and Nynnia the calm center of it all.

Sorcha could hear her heart beating in her chest, yet much as she hated to trust Nynnia—they had no other choice. And she had saved Merrick's life. Slowly both Deacons took their seats.

Nynnia turned her head and looked out the grubby window. "What else did you see in the waters?" she asked, her tone as distant as if she were asking about the weather or the price of embroidery thread.

"We saw Vermillion burning," Merrick muttered.

"Sorry to hear about Vermillion," Aachon said coldly, "but why should we care about the usurper's sister?"

Sorcha was about to open her mouth and reply when Nynnia suddenly flung herself across the table. The tumble was so unexpected that the others seated around her had only time to gape as she spun past them and collided with a man who had come up behind them.

For a second Sorcha thought the creature had gone quite mad, and she was ready to come to the aid of the other patron when she saw the gleam of metal in his hand. Then everything got more confused. Shouts rang out as Raed spun around to face the dozen or so intruders. The crew leapt to his defense, while Merrick and Sorcha scrambled to get out of the way as the giant Aachon picked up the table and threw it at those threatening his captain. A bar fight was obviously not an unknown situation for these men, but Sorcha also managed to get in a few punches while chaos reigned.

Yet it was Nynnia who was the center of the storm. Her lithe body, which had seemed beautiful but useless, now revealed itself to have the elegance of a deadly dancer. She spun and whirled, knocking men aside with graceful kicks that should have been set to music. While the crew of the Dominion fought with deft brutality, it was Nynnia whom Sorcha could not stop watching.

The fight was over quickly; the thugs who were not sent streaming from the tavern were lying unconscious on the floor. "Nynnia!" Merrick's horrified yell stopped the others in mid-congratulations. The slim woman was staring down numbly at the handle of the knife buried just below her ribs; blood was staining her petal-colored dress. It was a deadly wound, tilted upward into vital organs.

But before Merrick could reach her, Nynnia's father, who had stayed beyond the battle, moved to her. With a little grunt, Kyrix pulled the knife loose. After exchanging a glance with his daughter, he threw the dagger away without even looking at it. It clanged into the corner.

"Nynnia?" Merrick took her arm as if he expected her to fall over. She didn't stop him as his fingers gingerly explored the gash in her robe. Beneath, there was nothing but smooth flesh. "Nynnia . . . you should . . . What—" He paused to catch his breath.

"We have no time for explanations." She pressed the tips of her long fingers against the line of his jaw. "I am more than you think, that is true, but I also have the same aims as you—to stop the Murashev and save Vermillion." She looked around at the others. "Do you trust me?"

They looked at her hard, then around at one another. Sorcha didn't want to influence them, so she stayed silent. She'd made up her own mind. Whatever Nynnia was, she was powerful, and they needed all the friends they could get at this point. Still, if Raed and his crew rejected her, Sorcha would stand with them.

"She could have let the Captain get a knife in the ribs," Frith said in a low voice, and the others nodded in agreement.

Aachon's dark eyes didn't look as convinced, but he glanced at Raed. "It is up to you, my prince."

The Pretender shrugged, and pronounced his verdict with a broad grin. "Beautiful, powerful women don't fall into your lap every day—just what this venture needs, I say."

Sorcha heard Nynnia murmur a question to Merrick, but couldn't quite make it out. If they were going to face the Murashev, she found herself wanting him to have a little happiness.

"She saved your life once," Sorcha said reluctantly to Merrick. "Now she's saved Raed—what more does a girl have to do to get your attention?"

The young Deacon pulled Nynnia in and kissed her hard. Sorcha looked away; there was a limit. For once, the woman—if that was what she was—looked flustered, her cheeks rosy with a becoming blush. "We must move quickly. These thugs will be just the beginning."

Raed quickly strode toward the back door, but as the rest followed, Sorcha turned in the other direction. She grabbed hold of the publican who was carefully avoiding looking straight at them. He looked too guilty for her liking. With the careful application of force as taught to all novices, Sorcha had him facedown on his own bar in seconds. He winced slightly as his earthenware cups went tumbling to the floor; two smashed loudly. Sorcha knew in his tiny brain he was trying to work out how a woman two heads shorter than him had him pinned down. Before he could decide to put up a fight, she hissed into his ear. "What is happening at Brickmaker's Lane today?"

Obviously the question was as simple as he was, because a grin spread over his face and he gabbled an answer. "The Emperor and the Grand Duchess are opening the public fountain destroyed by geist attack last month." She patted the publican on the cheek, released him and followed the others out the back.

Brickmaker's was only three streets over. Catching up with them, she reported her findings. "Zofiya will indeed be nearby and probably in the next hour or so. She'll be officiating the reopening instead of her brother, since the little goddess Myr has jurisdiction over water."

"The fountain." Merrick was a smart lad; even with stars in his eyes for Nynnia, he recalled the case.

"What is the significance of the fountain?" Raed was checking the exit from the alleyway, but his mind was more than capable of juggling several tasks.

"It was destroyed by a swarm of rei." Sorcha was pressing her memory hard; it had seemed such a trivial event, the last dying breath of a cluster of crisis near the fringe of the city. Rei were generally thought to be the souls of the drowned, drawn to the energy of water and delighting in making mischief by disrupting it. Vermillion—like every port city—drew them, with its combination of water and people. Still, as annoying as they were, they could also cause real damage—destroying pipes was their particular specialty. No one liked their sewage being interfered with, but it was even worse when public fountains bore the brunt

of their mischief. Everyone was affected then, as no one could
drink safely from the lagoon.

"The rei swarm didn't just destroy the pipes." Merrick
snapped his fingers finally, recalling the rest of the memory.
"They wrecked the fountain and the pipe feeding it, right to the
mains. They had to spend weeks digging back to fix it—back to
the old ossuary, I think."

Sorcha's chest contracted as if she'd been punched, so much
so that she had to lean back against the wall of the building for
a second. The Bond vibrated so loudly with her new fears that
Merrick—and even Raed—gasped.

Her partner suddenly realized what he had said. "The ossuary! By the Bones!"

"Literally," Sorcha snapped, feeling the circle joining itself
back up.

"Again"—Raed crossed his arms—"with the lack of information."

Sorcha stamped her foot to illustrate her point. "Beneath us
right now is the First Ossuary. Vermillion is a very, very old city,
and two hundred years ago there were simply too many bodies
filling up all the graves—nowhere to put new ones. So they had
to fill the caves on the fringe with the bones."

Nynnia made a face. "Digging up the dead, in a city infected
with geists?"

"No, it wasn't pretty." Merrick squeezed her hand. "But from
the records of the native Order, they were eventually able to get
the city under control. Burning the bones would have been even
worse."

"That has got to be where the Murashev is being created."
Sorcha blinked, thinking of the last time she had been down
there; the endless rows of skulls and bones stacked upon one
another. The recollection made her shiver. Even though she'd
been a member of a Deacon Conclave, the looming menace had
still been palpable. The White Palace, the locals called it, as if it
was a mirror image of the Imperial Palace above.

"If the Grand Duchess were to be taken there and sacrificed . . ." Even Nynnia couldn't finish that sentence. It didn't
take too much imagination to consider the consequences.

Apparently, however, Frith had no imagination. "What's so
cursed different about her blood compared to ours? She bleeds
red just like every other person!"

"Certainly she does," Merrick replied, "but her line is rife with old blood. Ancient blood."

"They need it," Nynnia said, with a sidelong glance at her father.

Sorcha was beginning to suspect there was something more to that relationship. Feathers of eldritch blue light twined between the two. The flow of power from man to woman was like blood flowing through shared veins. Life force. He might call himself her father, and that could still be true, but he was also her foci, just like Raed and the Beast, or the children of Ulrich and the poltern. Whatever kind of creature she was, she needed her foci just like the rest. It was both a strength and a weakness; a foci meant she couldn't be easily dismissed back to the Otherside, but also bound them together so that her strength depended on his fate. No wonder she had wanted to reach Ulrich so desperately when they had first met.

Nynnia's eyes locked with Sorcha's, acknowledging the Deacon's observation and recognition. Sorcha's gaze did not flinch. "Don't you think it is a good idea for your father to be safely away from this?" she asked pointedly, while the men around them murmured among themselves blindly.

The slim woman nodded slowly. "Yes, you are right."

"Better make it quick," Raed commented. "There is a crowd gathering."

Sorcha stood at his shoulder and glanced out into the street. He was right: people were streaming in the direction of Brickmaker's Lane; they were suddenly surrounded by eager apprentices, mothers with wailing babies, gritty laborers and dyers with their hands stained the colors of the rainbow. The Emperor and his sister were coming out from the palace—not an everyday event.

The opening of a public fountain was not something that would have warranted the sovereign's attention, but having been so publicly attacked by geists, he was probably trying to reassure the citizens by appearing with the Grand Duchess.

"By the Bones, I need a smoke," she groaned, thinking miserably of the ones lost to Merrick's enthusiastic plan.

Wordlessly, Raed reached under his disguise and pulled two smooth brown Ilyrick reserves out of his pocket. Sorcha's smile was broad and thoroughly inappropriate for the situation. She took them, knowing her hands were trembling slightly. She tucked one into her pocket and tore off the end of the other. It was a cigar that

deserved better treatment, but she simply didn't have the time.
Raed lit it for her, and she leaned back for just a minute and drew
the smoke sensuously into her mouth. There was no time to enjoy
this cigar as it should have been enjoyed: slowly, on a balcony,
watching the stars and in his company. There would probably
never be such a moment for them.

Sorcha would take what she could get.

She pushed away from the wall, still sucking on the cigar, and
looked at Raed: her beautiful surprise. "Nynnia, get your father
out of here." Sorcha fell back on old habits of command. Pulling
up the hood on her disguise, she gestured. "The rest of us have
an audience to attend."

The crew, for once, did not look to Raed. Even Aachon fell
into step behind her as they blended in with the crowd. Nynnia
was talking with Kyrix, and they both looked distressed. As the
others flowed ahead of her a little, Sorcha hung behind, waiting
for Nynnia. She didn't want to lose the creature in the press of
the crowd.

All it took was one glance away; when she looked back toward
the pair, Nynnia was hugging her father one last time. She did not
notice as a towering man, who had looked like just another member of the crowd moments before, suddenly lunged forward. Sorcha darted toward them, but she couldn't reach them in time. The
man thrust a long knife under the old man's rib cage and gave a
vicious twist. Without a noise, Kyrix crumpled to the ground.

Nynnia cried out, but the Deacon grabbed hold of her arm
and tugged her into the crowd. The foci was already dead—the
attacker had known what he was doing. Their enemy, whoever
they were, must have realized something about the nature of the
woman missing from the Possibility Matrix.

Tugging the stunned Nynnia behind her, Sorcha zigzagged
through the crowd, trying to lose the attackers in the tumult. Her
heart was racing and her brain tumbling. How on earth were they
going to save the Grand Duchess from someone who could see
one step in front of them? Even Garil's gift was not this accurate.
Her mind still lingered on the sigil of the Emperor on that dispatch box that had started everything.

Catching up with the others, she thrust Nynnia's hand into
Merrick's. "Your beloved just lost her invulnerability in a rather
messy way."

The creature's chin tilted up in defiance. "I am still what I am.

You need me." She might have been in shock from having her foci ripped away, but she had determination in spades.

Sorcha began to warm to Nynnia. "I have no doubt of that."

"We should split up," Raed said as they drifted forward with the crowd's ebbs and flows. "They'll have less luck tracking us that way—we can blend in more."

"Not us," Merrick hissed, his hand still locked with Nynnia's. "You and I and Sorcha . . . the Bond . . . We should stay together."

Sorcha thought about it a second. Although she didn't like the idea of splitting up, there were going to be a lot of people at the opening, and without any idea of Zofiya's movements it was going to be difficult to position themselves in the ideal way to protect her. Also, the assassins would undoubtedly be looking for the group of them. The added difficulty of the Possibility Matrix was impossible to calculate. It could easily cloud her judgment so much that she would be swallowed by entropy. Best to move.

"The Bond gives us an edge," she muttered to Merrick while they were pushed backward and forward in the press of people. "We won't lose each other."

His look was suddenly not that of her partner, but of a young man caught in the middle of something he had not expected from his first case. Her sympathies went out to him. *By the Bones, I wish I could make this different for you—for all of us.*

I trust you. The answer came back as clear as the shouting and arguing around them, even though Merrick had not opened his mouth. His wise old eyes in that youthful face held hers steady.

Sorcha smiled back—for once grateful for this unusual Bond. Then she turned to Raed, sliding her hand in against his chest, for a moment luxuriating in the warmth and strength of him. She leaned in close, his smell of leather battling with the cigar still clenched in her hand. "We'll do as you say." She paused, took a long breath. "I trust you." She had to say the words, just in case he hadn't heard through their Bond.

Underneath her palm, Raed's heart was suddenly racing. It wasn't their dire situation that caused it, but his body's reaction to her nearness.

He jerked his head toward the crowd that gathered before the towering fountain. "I will get my crew to spread out over there. You, Merrick and Nynnia take up positions at the back—I want you to be invisible." His fingers wrapped around her chin, a gesture she would not have tolerated from anyone else.

Sorcha reached up and stroked the line of his jaw, his beard rough under her fingertips. "Take care of yourself, pirate. I'll be watching."

His kiss was hard and sweet, driving away fear with desire— at least for an instant. Then he turned and drew his men away from them into the crowd.

Sorcha, Merrick and the hunched Nynnia pulled up their hoods and drifted to the rear of the fountain. It was cold enough that they were not the only hooded figures. They found a spot mostly blocked by the bulk of the construction. Merrick's mind was now so wide-open that Sorcha's head swam. The Sensitive had not used any of his powers yet, but even so, the world was brighter through two pairs of eyes than one.

At the front of the crowd Imperial servants were beginning to hand out triangular flags in red and yellow: the Emperor's colors. As these were passed back through the throng, Sorcha noticed the first Guard arrive, dripping in scarlet and gold braid. She knew that they were incredibly well trained—but she was just as sure that they were not prepared for what they were facing. Toward the back, she saw the blue and emerald cloaks of the Emperor's own Deacons. Lolish and Vertrij, a good team—as far as she knew. If her dark suspicions of the Emperor were correct, then maybe not.

Nynnia was standing between them, and for the first time Sorcha noticed tears on her pale cheeks. Either the creature was an excellent actress or she had felt genuine affection for the foci she had called father. "You must not fail," she said softly, glancing up at Sorcha through red-rimmed eyes.

"I know!" Sorcha snapped, feeling enough weight of responsibility.

"No." Nynnia pressed close to her ear and whispered. "You *must* stop them summoning the Murashev—I have seen her. Your world would not survive her coming." When she pulled back, her face was a mask of real terror.

Sorcha believed her. She nodded wordlessly.

A murmur traveled through the crowd like a ripple of wind on water. The flags raised and waved enthusiastically.

"They are here," Sorcha whispered to herself, and the cold descended about them all.

TWENTY-THREE

A Worthy Sacrifice

Raed had lost sight of Sorcha in the crowd, and he told himself that was a good thing. If he couldn't see her, then maybe no one else could either. When the flag-waving began, he even lost sight of Aachon and the crew, but he knew they were close—watching his back as always.

It was sunny for a winter's day, and the press of people around him kept the wind at bay. The festive air of the square was certainly real enough—the citizens of Vermillion were genuinely excited to be seeing the Imperial siblings in the flesh, as was Raed. Putting aside the visions in the Possibility Matrix, it would be the first time he would lay eyes on the Emperor who had been dogging his family's footsteps for such a long time.

A cheer went up near the south end of the square, and the crowd turned as one to crane their heads in that direction. Raed, standing taller than most around him, caught a glimpse of a white horse surrounded by the tin soldiers of the First Guard. The Emperor arrived on a white charger—hardly original. His sister, the Grand Duchess Zofiya, was at his side on a coal black mare. From this distance it was hard to get a good look at them, but as they both dismounted and walked on foot into the Square proper, Raed's heart began to race.

It was a nice touch, Raed had to give them that. Mixing with the people on their level always made a sovereign look like he had a common touch—made him seem unafraid of his own subjects.

The Pretender watched as the Emperor turned and waved to the crowd. Kaleva, second son of Magnhild and now Emperor of Arkaym, was—even Raed had to admit—the very figure of a ruler. He was ten years younger than the Pretender who watched from the crowd. The Emperor was attired simply in white dress uniform, only lightly decorated with gold braid. The crispness of the outfit set off his dark coloring to best advantage, caramel skin and waves of jet-black hair. Yes, Kaleva was a fine-looking young man, the kind to inspire devotion from his citizens and probably send half the princesses in the realm running for their best dresses and most sparkling jewels.

His sister, Zofiya, was only slightly shorter, but a stunning beauty that gleamed like an exotic jewel at his side. Her ebony hair was elaborately tied and draped over one shoulder, standing in stark contrast to the scarlet of the Imperial Guard. Even on the open sea Raed had heard that the Grand Duchess was an excellent commander and a fine swordswoman.

They made a striking pair of siblings, and the Pretender finally understood what he was up against. Raed could hear his father's voice in his head, reminding him that the usurper had stolen everything that once belonged to their family.

We should destroy them all, the Beast slavered. When chaos erupted, it would be easy to kill both the Imperial siblings.

He let out a long breath through his nose and glanced over his shoulder as the Grand Duchess mounted the carved steps of the impressive fountain. Her brother pressed the flesh of the cheering crowd, surrounded by his Guard. Raed knew he would have to act soon.

Kill yourself if you like, but I will become your sister's burden.

The Rossin reminded him of the one fact that had stopped him jumping from the cliffs when he'd found his mother's blood on his hands. He loved his sister, and had sworn that he would never willingly pass his onus to her, but this was about more than his family's curse—this was the death of the realm itself. He couldn't stand by while that happened. Aachon, to his left and two ranks back in the crowd, was shrugging. Everyone seemed happy, waving their flags and cheering. The Grand Duchess stood, hands clasped behind her back, smiling slightly and waiting for them to calm down.

"Good people." Zofiya finally got their attention, and reluctantly the crowd grew silent. "Good people," she began again, her sweet, strong voice only slightly tinged with a Delmaire accent. "When this vital water supply was destroyed by geist attack over a month ago, my beloved brother promised that it would be restored in record time. You now see how he keeps his word."

In among the crowd, Kaleva turned and glanced back at his sister, but it was impossible to see his expression at this distance. The crowd, however, lapped it up.

It was hard not to watch the beautiful Grand Duchess—especially from the Pretender's perspective—but he turned his eyes deliberately back to the crowd. The First Guard were hard to miss, standing stiffly, half-turned toward the mass of people. They were watching Zofiya, but it was obvious that the Emperor Kaleva was their major concern. Some had their eyes turned upward toward the tottering buildings—after all, a shot could come from anywhere. Raed knew good troopers when he saw them, and he was just about to resume scanning the crowd when a flicker caught his attention.

For just a split second something seemed odd about the Guard to the right of the Grand Duchess, on the far side of the fountain. Through the Bond, Raed saw a glint of light dance across his face, as if reflecting off of something above them, and then disappear. The trooper was possessed.

He began charging through the crowd toward Zofiya, while the Rossin laughed, low and wicked in his head. To reach the Grand Duchess in time, the Young Pretender had to tap into the Rossin's power—at the same time holding back the Change as best he could. He had never tried this before, but the Bond with the Deacons gave him more control. The Guards facing the crowd barely had time to turn as he leapt over them, his body still between forms. The Bond was pulling him back, keeping him hanging right on the edge of Change, as the Pretender bent all of his will to reaching the Grand Duchess.

Out of the corner of one watering eye, he saw the possessed Guard raise his gun and fire. The Beast roared in Raed's head as he leapt upon the slender figure of the Duchess.

Hot lead pounded through body and bone as the two of them tumbled backward in the cool waters of the fountain. The Rossin snarled, caught between Change and Bond, its instincts to hold together the body it had lived within for so long. He caught a glimpse of the Imperial Guard hustling the Emperor quickly away—as focused on his safety as they should be.

The water turned red in an instant. Zofiya and the howling Pretender were eye to eye, caught in surprise and shock. The distant screams of the crowd and shouts of the Guards were still a long way off. But the Change was so damn close . . . The Unsung might get his wish to hurt the imposter's family after all.

Zofiya was looking around her at the blood now filling the fountain, realizing it wasn't hers. Understanding dawned upon her face. Raed jerked, feeling crushing pain warring with the rigors of the Change. "Go, go!" he gasped to the Grand Duchess.

He howled in pain as, instead, Zofiya pulled him out of the fountain and onto the cool surface. "Raed Syndar Rossin." She sounded puzzled rather than frightened. At least his fatal bravery would have a fitting epitaph.

"Raed!" Sorcha's voice was nearby; he increased his effort to hold back the Change. The pain was making it hard.

He wasn't so far gone that the rumble didn't reach him. Somewhere below the fountain, something was moving; the cracking was like gunshots. Now the screaming began in earnest as the crowd realized there was more going on than a madman's attempt on the Grand Duchess.

"Imperial Highness." Merrick's voice was calm as he appeared over Sorcha's shoulder. "Please get to safety."

Zofiya opened her mouth to protest, but then her retinue surrounded her. Gloved, urgent hands pulled the Grand Duchess away, despite her protests, using their own bodies as shields. They had their orders. She disappeared in a sea of scarlet uniforms, hustled away.

"It is too late." Nynnia was out of his narrowing cone of vision, but her voice was full of sadness. "You tried your best, mortal, but it was too late. There is no safety left for anyone."

Raed coughed on his own blood as Sorcha pulled him up into her lap. "Damn that," he spluttered, barely able to make himself heard through shock and the shivering edge of the Change. "I saved the bloody Duchess."

Sorcha had her hands pressed to the wound in his side, staunching it as best she could. The world seemed to be tilting. No one was explaining this phenomenon to Raed, and breathing was taking all his concentration.

"He did it; Zofiya is safe!" Sorcha was practically screaming to be heard above the wrenching of rock; she was as outraged as he at the unfairness of it.

"They needed royal blood." Nynnia shook her head, dark curls coming loose to spill down her cheek. Her eyes widened. "The fountain!" She pointed to it, the stone tilted at an angle. "It is draining into the ossuary."

"What are you talking about?" Sorcha pressed harder on Raed's wound, but the pain was distant now.

"The Emperor and the Pretender share much of the same lines . . . Ancient blood to wake the Murashev is pouring into the White Palace."

It was cruel to be dying and know it was for nothing. "It is rising," Merrick said as the ground again rumbled. "They must have connected the pipes to some sort of summoning circle below."

"I believe the expression is, Done"—Raed spat out a great clot of blood and grinned weakly—"and dusted."

"Do something!" Sorcha's expression was dark and dangerous under the wave of her copper hair, and it was turned on Nynnia. "He's dying."

"I can't heal without my foci," Nynnia said, her voice cold even while reality seemed to be getting hotter. "There is only one lord who can save him."

Raed felt the impact of her words and he knew what she meant immediately. Sorcha, however, was distracted by the madness around her, the groan of the underworld rising up to meet them.

It was Merrick who grasped it first. "The Rossin—by the Bones, you mean to use him."

"He has his part to play, as we all do." Nynnia shifted in his vision, for a second looking bright, like a glimpse of the sun. Raed knew he was dying, but by the Blood, he was going to die as himself, not as some raving beast. He tried to shake his head, but there was so very little strength left in him.

Out of the corner of his wavering vision, the Pretender saw Sorcha shoving her Gauntlets on in a sharp gesture. Her face was like stone. "Then we Merge."

Never been done with so many Bonds. Even Merrick's thoughts were hurried and full of fear. Images filled the Pretender's failing mind. To Merge and become one entity was the final act of desperate Deacons—ones who didn't expect to live.

Raed's mouth was full of the taste of iron. "What part of desperate do you not see about you, Merrick?"

The young Deacon was pale, and it was hard to tell if the shake of his hand was due to the tremors of the earth or his own inner fear. Yet he smiled back, a sharp flash of grim humor, the kind that Raed had seen plenty of times on other young men in the heat of battle. Courage was filling him: reckless understanding that this was the end.

Sorcha placed her Gauntlet-encased hand on his head; it was warm like her skin. *I cannot say how this Merge will go—the Rossin is unpredictable.*

No need to tell me. Raed closed his eyes. *I've been living with him my whole life.*

White light burned through his eyelids and the Pretender realized he should have been terrified—yet there was a moment of bliss as he let it take. He surrendered to it, as he never had to any battle in his life.

Four strands of base metal twined together in the forge of the Bond's making. The fear of being lost within one another was overcome by the giddy rush of joining. Flesh and mind were flayed open in pain and ecstasy until only one creature remained. One creature created out of four. The wild core of this being was the Rossin, the geistlord trapped for so long in the bodies of the line of kings. But the others were there; the young and brave Sensitive, the angry power of the Active, and the ancient strength of the Pretender. The Bond wrapped them tighter than twins or lovers, holding mind and flesh together. It not only had the power of the Rossin—it had the vision and runes of the Deacons.

The massive cat towered over Nynnia so that she had to tilt her head back to meet its eye. Standing larger than any feline that had ever walked, its hide was tawny rather than the black of the Rossin, but it was patterned with the runes of the Deacons—even the feared Teisyat. Its eyes flickered from blue to brown to hazel and then gold in a spiral of sparks. As the White Palace erupted around it, there was no fear in the Great Beast. The ground shook as the bones ruptured paving stones and houses, destroying all that humanity had built with shards of what they all eventually came to.

The Beast braced itself on its massive paws, and it roared. It was a sound that proclaimed its ascendancy and rivaled both the screams of the fleeing populace and the rumble of the arriving ossuary. Even Nynnia flinched from it, and the Beast was proud. It was more than the world had ever known; a Merging of the royal line, the geist and the Deacons.

And now it would hunt. The boneyard that punctured Vermillion like a white row of spears was but a sign. The Beast snarled, its curved scimitar canines sliding over its lips. It smelled something below, something that wakened ancient enmity in the deepest core of its brain. Something that made its claws flex and clench into the crumbling stone of the fountain.

When Nynnia reached out and laid her hand into the deep fur of its dark mane, it flicked its head around, ready to destroy her. She too smelled of this enemy; the scent more distant and muted by the wrapping of human flesh, but definitely there.

While the Beast recognized fear in its parts, it was full of its own pride and power. Whatever was below was prey and deserving of death. Even though the woman at its side was at least partly the enemy, her human form protected her from its rage. It even tolerated her hand in its mane. This was nothing to do with the Sensitive deep down relishing her touch. No, certainly not—no human could influence it.

"Come," she said, taking a step down from the broken dais and into the dust of the bones. "The Murashev awaits."

The Beast and the woman picked their way down the stairs into the White Palace, and there was an eerie beauty about it. Rows of skeletons were stacked up on each side; walls made of thighbones and topped with skulls. All of these bones were ancient, their domes crushed in and smelling of dust.

The Beast's scything shoulder blades brushed against the curved roof as it swung its head from side to side, inhaling. Humans had been here, humans that part of it recognized. Deacons had passed this way, smelling of old man and incense. A growl disturbed the massive chest.

The Beast could see better than a cat in the dark and could now make out a light ahead. Those swirling eyes narrowed to slits and the rumble in its chest threatened to become a snarl. The Rossin core recognized the light and was ecstatic. *The light of the Otherside—home.* However, the Deacons within and the uncrowned king were cautious. Something had already breached into this world.

The woman's hand slid out from its mane, and it paused to glance at her. "You must go on ahead," she said softly. "I have to get close to the Murashev without it seeing me." In the near darkness, there seemed to be a glow coming from her, even through the shell of human flesh.

It did not bother the Beast, though deep down the strand of the Sensitive was confused. The creature padded forward on paws of silent velvet through once-tidy rows of bones and skulls.

Whatever had just happened had thrown this section of the White Palace into disarray. Tumbles of ancient skeletons lay all around, and the Beast could not help but crush some as it drew nearer to the light. Not that it looked down; its eyes were riveted to the scene before it. It was obvious that a doorway had been opened because this chamber in the White Palace was full of shades, flickers of white mist hovering around the source of light like eldritch moths.

The Murashev was already here. The geistlord that was no geistlord. The one creature that the Rossin feared. She was such a small creature in this world that the humans in the meld registered astonishment. She stood in the middle of a growing pool of water; water that was pink with the blood of the Pretender. The Murashev was only as tall as the Arch Abbot standing next to her, yet she was the one that glowed. Even the Beast glanced away for a second. For, she was beautiful; more beautiful than anything this realm could offer. Her skin was the scintillating colors of the Otherside, a rainbow of running shades that entranced over a body that was at least humanoid. Long tendrils of what might be termed hair fanned out around her head, curling alternatively toward and away from Hastler. Behind, a long, curved tail twitched, the only addition to a form very similar to those it would burn and enslave.

The Rossin repressed its growl, crouched low in the wreckage of bones, and prepared to strike. Great muscles bunched and the Merged creature charged, ready to rip and rend the Abbot and the Murashev apart.

Then the new arrival turned her face to the Beast. It was the face of one who dwelt in the deepest parts of the Otherside, all beauty and deadly danger. The melded creature stopped midstride.

My new body is here. The Murashev's lips did not move from their wicked smile, but her words buried themselves directly like splinters into the brain. *The final piece fits.*

The Beast snarled and roared, held in place by muscles suddenly not capable of anything. The Murashev had not even gestured. She stepped out of the pool, blood-soaked water running down her shifting form, and she walked toward the Beast, trailing light. The white mist of dancing shades followed, leaping in the air with joy at this creature's arrival.

You have done well, Hastler. The mesmerizing eyes ran over the great shape of the Beast. *This scion of our line will indeed make a fine home for my power in this world.*

"As promised, great lady." The Abbot seemed to be made of shadow against the burning light of the Murashev. "Two of our best Deacons, and the Pretender to the throne; worthy material to make you a body for this realm."

The tendrils of light whipped about, moved by unseen winds, and that eldritch smile burned bright. *Indeed, I am the Opener of ways. Blood of kings brought me here, and I will bring fire— enough fire to consume every citizen of the Empire. Each one sacrificed will bring my kin back into this world.*

The Murashev burned too hot for this world—she would need flesh, and soon. The Rossin within howled at the trap. The Murashev's hand reached out and touched the Beast, and it was like winter invading the Merge. The four entities within cried out as tendrils pulled at them to make space for this much greater force. Sensitive, Active, and Pretender screamed as one.

As on the Otherside, the enemy was clever and cruel, more so than any geistlord. She sought to break them apart and find her own place in the Bond. She would become them. The veins of the Murashev twined through them all.

Merrick saw his father on that stone staircase, burning with the power of the Deacons. Raed saw his mother's face, the horror as she was pulled down into the Rossin's talons while he, buried so deep, was unable to do anything about it. Sorcha heard the siren cry of the Otherside, the one she had tried to ignore for so long; had tried to pretend held no attraction for her.

Ripping and tearing, the Merge was tested to its ultimate limit. The Murashev wanted *in*—to become part of them—yet they would not let her. The strain was intense, burning and physical for a long moment. And yet—it held. Sorcha and Merrick, who had thought their Bond only a temporary thing—found it so much more. And then Sorcha and Raed, the unexpected surprise, sudden like a storm. Even between Raed and the Rossin, a bond of fear and rage was still more than it had once been. All of these tangled bonds—some new, some ancient—held true against the assault of the Murashev.

She could not get in. Outraged beyond measure, the Murashev resorted to brute force. If she could not have the body she wanted, then she would destroy them and find another, but she would leave no geistlord behind to challenge her. The strand of the Rossin was too powerful, but the humans were weak. She turned her might upon them. Flesh and mind caught fire under her assault; the strands howled in agony. As long as they were together—they would all burn together.

Do not let me in, then. Her voice made the ossuary tremble like a struck bell. *I will unmake you one by one. It will be my first pleasure in this world.*

Finally human spirit could not take any more pain—they let go of the Bond and fell into brightness.

Sorcha staggered out of the light of the dissolving Merge, feeling as though her mind and body were still in pieces. Merrick was on his knees to her right, shaking his head like an animal emerging from hibernation. To her left, Raed—more experienced in shifting than the others—was getting up, his hand already going to his saber.

There before them was the Murashev, the bright creature of every Deacon's nightmare. And she did not look at all happy. Her tendrils danced and her tail lashed, and Sorcha was sure she had indeed smoked her last cigar. Ruefully she patted the remaining one in her pocket. Despite knowing that it was useless, she raised her Gauntlets.

Then Nynnia appeared, leaping out of the shadows like a cast spear. She attacked the Murashev, the light spilling from her in a very similar way to that of her opponent. Sorcha knew what that meant. Her form was too fast and lethal for her to be anything but from the Otherside. Merrick staggered to his feet and made toward the whirling females, struggling and howling as Sorcha tried to hold him back. The light flared around them, knocking them off their feet once more.

Within the bright globe, Nynnia and the Murashev fought while the flocks of geists spun around them. It was hard to see anything, but what she could make out gave Sorcha pause. The

Murashev's form was flickering—without a mortal body, it could not last long in this realm. Nynnia had the advantage of a physical form, but it was also a hindrance. Flesh burned where they touched, but she did not flinch or slow.

Sister, we can breathe again—this fighting is foolish. The Murashev's voice was a purr; soothing and calm.

"And they die for it." Nynnia's hair, scorched and burned in some places, stuck to her pretty face. "This is not our way."

The two females clashed again, sending showers of light cascading over the humans—four humans. For a moment Sorcha had forgotten Arch Abbot Hastler. She had wanted to forget the shock of seeing the head of the Order standing at the side of the great enemy. It had been easier to imagine him kidnapped.

However, she could not afford to hide in ignorance. Summoning the Murashev was a task that would drain any Deacon. She needed to act now. Sorcha's brow furrowed, and she took a careful step toward the Arch Abbot. Bile choked the back of her throat.

Raed made to go with her, but she shook her head. "This is my fight, my Abbot." His hazel eyes locked with hers; then one finger lightly touched her cheek and he let her go.

Hastler saw her coming, and his face, which she had once thought kindly, twisted into rage. As she strode toward him, her stomach twisted with fear, Sorcha called out. "I think you need to come in, Hastler. You really need to face an Episcopal inquiry."

"Weak," the Arch Abbot replied. "You always were a weakling with far too much power."

"And you relied on that when you sent us north." Sorcha's ear was tuned to the raging battle between the Murashev and Nynnia. "You moved us like pieces on a board."

His lips split in a cruel smile. "The Knot is tightening, and you may have slipped it twice, but it will find you again." His Gauntlets were already on, but as she got closer he tied on his Strop as well. The tooled leather turned him from a maddened old man into an eerie creature whose eyes were replaced by runes. Sorcha hoped he was more exhausted by the summoning than he appeared; Hastler was more than her equal. By the Bones, she hoped he didn't have it in him to open Teisyat.

She reached out along the Bond for Merrick, and it was like hitting a raw nerve. Merging had made the Bond as sensitive as a newly pulled tooth, but the world bloomed bright. Hastler was glowing in this world, but not as strongly as he normally would have. Blue tinges were emerging; he was reaching for Yevah. She had to act quickly—she summoned Seym. Her body filled with power.

Sorcha ran, and before Hastler could get his rune shield up, she was on him. When she wrapped her arms tight around him, she found him as cold as a piece of ice—dealing with the Otherside could do that to a person. A lesser Deacon would probably have died from such a summoning, but she had no time to compliment her superior on his fine achievement. Yevah was of no use to the Arch Abbot now—not while Sorcha was so close—but he still had plenty of reserves.

He's reaching for Pyet, Merrick howled in the back of her head.

"By the Bones," Sorcha grunted. For an old man, Hastler was strong and hard to get a handle on. She twisted and grabbed at his Gauntlets before he could bring the burning power of the rune to bear on her. She had no desire to find herself a piece of crumbling toast hanging on his back.

It felt wrong, and yet deeply good, to smash a fist into his face. Normally, punching an old man would have been the lowest of the low—but this was the man who had summoned the greatest danger to her city, made them outlaws and, above all, lied to her. But even as Sorcha tried to hold on, Hastler broke away from her; residual strength from the Murashev must have been aiding him. Once free, he turned the fire starter rune on her.

Try Shayst, Merrick hissed into her mind effortlessly—more an idea than words.

It was the rune that drew power from a geist, and as far as Sorcha knew it had never been used on a human before. But then, Hastler was only borderline human now, anyway. With a yell that contained all her rage and frustration, Sorcha summoned the rune of drawing and shoved her green-lit hands onto the Strop that girded the other's eyes. The sensation was like fire pouring into her head. Dimly she was aware of screaming, and realized that it was coming from both of them.

Her body was flung aside. She slid across the floor and smashed into the far wall of bones, but she barely felt the impact. Weakly, she struggled up out of the debris of the dead to see Raed charge the Abbot. His first blow was only just caught by Hastler as the Abbot raised Yevah, the edge of the Pretender's

blade slicing through the top layer of the cloak that Hastler had
no damn right to wear.

He seemed to have been slightly blinded by her drawing of
his power; he clasped one Gauntlet to his Strop, and the delivery
of the shield rune was awkward. Still, by the time Raed spun
and made a second strike, the Arch Abbot had recovered enough
to summon Deiyant. The Pretender was shoved backward as if
caught by a great wind. Sorcha struggled to her feet, her head
buzzing with an unfamiliar energy. Traditional weapons, then.
She rolled to her feet, though every muscle screamed a protest, and ran toward the Abbot as he advanced on the stunned
Pretender.

She had time to spare a glance back toward Nynnia and the
Murashev. The women were now impossible to see, their blazing light a sun in the ossuary. Merrick was standing nearby and
Sorcha could feel him feeding his energy to Nynnia—though it
would not be as effective without a Bond. Still, he turned and
looked at Sorcha. Their gaze, only a heartbeat long, pinned her
with a realization.

She is losing. His mental voice was calm—much calmer than
his physical one would have been. *You must kill the Murashev's
foci!*

By the Bones—he meant Hastler. It made sense; without a
physical body capable of holding her, the creature would need
some foothold in this realm, even after such a powerful summoning.

Sorcha gritted her teeth. Holding her palm outward, she
opened Chityre. The ground beneath Hastler's feet exploded. It
wouldn't get past his shield—but it got his attention. His grin
was maniacal on a face that had always seemed serene. This had
to be a terrible nightmare, Sorcha thought, as he turned Deiyant
on her.

Her attempt to raise her own shield was not quick enough—
even running on reduced strength, Hastler was still faster than
she. The manipulation rune closed on her throat as effectively as
a giant fist. Despite the fact that she knew it was pointless, Sorcha scrambled against nonexistent hands. Her vision dipped and
spun. Her own power was subsiding, her Gauntlets dimming and
waning as life drained from her.

She reached out for Merrick, but his power was twined
with Nynnia's and it was not enough. The Bond found her a

replacement. The Rossin, injured and depleted though it was, reached out to her with a heady flow of power directly from the Otherside.

With a gasp, she managed to light her shield rune underneath his—an impressive feat. Hastler's face twisted with rage as the recoil knocked him back a step or two. But when he righted himself, she knew just by the look on his face that he was going for Teisyat. The unknown quantity of what a door to the Otherside would do in the ossuary was enough to make her tremble with fear.

And then Raed struck, the curved scimitar smashing through ribs and back and emerging in a flow of blood that no cantrip could prevent. Hastler looked once at Sorcha in rage and astonishment. Raed twisted his sword and the old man crumpled. It was habit that drove her to his side—that was what she told herself.

The look on the face of the dying man, however, was not one of defeat. "You do not know it, but you are already caught," he gasped. "It will be just as I saw." His laughter was choked with blood, and he had a white-knuckle grip around a medallion that had fallen loose from under his shirt. Sorcha waited until he slumped back, finally dead, before prying it from his fingers. It was a knot of two snakes, twined around each other in a circle and eating each other's tails. Nothing else remained to tell what it meant. She put it into her pocket quickly, just as Raed struggled to her side.

And then the world tipped. The trained part of her knew that the banishment of a Murashev would not be easy, but she could never have prepared for the cacophony of sound and light that swept around her. The howl as the creature was sucked back into the Otherside was terrible. Without corporeal body or foci, there was nothing to keep her in the human realm when confronted with the void.

When the survivors straightened, Merrick was standing in a hollow blasted clear of bones. Of the Murashev there was no sign, but the Deacon was holding the burnt and disfigured body of Nynnia in his arms.

She protected me. Merrick's thoughts were like sharp pins in Sorcha's head, full of loss and foolish hope. Carefully, she knelt down next to her partner. She didn't need to ask why the creature had done what she had to save Merrick—in her eyes gleamed real triumph. Sorcha, however, still had questions that needed answers.

"You are like the Murashev, aren't you?" she whispered.

Merrick gave her a stern look, but the shattered remains of the beautiful Nynnia smiled. "Once again, you only see a part of the truth." Her once-sweet lips twisted in pain. "Like, but not like. The same . . . The same creature, but not all our kind agreed with its course of action. My path, being born as a human, takes longer, limits us—but I was sent to stop this."

"And you have," Raed said softly, his hand resting on Sorcha's shoulder.

Nynnia gasped, her body undoubtedly descending into shock. "Yes, I did. But I did not expect to find love here." Nynnia's smile was faint but victorious. "And neither did you, Deacon Faris."

Sorcha gasped, her memory flashing back to those dreams she'd had while sharing a room with Nynnia. What had the creature done? What had been whispered into her head while she slept on unaware? Were the feelings she had for Raed only part of some Otherside plan?

"Hastler was not the only one who could see the future," the dying girl whispered, "yet he could not include me in his calculations. I am not of your world, after all. My elders said I shouldn't have been born, taken human form, but I have no regrets . . ." Her hand fluttered up to rest against Merrick's lips. "None."

Merrick brushed her hair from her face and her scorched lips as gently as he could. "We're safe, thanks to you." His tears poured out of his gentle eyes.

"No—not safe," she gasped, lurching up in his arms, her fingers locking on his hand. "This will not be their last attempt!" Nynnia coughed and writhed in real mortal pain. "They will not stop." Her eyes were losing their luster; the light of the Otherside dimming in them. One final breath rattled out of her broken body. Merrick held her close, but there was no way for even a Deacon to hold back death. Whatever the creature had been, she died as a mortal.

Then there were only the three of them, staring into one another and surrounded only by bones and death.

TWENTY-FOUR

Into Apostasy

Merrick held to his training—it was all he had left. He gathered up Nynnia, knowing she deserved proper ceremony. She felt so light, as if her departed soul had been the heaviest thing about her—if she had possessed a soul at all.

Through his numbness, the logical part of him was still working. "We have to take Hastler's body too," he mumbled. "There will have to be an Episcopal inquiry. The Presbyters will need to see it, much as it should stay here to rot."

Sorcha's blue eyes, dark pits in the dimness of the ossuary, flicked to Raed. "Can you carry him?" She did not complain, but the way she held herself spoke of at least a broken rib. Wordlessly, Raed slung the remains of Hastler over his shoulder.

As they scrambled mournfully up into the light, around him Merrick could hear the creaks and groans of the White Palace, as if they were buried within an arthritic body. The ossuary was sliding back underground; drawn up by geist-power, it was returning to its natural place.

None of these facts made any impact on him. They were distant details to the cooling form in his arms. Perhaps he had been a fool to love Nynnia so quickly, and with so little thought, but he wasn't going to wish it had never happened. She had not told him what she was, but her actions spoke of a bright being that he would miss. Some inherent Sensitive part remembered her words and knew that in the shadows to come, they would need all the help they could get.

The blazing light of the sun made him blink through eyes still burning with tears and scarred from the light of the Otherside. The people were emerging from their houses—frightened, yes, but aching to see what had happened. Their faces, covered in dust, looked so alien that for a moment Merrick feared that Nynnia's sacrifice had not been enough; that they were surrounded by damned souls staring at the body of their Arch Abbot tossed so casually over one shoulder of the Pretender to the throne. His mind raced—something was very wrong in a day that had seen enough wrong—yet his mind was too numbed to make hasty connections.

Then the Order arrived. The trio was surrounded by the emerald and blue cloaks of Merrick's fellow Deacons, like ornamented crows. They moved swiftly between the survivors, shielding them from the view of Imperial troops and commoners. They took Hastler from Raed, and Sorcha disappeared from sight altogether. A knot of panic clenched in Merrick, and he knew it was not an entirely unreasonable reaction.

Their own Arch Abbot had been conspiring with creatures of the Otherside—who knew if this was an aberration or a new policy? Only his awareness of the Bond kept the young Deacon sane. He might not be able to see the others, but he could feel them. Sorcha was as numb as he was, while Raed felt resigned; he would not be able to escape from the Order now.

When kind hands tried to take Nynnia from him, though, Merrick stood tall, clasping her close. "I will carry her," he said, his voice cracking a little.

It was an uneasy return to the Mother Abbey, flanked by Deacons none of them knew if they could trust. He resisted the urge to fall gratefully into their arms. A lot had happened in a few weeks and he was not the green boy who had ridden out that day.

They took Sorcha and Raed to the infirmary, but Merrick they left alone in the mortuary to lay Nynnia out. He straightened her limbs, cleaned her face and carefully cut away her dress. It was burnt to her skin in many places, but he was able to remove enough to put her in a decent replacement.

He heard Presbyter Rictun come in, but did not acknowledge his superior until he was done. Turning around, he locked eyes with the man who was now, effectively, one of the heads of the Order in the Empire. With Hastler dead, the five Presbyters would speak for the Mother Abbey; and yet Merrick didn't know if they were as corrupt as the Arch Abbot had been.

It took the young Deacon a moment to recognize at the Presbyter's back were five others from the Order—a quickly assembled Conclave. Their linked minds were probing his, weighing every word for truth. Well, they were not the only ones who could do that.

Merrick's eyes narrowed. The woman he had been growing to love had died, the world had teetered on the edge of doom, and the man they had all trusted to lead them had proven false. Before they could stop him, Merrick thrust with his Sensitive power, which had never failed him in the ossuary, even for a moment. Indeed, it seemed to have grown stronger, and he slipped easily within the Presbyter's mind.

It was not a place he wanted to be, cool and perhaps cruel— but Merrick had his answer. Inside, the Presbyter was shocked and disgusted with Hastler, concerned with what this would mean for the Order, and cautious about what Sorcha, Raed and Merrick had seen in the White Palace. That was all.

The Conclave's attention swelled and he was unceremoniously ejected from the Presbyter's mind. One of the Conclave members muttered under his breath, no doubt displeased with the young Deacon's presumption.

Rictun's eyes widened slightly as he realized how easily Merrick had plucked his concerns from his mind, but surprise soon turned to anger. "So it was Hastler? You saw him consorting with the Murashev?"

The mental fingers of the Conclave pressed harder into Merrick's mind, holding him rigid like a bug as he said the words condemning their beloved leader. "Yes, it was Arch Abbot Hastler. He planned the death of Grand Duchess Zofiya to bring the Murashev into Vermillion. Why, I cannot say with certainty."

Rictun cleared his throat. "A full inquiry is being assembled for two days' time. There we will examine your partner's experience, but it has already been decided: the Arch Abbot's part in this will not be revealed to the public. The only person outside the Order to know of it will, of course, be the Emperor."

Merrick felt his jaw tighten, and his mind opened to Sorcha. *They're going to cover up that Hastler was behind all of this.* He felt her rage boiling over the edges of his own.

It must have been enough for even the Active Rictun to feel, because he raised his hand. "Think for a moment about this, Deacon Chambers. Think what would happen to the Order if we disclosed everything. Do you really want to go back to the bad old days before we came here?"

Merrick glared at him. "The truth is not an option; it is a necessity." His words echoed in the emptiness of the mortuary.

"Really?" Rictun grinned bleakly. "Think about it: none of the great unwashed would ever believe that the Order is not corrupt. They would never trust us again. They would never turn to us when the geists break through."

Merrick glanced down at his feet, thinking of his first taste of what geists could do to the unprepared. The bodies of the slain Tinkers haunted his nightmares.

"They would understand, if we explained properly." Even his own ears could discern the edge of uncertainty in his voice.

Rictun strode over and looked down at what remained of Nynnia, and then he delivered the ultimate blow. "You don't believe that, Chambers, and you know this woman's sacrifice will be for nothing if the people lose faith in us. We are the only defense they have against the geists."

Merrick felt his throat go tight, and he had the sudden awful feeling that if he spoke now, he might cry. Light from the one stained glass window was casting a soft rainbow glow over Nynnia's body, concealing her terrible wounds. His fingers drifted back to touch her now-cold hand.

He opened himself to Sorcha again, and felt reassured that despite her anger she had come to the same conclusion. Clearing his throat, he turned to face his superior. "A lie is a terrible thing, but what I have seen in the last few weeks is also terrible. One day, the truth will come out." Pausing, he squeezed Nynnia's hand as if she could still feel it.

Rictun's eyes narrowed. "But not today?"

"No, not today."

The Presbyter nodded. "A wise choice, Deacon." His concerns assuaged, his tone softened. "You and Deacon Faris will submit yourselves to the inquiry by day's end. There is much to be decided, if the Order is to survive."

"Naturally." Then Sorcha's concerns flooded over him. "Presbyter Rictun," he called. His superior paused at the door. "What of Raed Syndar Rossin? He was a great help to us. He even saved the life of the Grand Duchess."

It was impossible to read Rictun's expression. "He is also the Pretender to the throne, and one of our Emperor's greatest enemies. He will be locked in one of the civic prisons until his fate can be decided." He sighed. "But I believe our liege will be inclined to leniency, given the circumstances."

"Are you certain, or just confident?" Merrick asked, feeling Sorcha's rush of rage clog his throat.

Rictun gave him a stern look. "Today no one can be sure of anything, but I will certainly take the results of the inquiry to the Emperor and plead his case."

Merrick felt something else in Sorcha then, something that she only barely acknowledged herself: guilt.

Her partner asked where she could not. "And Deacon Kolya Petav, Presbyter? Will he be at the inquiry?"

The answer plunged Sorcha deeper into remorse. "No, he will not. He is still in a healing coma in the infirmary. The mess the Arch"—Rictun broke off with a glower—"Hastler made of your Bond will have to wait until more pressing matters have been dealt with."

It was enough for now. The Presbyter left Merrick to his mourning, and even his partner pulled back her consciousness. He was left alone with the ashes of his love and hope.

The Pretender slept fitfully in the comfort of the Emperor's prison, but it was not that his host was exceptionally harsh. The cell was clean and tidy, and surprisingly it contained a very comfortable mattress over the slotted wood cot. Nor was it his jailors, who seemed uninterested in torturing him. They fed him through the bars with simple but tolerable fare.

No, it was the chattering of the Deacons in his head that Raed could not stand. He turned over on the bed with many a sigh and tried to block out the whispers of the inquiry he was forced to share with Sorcha and Merrick.

It was impossible. Whatever floodgate they had opened in the ossuary, it refused to close.

In time, it will fade. The Rossin, too, was tired of the connection.

Eventually exhaustion won out over the drone of Deacons, and the Pretender managed to get a few hours' sleep. The noise of a crowd outside woke him. It was not the cheering noise from the day before, but the shuffle of somber feet and subdued whispering. Wiping sleep from his eyes, Raed stood on his bed and peered out the window.

The jail was on Silk Road, one of the main thoroughfares of Vermillion, and when he peered out into the early-morning light he could see it was already crowded with people. No flags were in evidence this day and everyone was dressed in shades of gray. Raed could, in fact, make out weeping.

Outside his cell, one of his jailors was about to slide a morning meal between the bars, so the Pretender ventured a question whose answer he feared: "What's happening outside?"

The man's lip curled, and his brows knitted together in an expression that he had not worn the previous day. "It's the funeral procession for the Arch Abbot."

Raed swallowed hard as dread built in every nerve ending. "A state funeral for a traitor?"

The jailor threw the tin tray containing Raed's breakfast against the bars. Some of it splattered onto him. That was a shock, but the sudden boiling rage on the man's face was too. "Shut your filthy mouth," he bellowed. "You're not fit to lick that sainted man's boots."

This was a very bad sign, but Raed couldn't help himself. "Fond of murderers, are you?"

The jailor's face grew crafty. "You might be singing a different tune by the end of the day." He left Raed alone with that prophecy hanging in the air.

Raed turned once more to the window to see how the Order took care of its own. He had to see how it would all end, despite everything. The crowd was filling every cranny of the street, hanging out of every window and clinging to any other vantage point they could find. The whispering was louder too, and there were plenty of angry faces among the grieving. Raed did not imagine it; one or two were turned in the direction of the jail.

The cortege was announced by the low drone of pipes, a fresh wave of weeping and the rattle of carriage wheels. Clenching his hands around the bars, Raed was able to pull himself up a little and see farther down the street. Four ebony Breed horses pulled a shining wagon on which was placed an elaborate brass and oak chair, surmounted by the emblem of the Order, the Eye and the Fist. It had to be Hastler's chair of office. Another carriage followed up the rear, and this one had a plain coffin on it.

Raed's dread now filled his stomach and bubbled behind his eyes. The ranks of Deacons followed, made all dark and somber by the fact their cloaks were turned about so that the black lining showed. Only a flutter of occasional emerald or blue indicated who was Sensitive and who was Active. It could have been only his imagination, but he thought he caught a glimpse of copper hair among the ranks. His eyes closed briefly as the Deacons gave way to files of aristocracy and Imperial Guard making up the rear of the cortege.

He'd been betrayed. He'd been stupid. Naturally, the Order would never reveal what their Arch Abbot had been! It didn't matter that he'd saved the Grand Duchess—such trivial details were of little account.

As the dirge receded into the distance, the Pretender's hands grew white, clenching harder around the bars. He was so consumed with his own rage that for a minute he took no notice of the change in the crowd. He didn't drop back when the first of the angry fingers were pointed in his direction—and by then it was too late.

A wave of outraged screams swelled up in the crowd. A deep bellow sounded from many throats, and then came the wave of missiles. Raed jerked back from the window, but the damage was already done. They had seen the object of their anger.

The rattle of objects thrown against the jail was far too loud to be merely soft fruit. It sounded instead as if the crowd, now turning itself into a mob, had pried loose some of the paving stones as well. The impact of these only grew, and now he could make out individual words.

Murderer! Assassin!

Raed glanced over his shoulder. There were thumps in the depths of the building, the rattle of angry fists on the doors of the prison. He strode to the cell door and, grasping it, made to call out to his jailor. The door swung in his grip. While he'd been occupied with the scene outside, his newly unfriendly captor had unlocked it.

So, his guardians were of the same opinion as the mob. The smell of smoke wafted up from outside just as the screaming reached a level to make his ears ring. Even if there was one jailor that didn't like the taste of a lynch mob, there was no way that man would risk his life for the Pretender. Raed slipped through the door and into the corridor, but after that his plan got very blurry.

"Not staying for the show?" The woman's voice was behind him, and it was the sweetest sound he had ever heard.

Spinning around, he caught Sorcha's grim smile—and she was not alone. Merrick, despite the fact that Hastler had tricked him into partnership with the older Deacon, remained true to his vows.

"It doesn't sound like my sort of party," Raed admitted, before kissing her. In his mind, there was always time for that.

"Quickly." Merrick grabbed them both and tugged them down the corridor in the opposite direction from the screaming of the mob. The alarming smashing now sounded very much like a door giving up its hold on its hinges.

Together the three of them ran past the row of cells full of cheering, howling prisoners. Down a spiraling staircase, they found the back door. It was smoking and lying on the ground. Raed shot Sorcha a surprised look, but she smiled back. "We were a little short of time."

He was not going to question her methods, because behind them they could now hear the sound of pounding feet. Dashing out into the alleyway, however, he found the rescue more than a little lacking. "I hate to be picky—but shouldn't we have some method of escape?"

Silk Road, to their right, was still packed with angry people; angry because they were unable to get to the front of the lynch mob pouring into the Imperial Jail.

"We had horses!" Merrick's face was pale.

"You can't leave anything lying about in this town." Raed shrugged, feeling that knot of dread tightening up once again.

There was nowhere to hide in this narrow alley, and several of the mob had become aware of the three of them. People had been swallowed by shared anger, losing all inhibition and control. It was now turning toward them like a great beast with many heads. Raed wondered how painful getting torn apart would be. He would have at least liked to have had a sword.

Sorcha tossed him hers without him having to ask, but her next action startled him. She shoved her Gauntlets on her hands and turned toward the onrushing mob. He recalled suddenly her outrage at Aulis when she threatened to use the runes on the public. And along the Bond he could feel her—it was not fear of death that she was feeling; it was something colder. She had lost her faith in the Order and what it stood for. Her concern now was purely about defending those who mattered to her.

Green fire sprang along the length of her spread fingers, and the stony look on her face was one he had never seen before—even when they had faced the Murashev. *Join her.* The Rossin was aroused by the promise of unfettered violence. *Unleash me.*

The mob bore down on them and the air tasted like sweat and electricity, as Sorcha raised her Gauntlets and prepared to break every tenet of the Order she'd been a part of since childhood.

"Sorcha, don't!" Merrick was usually the calmer, tempered one, but his voice cracked with such power that for a moment she did indeed pause. Or maybe it was the world itself—for it dipped into that misty moment that Raed had experienced before; the time before decision and death.

What happened in the next heartbeat, the Pretender could not quite identify. The walls of the alleyway distorted, bending in an optical illusion that stopped everyone short. And then the tide of emotion swept over them. Suddenly Raed was thrown back to that moment when he had awoken with his mother's blood all over him, her broken and torn body at his feet. The grief washed over him, as fresh and terrible as it had been in the moment when it had dawned on him what the Rossin had done.

At his side, Sorcha was curled in on herself, a strangled sound of utmost despair clawing its way out of her throat. Through his tears, Raed was able to see that the crowd—descending on them angrily only a second before—was also wracked with despair. They huddled on the street, sobbing and clutching at one another, in the throes of the emotional storm; a wash of misery that had been leveled upon them far more easily than anything Sorcha could have done.

Raed was only just able to nail that observation down before the waves of his own emotions crashed over him once more. The rawness of despair ran through his body, the depth of melancholy impossible to resist. That was, until Merrick's hand touched his shoulder. "Raed." His voice cut through the grief and pain, removing it as swiftly as it had come.

The Pretender climbed to his feet, noticing that Sorcha had also been pulled free of whatever had happened to them. She was brusquely wiping away her tears, turned slightly away; embarrassment burned along the Bond.

Merrick's Strop dangled from his fingertips, tucked behind his back as if he were ashamed of it. A flicker of rainbow light played across its surface and was gone. Raed had studied the ways of the Order, and he had never heard of any Sensitive doing any such thing. Yet there it was; Merrick had leveled a lynch mob by reaching in and twisting their emotions—hard.

The three of them stared at one another, and then Deacon Chambers folded his Strop and tucked it inside his shirt. His expression was as flinty as his partner's had been when she had faced the mob. "It won't last long." He flicked his reversed cloak around his shoulders and began picking his way through the still-weeping crowd.

Sorcha and Raed followed after. They had to be careful; people were rolling around sobbing, crying the names of dead relatives, and merely howling incoherently. No one paid the three of them any mind.

The circle of this emotional storm was three streets wide, leveling every citizen—even those beyond Silk Road who had not been involved in the lynching. Sorcha draped her cloak over Raed as they found the edge of the effect, lifting the hood to hide his features. Ahead of them Merrick was still striding, not looking over his shoulder, his back ramrod straight.

"Do you know what that was?" Raed whispered, clenching her cool hand in his.

She shook her head, her eyes wide, concerned and still a little red from the sudden tears. "There are many things that Actives do not know, about what Sensitives do," she muttered, "but I do not think this is taught in any class at the Order."

"And by the looks of him, now is not the time to ask." Raed lifted her fingers and kissed them lightly. "But I appreciate the rescue."

Her smile was bright, sudden, and concealed immediately. "It was not quite as planned." She did not say it, but Raed could hear her thoughts. *Consequences be damned.*

Eventually they passed through another section of narrow alleyways and into the Artisan Quarter. Weavers hung their wares out in front of stores while talking with passersby. It was loud and vibrant, and stood out in stark contrast to the weeping mob they had so narrowly escaped. Merrick flicked aside a tapestry that, ironically, showed the achievements of the native Order, and led them into the depths of one of the shops.

In the basement Raed felt the last of the melancholy lift from his shoulders. "Aachon!" He crossed the short distance and grabbed hold of his first mate before the man could move. The slap on his back was gruff but heartily meant. The Pretender laughed loudly as the rest of his crew crowded around him; not a single one was missing.

Over the tops of their heads, he glanced back and saw the Deacons standing as still as herons by the door. They, Raed realized, had risked a great deal to get him to safety. To extend such loyalty to someone not in the Order was something he had not expected. But the Bond was still there. He might have wanted it gone, but it had saved them all.

Raed cleared his throat. "What now?"

Sorcha's hands clenched at her sides, and her voice was soft. "There is a ship leaving tomorrow morning, with a captain who asks no questions. He is heading north to Ulrich. You are safe here until then." She pulled her cloak about her and, with a look at Merrick, jerked her head toward the door.

They slipped out before Raed could say anything, but he wasn't exactly sure what he would have said, anyway.

TWENTY-FIVE

Comfort in Eschaton

The summons to appear before the Presbyterial Council came before nightfall. Apparently attending a state funeral had not worn out its members—something that Sorcha had counted on as protection at least until the morning.

Rictun sat to the right of the glaring gap in the circle where the Arch Abbot's chair had been. He was very close to coming to power and Sorcha knew that his position now was merely a formality. In the next week, Rictun would be the new Arch Abbot. For now, though, she was too busy fighting for her place in the Order—hers and Merrick's—to be concerned by Rictun's imminent promotion.

When they had slipped out of the ranks of mourning Deacons, they'd both known there would be consequences, but she had made sure that it was she alone who stood before the Council. She had said nothing about what Merrick had done; she didn't know what it was anyway. All that they knew, all that had been reported to them by those Deacons who witnessed her, was that she had nearly used the runes against civilians—even if those civilians were about to rip her apart.

To cover up his actions, the Council had claimed the wave of sorrow that had followed was the sainted Arch Abbot Hastler intervening so that no violence would be done in his name.

Sorcha knew the beginnings of a martyrdom legend when she saw it. By the end of the week there would be miracles in the tomb and sobbing mothers taking their sick children there to be healed. Her role in this myth-in-the-making, she also suspected.

"The only reason you are still wearing the symbol of the Order"—Rictun stood and looked around at his fellow Presbyters—"is because of what you did in the ossuary."

"Very glad you still remember," Sorcha muttered, so far into her rage that even Merrick's soothing presence through the Bond could not stop her.

"Deacon Faris," Presbyter of the Young, Melisande Troupe, leaned forward, her white-gold hair cascading around her shoulders. "No one can deny that you saved Vermillion from destruction, nor would anyone have argued against your freeing the Pretender Raed Syndar Rossin, since the Emperor himself was planning to do the same thing. You are here for the use of runes on the general population—something expressly forbidden by the Charter."

"But I did not—"

"You would have." Presbyter of Sensitives Yvril Mournling's gray eyes drilled through her where she stood. "The action would have occurred if it had not been for a turn in the crowd."

Sorcha frowned. Surely Mournling of all people should know what had gone on, but something in his expression, something subtle, begged for her silence. *How can he know, when even I do not?* Merrick's voice whispered in the back of her head. Even there, his tone was thin and sad.

Her throat tightened. A wild talent, then, like Garil's, and if anyone were to discover it . . .

"I admit," she said, tucking her shaking hands behind her back, "I did act without thought, and in a moment of self-preservation I was tempted to use my gifts on the mob." She hung her head. "I let my primitive instincts take over, and I stand ready to be punished for it." Hopefully they would ask no more questions before her dismissal.

When Sorcha glanced up, the look of shock on Rictun's face made the admission worth it. He cleared his throat. "That is very well, but you have sullied the good you did. The people of Vermillion will not forget—"

Presbyter of the Actives, Zathra Trelaine, raised one scarred and crooked hand, stopping Rictun in midsentence. He stood and walked haltingly to Sorcha. As a Deacon, Trelaine had earned every one of his injuries in service to the Arch Abbot—his pain at the betrayal was deeper than most and she could read it on his face.

He looked Sorcha up and down, and the tremble in her hands worked its way up her arms. "You do not understand, Deacon Faris—control has always been our greatest concern with you. Despite your power, which none even among the Council can match, you still have a tenuous grip on it."

She opened her mouth to protest, but then closed it with a snap. She disliked being wrong; it curdled her stomach and brought a thousand excuses to mind, but there it was—the bald truth of it.

"Your service to the Order in the ossuary was exceptional"— Trelaine's eyes narrowed—"and I was one of the ones in this session that championed your ascension to our ranks."

Sorcha swallowed hard—a Presbyter . . . They meant to make her . . .

Her superior shook his head. "Naturally, that is now out of the question, and you will have to remain within the Mother Abbey for a good few months until the rumbles of your actions have died down."

A wave of relief made Sorcha dizzy. "Then . . . then I may remain a Deacon?"

Trelaine crooked an eyebrow. "You are too powerful for anything else, and perhaps with the right partner"—his emphasis on "right" brought a rush of reality to her giddy moment—"you may yet learn something."

The Presbyter turned and limped back to his chair, apparently washing his hands of any further comment.

"But there must be punishment for such transgression," Rictun barked. "To even contemplate . . ."

"Yet that was all she did." Presbyter Mournling folded his hands and leaned back in his chair. "And only a day earlier she stood against a Murashev. When you are Arch Abbot, Presbyter Rictun, you will quickly learn that there is no such thing as black or white."

Behind her back, Sorcha clenched her hands tight on each other. Working with this man was going to be punishment enough. The tension in the air was palpable; Rictun had not made friends in the Council, but he was, unfortunately, the only one of them strong enough to take up both the Gauntlet and the Strop as an Arch Abbot was supposed to do.

He smiled grimly at her. "You may return to your duties, Deacon Faris."

It should have been a victory, but her heart was no lighter than when she had stepped into the chamber. She gave a bow to each in turn and then turned for the door. Rictun stopped her with words that cut to the core. "The matter of your partner—or rather, partners—will have to be untangled at a later date. It is quite a mess."

As she left the chamber and headed down to the icy garden where Merrick waited, her heart was racing in her chest. The young man turned, and, despite everything, she smiled at him as if all was just as she wanted it. And suddenly she was sure of one thing: she wanted this brave young man as partner, not Kolya. She might not be able to have everything she wanted with Raed, but this was different—this was a relationship she could fight for.

They left the Mother Abbey; it bustled with life like a disturbed hornets' nest. Merrick kept his Center open and they circled back through the streets many times before making their way to the Artisan Quarter. In the little weaver's house they found Raed and his crew at a game of cards. The Pretender smiled at her, making her every nerve ending come alive. He was so much to her, and yet he could be nothing.

Coldly, she held out her hand to him. "It's time to leave."

Despite the Council's assurances that the Emperor would have given Raed safe passage out of Vermillion, Sorcha was still cautious. She led the little group through every alleyway and double-back she knew, until at last they reached the port.

Merrick, without having to be asked, led the crew down toward where the ship waited so that his partner could say her good-byes to the Pretender. "The Captain will take you north, but in case there is ice blocking your route, this should buy you horses or carriage fare." Slipping out a small pouch of gold, she pressed it into his hand. "Make sure not to gamble it all away."

Raed's eyes dropped, and his melancholy across the Bond was an echo of hers, though he tried to conceal it. "I am sure I could double your investment." The smile was broad, but uncertain.

"You have already repaid me," Sorcha replied, not letting go of his hand.

His bravado dropped away, and his fingers tightened around hers. "If I could, I would stay—you know that."

It was a pretty dream, but both were old enough to know this was not the time for dreams. The Emperor's largesse would not extend to allowing Raed to linger, and Sorcha had an Order to rebuild. He had to go. She had to stay. They both knew these things, and yet she was using every ounce of her control not to let her disappointment show on her face.

"I know, Raed. If wishes were horses—"

"I would never have to walk again." He laughed, but his smile was bittersweet; he heard her thoughts as well as she could hear his. The Bond was making this so painful that both wanted it to be over, and yet they yearned for it to go on forever. "Indeed, Mistress Deacon, I should be going." He leaned down and brushed his lips against hers, a sweet memory sweeping over them both for a moment.

When he let go of her, Sorcha realized he had pressed something into her hand in return. It was a captain's ring, marked with the sigil of his house: the rampant Rossin.

Wrapping her fingers around it, Sorcha smiled up at him. "No promises?"

He brushed her hair away from her cheek, the gloved back of his hand stroking her skin. The Deacon ached to lean into his touch, but managed to hold herself stiff. "Promises, no," he said, his hazel eyes gleaming with light reflecting off the water. "But plenty of hopes."

Then he turned and walked away from her. Sorcha watched as the vessel was made ready, and cast off to the ocean. She didn't move, even when Merrick walked back up the pier to her. She felt her partner's concern wash over her, but he wisely said nothing as she stood there, watching the tiny vessel sail away, the unreality of the moment giving way to gaping realization. Raed was gone, though she could feel where he was like a tiny lodestone nestled in her head. The Bond surely would weaken with time—which should be a good thing . . . It should be.

"I'll meet you back at the Abbey." Merrick's touch on her arm was strong, a good, hearty squeeze that was unlike the feather touch of his mind on hers.

Her partner, who was more than she had ever expected in one so young, pulled the hood of his emerald cloak up against the wind and left her alone with her thoughts. He was thinking of Nynnia as he went, the pain white-hot in him, though nothing showed on the outside. Whatever the creature had been, he had loved her.

Sorcha's fingers traced the sigils on her Gauntlets idly. They all had scars and injuries—it came with being an adult, messy and awkward as that could sometimes be. And right now it came from being a Deacon. The chaos that Hastler had made of the Order, the ruin to both its reputation and its ranks, could not be underestimated. Whatever he had done, she knew deep down that he had not done it alone.

Sorcha pulled out the badge she had taken from the traitorous Arch Abbot; two twined snakes in a circle, eating each other's tails. She had scoured the library, asked Garil and found nothing about it. She flipped it over and looked at the one thing she did recognize—five stars imprinted on the back, the sign of the old Order. It filled her with a dread she could not shake. She tucked the badge into a pocket with Raed's ring.

Her fingers brushed against the smooth surface of the remaining Ilyrick reserve that Raed had given her. This was as good a time as any to smoke it. It would be a poignant moment to do so, while watching the Pretender sail away from her—yet she stopped. Optimism won out over her natural skepticism. For some reason she dared not examine, she would save the Ilyrick for some other day.

Reaching deeper into another pocket, she found the Fabvre she'd retrieved from her cell at the Mother Abbey. This was a good cigar, not as good as the Ilyrick, but it would do.

She dropped down and seated herself on the edge of the wharf, legs dangling over the water. Slipping on one Gauntlet, she summoned Pyet between her fingertips and gently lit the cigar. The sun was emerging over the horizon, bathing Vermillion in blues and pinks that softened even the city's darker lanes and alleys. Her mind was unable to stop thinking of Hastler's last words. The twisted smile on his lips. *You do not know it, but you are already caught.*

Logic said his threat was meaningless—they had repelled the Murashev—but instinct would not be satisfied. Some part of her wondered if they had really found the depth and width of such well-laid plans.

Yet Raed was gone. One less complication in her life—she should have been grateful for that. Sorcha drew a sensuous cloud into her mouth, letting the taste fill her like memories. Ahead lay her own personal questions of Kolya and Merrick; her marriage—her partnership. But as terrible as things would become there, she was also sure that the Otherside was not done with the Order yet.

For now it was merely a moment to draw breath and appreciate the little things in life. "Keep sailing, Young Pretender," Sorcha whispered, raising the cigar to her lips. "You know where to find me, have you a need."

ABOUT THE AUTHOR

Philippa Ballantine is a writer, podcaster and librarian. Her podcast of *Chasing the Bard* won the Sir Julius Vogel Award in 2009, and two of her novels have been short-listed for it. She is currently living in her hometown of Wellington, New Zealand, where her two Siberian cats keep her in line. Visit her website at www.pjballantine .com.